THE
MASTER
OF TIME

ROADS TO MOSCOW
BOOK 3

DAVID
WINGROVE

DEL REY

1 3 5 7 9 10 8 6 4 2

Del Rey, an imprint of Ebury Publishing
20 Vauxhall Bridge Road,
London SW1V 2SA

Penguin
Random House
UK

Del Rey is part of the Penguin Random House group of companies whose addresses
can be found at global.penguinrandomhouse.com

First published in the UK in 2017 by Del Rey

www.penguin.co.uk

A CIP catalogue record for this book is available from the British Library

ISBN 9780091956202

Typeset in India by Thomson Digital Pvt Ltd, Noida, Delhi

Printed and bound by Clays Ltd, St Ives PLC

Penguin Random House is committed to a sustainable future for our business,
our readers and our planet. This book is made from Forest Stewardship
Council® certified paper.

MIX
Paper from
responsible sources
FSC® C018179

To my dear friend Andy Muir,
for forty years of fellowship.
Awrabestfurnoo!

Contents

CHARACTER LIST

Angels — time agents from Up River. Not even born yet.

Anna — daughter of Otto and Katerina.

Aristotle — Greek philosopher and scientist, born 384 BC, died 322 BC.

Arizhelika — female Russian time agent.

Arminius — German tribal leader (died AD 21), chieftain of the Cherusci, also known as Hermann. Defeated the Roman army in the Battle of the Teutoberg Forest, AD 9.

Augustus, Gaius Octavius — founder of the Roman Empire and first Emperor. Ruled 27 BC to AD 14.

Aurelius, Marcus Anthonious Augustus — (reigned AD 161 to AD 180) Emperor of the Roman Empire.

Baetorix — German chieftain, in AD 9. The warrior who fights Urte.

Behr, Otto — our narrator. A German *'reisende'* or time agent. Voted Meister by the *veche*, or 'council'.

Beskryostnov, Mariya — fortune-teller in Baturin, in 1808. Twin to 'Jamil'.

Blagovesh — the Bandit King; leader of the Marsh bandits in thirteenth-century Russia.

Bobrov — Russian time agent and killer of at least a dozen German agents. Member of the *veche*, or 'council'.

Burckel, Albrecht — German time agent, or *reisende*. A 'sleeper' in the Greater Berlin of AD 2747.

Bush, George — Vice-President of the United States of America, November 1984.

Charles XII — King of Sweden, defeated at the Battle of Poltova in 1709.

Chkalov, Joseph Maksymovich — otherwise known as Yastryeb, 'the Hawk'. Grand Master of Time for the Russians.

Curie, Marie — Polish-born physicist and chemist (1867–1934).

Dankevich, Fedor Ivanovich — Russian time agent, and archenemy of Otto. Member of the *veche*, or 'council'.

Darre, Richard Walther — SS *Obergruppenfuhrer* and Reichminister of Food and agriculture, 1933–1942 (Born in Argentina).

Darya — female Russian time agent.

Da Vinci, Leonardo — Italian polymath. Inventor, painter, sculptor, architect, musician and mathematician (1452–1519).

DeSario, Joseph P. — owner of the apartment in New York in November 1984.

Dick, Kleo — wife of Philip K Dick. Deceased.

Dick, Philip K. — President of the United States of America in November 1984. Also science-fiction writer.

Diedrich — German time agent, and Four-Oh's physics expert.

Dietrich — Grand Meister of Altenberg, responsible for Prussian crusades in the thirteenth century.

Dimitri — Russian time agent from Up River.

Dirac, Paul – English theoretical physicist and specialist in quantum mechanics.

Do hu — 'domesticated humans', genetically adapted servants, from Greater Germany.

Doppelgehirn — experimental use (in Greater Germany) of two heads connected to a single body. Preliminary tests AD 2320–2370.

Edison, Thomas — American inventor and businessman (1847–1931). Invented the light bulb and photographs.

Eichel, August — silver-haired master of genetics. Professor at the Berlin Akademie (where he laid the foundations that allowed the development of the Guildsmen).

Eicke, Theodore — Commandant of Dachau (1892–1943).

Einstein, Albert — German-born theoretical physicist, famous for his general theory of relativity (1879-1955).

Ernst — see *Kollwitz.*

'Ernst' — a parallel timeline version of Otto's best friend, a gang boss who does not know Otto's Ernst.

Feynman, Richard Phillips — American theoretical physicist. Developed the theory of quantum mechanics (1918–1988).

Fischer (Theoretician) — leading figure at the Scientific Akademie in Berlin in 2343. Expert in genetics.

Frank, Karl Hermann — prominent Sudeten German Nazi, stationed in Czechoslovakia (1898-1946).

Franke — second 'personality' that makes up the *doppelgehirn* known as Reichenau.

Franklin, Rosamund — English chemist and X-ray crystallographer (1920–1958). Partly responsible for the discovery of DNA's double helix.

Frederick The Great — King Frederick II of Prussia, known more commonly as 'Old Fritz'. Fighting against overwhelming odds, he helped Prussia survive the War of the Austrian Succession (1740–1748) where he was faced with the alliance of France, Austria and Russia and defeated all three. A hero of Europe.

Freisler — German *reisende* or time agent. Meister Hecht's special henchman – his *'Jagdhund'* or bloodhound – responsible for doing all of Hecht's dirty work.

Galileo Galilei — Italian astronomer, physicist, engineer, philosopher and mathematician (1564–1642).

Gehlen, Hans — aka, 'The *Genewart'*. Architect of Four-Oh, scientific genius and inventor of time travel. Has existed for two hundred years as a gaseous presence in the midst of Four-Oh's artificial intelligence.

Golitsyn — the Regent Sophia's lover.

Golubintzev — cossack in Baturin, 1708.

Gress, Ulrich — senior member of the *Schufzstaffel* – or SS – in AD 2343.

Grigor — time agent from Up River.

Hammill, Kurt — Master of the Guilds, Greater Germany, twenty-fifth century.

Haussman — geneticist and author of *Against Random Choice*. Chief progenitor of future Greater Germany.

Hecht, Albrecht — Master Hecht's older brother and keeper of the archives at the haven, way back in time.

Hecht, Meister — 'The Pike'; Master of the Germans back at Four-Oh. Deceased.

Heinrich — ex-Russian time agent. Reichenau's right-hand man from the twenty-eighth century. Also Burckel's friend. A revolutionary (*Undrehungar*). Also present in 1950s California.

Heydrich, Reinhard Tristan Eugen — high-ranking Nazi – one of the main architects of the Holocaust. Assassinated 4 June 1942.

Himmler, Heinrich — *Reichsfuhrer* of the *Schutzstaffel* [SS]. Leading Nazi.

Von Hindenberg, Paul — German Field Marshal and President of Germany (nineteenth–twentieth centuries).

Hitler, Adolf — Fuhrer ('leader') of the National Socialist or Nazi party in the twentieth century.

Huber, Franz Josef — (1902–1975); Chief of the Munich Police. Prominent Nazi.

Hypatia — (female) Greek mathematician, astronomer and philosopher – originally from Egypt (b. AD 415).

Ilyusha — Kolya's helper at Krasnogorsk.

Iranov — 'priest' at Cherdiechnost in the thirteenth century.

Irina — daughter of Otto and Katerina.

Izolda — female Russian time agent.

Stewart, James II — King of England, Ireland, Wales and Scotland, early seventeenth century.

Joe — owner of the bar in New York City, November 1984.

Von Jungingen, Hockmeister Ulrich — (1360–1410); twenty-sixth Grand Master of the Teutonic Knights, from 1407 to 1410.

Kabanov — Russian time agent. Traitor.

Kaminski, Nikita — Russian time agent both from the period of Catherine the Great (1762–1796) and the Mechanist Age (c. 2450–c. 2650).

Kavanagh, John Patrick — American agent and gun salesman, based in New York in November 1984.

Kepler, Johannes — Italian astronomer and mathematician (1571–1630).

Klara — female Russian time agent.

Klug, Hans — from AD 2343. German geneticist and scientist, responsible for creating the ruling royal family's bloodline.

Koch — President of Greater Germany. Assassinated.

Kollwitz, Ernst — a *reisende* or time agent. Otto's best friend and travelling companion; damaged in the Past. Member of the *veche*, or 'council'.

Kolya — archenemy of Otto Behr.

Krauss, Phillipe — German *reisende*, or time agent. A traitor to his own agents.

Kravchuk, Oleg Alekseevich — agent of the Mongols in thirteenth-century Russia and – in some timelines – married to Katerina.

Kroos, Meister — Fake ID/alias Otto uses when in AD 2343 Greater Berlin.

Kurdin, Igor — Russian time agent and member of the *veche*, or 'council'.

Leibniz, Gottfried Wilhelm — German polymath and philosopher (1646–1716).

Lersch — Friend of DeSario's, New York, November 1984.

Lishka — a haulier in thirteenth-century Russia.

Loki — god of Norse mythology and a malicious troublemaker.

Ludendorff, Erich Friedrich Wilhelm — German general, victor of the Battle of Liege (1914) and the battle of Tannenberg (1914). Chief architect of German military activities in the First World War.

Ludmilla — female Russian time agent.

Makarov — Moscow Central's expert for the period of Russian history that includes Fredrick the Great.

Malya — Kolya's helper at Krasnogorsk.

Mannfred — King of Greater Germany, and tenth in his genetic line.

Maria — woman in the apartment next door to Otto, in New York, 1984 – with son and daughter.

Martha — lost daughter of Katerina and Otto.

Master, The — owner of Cherdiechnost B.

Matveyev, Artamon — influential friend of Frederick the Great, murdered by the Streltsy in the Moscow Uprising of 1682.

Maxim — Russian time agent from Up River.

Maxwell, James Clerk — Scottish scientist specialising in mathematical physics. (1831–1879).

Meisner — German time agent and member of the *veche*, or 'council'.

Meitner, Lise — experimenter on radioactivity and nuclear physics (1878–1968).

Menshikov, Alexander Danilovich — Russian general and friend of Peter the Great, victor of Poltova (1709).

Mondale, Walter — Democratic opponent to President Dick, November 1984.

Moseley, Henry — English atomic physicist (1887–1915).

'The Mouth' — Mafia soldier, New York, November 1984.

Muller, Heinrich — Chief of the Gestapo in Nazi Germany (1900–1945).

Muller, Kurt — German time agent, responsible for de-briefing Galileo and Einstein.

Natalya — daughter of Katerina and Otto.

Nemsov — Russian time agent and member of the *veche*, or 'council'.

Nevsky, Alexander Iaroslavich — Russian Orthodox Prince of Novgorod in the thirteenth century. Victor of the Battle on the Ice (on Lake Peipus) in April 1242, a battle that effectively ended the expansive Northern crusades.

Newton, Isaac — English physicist and mathematician (1643–1727).

Otto — see 'Behr'.

Patricia — woman Kavanagh is seeing in New York City, November 1984.

Pauli, Wolfgang — Austrian-born theoretical physicist (1900–1958) – the father of quantum physics.

Pavlusha — Russian time agent.

Peter the Great — six foot six ruler of Russia from 1672 to 1725. Architect of modern Russia.

Petr — Alias Otto uses in Cherdiechnost B.

Postorsky — Russian time agent and traitor.

Publius, Quinictilus Varus — Commander of the three Roman legions in the campaign into the northern forest in AD 9. Lost the Battle of the Teutoberg Forest.

Puskarev, Kebba — big African from the Gambia. A 'free man' at Cherdiechnost in the thirteenth century.

Razumovsky, Katerina — eternal love of Otto Behr. Daughter of Mikhail Razumovsky in the thirteenth century at Cherdiechnost.

Rakitin — Russian time agent.

Reagan, Nancy — widow of President Ronald Reagan.

Reagan, Ronald — President of the United States of America. Assassinated in November 1984.

Rehnskjold, Carl Gustav — Field Marshal of Charles XII's Swedish army. In command at the Battle of Poltava (1709) and captive of the Russians until 1718.

Reichenau, Gudrun — daughter of Michael Reichenau (so he claims).

Reichenau, Michael — *doppelgehirn*, also supervisor of Werkstatt 9. Somehow involved in time travel. Product of a genetic experiment, he has two skulls 'hot-wired' together.

Rutherford, Ernest — British physicist, known as the father of nuclear physics (1871–1937).

Samsonov, Alexander — defeated Russian Marshal at Tannenberg.

Saratov, Sergei Ilya — Harbourmaster at Tver in thirteenth century Russia. Time agent on some timelines, and member of the *veche*, or 'council'.

Schafer, Adelbert — President of Greater Germany.

Schikaneder, Jakub — 'sleeper' time agent in 19th century Prague. Painter and exile. Also known as Klaus Hecht.

Schmidt, Hans — German time agent and member of the *veche*, or 'council'.

Schnorr — 'Old Schnorrr', Master at Four-Oh in charge of the project to trawl time for common/familiar faces. One of the Elders and a member of the *veche*, or 'council'.

Schwab, Meister — Speaker of the Reichstag and President Schafe's Chancellor (twenty-fourth century).

Schwarzenegger, Arnie — Hollywood film actor, November 1984.

Shafaravich — Russian time agent; henchman to Yastryeb (the Hawk), Grand Master of the Russians.

Shaklovity, Fedor — Russian diplomate of the seventeenth century.

Shakespeare, William — also known as 'Will'. Poet and playwright from the sixteenth and seventeenth centuries.

Shelley, Peter — UK punk singer/songwriter, November 1984.

Shepnikov — Steward at Cherdiechnost B.

Simon — the smith at Cherdiechnost B.

Sofia — female Russian time agent. Senior member of a squad of five.

Sophia — Regent of Russia in the seventeenth century (on behalf of Peter).

Stahlecker, Walter — doctor in charge of *Einsatzgrupen A*.

Stalin, Joseph — AKA Iosif Vissarionvich Dzhugashvili; leader of the Soviet Union until 1953.

Steiner, Felix Martin Julius — General of the Waffen-SS and prominent Nazi (died 1966).

Svetov, Arkadi — Russia's chief agent in the twenty-fourth century. Member of the *veche*, or 'council'.

Talianov, Sergei — Russian psyche expert.

Tavener, Jason — character in a Philip K. Dick science-fiction novel.

Tesla, Nikola — Serbian–American inventor and electrical engineer/physicist (1856–1943).

Todd — Boy-actor in Shakespeare's troupe of players.

Tomas — young German student at Four-Oh.

Tupayeva, Alina — Russian time agent and member of the *veche*, or 'council'.

Turing, Alan — pioneering British computer scientist, cryptoanalyst and theoretical biologist (1912-1954).

Tyutchev — Russian time agent.

'Ugly Fucker' — Mafia soldier in New York, November 1984.

Urte — one of the women at the platform in Four-Oh (and subsequently Moscow Central). Also an expert physicist, technician and mathematician. Member of the *veche*, or 'council'.

Vasilia — Russian agent and markswoman.

Wallis, John — Mathematician who originated the use of 'infinity' (the lazy eight) as a mathematical symbol in 1655.

'Will' — see Shakespeare.

Yastryeb — see Chkalov, Grand Master of Time for the Russians.

Yusupov, Irina — Russian time agent and member of the *veche*, or 'council'.

Zarah — fifth and youngest daughter of Otto and Katerina.

Zarah — most senior of the women who run first Four-Oh and then Moscow Central's operating systems. Sweet on Otto.

Zasyekin, Petr — Russian time agent.

Zieten, Hans Joachim von — Cavalry general in Prussian army and advisor to Frederick the Great.

Part Eleven
Exiles

'It would be funny, he thought, if it were happening to someone else. But it's happening to me. No, it's not funny either way. Because there is real suffering and real death passing the time of the day in the wings. Ready to come on any minute.'

– Philip K. Dick, *Flow My Tears, the Policeman Said*

For a time I just lie there on the bed, facing the wall, the tears trickling slowly down my face. The hurt is simply too much, the pain too fierce. I try to fight it, to be 'manly', only I keep seeing their faces, their eyes wide with fear, pleading with me – Katerina and my brave Natalya, young Irina and Anna, and Martha and my darling little Zarah – and an overwhelming sense of hopelessness, of sheer, soul-numbing impotence, stops me dead.

How can I live without them?

I can't. But giving up will not save them. Only by living can I help. Only by forgetting the hurt and setting it aside. But it's hard. Perhaps the hardest thing I've ever had to do.

I sit up and look about me, trying to think, trying to function like the time agent I am. I used to be good at this – at living off my wits – but it seems I've grown soft.

I know two conflicting things for certain. First, I am trapped in some cul-de-sac of Time; trapped and unable to escape. Second, I can't possibly be trapped, because I'm still in the loop. How, for instance, can my children have been stolen from me when they do not yet exist? For surely, unless I escape from here and conceive them, they cannot come into being?

Or am I missing something? Has Kolya, perhaps, robbed me even of that?

I stand unsteadily, then begin my explorations. First I must know where I am and when. The newspaper on the floor – a *New York Times* – suggests I'm in that city in November 1984, but is that so, or is it a false clue left by Kolya?

Yes, and why here? Why now? Or was this hastily contrived?

I think not. I don't think Kolya does anything hastily or without a reason. At least, that's my experience so far. He's a control freak. Perhaps the ultimate control freak. A control freak with the ability to travel in Time.

I walk across and try the left-hand door. It's locked. I put my ear to it and listen, and sure enough I hear movement out there.

Turning, I walk over to the other door and try it. It opens. Beyond it is a short passageway with rooms off: a bathroom, a kitchen and a lounge. Four rooms, then. And not a hotel by the look of it. An apartment. But whose?

Not knowing when someone will return, I decide to search the lounge. There's a TV and a big leather sofa – an old white thing, well kept and relatively unscuffed – only what interests me most is the standing shelves.

Whoever this guy is – and I'm almost certain from the décor that it's a male – he's heavily into his military history, though there's a smattering of books about various media and sports personalities, as well as politicians. The few novels are cheap thrillers of the kind you'd buy in airport lounges. Well-thumbed paperbacks.

What else? The carpet's wine red, the curtains the same. There are no pictures on the walls, and no photographs on display. Not anywhere. It's neat rather than fashionable and suggests our tenant is single. A very organised man.

I walk through to the kitchen. Again it's neat, everything in its place. But what stands out? A coffee grinder and, nearby, an espresso machine. One of those expensive, Italian jobs. Three big mugs hang from hooks below one of the wall units. The bowl in the sink is empty and there's no washing up on the drainer. I turn, looking 360 about me. No. There's nothing here that gives him away. Nothing except the coffee machine, which suggests expensive tastes.

The bathroom is a surprise. Marble. Real marble, not fake, and a top-of-the-range shower unit with one of those variable heads. This guy likes to shower. It's the nicest room in the apartment, and speaks volumes about his habits.

I look in the little wall unit over the sink. There's a shaving kit here, but it looks like a spare. I'd guess he has his best kit with him, wherever he is. And no sign of colognes or aftershave. Even the soap is unscented.

I nod to myself then move quickly on, returning to the bedroom.

It's hard to see this room without thinking of Kolya's presence. He jumped in here with me, so he knew this room. He'd been here before. So what's the connection? Does he know the tenant? Or is this one of *his* apartments?

Somehow what I've seen doesn't fit with Kolya's 'profile'. I can't see him being obsessed with showering, for a start.

I walk over to the bed and, crouching, drag the case out from underneath. It's locked, but that doesn't trouble me. As I click the locks open and push the lid back, I frown. It's full of old newspapers, some of them going back to the fifties. If they belong to our tenant, then that puts him, I'd say, somewhere in his forties.

Without studying them in depth, I can't see any obvious connection between them. They come from all over the USA, and the dates seem random, though I'm sure they're not.

Closing the case, I return it to under the bed, then go over to the desk, flicking through the papers there. And get myself a name. *DeSario, Joseph P.*

It's there, on three of the bills, and on two of the letters.

Not only that, but there's an address – presumably the address of the apartment where I am right now.

Apartment 8D, 357, 75ᵗʰ Street, New York.

The desk has three drawers on the right-hand side. I try the top drawer first, and find it full of the usual kind of stuff – paperclips, biros, scraps of writing paper and a packet of gum. There's a stapler, too, and in the corner at the back a small glasses case.

I take the last item out and open it. The glasses look ordinary enough, only when I try them on, I realise that they're not spectacles at all. The glass is plain, the lenses perfectly flat.

I put them back, then try the middle drawer. Empty.

I slide it closed and, not expecting anything, pull the bottom drawer out.

And almost smile.

There's a handgun. A .357 Magnum, if I'm not mistaken. And beside it a box of bullets. I open it and, sure enough, they're .357s. Live ammunition, not blanks. Careful not to touch the gun, I ease the drawer right out, peering into the back of it, and am rewarded with the sight of something else.

A small diary with a black leather cover.

I reach in and take it out. But there is no revelation to be found within its pages. The diary is mainly blank. There are barely any entries at all, only hand-drawn lines linking blocks of three, four or five days, with the word 'OUT' at the start and 'BACK' at the end. Business journeys, presumably. But doing what? The bills give me no clues, nor do the letters. Only I know now when our friend, DeSario, will be back. Three days from now, if the newspaper is accurate, on the eleventh of November.

And then I think about that. According to the diary he was 'OUT' on the eighth, so he probably left the newspaper on that day. Which would make it . . .

I go through to the lounge and switch the TV on, changing channels until I find a news programme, and there – beneath the headline – is the date. The tenth of November, 1984.

Back tomorrow, then.

I'm about to switch it off and go back through, when I realise what I'm watching. It's a state funeral. There's a gun carriage, pulled by two black horses, and on it is a coffin draped with an American flag. There are lots of troops and important-looking men in sombre coats, and there, walking just behind the coffin, next to a small, slim woman in her late middle-age, his head bare, his whole demeanour immensely sad, is Phil.

I stare and stare, beginning to understand, beginning to remember what I know about this period. The guy in the coffin . . . Reagan . . . in our timestream he went on to win a second term, his running mate – Bush, was it? – following him as president. But in this timeline Reagan has died somehow, and instead of Bush for a running mate, he had Phil.

The idea is so preposterous that for a moment I entertain the idea that I've been drugged. Reagan, if I remember rightly, was a Republican. And remembering Phil . . . well, I don't know what his politics were, really, but they certainly weren't Republican. He hated all that authority stuff.

I'm still watching as something flutters into camera view and lands on Phil's shoulder, perching there, preening itself even as he walks on, his step unchecked, behind the gun carriage.

An owl. A snowy owl.

I switch it off then hurry back to the bedroom. Picking up the *New York Times*, I flick through it until I come to a full-page article that fills me in with some of what's been going on.

The man in the coffin was indeed Reagan – Ronald Reagan, the thirty-ninth President of the United States of America – and the woman walking beside Phil, following the carriage, was his widow, Nancy.

Having survived one assassination attempt just two months into his first spell as president, Reagan was shot a second time while touring Wisconsin, only weeks before a poll that, most commentators agreed, would have seen him re-elected with a landslide victory over his Democrat opponent, Walter Mondale.

I read down the page, looking for details, then find what I'm looking for. According to this, Reagan was in a coma for the best part of six days before he died, while his running mate, the senator for California, Philip K. Dick, took over the campaign, choosing a relative unknown, the Governor of Texas, George Bush, as the new prospective vice-president.

The sympathy vote was huge. Dick, seen by many as a strange choice for running mate, representing, as he did, the softer side of Republicanism, had carried the day, not only riding the tide of Reagan's popularity, but coming into his own with his dignity of bearing and his clear, straight-spoken manner.

I close the paper and sit back, trying to think this through. If I'm to get out of here, I've got to find out just how far back the changes go, because that's where I'll find my way out of here. That'll be the point – the one and only point, in fact – where I can jump back to Four-Oh, back to the main trunk of the Tree.

Only there are two problems. One – I don't know enough about the specific history of this time and place to make that judgement and isolate that point where the changes began. And two – even if I did, how in Urd's name would I get back there?

I go over to the door again and rattle it, hoping maybe that the lock will prove weak enough to give, only it doesn't. It feels good and solid and secure.

And there's no way I can use the windows. There's a straight drop of eight floors to the sidewalk.

I walk back through to the kitchen and check the fridge. There are one or two bits of food, but barely enough to feed me for a day. Searching the wall units I come across a few cans and various packets, but again there's not much. If DeSario doesn't come back tomorrow, then I'm going to have to try to break out of here, if only to feed myself.

I go back into the lounge and stand in front of the bookshelves again, staring at them, as if the answer's there. Then, some kind of instinct driving me, I go over and start pulling books out and looking behind them. It's fairly random at first, but then I notice something. There's a small section on the bottom shelf where the book spines seem pushed back a little in one place.

I crouch and remove a couple of them, and there it is. A small wooden cigar box. And inside? I smile, knowing already that they're going to fit. For it's keys. A set of keys to this apartment.

320

I spend the next day and a half mainly on the sofa, the door open, giving me a clear view of the passageway and the front door, the TV on low, the .375 Magnum resting on my chest. Loaded, of course. Just in case.

Because what's a man doing with a 'thirty-eight' Magnum if he doesn't intend to use it?

I've tried the keys and they work. Not that I intend to go anywhere just yet. Not until DeSario returns.

And if he doesn't?

Then I'll go out. See what's to be seen. Buy myself a steak dinner, maybe.

Because I've got cash now. Over eight thousand dollars. Money that was in the box where I found the key, in a sealed envelope marked 'expenses'.

I don't intend to steal it. Just borrow it for a while.

For a while I channel surf, getting a feeling of this age through its images and idioms. It's very different from the fifties, and not just in its degree of sophistication. This is an age that has recently discovered sex, and in what I see and hear there's a constant battle raging between those who think things have gone too far and those who don't think things have gone far enough.

I stop at a music channel – MTV, it's called – and watch for a while. The music's bland to my ear, the beat repetitive, the tunes insipid. Even jazz, I think, is better. But what do I know? Besides, at the volume I've got the TV, who can tell what the dynamics of the music are?

Only I've sat in the same room as Beethoven and seen him play piano, like a man possessed, and know what I'm seeing on the screen before me is not the best humanity can do.

I wait all of that day, and all of that evening, too, and still he doesn't come. DeSario is late. Either that, or he doesn't actually exist. Maybe this is all a construct, created by Kolya to keep me occupied. But why would he do that?

Is he watching me? Is that what this is? A controlled environment?

I decide to risk going outside, onto the streets. I've money and a key, and a gun. What harm can come to me? And if this *is* a construct, I'll find out quick enough. Kolya doesn't have the resources to people a whole city for my benefit.

I go to the window, to check out the weather, then return to the bedroom to search through DeSario's wardrobe. Looking through his clothes, I note that he's no style guru, but that doesn't really matter. What does matter – and *is* it just coincidence? – is that he's my size, right down to our matching shoe size.

Slipping out of my old clothes I get dressed, then study myself in the bathroom mirror. It's far from perfect – denim jeans, a black T-shirt and a pair of casual slip-ons – but it'll do.

Last of all, I look for a coat to wear against the weather. There's one dark woollen jacket that'll do me and I pull it on, noting how snugly it fits.

I pocket one of the hundred-dollar bills, slip the gun into my jacket pocket, then pick up the key. I'm about to go out when I hear noises from outside, in the hallway.

There's a peephole in the door. I go to it, placing my eye against the glass.

There, in that shadowed space between the apartments, two men are gesturing violently and shouting at a woman. It's not a pretty sight. She has her arms up, as if to defend herself, and they keep leaning in to her threateningly, leaning in and shouting, until, finally, one of them shakes his fist at her and turns away, quickly followed by the other.

I watch her watching them go, real fear in her eyes, then see how she slumps, one hand gripping the half-open door behind her, as if she's about to collapse. There's a part of me that wants to throw the door open and go out to help her, but I don't know whether this isn't yet another of Kolya's little games.

I step away, then turn, my back to the door, waiting, *listening*. And in a while I hear the door to her apartment slam shut.

I give it a minute, then slip out, locking the door behind me. Whatever it was, it'd be best not to get involved. For all I knew she might have been at fault. Only I don't think so.

I make my way down the stairs and out onto the grey streets of New York City. It's cold, a faint flurry of snow in the air. On the corner, just across from me, is a grocery store, its cluttered interior lit up against the encroaching darkness. I go across, buying myself groceries, a torch, a notepad and a packet of pens, the old guy on the till growling in his best New York fashion.

'You not got something smaller, buddy?'

I make an apologetic face. 'Sorry, friend. It's all I've got.'

The old guy makes a face, then rummages through his till, hiding the hundred-dollar bill beneath the tray, before handing me my change.

I was going to head straight back, settle in and make myself supper, only I notice a bar, a few shops further on. A cosy-looking place. The kind you find scattered all over New York in this place and time.

Why not? I could have a steak and a beer, perhaps.

Yeah . . . but what if DeSario turns up while you're gone?

That's a risk I'm going to take. Besides, the mere thought of a steak is too much for me after all I've been through.

Okay. Let me make this clear. There's not a moment I'm not thinking of them. Agonising. Wondering how I can get out of there and rescue them. Only . . .

Only a man has to eat. Whatever age he's trapped in.

I walk across. There's a neon sign above the window. *Joe's Bar*, it reads, as if it could be called anything else.

I go inside.

It's small. One long room with a bar to the left and a row of tables and chairs to the right. It's also unexpectedly empty. Or almost so. There's a barman cleaning glasses, a small, stout, bald-headed man in his forties, and, sat on a stool at the far end of the bar, his one and only customer.

My instinct is to turn about and leave. Only that would seem strange, impolite. Not that the barman seems to notice that I'm there. He doesn't even look up, just continues to clean glasses, the clink of which is just about audible over the sound from the small TV screen that's just behind the bar.

Yes, and to add to my awkwardness, I've a heavy bag of shopping. I've only taken two steps towards the bar when I'm hailed. 'Hey, buddy! Let me buy you a drink!'

There's a small part of me that's deeply suspicious. I don't know the fellow, after all, and what better way for Kolya to keep tabs on me than to have his men scattered all about the area? In bars and shops and on the streets nearby. Watching me. Keeping tabs.

I go across. He's younger than the barman. Mid-thirties at the most. A tall, rather handsome young man, in a dark grey suit, the jacket of which is laid over the back of the bar stool, a packet of Tareyton Long Lights – cigarettes, I'm guessing – on the counter next to his wallet.

'Hey,' I say, setting my shopping down and offering him my hand. 'Name's Otto—'

He smiles. A pleasant smile. 'Hey, Otto. I'm John. John Patrick Kavanagh.' And he takes my hand and shakes it firmly. 'What'll you have?'

I note that he's drinking a Coors Lite. A lager, by the look of it. I nod towards it.

'I'll have what you're having.'

He looks past me. 'Sure . . . Joe! Another Coors!'

And so our friendship begins. And within half an hour any doubts I had about the man are gone. He no more works with Kolya than I do. In fact, he's a lawyer, and that accent in his voice that I couldn't place is from Illinois, from downtown Chicago, to be precise, where he works in corporate law. When I ask what he's doing in New York, he laughs and, drawing from his cigarette, tells me.

'I'm attending subcommittee meetings of the NAIC. That's the National Association of Insurance Commissioners. But in my spare time I'm visiting the Museum of Modern Art. Oh . . .' And he leans towards me, lowering his voice confidentially, '. . . and cranking a woman named Patricia. She's from Chicago too. Moved out here after her divorce.'

By 'cranking' I assume he means having sex. And for some reason I think of the woman in the apartment across from where I'm staying and a cloud falls over my face, which he sees.

'Hey, buddy. What's up?'

I tell him what I saw, and he takes a long draw on his cigarette while he mulls it over, then, nodding slowly to himself, meets my eyes.

'You know what? I think you were right not to get involved. This is a hard town, Otto, and there're some hard people out there. You cross them and you'll end up dead.'

I can believe that. Only now that I've had a few beers, I feel like telling him more. Telling him *all* of it, in fact. Only then he'd think I was insane. That I'd escaped from some asylum. And then I'd be alone again. And I don't want to be alone. I realise that now.

'I'd better get back,' I say. But I sound only half convinced. There's part of me that wants to stay here and get drunk, and Kavanagh, realising that, buys me another drink. And another. And all the while he's telling me all about what's been going on – as he sees it – as if I've spent the last ten years on the dark side of the moon, which is near enough the truth – and I begin to get a picture of this time and place. And there's yet another part of me – the part that is *Reisende*, time agent through and through – that takes all of that raw information and makes a pattern from it. A *gestalt*.

And then – and who knows how it came about? – I'm saying goodbye to Kavanagh in the snow outside the bar, shaking his hand with my one free hand, the other clinging on to my groceries, then watching him as he disappears into the night, like a spectre. Or like some figure from a dream. And I return to the building where I'm staying and unsteadily climb the stairs back up to the unlit apartment on the eighth floor where I have washed up, like a sea-sculpted spar from some shipwrecked vessel.

And DeSario?

Of DeSario there's no sign. Not that I expected anything. Because I know now. There *is* no DeSario. That's just a name. A peg for my imagination. And all of this is a construct, to keep me busy, guessing, running about like a hamster in a cage. Going nowhere fast. All for Kolya's sick amusement.

And, locking the door behind me, not bothering with the lights, I throw myself down on the big double bed and weep once more. For my girls. And Katerina. And because, despite all of Kavanagh's kindness, I am alone in this alien place.

321

I fell asleep, then woke, gasping, the apartment in darkness, the timer on the bedside alarm showing it was just after five.

The dream in my head was still fresh, still raw.

I had been watching them die, one by one. Bound hand and feet, my mouth gagged, I had been forced to witness it all, while beside me, gripping my arms, keeping me upright, even as my legs gave way, was him.

Kolya. My enemy.

A dream? It didn't seem so. No. It had felt too real, too awful to be other than real. Not here, maybe, but somewhere in Time.

Barefoot, I went through to the kitchen, where I filled a kettle and placed it on the hob to heat. And, as I stood there, so the daylight leaked slowly back into the world.

I had stopped trembling. Only I knew this couldn't go on. My fear for them was slowly sapping me. Destroying me. Another week of this and I would be fit for nothing. And maybe he knows that. Maybe that's why he's trapped me here.

I make coffee, then I make plans.

The bag of groceries is where I left it last night, on the floor by the door. I pack them away, then, taking the notepad and a pen, sit on the sofa, meaning to sketch out a plan of action. Only what's to be done? Unless Kolya takes pity on me, I'm here and here I'll stay. Until the sun grows cold.

Even so, I open up the pad and begin to write, noting down everything that happened, looking to see whether I've overlooked something. Something obvious.

An hour later and all I have is a series of sketches of my girls, hand drawn from memory – Martha and Zarah, Natalya, Anna, Irina, and, of course, Katerina. And I wonder why I am tormenting myself. Why, when there's nothing I can do, I am wasting my time making plans, because we are beyond plans, beyond all practical measures. No. There is nothing I can do. He doesn't even have to watch me. Because there *is* no way out. No trapdoor exit for me to find. Why, he didn't even have to kill me, just leave me to this torment, a member of the living dead.

I'm on my third coffee when I realise that there's a question I haven't answered yet. What does Kolya want? Having effectively ruled me out of the Game, what will he do next? Where will he strike? And why? Not that, if I *had* the answers, I could do anything about it. Yet I still need to know.

I make breakfast, the big Magnum on the worktop beside me. In reach. Just in case.

I've just finished and am clearing up when the phone rings, startling me. I go across and stare at it, then pick it up.

Nothing. Or rather, the sound of emptiness itself.

Kolya?

The line goes dead.

Today, I think. *It's going to happen today.*

16

Only that's my gut instinct, and I've ceased trusting my gut instinct. Look where it's got me, after all!

I spend the day doing nothing. Watching the breaking news. Walking about the flat, like the lost soul that I am. Dozing, on and off.

And so the day passes, and the dark comes down again. And I venture out, to buy myself a six-pack and a microwave meal of some kind.

Only, passing Joe's Bar, I realise that I don't want to go back to that apartment. That I can't face that sense of overwhelming futility I have when I'm there. And so I go inside, and there, at the far end of the bar, sitting there as if he's been waiting for me, is my new friend Kavanagh.

And what if he has been? What if he *is* Kolya's man?

I go across and sit beside him at the bar, and we share a beer or two and watch the baseball on the TV – the Boston White Sox, his team. And oddly enough, his simple kindness raises my spirits, and when I leave him, I feel a different man to the one I was barely two hours before.

Only they're there again, the two men I'd seen before, harassing the woman on my landing. I halt on the landing below, listening, wondering what's best to do, then press on, climbing the last two flights.

One of them turns to stare at me as I come to the top of the stairs, challenging me, his scowling face prodigiously ugly, his dark, Italianate eyes threatening me to make any kind of comment, and I know for a certainty that these are mob men – gangsters, as they call them here.

The other one's busy, his face pressed up close to the woman's face, and from what I hear he's giving her two days to come up with what she owes them. *Or else.*

I skirt them, shaping my body language to make myself seem apologetic, when all I really want to do is knock their heads together and throw them down the stairs one at a time with my boot planted up their arses.

And the woman? Our eyes meet briefly, even as I unlock the door and slip inside, and I see, in that single glance, how desperate she is, how terrified. Only I can't help her. Because her problems aren't mine. And even if my own cause is quite hopeless, I don't want to throw it away. Not for someone I don't even know. Because I'd never forgive myself.

Only I feel like I'm the lowest of the low for not intervening. As if I've let her down badly, and I find myself watching her through the peephole even as the one I didn't see, the one who had his back to me all the while, reaches out and, taking the skin of her cheek between thumb and finger, tweaks it hard, making her cry out.

'Two days,' he says for emphasis. And then they're gone.

322

I sleep poorly and wake to find myself covered in a sheen of sweat. It's not that the flat is too warm – it's New York in November, after all, and I've not got the heating on – but I'm burning up anyway. I shower and then dig out some more of DeSario's clothes, more convinced than ever that the guy simply doesn't exist.

Which is when I get the phone call, asking for him. Leaving him a cryptic message, which I write down there and then.

'Tell Lersch that Chinese is fine. Will meet as scheduled.'

For all I know this could be perfectly innocent, only I don't think so, and, sitting down in front of the muted TV, I begin to sketch out everything that's happened to me that doesn't make sense. I head the page up 'Loose Ends', but after a while I realise I need a bigger piece of paper, so that I can make some kind of chart, and I go out to get some – and some more groceries.

And come back to find the front door open, and no sign of it having been forced.

Nothing seems to have been disturbed, but someone has definitely been there. DeSario? If so, then why didn't he stay? And why leave the door open? Unless it's to let me know that I'm being watched.

I go through the yellow pages and find a locksmith. He's there in half an hour to change the locks. I pay him off and pocket the keys, and as I do, so I note that the door to the woman's apartment is open several inches, though as soon as I look across, it eases shut again.

I wait for the man to leave, then go across and knock.

She doesn't answer at first. I knock again, and, after a moment, the door opens just a crack, just enough to let me see one of her eyes.

'Yes?'

The tone's suspicious, the accent vaguely Russian with a New York twist.

'You okay?' I ask. But I already know she isn't. I saw it in her eyes the other night. She's terrified.

The door opens a little wider. She's a fairly ordinary-looking woman, and I wonder what kind of trouble she's in with the mob. Has she borrowed money and can't now pay it back?

'I . . .' She hesitates, then clearly changes tack, her eyes looking away from mine. 'Look . . . there's nothing you can do, okay?'

But her eyes say otherwise. She wants me to rescue her somehow.

'Those guys . . .' I begin, but she shakes her head.

'Don't get involved.'

19

It's then that I see them. Two kids. A boy and a girl, the eldest ten at most, behind her in the doorway to the bedroom. They too look terrified.

Hostages to love, I think, and experience a moment of pure dread, thinking of my own and wondering where they are and what was happening to them right then; seeing them as I'd seen them in my dreams, bound and bloodied, slaves to that cunt Kolya.

'Look, I . . .'

Only I don't get a chance to say anything more. The door slams shut.

I stand there a moment, wondering whether I should knock again, then turn away. *None of my business*, I tell myself. Only I don't believe that. In other circumstances I'd teach those bastards a lesson. In other circumstances.

323

'Hey, Otto . . . how's tricks?'

I put my carrier bag down on the floor by the bar and reached out to take Kavanagh's hand, realising, as I do, that I've rarely seen him off that bar stool, not even to go to the 'can', as he calls it. It's like he's glued there, just as his wallet is glued to the bar itself. Only there is a difference this time.

'I'm fine.' I indicate the glass in front of him. 'What's that you're drinking?'

Kavanagh smiles. 'That? That's a kir on the rocks with a twist.'

I raise an eyebrow and he explains. 'Basically, it's a glass of white wine with a splash of Chambord – a blackberry liqueur – and a twist of lemon peel. With ice, of course.' He sits back and takes a small sip. 'It's all the rage.'

I turn, looking to the barman. 'Two more of those, thanks, Joe.'

And while he sets to making them, I plant my butt on the bar stool and smile at my only friend in this corner of the multiverse.

'Busy day?'

Kavanagh's smile broadens. He's clearly been cranking his friend Pat all afternoon. 'Thing is,' he says, seeing that I'm following him, 'it's a bit like fucking an inflatable love doll.'

We both laugh at that, but I can't entirely hide my awkwardness. It's not that I'm prudish, it's just that I can't make light of the subject. That would be a grave disservice to Katerina and what I have with her. Fucking? No. We never just fuck. It's more like some passionate ritual, a *losing* of ourselves. And talking about that isn't for bars like this.

Which is why I've not spoken of it to Kavanagh. As far as he's concerned, Katerina does not exist. Nor does a single one of my daughters. No. to him I'm a single man, a divorcee, and I work for one of the big corporations. I've kept it vague, and he's not pushed for more. Which is good. We stay within our comfort zones, and that's fine for both of us.

Joe brings the drinks and I slip a ten-dollar note onto the bar in front of me, following the local custom. We clink glasses, then drink.

It's good. I can see why it's so popular.

'How's that woman on your landing?' Kavanagh asks.

I consider that a moment, then shrug. 'It's a tough one. By the look of them, they're gangsters. Mafia, I'd say. The other night, after I'd left here, I had to squeeze past them on the landing. They were threatening her again and she looked terrified. I spoke to her this morning but she didn't want to know. She's got two young kids, however, and they look terrified too. The mobsters . . . they warned her she's got two days.'

'Two days?'

'My thinking is that she owes them money.'

'Ahhh . . .' And from the sound of it, I'd say our friend Kavanagh has had similar problems in the past.

'The thing is, I don't know quite what to do.'

'What do you mean?'

'Whether to get involved . . .'

'With the Mob? Get serious, my friend. They're unforgiving. Besides, violence isn't the answer to this. Why? Because they're better at it than us.'

It's hard to argue with that. Violence probably isn't the answer. It'll simply draw attention to me. Like that time with Katerina on the river. But I'm out of patience. Just three days trapped here in this cul-de-sac of Time and I'm already climbing the walls.

'You ever killed a man?' Kavanagh asks, his whole being suddenly serious.

And I want to say yes. Hundreds of them, in dozens of different fashions, and that it's what I do and what I'm best at. Only I can't tell him that, so I shake my head and lie.

'I've got a gun,' I say and make to show him it. Only, seeing what I'm pulling out of my jacket pocket, he leans across and pushes it back down again.

'Not here,' he says, his eyes registering an element of shock. He leans closer, lowering his voice. 'Is that loaded?' And when I nod, he whistles.

'Look,' he says, after a moment's thought. 'This is not something I'm comfortable talking about in public. You say your apartment's nearby?'

'A hundred yards.'

'Then let's go there. You got some beers?'

'A six-pack of Coors.'

'Then we're set. And Otto . . .'

'Yes, John?'

'Keep that thing in your pocket, will you? Till we're safe indoors.'

Back at the apartment building, there's no sign of our Mob friends. So we go inside, into DeSario's, where, emptying the chamber, he examines the Magnum, nodding his approval. Only then, to my astonishment, he presents one of his own, setting it down beside mine on the tabletop. They're like twins. Two wonderful examples of Smith & Wesson's finest craftsmanship.

'Courtesy of Bell's Guns, Franklin Park, Illinois,' he says and laughs. 'I don't often carry it. But I had a hunch that I might need it today. Guess I was right, huh?'

I don't know what to say. And then I do.

'I thought you were the one who said violence would solve nothing?'

'You ever found that to be true?' he asks, and we both laugh, a relaxed laughter this time. The laughter of friends.

'Look,' he says, after a moment. 'I'm going back to Chicago in two days' time. My woman's phoned and all's well. But in the meantime . . .'

I'm not precisely sure what he means, nor how he proposes to go about helping the woman across the landing, but we've at least evened-up the odds a bit. Two guns against what? Thirty? Forty?

Anyway, they'll not be back for another day, so we can relax a little, and formulate our plans.

'Nice place you've got here,' he says, walking from room to room.

'It's not mine. I'm borrowing it. Belongs to a guy named DeSario.

At that, his eyes fly open. 'You're kidding! Joe DeSario?'

I'm shocked. 'You know him?'

'If it's the same guy. I don't see him often, but . . . well, he's a lawyer, too. Works from an office on Fifteenth Street. He wants to write thrillers. That is, if it's the same guy.'

The coincidence wrongfoots me. It's too close to home, and it makes me reconsider what I know about Kavanagh. If that's his real name and not DeSario. Because now that I think about it, the guy has a similar build to me, right down to his shoe size.

Okay. But why? For what precise purpose would Kolya be doing this?

'You okay, Otto?'

I nod. Then, because I haven't thought of a better strategy, I ask him if he wants a beer and he says 'Sure' in that rich, Illinois accent of his. I get two from the fridge – the last of last night's six – then slide the others onto a shelf and shut the door.

I turn to find him watching me intently.

'You're not from here, are you, Otto? I've been trying to work out what that accent is. It sounds a bit . . . *Germanic*, but there's a bit of Russian in there too.'

I smile. Or try my hardest to. 'I'm from Berlin, but my mother was Russian.'

Not that I know who my mother actually was.

But Kavanagh is smiling now. 'There are a lot of Germans in Chicago. Almost one in four of the population. In fact, my great-grandfather, on my mother's side, was German. He came over from Hamburg in the 1840s.'

He pops his can, the hiss of the gas in the beer filling the silence between us. A moment later, I do the same, and we raise our cans and touch them, to toast each other. But whether we're friends or mortal enemies, I'm no longer sure.

All goes well. We drink beer and talk and watch TV, and I'm about to call it a night and go to bed, when there's a commotion outside in the hallway; the sound of someone trying to break down a door.

Our friends are back. Slightly the worse for wear, it would seem, having consumed a few too many bottles of *vino rosso*. I look through the peephole and see that it's the two who were here earlier, then turn to Kavanagh.

He's holding out my gun to me, his own tucked into his waistband.

'They're both loaded,' he says quietly, suddenly more sober than I thought he was. I nod and take it from him, but I check the chamber anyway.

It's loaded.

I turn back and look again. The bastard's banging on the door now, not caring who he wakes. And beneath his Sicilian bellowing, I can hear the children screaming.

I look to Kavanagh. His face seems determined. 'You ready, John?'

He smiles. 'Sure as fuck am, Otto.'

'Okay. You take the ugly fucker, I'll take the mouth.'

These are the pet names we've adopted for the two while we've been talking about them. But knowing who we're each targeting is a necessity. We don't want to be focused on the same guy.

I throw open the door and step out, gun raised, aimed at Mouth's head.

'Can I help you, gentlemen?'

The two thugs turn as one, reaching to draw their weapons. And freeze, seeing the two big revolvers we're pointing at them.

'Who the fuck are you?' Mouth says belligerently. 'This ain't none of your business!'

I cock the gun and take a step closer, aiming the gun at the centre of his forehead.

'I'm a friend of the lady, and if you're not gone from here in thirty seconds, I might just blow your damn head off!'

'Ditto,' Kavanagh says, coming alongside me, cocking his gun in the same fashion.

'This ain't none of your business,' he says again, and glances to his right.

I follow his line of sight and see there's a window there. Maybe there's a car outside the building, and reinforcements. Maybe that's what he's thinking. To shout down to them and have them help him out. If so, he's mistaken.

I yell at him, the force of my voice surprising him. 'Now go! *Now!*' And he jerks, and then, narrowing his eyes, the scowl returning to his face, he leaves, tailed by his buddy, the ugly fucker. 'I'll be back,' he says. And beside me, Kavanagh laughs, as if what the guy said was funny somehow.

'*Terminator,*' he says, after they've gone. 'You haven't seen it? You see . . . there's this guy from the future and—'

I turn abruptly, staring at him. '*What?*'

'It's just a film. With Arnie Schwarzenegger. You must have heard about it. It's one of the biggest films of the year.'

Only I haven't. And now I feel I ought to. 'Guys returning from the future, huh? Now how likely is that?'

'Oh, he's not human,' Kavanagh says. 'He's some super-android and he's lethal.'

'Fine,' I say. 'Only what are we going to do now?'

I turn and look to her door. It's almost off the hinges. One more kick and it'd be gone. I walk across and knock. 'Lady? You there? You can come out now. They've gone.'

It takes a while, but she comes out, the door almost falling away from her as she opens it.

She looks confused, and I can almost read her mind. Are we police of some kind? Special agents, maybe? Because ordinary citizens don't get involved.

'You can't sleep in there,' I say. 'Not with the kids. Bring them through to mine.'

'I . . .' She makes to argue, then sees the sense in it. 'You think they'll come back?'

'Not tonight. But we need to get your front door secured. I'll phone first thing tomorrow. Arrange it.'

'Thanks . . .'

I turn and look to Kavanagh. 'John . . . thanks, but you'd better get back to your hotel. I'll be fine.'

'You sure?'

'Yeah. They won't come back tonight. They'll expect us to call the police. And I suspect it was the wine that brought them here. Maybe they thought they could rough her up. You know how these guys are.'

'Rough her up and . . .' But he falls silent and doesn't say what else, because suddenly she's back, the two kids in tow.

'Go through to the bedroom,' I say to her. 'I'll have the sofa.'

She nods her thanks and goes inside. I turn back and see that Kavanagh's watching me again. 'You're sure,' he says again, and I tell him, yes I'm sure, but if he wants to come back in the morning . . .

'Take care, buddy,' he says and pats my back and goes, the Magnum tucked into his waistband, beneath his coat, like he's some ancient gunslinger. And I realise that he enjoyed it. As, strangely, did I.

Doing nothing. That's why I felt so low. It wasn't just thinking about Katerina and the girls, it's what I am. A *Reisende*. Yes, and a bloody good one, too.

I close the door and, going through, briefly check on them before closing the door on them and stretching out on the sofa, the Magnum close at hand.

'I'll be back,' I hear him say.

'Yeah,' I say quietly to the darkness surrounding me. 'And if you do, I'll blow your fucking head clean off your shoulders!'

325

She comes to me in the night. She's half-naked and smelling of some cheap perfume and she wants to say thank you in the only way she can think of. Only I can't. I already have a woman, even if she's lost to me.

I tell her this. Try to explain. 'She's lost,' I say. 'We got separated, in a country far away from here. But she's still mine, and I'm hers . . . for ever.' And the woman looks at me in awe. I can almost hear the thoughts that are going through her head. How lucky Katerina is to have a man like me.

'Look,' I say quietly. 'What do you owe?'

She glances down, disturbed. It's clearly not something she wants to discuss. But I press her on it.

'It's just . . . well, if it's only money, then I can help you. I've five thousand dollars, if that'll help.'

At which her eyes widen even further. No one's ever offered her so much, or taken so little in return. 'I . . . I can't.'

I take her hands in mind. 'You can. You have to. For the children.'

She looks down, abashed. 'Thank you,' she says, then looks up, meeting my eyes. 'Are you sure . . .?'

'I'm sure.'

Only I notice for the first time how aroused she is. For all I've said, she still wants me to take her. As my reward. To thank me for standing up for her. Yeah, and maybe because she simply wants me.

'What's your name?' she asks, and there's the faintest smile on her lips; the first I've seen. It transforms her. Makes her face seem pretty in the half light. Only I've no intention of 'cranking' her. Not even if my body cries out for it. Because there's only one woman for me, in the length and breadth of all the universes that exist.

'My name is Otto,' I say, ignoring the warmth of her where she leans against me on the sofa.

'Maria,' she says, and squeezes my hands.

Maria. It's a pretty name. Only she has to go, now, before I succumb to her.

Her voice is low, almost a whisper. 'Otto?'

'Yes, Maria?'

'Won't you hold me? Just hold me.'

326

There's a song playing on the radio. an example of what they call punk, and while I don't care too much for the tune or the way they play it, a line of it catches my attention and I write it down – *It's the aim of existence to offer resistance to the flow of time.'*

My life, defined in a single line!

I determine there and then to find out more about the guy who wrote it. Some guy named Peter Shelley. Maybe he was an agent. Or knew one.

Maria has gone, hours back, along with her children, the door to her apartment repaired, new locks fitted.

Yes, and I'm glad that she stayed, for I needed someone to hold on to in that dark night of the soul. Someone to give me comfort. And no, I didn't fuck her, much as my body wanted to. And I know that Katerina would have understood.

But for once the dreams didn't come, and for that I am immensely grateful. Even so, I didn't sleep well, and, having sorted everything, I went back to bed, the smell of the woman, Maria, on the sheets, the memory of her eyes, so like Katerina's eyes, haunting me still.

I slept. And woke to a hammering on the door.

It's Kavanagh, who, unknown to me, has been watching the front door of the building. I try to calm him down, because he seems to be panicking, only he's got good reason to. There are two big black cars – limos – downstairs and half a dozen or more black-suited thugs, big men bristling with guns, and Kavanagh thinks that they're heading my way. And that's extremely likely. Only suddenly I can't find my gun. I thought it was on the bed beside me, but it's gone, and I wonder what that means.

Only there's no time. I can hear them on the stairs, huffing and cursing, and suddenly they're there, in the apartment, shouting and gesturing with their guns, and as one of them grabs hold of me, another slips a needle into my arm.

Kavanagh, too, has been taken, kicking and struggling, and as we're dragged away, so I glimpse the woman's apartment, see that the door's wide open and that there's no sign of Maria or her kids.

And then the drug hits me, and I slump . . .

327

. . . And come to, in a room in Washington, DC. Through the window to my left there's a view of the Lincoln Memorial.

'So what happened to DeSario?'

I shake my head to try to clear it, because this is surely a hallucination.

'I beg pardon?' I say, and Phil, who's the man in the chair facing me, repeats it slowly, word for word, like it's something I would know.

'What . . . happened . . . to . . . DeSario?'

'I've never met him.'

Phil leans towards me, his dark eyes studying me. 'So why were you in his apartment? And why don't you have any identification on you?'

'Just why am I here?'

He laughs. 'Don't you know?'

I'm silent for a moment, then: 'I gave you the owl.'

'You gave me . . .?'

'You were living with Kleo. I came to see you one morning, with a gift. Remember?'

Phil's eyes open wide. 'That was *you*?'

Only, now that I think about it, it can't have been, because if it had, this wouldn't be a cul-de-sac timestream. Unless . . .

Well, maybe what I've done is to create a major alternative timeline by giving Dick the owl, unless this has become a central reality – the main trunk of the Tree of Worlds – and just how likely is that?

'I slipped over,' I say. 'Like Jason Taverner.'

Phil laughs. 'You've read my stuff, huh? A lot of people have. But I don't write that kind of thing any more. Not since . . .'

Since Kleo's death, I guess. But he doesn't say.

It's then that I remember something.

'Someone phoned,' I say. 'Left a message for DeSario.'

'And?'

I close my eyes, trying to remember the exact wording, but the drug has muddied my memory.

'He said . . . Tell Lersch Chinese is fine. Will meet as scheduled.'

Phil jumps up at that and claps his hands, a big beam of a smile on his face. It's almost like this is what he's been waiting for, only he makes no attempt to explain.

31

'Who are these people?' I ask. 'Are they agents? And where's Kavanagh?'

But Phil's not listening. He goes to the door and, flinging it open, speaks to the two men who are standing out there in the corridor.

'He's sent the signal.'

I try to turn my head, to see what's going on, but the effects of the drug prevent me. Even so, I'm wondering what I've got myself into here. I thought these guys were mobsters, and it turns out they're government agents – CIA, in all probability.

And Phil, as president, in charge of it all.

So just what *is* going on?

Phil comes across, looking down at me where I'm seated, like he's a mile high. 'Kavanagh's safe. For now. He's waiting for you, in fact. Back at the apartment. But you, Otto . . . It's almost like what you said was true. You're a bona fide mystery. It's like you appeared out of thin air . . . like Schwarzenegger in that movie. Our guys have tried to trace you, but . . . Nothing.'

'*Terminator*,' I say, and he nods and places a hand on my shoulder, like he's an old friend. Which is the truth. Only not here. Not in this timeline.

'I'll be back,' Dick says, in a mock Austrian accent. And then he laughs.

328

Three hours later and I'm back in New York, in the apartment, Kavanagh cooking up some scrambled eggs for the two of us while we chew over what has happened.

Kavanagh, it seems, was questioned for more than six hours, then released after signing a 'good conduct' document. I don't know whether I believe his account – I find it easier to believe he's an agent – but I keep my doubts to myself.

And me? I've been told by Phil to behave myself and not leave the locality. More ominously, they say they're going to be watching me all the while, and maybe that's a good thing – especially if the two guys *were* Mafia.

Speaking of which, Maria's apartment has been boarded up, a heavy padlock securing it. Of Maria herself there's no sign, and when I mentioned her to Phil earlier on, he didn't seem in the least bit bothered with her. Which seemed strange, though I'm not sure why.

The scrambled eggs are good. I wolf them down, then, when he asks if I want some more, hand Kavanagh my plate. I'd forgotten just how hungry I was, and the thought of it reminds me of my plan to have steak, and I mention it and Kavanagh says he'll buy me one, then adds – as if in explanation – that he's heading home tomorrow, a day earlier than he planned. And the thought of being on my own again hits me hard, and I tell Kavanagh about Katerina – my story doctored to make it believable – and he sympathises in a friendly way, and yet again my doubts about the man vanish, and we end the evening at Joe's, both of us tucking in to one of his wonderful sixteen-ounce steaks, with all the trimmings.

And there, on the TV behind the bar, my old friend Phil is suddenly on-screen, announcing a new treaty with China, and also a new phase of NASA's space exploration programme, which aims to have a rocket land on Mars by the year 2000 – another US–Chinese collaboration. And, hearing that, Kavanagh turns to me and laughs.

'Now that really is weird, huh?'

Which is true. But only if you haven't read any of Phil's books.

And then he's gone – vanished into the night – with the promise of calling in on me before he leaves tomorrow lunchtime.

And I turn, facing the building, noting how still, how quiet it seems at that late hour.

329

The door across from mine is open, the padlock gone. I stand there for a moment, wondering what that means. Someone's been here, certainly, but why?

I know that I ought to ignore it. To walk on by and lock my door behind me. Only I can't. I need to know what's happened. Whether she's safe.

Only I *know*, even before I find her, there in the bathroom, the white tiles spattered with her blood spray. Her skin's as white as alabaster. Her tights have been pulled down over her ankles where they've raped her, her breasts exposed, her right eye put out on the edge of the sink. There's clotted blood in her hair and her throat has been cut from ear to ear. Finally, the bath, over which her body's draped, is filled with her blood to a good two inches' depth.

But worst of all is her eye – a single dead eye that is open wide, as if staring into the eternal nothingness that ultimately swallows everything. And it reminds me of the awful dream I had, where Kolya put out Katerina's eyes.

I swallow, feeling nauseous, then go through to find the children. They're in the bedroom, lying side by side on the bed, holding hands, a single bullet hole through each of their tiny foreheads, two big, circular patches of congealed blood on the blankets beneath their heads, the browny-redness overlapping to form a lazy eight, that universal symbol of infinity.

Kolya's calling card.

The sight of it makes me groan. This is my greatest fear. That I can do nothing to help my girls; nothing to prevent this from happening to them. I can see it plainly. How one of them kept them here, while the other did that to the woman. How then he'd shot them; the boy first maybe, and then the sister. And as I think it, so I notice what I missed at first glance. They are not holding hands. Or not just. No. The bastard wired their wrists together, the steel wire cutting deep into the flesh where they had tried vainly to escape.

And instinctively I know that this is Kolya's work. That he's exercising my imagination through the woman and her children. Stripping away another layer of skin.

Why else would he leave his sign?

I leave them there, returning to my apartment. Only for once I don't know what to do, how to respond. I've not even got a gun any more. Phil took that from me.

I look about me, lost, my mind a sudden blank, when I see it, there on the cupboard by the front door. Kavanagh's business card.

I turn it between my fingers and see that he's written down the name and number of the hotel he's staying at, and ask myself whether he had any part in this. Only I know he didn't. Kavanagh's a decent man.

I go through and sit there while I dial the number and wait, and when the concierge answers, I ask for Kavanagh, in as steady a voice as I can muster. He puts me through, and I wait while it rings and rings, and suddenly Kavanagh's there on the other end of the line, his voice heavy with sleep.

'Otto? That you?'

'Kav?

'Hey, buddy . . . what's up?'

I hesitate, wondering just how much to tell him over the phone. In all likelihood this line is tapped. But I need his help.

'It's the woman. She's . . . she's dead.'

'Jeeze! You sure?'

'I'm sure.'

'You still in the apartment?'

'Yeah . . . look . . . I really don't know what to do.'

'Otto. Listen. Just stay where you are. Lock the door and wait. I'll be there in twenty.'

And the phone goes dead.

And as it does, so I wonder – have I done the right thing? Only what else could I do?

I think about the situation, aware, suddenly, that something's wrong. There would have been noise, lots of noise – the kids screaming, and the two gunshots. So why aren't the police here? Surely *someone* would have phoned them.

Kavanagh's there in fifteen. He's carrying a big suitcase, and as he sets it down on the sofa, so he looks at me with a pained expression.

'Otto . . . I've got something to tell you.'

'Yeah?' And I wonder if it's one of the scenarios I've run through my head the last few days. 'You're an agent, right? CIA?'

'Fuck no. But I'm not a lawyer, either.' And as he says it, so he springs the lock on the case and it eases open. And inside . . .

Guns. The whole case is full of guns, everything from handguns to what look like fully automatic army-issue rifles.

I laugh. 'You sell guns?'

Kavanagh smiles. 'Handy, huh?'

And I reflect that that's true. Mighty handy, in fact.

I reach past him and take one of the big guns. A Heckler & Koch G41. It's a German 5.56mm assault rifle. A civilian version of a battlefield weapon.

'You *sell* these?' I ask him as I test the unloaded gun.

Kav smiles and nods, but his eyes are taking in how familiar I am with the weapon. Which is the truth. I've used it many a time, back in the past. It's a beautiful weapon.

'You got shells for this?'

In answer, he shows me the munitions belt he's wearing under his coat, and I laugh.

'Who are you working for, Kav?'

At which he looks hurt. 'Hey, I know I've spun a lie or two, but . . . well . . . this is what I do. I sell guns. And a good living it is, too.'

I slowly nod, taking in what else he's got there in the suitcase. It's a regular little armoury. The only thing that's missing is a laser rifle. And that's only because it's 1984 and far too early for that kind of weaponry.

'So what do you want to do?' Kavanagh asks me.

And in my head I answer him. I want to blow their fucking heads off, that's what I want to do. But I'd have to find them first, and I've a feeling that could be more than a little bit difficult. Only Kavanagh, once more, is way ahead of me.

'Can you use that thing?' he asks me, gesturing towards the gun.

I nod.

'And you seriously want to take these fuckers on?'

I hesitate, then nod again.

'Then I'll take you there. They've a building on Seventh Avenue.'

'How do you know this?'

'They were good customers of mine . . . In the past.'

'What happened?'

'We fell out.'

I don't ask. No. Now that my mind's made up, I get a trench coat from DeSario's wardrobe – bulky enough to hide the fact that I'm carrying the Heckler & Koch, and one or two other items I've selected from Kavanagh's suitcase – and slip it on.

I turn, to find that Kavanagh's busy loading the guns. And not just mine, but his.

'What are you doing?'

He smiles at me. 'You think I'm going to let you go in there on your own? Who d'you think you are? Arnold Schwarzenegger?'

I can see I'm going to have to watch this movie. If I'm still alive, that is.

Five minutes and we're ready. But before we leave the building, I take him inside and show him what those bastards have done, and witness for myself how he's affected by it.

As we step out onto the New York streets there's no outward sign of the weapons we're carrying, but there is something menacing about the look of us. That said, it's dark now, the streets almost deserted, and we seem to melt into the shadows.

'You don't have to do this.'

He looks sideways at me. 'No?'

'What about the woman, back in Chicago?'

'What about her?'

'I thought . . .' Only I don't know quite what I thought. And I'm incredibly grateful to Kavanagh for being there with me. For sticking around. Yes, and for sharing the risk.

Because in all likelihood, neither of us are going to see another morning. And that's asking one hell of a lot of someone you've only known a day or three.

Not that getting revenge for a woman I barely knew makes any kind of sense. Only how could I possibly let that go? How could I let those bastards get away with it? Especially if it *is* Kolya.

The further south we go, the busier it gets. Things are much more lively here. There are whores a plenty, and their pimps, not to speak of the drunks and addicts to whom this late hour is the beginning of their day.

And then suddenly we're there. It's an eight-storey apartment block, and from the lights that are on in a number of its windows, I'd guess that the evening shift was on.

I look to Kavanagh. 'You sure this is it?'

'Uh-huh.'

'And you still want to go along with this?'

'You changed *your* mind, Otto?'

I look back at him, for the briefest moment wondering whether this makes any kind of sense whatsoever. Only if I *am* trapped in this alternate world with no way out, then why not make this ultimately futile gesture? Why not try to clean the streets of some of these motherfuckers and scumbags? Because the authorities sure as fuck aren't committed to the task.

The Heckler & Koch feels reassuringly warm and firm beneath my fingers. I click off the safety and smile at Kavanagh one last time.

And, turning back, facing the big, glass-panelled doorway, we go inside.

330

As we stand there, waiting for the lift to descend, I say a silent goodbye to them all – to Katerina and my girls – because this isn't the kind of adventure where everything turns out well. Nor can it be put right by jumping back in Time. That option simply isn't open to me this once. If they kill me, I stay dead.

Kavanagh, beside me, is quietly whistling to himself. He seems almost cheerful. As for me, I've done this far too often to feel any nerves. I'm not afraid of death.

As the bell pings and the lift hisses open, two of them – big, Italian bastards in black suits and dark glasses – make to exit. There's a moment shocked surprise as they register our weapons, and then they reach for their own.

Only it's too late. Kavanagh takes the big fucker on the left, blowing the top of his skull off, while I rake the other one, the power of the 5.56 millimetre shells making him jerk backwards in an obscene dance.

Stepping over the bodies, we enter the lift.

'Eighth floor,' I say, and Kavanagh obliges me. The doors hiss shut and the big cage begins to ascend.

Kavanagh watches me, a faint smile on his lips now. 'You think they heard that, up on the eighth?'

I shake my head. Only I'm not taking any chances. Whatever advantage we had is being used up fast. They don't know who we are, nor how many of us there are, but they'll know pretty soon that they've been infiltrated.

We're there in thirty seconds. By my calculations, it's not time enough for a message to be phoned through; even so, I have Kavanagh position himself on the far left of the lift.

'Cover me,' I say, and, as the doors begin to open, I'm through the gap, gun raised. Only no one's covering the lift. There's a broad corridor with five doors off of it, two of them facing me directly. It's through these they come, four tough guys, armed with handguns. Kavanagh takes out one of them even as I open up with the Heckler & Koch.

So now they know we're here. From this point on we're in hostile territory. We miss a single one of these fuckers and we're dead.

'You okay?' I ask Kavanagh.

In answer to which he swings the big gun round and fires off a stream of bullets, the closeness of which reminds me just what a knife-edge we're on here. But that's two more dead, and one life I owe Kavanagh.

'How're we going about this?' he asks. 'Room by room, or do you wanna wait right here and pick them off two by two?'

'Down,' I say. 'We keep moving and they can't anticipate us. We stay here and we're dead.'

'All right,' he says. 'You seen the guys who did it yet?'

I shake my head, realising, as I do, just what I'd like to do to those two. More than just kill them.

I indicate the left-hand stairs. 'Down there,' I say quietly, and, as one – as if we've been partners this last dozen years or more – we descend, side by side, our big assault rifles searching for targets.

And almost run into three more of them. It's only the fact that we're silent, and they're talking – a nervous, uncertain chatter – that gives us the edge.

We open up as they come round the corner of the stairs, the noise deafening in that small space, but the second or two advantage means that they don't get off a single shot.

So far, so good. Only now we can hear heavy footfalls on the stairs below, and shouting, and, somewhere, a telephone ringing urgently.

We've killed eleven of the bastards, but if Kavanagh's right, there's a good thirty or more of them in the building, and we sure as hell aren't going anywhere. They'll have sealed off all of the exits by now, and even as we slowly back up the stairs, we hear the power to the lift cut off.

Kavanagh glances at me, a kind of 'what now?' look, and I gesture toward the floor above.

It's identical to the eighth, with five doors, two of which face the lift. I gesture towards the end door and we run across. Kavanagh jerks the door open, and we're met by the shocked stare of a secretary: a young woman in her twenties, who, by the look of it, is on the phone to someone. She's alone in the room, and I go to turn away, when she makes a grab for the gun on the desk beside her.

It's mistakes like that that are fatal, and I deserve to die for making it. Only Kavanagh is on the case, thank Urd. As she lifts the gun and aims it at me, he blows her head off.

Two lives I owe him now.

'Out!' I say urgently, and, both of us taking a long breath, we kick the door in and go in guns blazing.

And take out a big, fat guy in a vest, who falls with a massive thud on the carpet beyond his desk.

'Jeeze,' Kav says, looking at the big guy. 'You know who that is?'

I haven't time. 'Out!' I say. 'Now!'

And we go out again, directly into a firefight. For a minute or two we're pinned down, but then we get lucky and another group of their guys – unnerved, possibly – come up the other stairway, firing as they do, and for a moment the two groups are blowing each other to kingdom come, until one of them realises what's going on. But it gives us the chance we need, and suddenly we're out of there, hurtling down the stairs, shouts and gunfire following us down.

'Where to?' Kav yells.

'Fourth floor,' I answer him breathlessly, praying to the gods that there's not a welcoming committee there. We're lucky. The fourth floor's empty.

But not for long. The circle's closing in on us. We can hear them, up above and on the floors below, shouting, getting closer by the moment.

I turn and kick one of the doors open. The room is empty.

'You know who that was?' Kav asks again. 'Up on the seventh. The fat guy?'

I shake my head.

'That was him. The Big Boss himself.'

'Yeah?' Only I'm looking about me and thinking what a shithole this is. What an awful, shabby cesspit of a room to die in. Because die we shall. They're closing in by the second.

I change the clip in my gun then look to Kav.

'Hey, bud . . . I owe you . . .'

Kav makes a vague sound in his throat then goes over to the window.

'Shee-it!' he says, and the way he says it makes me go to the window to see. And what I see makes me more sure than ever that were going to die. Because there are three, no four big limos pulling up, and lots of black-suited guys pouring out of them.

Only suddenly there's gunfire down there.

'What the . . .?'

The door behind us crashes open and there's sudden gunfire. Kav, I know, is down, but even as the guy in the doorway looks to me, I let loose, a dozen or more shells slamming into him, blowing him out into the corridor.

There's a moment's silence, and then the gunfire starts up again, but far below this time, out in the street and on the lower levels, and for a moment I don't know what the hell is going on. All I know is that, for that brief instant, I am safe. Hurrying across, I kneel beside my fallen buddy and see at a glance that he's not going to make it. Not with those wounds. But I do what I can, holding him and comforting him in those last few moments; telling him I couldn't have done it without him, that I owed him my life.

And then the door crashes open again and the big men with guns are forming a circle about us, even as Kavanagh takes his last, long, shuddering breath, and dies.

A real death, I think. *A meaningful death. One that you don't come back from.*

And, after wiping a tear away, I let them cuff me and lead me away.

'I'll be back,' I say, and the two guys holding me look at me and laugh. 'Fucking comedian, huh?'

331

Four hours later, I'm sitting there with Phil again, only this time we're in the Oval Office, Phil's snowy owl settled sleepily on his shoulder. He stares at me a while, then shakes his head.

'Who are you, Otto? Who are you working for?'

Behind Phil, on a pull-down screen, they're running the edited CCTV footage of our attack on the mobsters' HQ , the sound muted.

'You want the truth?'

'You want to tell me the truth?'

I study him a while. If there's one person in the entire universe who might believe me, he's seated in front of me right now. Or, at least, the old Phil might. This new guy, the one who's president . . . well, he might just think I'm crazy.

'I don't come from this time,' I say, watching his face for his reaction. 'I'm not from the twentieth century.'

He laughs. 'Okay. I get it. You've seen the film. *Terminator*.'

I shake my head, but already I'm thinking that I might have made a mistake.

'Look . . . I realise that what I'm about to tell you sounds like the blatherings of some crazy man, but it's all true. It all happened.'

'And you can prove it?'

'No. I can't, but it's true nonetheless. I'm a *Reisende*.'

'A *Reisende*?' he says, taking great care with the pronunciation of the German word. 'A traveller?'

'That's right. A *time* traveller.'

'Oh . . . of course.'

I look past him, noticing a small movement, there in the shadows of the room, and realise that they're taping this. Of course they are. I mean, after all, I'm sitting with the President of the United States.

'There's this war, you see . . . .or was . . . between us and the Russians.'

'You being . . .?'

'The Germans.'

'The *volk*,' he says. 'You're talking *Rassenkampf*, yeah? A race war throughout Time?'

'That's it. That's it exactly. Three thousand years of time, anyway. Only I've been dumped here . . . here in this cul-de-sac of Time, and I can't get home.'

'And home is . . .?'

The thirtieth century . . . and the thirteenth . . . Only I don't say that.

'To Katerina.'

'Ahhh.' And he smiles, as if he understands. 'A woman. I thought there might be one. Your very own Helen of Troy, yes?'

I'm about to say that Helen has nothing on my darling girl, only there's a sudden knocking and, a moment later, Phil's aide-de-camp pokes his head round the door.

'Mister President . . . the press are going mad out here. They want to know what in God's name's been going on.'

Phil raises a finger, as if to ask for my indulgence, then answers the young man.

'Tell them I'll make an announcement later on. At eight, let's say.'

'But Mr President . . .'

'At eight.'

When the young man's gone, Phil looks to me again. Then, as if he's reached some kind of decision, he nods.

'Okay. Tell me straight, from the top. How you met this Katerina, and why you're trapped in this so-called cul-de-sac of Time.'

And I tell him, and his eyes show a pained understanding. I talk about the two great Masters, and the great war in Time and about Katerina and the girls . . . even about Reichenau and Kolya. And I know it sounds real whacko, but Phil just nods and listens. And then, when I fall silent, he tells me about his own VALIS experience and about the figure at the end of his bed. And he says all this despite the cameras watching, recording it all.

'I understand now,' he says finally. 'This reality of ours wasn't meant to be, was it? You shifted it.'

'Yes,' I say, understanding it for the first time ever. 'By loving her.'

'Then find her again. And save her.'

I'm silent a moment, then, 'Did your agents take my charts?'

'Charts?' He looks up, knowing that they're listening in.

A voice answers him. 'No, Mr President. There were no charts of any kind in the apartment.'

Phil looks to me again. 'Are they important?'

'Maybe,' I answer cryptically. Only I know the solution is there, somehow, among my loose endings.

I look to him again. 'What are you going to say? To the press, I mean.'

Phil smiles. 'We'll make something up. And hey . . . it'll even have an element or two of the truth in the mix.' He pauses, then, 'You know . . . you solved a big problem for us today, Otto. The guys you killed . . . the Mafiosi. We think they were behind the assassination of President Reagan, only we couldn't prove it. Now we don't have to.'

'Phil?'

'Yes, Otto?'

'Can you place me back there? In DeSario's apartment.'

'Are you sure that's where you want to be? If this Kolya fellow is watching you . . .'

But I'm certain now that he is. Or one of his agents.

'Can you?'

Phil hesitates, trying to work me out, and then he smiles. 'Okay. But we'll have to smuggle you out on the graveyard shift. We've half the world's press out there, clamouring for answers. Oh, and Otto . . .'

'Yes, Phil?'

'It must be real neat, going to all those times and places, meeting all those great men and women. Making changes.'

'Then you believe me?'

But Phil doesn't answer that. Maybe it's too incriminating. Instead he gets up, then leaves the room, the snowy owl fluttering on his shoulder as he goes.

332

That night, an hour before the dawn, I am in DeSario's apartment, stretched out on the big double bed, pretending to be asleep, when a ghostly figure appears in the room. It's no one I know, but I know who he's working for. Kolya. It can be nobody else.

Through half-lidded eyes, I watch him quickly search the room, and as he turns to go through into the living room, I spring up and grab hold of him. He tries to shake me off, but I cling on for dear life.

And as I do he jumps . . . out of that cul-de-sac world and back . . .

To Four-Oh. And it's there that he finally manages to shake me off, and immediately jumps again. Leaving me alone. Only I'm suddenly not alone. Because Freisler is there, like he's been expecting me all along. And he hands me a handwritten note from myself with a set of time coordinates on it. And I turn and see that Zarah too is there, and she takes the note from me and keys it in, before wishing me 'Strength'.

David Wingrove

And I jump, not knowing where I'm going or why, simply trusting to my future self.

The crazy man. The mafia killer. But more than any of these, the *Reisende* once more. And I grin, even as I move between the worlds. And, remembering my buddy Kavanagh, offer a thanks to the air. Three lives. I owe the man three lives.

48

Part Twelve

Perpetual Change

333

And jump into darkness, the smell of wet grass and campfires filling my nostrils. For a moment I stagger, unable to keep my balance, then steady myself, even as a tall figure appears from the other side of the clearing, cloaked and brandishing a fluttering torch.

As he comes towards me, I raise a hand to protect myself, then let it fall, laughing, astonished.

'*You!*'

It is indeed 'me'. Or some future version of myself. Older. Greyer. Hopefully more wise.

'Where are we?' I ask.

'Russia,' I answer.

'More precisely?'

'Poltava . . . Where else?'

Where else indeed. For Poltova is where it's won or lost. For us in Time, and for Peter in his reality.

Yes, the emperor, Peter, otherwise known to history as 'The Great', that six-foot-seven giant among his diminutive fellow Russians.

'When's the battle?'

'This morning,' he says, and I know from that that it is the twenty-sixth of June, 1709, and that the fate of two great empires is to be decided in the next twelve hours.

I look around me, taking it all in properly for the first time. There's a force of close on fifty thousand men encamped upon the low hillside overlooking the valley, and it's an uncomfortably warm night.

I turn to him again. 'Okay. But why here? What's happening?'

'The Russian agents are fighting among themselves.'

'Fighting?'

'Yes. It's civil war.'

That, more than anything, surprises me. 'Why now? I mean, what's going on?'

'I . . . Look . . . they're waiting for us.'

'Waiting? Are you sure this isn't a trap?'

And then I realise that in all probability he *is* sure. Only he can't tell me, because I've got to experience this – as he already has – before we move on in the loop. And any doubts I have about these renegades falls away. If I'm alive in the future, then it means that I've lived through this once already. Then why do it? Why have my future self there to greet me? Maybe so that I don't just jump straight out of there?

The inn's a mile away. There, in the cramped back room, three Russian agents are waiting for us. I know all three well. I've fought them many a time. Bobrov, Zasyekin and Svetov. They are dressed like peasants from the late Tsarist period, as if they've come directly from that time.

'Okay,' I say, looking from one bearded face to the next, as suspicious of them as I could possibly be. 'What the fuck is going on?'

I expect some kind of angry counter from them, telling me, perhaps, where I can stick my question, but all I get from them is respect. A respect that borders on reverence. And that, more than anything, makes me think something's badly wrong.

'So just what *do* you want?' I ask, after an awkward silence.

Bobrov looks to the other two, then back at me. 'We need to know what to do.'

I laugh. 'You want *me* to tell *you* what to do?' And I look to my other, future self, to see if I heard it right, or whether I've started hallucinating. Only he seems as serious as they.

'What's happening?' I ask him a second time. Then, to Bobrov and the others. 'You want to surrender to me, is that it?'

My future self looks to the Russians, then answers me. 'That's not it, Otto. That's not it at all. You see, the rules have changed. The Game . . . it's ending. Not everyone can accept that, but it's true. That's why they're here. To begin the process.'

'Process?'

'Of making the peace between us.'

I stare back at my older self, open-mouthed, not quite able to believe what he's just said, even though it's me who's said it.

'It's true,' Svetov says, his eyes imploring me to accept the situation. 'This now . . . this meeting . . . this is the start of something. Where it goes we don't entirely know just yet, only . . .'

'Only I don't trust you.'

Their heads go down, like they're disappointed.

'Only you must,' my future self says, reaching out to hold my arm. 'You *have to* trust them. There's no going forward without that.'

I want to jump right out of there. To see Hecht to discuss this. To argue it through. Only Hecht is dead and I'm Meister now.

I turn back. 'How many of you are there? Just you three?'

Svetov smiles. 'No. There's more than fifty of us. And more joining by the hour. Word's getting round . . .'

'Word? Word of what?'

'Of what you did, at Cherdiechnost.'

That stops me dead. They *know* about Cherdiechnost? The mere thought of it terrifies me. And I jump. Back to Four-Oh, praying that there's something I can do.

334

Back on the platform, Old Schnorr is waiting for me, bristling with excitement.

'Look, Otto!' he says, thrusting a bulky file at me. 'They're coming back. Dozens of them. Ours and theirs.'

'I haven't time—' I begin, only Old Schnorr interrupts me.

'Agents, Otto. That's what I'm talking about. *Reisende.* Coming back from the future.'

'But they can't . . . It isn't possible.'

'Things are changing fast, Otto. Someone must have come up with some new time equations. Something that allows this new phenomenon.'

I glance through the file, noting the endlessly repeated faces. Old Schnorr is not wrong. It's actually happening. Only how is this tied in to the renegade Russian agents – to Svetov and the rest of them? And why are they asking *me* what they should be doing?

'Oh, and Otto . . . one more thing. One of them came back here, to Four-Oh. He says he knows you. He's waiting for you in your rooms right now.'

335

I step inside, not knowing who it might be. And pull up sharply, shocked.

'How in Urd's name . . .?'

Because it's not an agent, it's Saratov. Sergei Ilya Saratov, who I last saw in northern Russia in the thirteenth century. Saratov the native guide, who helped us make our way upriver.

He is beaming. The same smile I remember so well.

'I'm sorry I had to conceal things from you, Meister, but I was under strict orders. We had to keep you alive, you see. If we hadn't . . .'

And he too hands me a file – a report on the journey through northern Russia we made with him.

Only it isn't. The report is different in a number of important ways. This charts a journey I didn't make. Or rather, one I don't remember making. One that was erased from Time, the only record of it here, and maybe in Sergei Ilya Saratov's mind.

'This happened?' I ask, looking up from the final page.

Saratov nods. 'As I said. We had to keep you alive. That was our priority. Because without that . . .'

But Saratov can clearly say no more. I ask him on whose orders and he's quiet a moment, before finally telling me.

'On yours, Master.'

I frown at that use of my title. 'So what now?'

'You have to *become* Master.'

'But I *am* Master.'

'No. Yastryeb is dead. *You* must be *the* Master now. Master of Russia *and* Germany.'

336

And so I go back, to Poltava, to meet my future self again and debate what must be done.

It is only four in the morning, yet the battle has already begun. The Swedes, under Rehnskjold and Lewenhaupt, have already advanced beyond the first two of the big earth redoubts Peter has had thrown up to delay them, meaning to gain the advantage of surprise over a Russian force twice their size. But the fatal mistake lies ahead. That is, if this is how things originally were, and circumstances have not been radically changed. For, you see, last time I was here – here under Hecht's strict orders – things had changed in four or five utterly critical ways, and Peter – against all historical precedent – was about to lose.

I know both men, of course I do, that's my job, only this once I am not there to meet with either of them, but to find out just how deeply Reichenau is involved in all of this.

I know immediately where we are – five miles north of Poltava, where Charles has his headquarters, on the hillside near the tiny village of Yakuvtsy. Menshikov's forces are to our west, strung out in a long line behind the redoubts, while to the north are Peter's forces.

My future self steps out from the trees behind me, cloaked and empty-handed. He greets me with a smile, but I can see the weariness in his eyes. He, much more than me, has clearly had a long day.

'And so it begins,' he says.

There's much that does not need to be said. He knows all that I know, after all. But there are things he needs to say, simply to feed the loop we are all in.

'Reichenau *is* here,' he says. 'Somewhere. At least . . . we think he is. We almost captured one of his men.'

'Anyone we know?'

He shakes his head. 'No. But they're clearly the ones who've been meddling. With a little help from our friends, the renegades.'

'About the renegades . . .' I begin. But my older self, of course, already knows, and answers what I would have asked.

'It's the older agents, mainly. Those of them who find it hard to adapt to the new order of things. The new guys – from the future – they don't have any problem with it. And it's them – a core of them, anyway – who are driving this. But the older men . . .

well, it's hard to persuade them that it's all been one huge mistake. They don't like it. It invalidates their whole lives. All those long years of struggle. All of those deaths. For that to mean nothing . . . that's a hard notion to swallow.'

'I can see that.'

'Good. Then be patient with them. Oh, there will be some – many, even – who will *never* be able to accept what is happening, who will fight on, in the old fashion. But the majority will come around.'

'And our role in all of this?'

'Our role . . . or *my* role, if you'd prefer . . . is to be the focal point, the *gathering point* of the new order. To be the figurehead of this new movement. To which end, we're convening a conference, to formulate policy and cement relationships.'

'When is this to be?'

My future self smiles again, brighter this time. 'When better than right now? The table's already set, dear self.'

'And where will it be held?'

His smile broadens. 'On neutral ground, Otto. In Tannenberg.'

337

We jump through, to a vast, sloping field with a panoramic view of broad, steeply trenched valleys and bright-running rivers, and, more distant, mountains, stretching away into the haze of the south. The grass is waist high, and when I turn, to look up the slope, I see, for the first time, framed against the backdrop of the pine forest, the massive dark wood farmhouse and, on the spacious deck that extends from beneath the building, two large wooden tables that have been pushed together to seat the two dozen guests who will shortly be arriving.

The sky's a dark slate East Prussian blue, great fists of cloud drifting slowly from one horizon to another. It could be any time, any year. Otto wishes me luck, then jumps again. And is gone. Leaving me singular.

Tannenberg. The very name resounds with our dark history. It was here, in 1410, that the Polish and Lithuanian armies took on the might of the Teutonic Knights under Hochmeister Von Jungingen. And beat them, leaving 18,000 dead on the battlefield. It was here also, in the first week of the Great War of 1914, that the German Eighth Army under Von Hindenburg and Ludendorff, took on the Russian Second Army under Marshal Alexander Samsonov. And destroyed them, taking 92,000 prisoners, and killing or wounding 78,000. Rather than report the defeat to his Tsar, Samsonov committed suicide. And here, too, in July 1944, a vast Russian army took on the combined battalions of the German SS and eventually defeated them, losing between two and three hundred thousand men in doing so, compared to twenty thousand German losses.

Men have fought and died here. And for what? To prop up kings and tsars. To defend the notion of empire. So much suffering and sorrow. For every man dead, a dozen grieving.

Well, now we had a chance to put an end to that. To forge another way.

There is a moment – seconds turning slowly into minutes – when I am alone there. When, as I am wont to, I think of Katerina, and whatever joy I have in life is bleached from me, leaving only a great dull ache. For without her what is there? She is my world.

And then they come, homing in from Time itself. From far and wide, and times innumerable.

The first to appear is Ernst, dressed in his Russian furs.

We embrace warmly. 'I'm sorry—' he begins, but I shake my head. 'Not now. There'll be time. Later.'

They follow quickly after that. Bobrov, Nemsov and Svetov, Meisner and Schmidt, my old friend Burckel, and my much older foe, Dankevich, whom I thought dead. Two Russian women are next, strong beauties in matching scarlet dresses – Irina Yusupov and Alina Tupayeva – accompanied by Igor Kurdin. They are followed by two more of my compatriots – Old Schnorr himself and Hans Zieten.

And then, totally unexpected, but why so? Zarah and Urte appear arm-in-arm from the air, grinning at the sight of me.

When we're done, there are twenty-four of us, including myself. Twelve Germans and twelve Russians, eighteen men and six women, fifteen old-timers and nine from Up River. The core of our new movement. An assembly that, a mere three weeks ago, would have been unthinkable.

Most, I note, have not even stopped to change. They are in the garments and uniforms of two dozen times, two dozen ages. Summoned back from history.

I greet each one of them in turn, though some more warmly than others. My future self is right. It's hard to trust those you've been at war with for the best part of two centuries.

Dankevich especially.

I take my seat at the centre of it all, like Christ at the last supper, and we begin. I go to speak, only Arkadi Svetov, seated at the far end of the table, to my left, stands and, looking to me, speaks to the gathered company in his rich, deep voice, his whole weight resting on his hands, which press palm-down against the tabletop.

He is a big man, full-bearded with a barrel chest, and his thick and heavy fur makes him look like some warrior of the far north.

Which, of course, he is. In several of his 'lives'.

He addresses us in twenty-sixth-century American, a neutral language, chosen so as not to offend either group of agents.

'Forgive me, Otto. But you will have your say. All this is fresh to our experience, and I wanted to address that. To speak openly of it, if you like. You see, to *not* be at war, that is strange indeed, and we must face that strangeness. We must learn to give up old habits, old instincts and re-forge our most basic relationships. We must learn to work with rather than against. *That* – that difficult adoption of new ways of thinking and feeling – is the challenge we face in the days to come. Not the renegades, but our own selves.'

He pauses, looking from face to face about the table, and as he does, so I wonder why they have chosen me and not Svetov for their Master. For Svetov is the real thing. A leader among men. And me? I am a lone wolf. Not a team player at all. I make to say this, but again he talks over me.

'Forgive me, Otto, I know how anxious you are to have your say, but there are things that must be said before you do. Things that must be laid before this council – this *veche* – and acknowledged. Let us have no doubt about it. This is a historic moment. We who are gathered here today have taken that all-important first step. That said, a long journey lies ahead of us. We face a long, hard struggle before the peace we seek becomes a living reality. And unless we recognise that, unless we take that into the equation when we formulate our strategies, we will undoubtedly fail.'

Svetov pauses, slowly nodding his head.

'Hard times lay ahead of us, dear friends. Difficulties unimagined when it was simply Us and Them. No. We must become different people. Kinder, *better* people. And to achieve that, we need to reconstruct who we are. To cast off old ways, old prejudices. As Otto did . . .'

I am on my feet at that, but still Svetov will not let me speak.

'Oh, let us have no doubt about it. Without Otto's example, we would still be at each other's throats. Still playing war games.

Letting that man and his abominable progeny blind us to the truth—'

'Which is?' someone calls from the far end of the table.

'That we are brothers, not enemies—'

'And sisters!' Zarah calls out, laughter following her words.

'And sisters,' Svetov echoes, smiling broadly. 'And that's another thing some of us need to learn. As Russians we have long known the true value of our women and have involved them at every stage—'

There are dissenting sounds at that, and the same voice from the far end of the table – Zieten, I think it is – calls out once more. 'You seek to criticise us, Arkadi Svetov?'

'Not at all, no, not at all, dear friend. Just that we must learn not to accept the old ways of doing things . . .'

'And if those old ways are *better* ways?'

I can see, already, what difficulties lie ahead. But Svetov smooths things over.

'Then we will consider keeping them. I only mention the question of our female comrades because their . . . *frustration*, let us call it . . . was very much a contributory factor behind this movement towards the reconciliation of our two parties.'

I look to Zarah at that, surprised. Is that so? Have they really been working towards this all this time?

And, strangely, unexpectedly, I feel a twinge of guilt. All of this, after all, is a kind of betrayal. Of Hecht and what we have been brought up to believe.

Which it is. Only that doesn't mean we're wrong. Because there has to be a better way of conducting ourselves in Time. Some kinder, *more humane* way of resolving our differences.

And so it begins, as the afternoon draws on and two dozen very different – and very vocal – individuals express two dozen different opinions on each matter. Unprepared, I find myself not speaking, but listening for once; taking it all in, and glimpsing, early on, just how difficult a task this is likely to be. For all their determination, creating a new design for living – one that breaks away from the old patterns of being – is not likely to be easy, for there are sharp divisions on many subjects. One thing alone unites them presently: a desire to hunt down and kill that bastard Reichenau. For they know now. Know that it was he who kept the Great Time War going; he who, like the mischievous half-god Loki, meddled in mankind's affairs and caused the great rift between the tribes.

Or not caused. No. That's taking things too far. Because *Rassenkampf* was real, back at the start of things. Back when things were raw. No, *caused* is wrong. *Maintained* expresses it much better. As a fire is fed.

Yes, and now they're out there, our agents and theirs, the older generation mainly, fighting throughout Time to keep things as they were. And no doubt Reichenau is involved once more, recruiting from our ranks. Promising them glory and revenge.

And that worries me more than anything, for that older generation – *my* generation – are a lot tougher and more experienced than the young ones coming from Up River. We have no names yet – no idea who it is that's leading the resistance, or even if there *is* an organised resistance as such. But one thing is certain. There have been deaths. Ambushes in Time. Yes, and though the platforms have been denied to them, some of them, we know, are still making jumps out there, which suggests – to me, anyway, and to Old Schnorr – that they have somehow obtained some of the jump pendants. Now, whether that's from Up River, or whether they've been given them by Reichenau, we know for certain that they're trying to cause as much trouble as they can.

I am about to say something in this regard, when a figure shimmers into being next to Svetov. It is my future self, dressed for the Russia of the early eighteenth century. The table falls silent.

'Forgive me, Arkadi,' he says, placing his hand on Svetov's shoulder briefly, 'but I must borrow myself for a while.'

'Is there news?' Svetov asks, half turning, looking up into his face.

My other self hesitates, and I wonder why. Then he shakes his head. 'I'll return Otto, ASAP,' he says, and, looking to me, gives me the slightest nod. And we jump.

338

Back to Poltava. In those narrow streets, surrounded by the Swedes and their allies, as the sun begins its long climb up the sky, I strain to hear the sounds of battle, but there are none. It seems we have jumped in several days before the two great armies engage.

We are not here to alter that. No. We're here to take one of Reichenau's men. To capture him and take him back to Four-Oh, there to question him.

We go to an inn, to which two of our agents – young men from Up River – have traced the man. From what they can make out he is in his room even now, asleep after a long night of debauchery. Personally, I wonder why we're waiting. Why it needs two of me to take this one. But it seems they wanted to be sure. To receive my orders before going in. And this small incident makes me realise how uncertain our forces currently are. How in need they are of strong leadership, with both Hecht and Yastryeb dead.

And that's my task. Lone wolf or not, I must at least act as if I know what I'm doing. As if I had some kind of plan.

'You, Grigor. Is the door locked?'

He shrugs.

'Okay. Well, the first thing I want you to do is try it. See if we can go in there any other way but jumping.'

'But . . .'

'No. We keep it simple. We go in there, remove his pendant, and replace it with one of our own. You have it, Otto . . .'

And I turn to my other self who, searching his pockets, is surprised to find one of the new jump pendants there.

I take it from him and hand it to the other. Dimitri.

'It's like this. You hold the man down, Dimitri, while Grigor removes the pendant. Cut it from him if you must, but don't let him jump. Then get the new pendant about his neck, so that when he jumps he's going nowhere but back to the platform at Four-Oh.'

'Yes, Meister,' they say, as one, and now that they've a task, they seem very different men, full of enthusiasm.

'Good. Then I'll see you there.'

And I jump. Back to Four-Oh, stepping from the platform even as the two young men appear in the air, their captive held between them.

There, I think. *Simple.*

Only the captive agent is one we've never seen before – even Old Schnorr fails to recognise him – and, perhaps more tellingly, he's mute. No tongue at all in his head.

I curse. Is this Reichenau messing with our heads again?

'Question him,' I say, taking the two men aside. 'Use chalk and slate to ask him questions, if you have to. He may have no tongue, but I reckon he can spell well enough. And if he proves reluctant, then hand him over to Freisler. He'll find a way to get him to tell us what he knows.'

I say that, not thinking properly, not actually knowing whether Freisler has joined us or become a renegade. But my guess is that he has. After all, he has always been loyal to the Meister. And I'm Meister now, so . . .

So I simply don't know. And that's the truth. Maybe Old Schnorr can draw me up a list of ours and theirs. If that's at all possible.

Thinking of Old Schnorr makes me realise – the conference is still going on. Important matters are being discussed, a new order being constructed, piece by piece, and I ought to be there, directing that process, playing peacemaker to the various factions.

I turn, meaning to summon one of the women, only to find Zarah standing there, waiting for me.

'It's okay,' she says. 'I've come to take you back.' And, taking my arm, we step back onto the platform and, just a second or two later, are back on the grassy slope beneath the farmhouse in Tannenberg, everyone at the two big tables turned to witness us appear from the air.

As Zarah and I take our seats, they wait, all eyes on us, only the faintest murmur of insects disturbing the ancient silence of the afternoon.

I sit, then look about me. 'Okay. So what did I miss?'

Svetov grins. 'We've been hearing about how things are, Up River. But then you know all about that stuff. Saratov briefed you, didn't he?'

'He did. And is that all?'

'No,' Urte, the smallest of us says, leaning forward. 'We've a problem.'

'I wouldn't call it that,' Svetov begins, but she interrupts him.

'D'you want this to work, or don't you?'

Svetov frowns. He's clearly not a man who's used to contradiction. But he swallows it this time. For the sake of making things work.

'A problem?' I look about me, seeing how every face wears the same look of pained concern. 'What kind of problem?'

'It's Freisler,' Ernst says. 'He's gone. There's simply no sign of him. It's like he's fallen off the map.'

'What if he's dead?' I ask. 'What if one of us has killed him, up the line?'

'Maybe we have,' Svetov says, with the slightest glance at Urte, as if he's checking whether it's okay for him to speak. 'But what concerns me – and others here, I'm sure – is the timing of things. For him to vanish as he did, at the moment we convened this meeting . . .'

'You think he's Reichenau's man?' I ask. 'You think he's been working for him all along?'

'I don't,' Svetov says, surprising me. 'I'd have said there was no more loyal man than Freisler. Only his loyalty was to the *volk*. He was Hecht's man, Otto. Never yours.'

I nod, taking that in, wondering what damage Freisler was doing even as we sat there, prevaricating. And as I did, I realised that they were waiting once again. Waiting for me to come up with a solution, or at least a strategy for dealing with the man.

'What we need right now,' I begin, 'more than anything, is information. We need to identify *who* our opponents are and *where* they're based. Because they must be based somewhere. Somewhere they can eat and sleep in safety and, well, someone who's organising all of that.'

Zarah raises a hand, fingers splayed.

'Yes, Zarah?'

'All that's to be discovered. Who they are, where they are. But what is *most* urgent is for us to protect what we have. Our platforms – Four-Oh and Moscow Central – particularly. Because without those we simply can't function. And they've never been so vulnerable, so accessible to our enemies, whoever they are.'

And even as she says it, some part of me knows it has already been attended to – or is just about to, which pretty much equates to the same thing in Time.

'As I see it, it's all very simple,' I say, thinking aloud. 'We need to out-think them. To anticipate and use the skills we have. To track them down and eliminate them, one by one. Until the job is done.'

Yes, and to find Katerina and my girls. Only I don't say that, even if everyone at that table knows what drives me.

'So what first?' Svetov asks. 'Freisler? Should we form a team to track that bastard down?'

'A mixed team,' I say. 'Germans *and* Russians. Good, reliable men who've had no exposure to Freisler. Because the last thing we want is to have our agents "turned" against us.'

Further down the table, across from me, Dankevich laughs and then leans forward. 'It seems to me that that's the biggest problem we have. Bigger than Freisler. Bigger than defending the platforms. Knowing who to trust. Get that wrong and . . .'

I stare at him a moment, trying to read what's behind the surface of his eyes, but it's no good. If there's one man at that table that I don't trust, it's Dankevich. Yet he comes with the endorsement of all the Russian camp. They tell me he's a man to be relied on, absolutely and to the death.

Well, we'll see, eh? In the meantime I resolve to place a man on him, to keep tabs as to what he does and where he goes. Yes. Maybe I'd even delegate that task to Zarah. Put her and Dankevich in a team for some purpose or another – nothing critical, but somewhere he could prove his worth to us.

My instinct, of course, is to kill him. Now, before he can betray us. Because I have a very bad feeling about Dankevich. I've killed him far too often to feel at ease with him covering my back. No. But I could limit any damage. Until we'd proved his loyalty . . . or lack thereof.

'Okay.' I say, looking about the table, shutting my mind temporarily to all such doubts, focusing on the task in hand. 'What's next on the agenda?'

339

We take a break. The first of many. Breaks to go and consult experts. Breaks to set things in motion. Breaks simply because we needed a break, the tension was running so high. But, more than anything, breaks to keep checking to see what effect our actions were having on the Tree of Worlds.

I'd noticed it earlier, at the platform of Four-Oh. How the operators were mixed now – half men, half women. And how respectfully they stood, heads bowed, whenever I entered that massive room.

Things were changing, especially now that we shared DNA access to each other's platforms. Slowly as yet, but with a sense of inexorable progress. A whole new way of doing things. One aspect of which was my first visit to Moscow Central. There, even more than at Four-Oh, I was greeted with an enthusiasm I found hard to comprehend.

I turned to Svetov. 'What *is* this, Arkadi? Why was *I* chosen?'

The big man laughed, then placed his hand on my shoulder, his eyes meeting mine, an almost fervent look in them.

'Because you chose Katerina.'

He is about to say more, to explain it all to me, when Dimitri shimmers out of the air.

'The mute has spoken,' he says breathlessly, handing the slate to me, on which there is a single word. Or, rather, a name.

Shafarevich.

If Freisler disappearing was bad, this is many times worse, for Shafarevich was the Russians' best agent. And, if what Reichenau's mute says is true, it's he whom the renegades have chosen for their 'Meister'.

Yes, but in charge of whom? Just a handful of Russians, or more than that?

'We must ask him for more. For other names and the number of his accomplices. For whom he answers to, and . . .'

I stop. Dimitri is shaking his head. 'We can't. He's been taken.'

'*Taken?*' Only I can see it, even as I frame the word. Reichenau, there in the cell with him, taking our pendant from his neck and putting his own in its place.

Reichenau, then . . . and Shafarevich . . . and Freisler . . .

The thought of those three working together, causing trouble together, chills me. Makes me think, for the first time, that we just might lose this one.

Only I can't say that. Can't even suggest it. Not if we're to win new converts. Not if we're to convince the un-persuaded that we *can* win. Because, right now, it's all balanced on a knife's edge, and while we have the massive tactical advantage of the platforms, that may not last. As Zarah said, they've never been so vulnerable. And none of those unholy three are idiots. Why, they'll be working right this moment on some scheme to grab them from us and set themselves up as time lords.

'Otto?'

'Yes, Arkadi?'

'There's something I need to say. Something I haven't told you about.'

'Then speak.'

Only it seems Svetov isn't going to tell me, not without telling everyone else. And so we return to Tannenberg and that long and crowded table, all of whom fall silent when Svetov and I reappear.

'Comrades,' Svetov says, remaining standing even as I take my seat. 'We have spoken many times now about what was wrong with "The Game". Of our general feeling that the wrong path was taken. That changing the past merely to destroy one's enemies was not the answer. It is why we are here. To repair what has been done, and to forge a new path. And so we shall. But first we must make sure that there *is* a path into the future.'

Svetov pauses, almost theatrically, I think, then looks at me, his whole demeanour changed. 'You see . . . It has already begun. In the last hour alone, twelve agents have died. Five of ours, and seven of theirs. And why? Because they recognise where our greatest weakness lies. Not with the platforms, but with the one I'd have you all call Meister. With Otto here . . .'

I expect there to be turmoil, only the mood around the table now is subdued. Every eye is on me, as if to judge my response.

'I mean,' he continues, 'that new information has reached us.'

'Information?'

'As to their strategy.'

Svetov needs to say no more. I understand.

'They mean to kill me, yes?'

Svetov nods.

'And that's the whole of it, right? No other plan than that?'

Svetov hesitates, then nods.

'And have they succeeded?'

'Not yet . . . but things are changing. Even as we speak, news is coming from Up River. It seems they're sending in teams to try to track you down.'

'So what's our answer? To surround me with agents?'

'We're doing that already.'

'And that's the all of it? The sum total of their strategy?'

'As far as we can make out. New information is coming through all the time, and some of it is . . . well, hazy to say the least. But one thing's clear. They mean not to stop until you're dead.'

'Then let them come.'

There's a rumble of disagreement from about the table, but I raise my voice and all there fall silent once more.

'No, really: let them come. What easier course is there? I meant to track them down, one by one, but if this is true . . . well, then, they'll come to me.'

Like lambs to the slaughter. Only I don't say that. There are still some here, even at this gathering, who still find it hard to see the renegades as their natural enemies. They've worked alongside these people far too long to find any of this natural.

But so revolutions are.

340

When we next take a break, I take Svetov aside and ask him what I've wanted to ask him since his first mention of it.

'You spoke of Cherdiechnost . . .'

'You want to go there?'

His words shock me. 'Can I?'

'Of course. The only question is . . . when?'

I stare at the big man, and find myself full of questions. But only one is of any real importance.

'Will *she* be there?'

His dark eyes are smiling now. 'She will.'

'Then . . .'

'Come,' he says simply, taking my arm, and in an instant we are there.

Cherdiechnost . . . So like the paradise I'd pictured in my dreams and memories, that, seeing it again, I almost break down crying. For this is home.

Even so, I don't properly understand it. Svetov is a Russian, after all, and up until a day or so ago, he was my enemy. So why does this exist? Why, if they knew of it, did they allow it to remain unscathed?

I turn to face him. 'I don't understand. You knew of this, and yet . . .'

'We had agents there. Trailing you and Ernst. Keeping watch on you. Reporting back to the *veche*. To start with we let things be. Then there was all that business with the small man . . . Kravchuk.'

Hearing that name I bristle. 'You saw all that?'

'Barely any of it. But your behaviour, Otto. It shocked us. Most of us, that is. But several of us were intrigued. And so we let things go. Saw how they developed. And then you made this.'

And Svetov gestures, his arms encompassing the whole of the estate, bathed as it is in the afternoon sunlight.

'It's beautiful, neh?' I say quietly, in awe of what I'd made of this place. 'Even so . . .'

Svetov laughs. 'We protected it.'

'You *what*?'

'Yes. There were debates . . . heated debates . . . in our *veche*. Some wanted it destroyed, along with yourself, Otto. Others . . . the majority, in fact, wanted to protect it . . . while we could.'

'But why? I was your enemy.'

'Our *enemy*?' Svetov laughs again and looks about him, his eyes drinking in the scene. 'Why, I've never seen a man more thoroughly Russian than you, Otto. And your girls . . . they were so beautiful . . .'

I note that *were*. 'I need to get them back,' I say. 'I need . . .'

Only he knows what I need. 'You want to see them?' he asks.
I am afraid even to nod, but my eyes say yes.
'Then come. We can't stay long. Not this time.'

341

I am there less than an hour, and in that brief time I do not get to
meet with them. But they are there, and from our vantage point,
hidden above one of the great barns, Svetov and I watch Katerina
as she goes about her tasks, shepherding our baby girls as she makes
her way here and there about the estate, organising everything in
my absence, so beautiful she takes my breath.

And afterwards, back in Four-Oh, I sit there for a long while,
in a daze at what I've done. For it is true. Our love was *meant*.
Was the very means by which the great breach between the tribes
was healed. My love for Katerina, it seems, is central to everything,
even Time itself. Whether this was always so, or was the result of
my meddling and rule-breaking, is no longer pertinent. So it is.
And nothing, it seems, can change that.

Unless, that is, I die. Unless I cannot find them all and bring
them back.

I return to the conference table, heartened by my brief vacation,
understanding now just why this strangest of meetings came about.

All for a pair of eyes.

But, much as I'd like to, I cannot dwell on that right now. There's
much still to be done. And so we draft an agreement to close down
all of our projects – Russian and German alike. All of those petty
schemes to change each other's history. All of those once-important
ventures into Time, ended in an instant, at a show of hands.

And in its place? New to-be-formulated schemes. Better ways
of doing things. Or so we hope.

We are about to wind things down when a messenger arrives. He bows before me and reports.

'The rebels have made their move, Meister. We need to intervene.'

'Where and when?' I ask, half-anticipating what he'll say.

Thirteenth-century Russia. On the way from Novgorod to Moscow.

I look to Svetov, who nods and hurries away, to organise a team of German and Russian agents to make sure we survive that journey, and to keep the rebels from capturing Katerina and me. Which I know they will. For all of this is in the loop. It will happen because it has already happened.

And, joining them, I find myself on the forest path to Sycevka once again, watching from a distance, as, in the valley below us, Lishka and his old horse and cart accompany Katerina and my former self across that heavily wooded terrain, making for Rzev, two weeks off.

It is strange, seeing my former self, and knowing what's to come. The cesspit of a village that is Sycevka is only half a mile ahead of us now, on the southern shore of the lake, and it is near there – barely another mile further on – that we will be ambushed. There that we so nearly died.

Svetov stands close by, his hand raised to shield his eyes against the morning sunlight, even as our earlier selves hurry through the village and on.

'Here,' my Russian friend says, handing me a pair of high-powered field glasses. 'Any moment now . . .'

And, even as he says it, so, through the glasses, I see myself go down, clutching the back of my bloodied head, where that little bastard with the slingshot has hit me. For a moment I lie there, stunned, then, giving a small, shrugging motion, begin to haul myself up. I look for Katerina with the glasses and find her, seeing how she ducks beneath the swipe of one of the attackers and plunges her knife deep into his guts.

And Lishka? I see him grin, laughing manically as his stave sweeps through the air and catches the axeman, taking out the man's teeth in a spray of blood and yellowed enamel.

But we are heavily outnumbered, and though I have already lived through this once, I still fear for us. What if they've altered the past just that tiniest amount? And what if that alteration means our deaths?

I watch my former self stand over the boy, even as he makes to load another rock, and catch him full in his face with his boot. *There, you little cunt!*

But I am swaying now, close to collapse, and as I turn, so Katerina cries out – as I knew she would – and feel my heart ripped from me a second time as some bastard sticks her once, then once again with his knife.

Svetov grabs my arm, stops me hurling myself down the slope to help them, hissing the words into my ear.

'*No, Otto! This* must *be.*'

And as I look back, so I see how I lift the axe and, bellowing with anger and pain, bury it in the bastard's forehead, almost splitting the fucker's skull in two.

The others flee, the four of them running for their lives.

Just as before, I think, and hand the glasses back. And jump – out and back again, only later – to look on from a distance once again, as my past self tends to my Katerina, making her well again.

And between those two moments? A battle, of sorts, with Svetov and I and twenty other men fighting off the Polovtsy, who, had we not been there, would have come this time and finished the job. Only *we* ambushed *them* this time, taking no prisoners.

Svetov stays with me a while, taking in the scene in the cave's mouth, watching as Otto builds the sled that will be used to carry Katerina, then seeing him go to the medical box and swallow several of the yellow pills that will give him the strength and energy for the journey to Rzev. All as before.

And then I am alone, Svetov gone, watching as the dark Russian night falls and the heroic Lishka makes up a fire. And in that fire's glow, I feast on the sight of her, alive, thank Urd, alive, her long, dark hair shimmering with warm tints of gold.

And, sitting there, knowing that my former self will see me before the night is out, I smile, knowing the worst is now behind us. All roads to this point are guarded now. Small squads have been posted ahead and behind in Time, our scouts moving like silent shadows among the trees, making sure that we are safe.

342

Four-Oh is buzzing with the news when I return. There has been a battle – one further battle, after the one we won. And indeed, we won this one – if we can call such a pyrrhic victory a success of any kind.

'What happened?' I ask Svetov, who was involved in the tail end of the fighting.

'Shafarevich happened,' he answers. 'And a crack team of renegade Russians with advanced weaponry.'

'Advanced? How advanced?'

'Like . . . twenty, maybe thirty years up the line?'

I register what that means.

'*Shit!*'

'Yes. We out-numbered them three to one. Even so . . .' He sighs. 'I've nine men missing, Otto. Presumed dead. And word of it has got out. The platforms are buzzing with it.'

'Where was this?'

'The fight? In Baturin.'

'Let me guess. The thirteenth of November 1708?'

Svetov nods. It's the day the Russians burned the Cossack town to the ground, killing thousands. The same day Reichenau has been sniffing about in.

'I see. But it's over, yes?'

'Not yet. One of the rebels is still holed up inside a house at the edge of town.'

'On his own?'

'Yes.'

'Not possible,' I say. 'Why can't we take him?'

'We think it's Shafarevich himself.'

'You think?'

'Who else could it be?'

Kolya, I think. But I don't say it.

'Okay,' I say. 'Find out what you can, then report back.'

'And you, Otto?'

I smile. 'Right now I've an appointment with myself.'

And jump . . .

343

To the cave, somewhere north of Sycevka, where, knowing that my travellers won't wake, I stand over them a while, then gently stoop, kissing Katerina's pale cheek, feeling such love for her at that moment as might fill whole worlds.

Alive, Urd be thanked.

It is a cold night – winter is coming – but the cave is warmed by the dying embers of the fire Lishka built up earlier. Lishka himself is sprawled nearby, exhausted after the fight.

I look again at my beloved, seeing the bloodstains on her dress, and lift the cloth gently, studying the slightly swollen wound, wincing at the sight; noting how that bastard's knife just missed the child within her.

And let the cloth fall.

I stand, looking about me at the cart, the horse, the three sleeping figures. I can see from the way they lie there just how much the fight took out of them. It was a minor miracle that they survived at all *first time round*. But all is well, now that I'm here.

Stepping back, taking in my last sight of her for what I know will be some while, I back away, walking round behind the resting horse. Because this is what happened last time.

I hear my past self wake, groaning softly as he sits up and looks about him.

And jump out again, jumping back in where I know I've stood before, fifty metres distant, staring back at myself as my other self sits there on a rock, keeping guard at the cave's mouth.

Fulfilling the loop. Because there's no alternative. Day by day, I realise, the loop grows stronger, channelling us. Making us do things that we'd much rather not do. Because we must. For without this – without following this predetermined path – all is lost.

And there and then it comes to me. *Kolya knows this. And yet he leaves it be. Why?* Or is he too trapped within this loop? Is he, too, waiting for the moment when action can be taken? I've no clear answer yet, but I *shall* find out.

The night draws on. I shiver and pull my cloak about me against the cold, remembering how I've spent this night before, staring back into the darkness of the cave's mouth, the shadow of what lies ahead – of Krasnogorsk and those two corpses on the cart – souring my mood, its dark memory poisoning my thoughts.

Time alone will solve these riddles.

Morning sees me back at Four-Oh, on the platform, preparing to jump back into Baturin as Svetov debriefs me.

'It's Shafarevich all right. Moscow Central have confirmed it. They've been tracking him these past few hours.'

'D'you think we can talk him round?'

Svetov narrows his eyes. 'You want to? I mean . . . if he's betrayed us once . . .'

'It's a risk, I know, but . . . is there really no other solution? Do we *have* to kill them all?'

Svetov looks away, clearly discomfited by the thought.

I shake my head. 'The idea of peace . . . it frightens them. But if we can show them that it works . . .'

'And just how do we go about that? No, Otto. For once our hands are tied. They'll fight us to the last. You know they will. And we've no alternative. We must hunt them down and kill them. Without mercy. To make the future safe.'

I want to argue, but it's true. Leave but a single one of them out there in Time and it could jeopardise our whole venture.

'So what's the plan?'

'For Shafarevich? We go in mob-handed. Thirty agents, armed to the teeth. We catch him, chain him, bring him back.'

'Back?'

'For the trial.'

It's the first time the possibility has been raised, and I'm not sure I'm keen on the idea. It seems somehow too *liberal* a way of doing things. But isn't that what this whole experiment is about? Doing things differently? Adopting new ways?

'You've discussed this?' I ask.

'Not yet, but we shall. This afternoon, I believe.'

'And Shafarevich . . . he's to be the first to be tried?'

'If we take him.'

'And if we find him guilty?'

'*Then* we blow his head off.'

The way Svetov says it makes me think of show trials and Stalin, and there's part of me that doesn't want to get involved in any of that. If the man's a traitor – and he is – then it's best, surely, to deal with him in the field. Not to give him the slightest chance. Blow his head off the first moment that we can, before the bastard can get the slip on us again.

Only we're a democracy now, it seems.

I meet Svetov's eyes. 'Are we ready to go in?'

Svetov listens to his earpiece a moment and then nods. 'All set.'

And in we go.

And as we do, so, on a screen in Moscow Central, the trace on Shafarevich blinks out, even as three of our men jump into the room he was in just an instant before.

Standing in the room next door, I get the news ten seconds later.

'Meister Otto . . . he's gone!'

'Gone? He can't be gone. The focus—'

'—vanished with him.'

While the rest of the men search the place physically, Svetov and I jump back to Moscow Central. There, we watch the on-screen memory of the event. How the trace was there one moment, and then – suddenly – was gone.

'Like it was triggered,' Svetov says.

'Yes, but how? He didn't come here, and, as far as we know, he didn't go to Four-Oh.'

We send an agent through to check, but there's no trace of him using Four-Oh.

'Reichenau,' I say. 'It has to be.'

But how? No. It makes no sense. He's gone. Our agents, coming back from searching where he was, confirm it.

'Go back before, then . . .'

Only they've done that. He's gone completely from that time-line, like he's been erased. And I can't see how Reichenau could have done that. Triggered? Yes, but how?

And, more to the point, *why*? To make us paranoid?

'He's joined them,' Svetov says, pulling at his beard. 'The bastard's fucking joined them.'

And if he has?

I look to Svetov. 'From now on we keep a five-man guard on each of the platforms. Three-hour shifts day and night till this is over.'

Day and night. It seems an incongruous thing to say in the context of where we are, only Svetov knows what I mean.

'And you, Meister?'

'Back to Four-Oh,' I say, looking up at the watching cameras. And jump. Because this is something I really need to think through.

345

Sat there in the Tree-lit darkness of Hecht's rooms, I mull things over. Reichenau is the key to all of this. Wherever *he* is, that's the centre of their operations against us. And Kolya? Kolya, I think, is playing a deeper, subtler game. What that is I don't know. Not yet anyway.

But Reichenau . . .

I laugh. It's obvious. Of course it is. We've the six pendants that we found in Kolya's house back in 1952 California. They're there in Four-Oh's safe. If anything's the answer then they surely are. Because they must, in some way, be connected to his platform. Connected by some code or password or . . .

Gehlen would know.

Or maybe I could jump back, to where we found the pendants in the drawer of his desk, go back a month or so before I last went in and see what else I can find.

Yet even as I think it, I know they won't let me. They'll say it's too dangerous for the Meister to go in alone. But that's not a problem. I can have an agent do it all for me. Be my eyes and ears. Delegate it for once.

And even as I think that there's a knocking at the door.

'Yes?'

It's Ernst. 'He's back,' he says. 'The agent you sent. He says—'

Only I don't get to hear what he says, because right then Gehlen summons me. His voice echoes in the air of the room, telling me I must come at once. And, telling Ernst I'll not be long, I leave him there and make my way . . .

. . .stepping through nowhere, into that cold, refrigerated space few ever get to visit, the curved walls rimed with ice, the inside the purest sapphire blue, shot with patches of vivid, pulsing red and orange and emerald green. This is the *genewart*: that gaseous presence that controls Four-Oh, its blurred interior containing the artificial intelligence that once was Hans Gehlen, inventor of time travel and the greatest scientist our world has ever known – long dead, but here resurrected. In a fashion.

'Ah, Otto . . .' the voice says, deep and mellow, like an organ note sounding in the air. 'I have a task for you.'

I am surprised. I have never known Gehlen to ask for anything. Then again, this might have been a regular thing when Hecht was still alive. I put my hand out, holding it a palm's width from the wall's cold surface, feeling how intense that coldness is.

'A task?'

'We've been falling behind.'

I haven't a clue what Gehlen means by that, but keep my silence, waiting for him to elucidate.

'The future weaponry . . .'

'What of it?'

'I have an idea . . . how to cope with it.'

'Go on,' I say, intrigued by the notion of it thinking these things through. Is this the only thing it's been thinking of?

'The technology we've been encountering lately. The new stuff from the future. The answer's simple. We have the new pendant foci now, so why not use them? We can move people about in Time, without needing to put foci in their chests. So let's do that.'

There's the briefest moment where I don't follow him. People? What kind of people does Gehlen mean?

'Scientists,' he says, as if he's heard my thoughts. 'Great men. Let's convoke a conference of all of the greatest scientists there have been and have them brainstorm some answers for us.'

I stare for a moment at the pulsing pool of colour that confronts me, and then I grin. 'Okay. Give me a wish-list and I'll see what we can do.'

'It's on your desk already,' Gehlen says, his pulsing presence drifting up until it floats there just beneath my hand, its intense light bathing my body in brilliant colours. 'Six names. I'm certain Master Schnorr will find them for you.'

And that's it. I watch it drift away, merging with the blue until there's nothing but blueness.

Great men . . . And I laugh, wondering who would be on that list.

346

Ernst is waiting for me when I return. He holds a sheet of paper out to me and frowns.

'Is this what I think it is?'

I take it from him, reading the listed names, then laugh. 'You want to arrange it, Ernst?'

'Shouldn't we debate this . . . in the *veche*?'

'You think we should?'

He hesitates, clearly in two minds, then shrugs. 'I don't know . . . what you're suggesting is the kidnap of some of the greatest men there have ever been. Removing them from their natural place in the timestream. Have you considered what that might entail? The potential damage it might do?'

'Not if we're careful.'

'Careful?'

I've already thought this through, in that brief time it took for me to return.

'It's simple. We take them out of the timestream for . . . well, it doesn't really matter how long if they're going to be based here in Four-Oh . . . but then, when everything's been resolved and they've served their usefulness, we put them back in again . . . only this time a moment before we took each of them out originally. That way they'd recall nothing of what happened to them. None of the new stuff that they'll have brainstormed into existence. You see, Ernst? That way there'd be no sullying of the timestream. All would be almost exactly as it was.'

'Even so . . .' Ernst begins.

But I'm not going to waste any more time discussing the matter.

'Look . . . If I give you the pendants, can you organise that for me? I'll give you a written order if you want . . .'

Ernst knows I'm close to being condescending here. But I am Meister, after all, and I really can't see why we should have to debate every last little thing.

'Otto, I—'

'Our agent,' I say, changing the subject. 'The one we sent into California in fifty-two. What did he say? You were just about to tell me when Gehlen summoned me.'

'Oh . . . Just that he thinks you ought to look at things yourself.'

'He does, does he?'

'He's posting a report, but he thinks, as you've been in once before and know all the people involved . . .'

'. . .I should be the one to take a better look?'

Ernst nods. 'Otto, this business with the great men—'

'Is an excellent idea, no? Gehlen himself has endorsed it. And, providing we're careful, and I'm sure that in your hands we'll be just that, it harms no one. So do it for me, eh? Let's not prevaricate. Let's even up the odds while we yet can. Get some of that future weaponry into our hands. Things our enemies don't have. Let's steal a march on them, yes?'

I can see that he wants to argue, but then he owes me several lives.

'Okay,' he says, sighing, knowing he ought to contest the matter more than he's done. Only I *am* Otto, and he *is* Ernst, and our friendship means everything. And so we go, at once, to visit the safe and get things moving on both fronts, because I know that, whatever the outcome, it's better to act than to endlessly sit on your hands.

And, a mere half an hour after my audience with Gehlen, I am up there on the platform once again, ready to jump . . .

347

. . . into the hallway of the Kolya house in Berkeley, California, in late January of 1952.

It all looks much the same as when I last was here, but at once I am aware of one important difference, of the noise, coming from the room in which I found the pendants and the map and the list of time coordinates.

I stand there, in the shadow beneath the stairs, listening through the wall, then watch as the door creaks open and various people – most of them men, but with the odd woman or two – emerge, one by one.

One in particular I know. It is the traitor Phillipe Krauss, a fellow *Reisende*, who sold his own brothers to the Russians, and whom, it seems, has been working for someone else all along.

As he closes the front door behind him, there is a sudden silence in the house that suggests that all of the guests have gone. But who have they come to see? Who, if anyone, remains within that room?

I tiptoe across and take a peek inside. This is Kolya's house, so it is Kolya I expect to see, seated at the desk, writing. Only it isn't. It's Reichenau, his massive, swollen head moving slowly, gently bobbing as he concentrates on each word.

I step back, out of sight again, then turn and, taking the opportunity, make my way upstairs, looking for signs of habitation.

It's a big house. The second floor has eight rooms, and all but one are empty. This, it's plain to see, is Reichenau's room. Perhaps the very place he sleeps. Only if I was him, I'd change where I slept every night. Just to be sure.

I walk across, then kneel, rifling through his portmanteau, looking for something – anything – that might be of interest. I note at once that he must have his shirts specially made, and wonder whether that might not be one way of tracing him. It's a small thing but significant.

Yes, but why not take him here? Take a dozen men in with us and take him when he's sleeping.

Only that's what we tried to do with Shafarevich, and look how successful we were there! No, we need to be more subtle. We need . . .

. . . *to find out how he continually pre-empts us.*

And how he triggers things.

As I go through his wardrobe, I am thinking about what I overheard earlier. About their plans for infiltrating both the Russian and German camps. Mention, too, of cusp moments in our history – Poltava among them. Evidence, all of it, that Reichenau is still meddling in Time, still playing the Game – even though we, for our part, have ceased to do so – still deliberately stirring up trouble between the Russians and the Germans.

I stop, my fingers closing on a small, cool object that's in one of the man's coats. I take it out and stare at it, recognising it at once. It's the lazy eight, only this one is made of some kind of crystal, its deeply green coloration making it seem like something natural.

It was cool, I say, but suddenly it is warm, that warmth increasing until . . .

I throw it down on the carpet, where it glows intensely for a moment and then dulls.

There is a burn mark on the carpet now, the tiniest drift of smoke lifting from the glowing fibres.

What the fuck?

I don't know what it is, or what its purpose is, but I sense very strongly that I should somehow get it back to Four-Oh. Or is that what he wants me to do?

I turn, looking about me, the sudden sense of being watched making my neck hairs stand on end. There's the faintest burning smell . . .

Downstairs the telephone sounds. I hear the creak as Reichenau gets out of his chair, then listen as his heavy footsteps cross the room.

I go across and, holding on to the door-jamb, listen.

Abruptly the ringing stops. 'Reichenau?'

I'm surprised. I'd have thought he'd use another name. But then again, he'd not be going outside much, not with that great pumpkin of a head.

He listens a while, then grunts. 'I wouldn't bother,' he says. 'I really wouldn't bother. If he wants me he can come and get me. Until then . . .'

There's more from the other person – nothing that I can hear – and then Reichenau puts the phone down.

I stand there, waiting for his footsteps, waiting for him to return to where he'd been sat, only I realise suddenly that he's gone – jumped – and that I'm alone in the house.

I turn, looking at the strangely shaped jewel, then quickly cross the room and, gingerly picking the thing up, pocket it. And jump. Back to Four-Oh, the jewel burning a hole in the fabric of my coat.

348

Zarah rubs an antiseptic paste onto the burn on my upper thigh, then looks up at me and smiles.

'What *was* that?'

'I'm hoping to find out. I found it among Reichenau's things.'

'We went back in, you know . . .'

'I know.'

And found nothing. The house deserted. As if no one had ever been there.

Zarah screws on the lid, then straightens up, even as I pull my trousers on again.

'They're waiting for you, Otto. At Tannenberg. That idea you and Gehlen had. They want to talk to you about it.'

I almost swear. 'I gave that to Ernst to deal with.'

'And he came to us.' She pauses, then, 'You can't do that, Otto. You can't ignore us. You're doing things the old way, and that's not on. Not now that we've changed things. You've got to get everyone behind you before you change things like that. To take the Great Men out of history . . . Urd protect us, Otto. What if it went wrong?'

'It won't go wrong. Not if we're careful.'

'So Ernst said you said. But is it really worth the risk?'

'I think so.'

She huffs, clearly frustrated with me, angered that I've not been playing by their rules. But what did they expect?

'They're waiting?'

'At the farmhouse in Tannenberg. We can jump there.'

I hesitate.

'Well?' she asks. 'Are you coming willingly or do I have to drag you?'

'One thing,' I say, 'and then I'll come.'

She stares at me a moment, trying to work out what I'm up to now, then shrugs and – in an instant – is gone.

I let out a long breath. 'Urd help me . . .'

'Otto? Are you in there?'

I turn to face the door as it hisses open, surprised by my visitor. 'Master Schnorr . . . I was just about to pay you a visit.'

'Oh yes, and why's that?'

'That bauble I brought back. The thing that burned me. Have we any idea what it is?'

He comes in, the door hissing shut behind him. 'Not yet, Otto. But we shall. Odd that it's shaped like that, no? That's Reichenau's symbol, isn't it?'

'It seems so.'

'But look, that's not why I'm here. I'm here to warn you.'

'*Warn me?*' I almost laugh. 'My wife and children are gone – kidnapped – and I've a whole army of rebels out to kill me—'

Old Schnorr puts up a hand to halt my protests. 'I know, I know, but . . . well . . . look for yourself.'

And he hands me a slender packet of photographs. Old-fashioned things, taken, one would have guessed, in the early years of photography. Only the subjects of these photos are scattered across the millennia.

'Where in Odin's name did you get these?'

'They were left for you.'

'And who was the messenger?'

'We don't know. One minute they weren't there, the next . . .'

I look at them again. Like many of the shots that were in the album Reichenau had had, these photos are of me. With one important difference. Kolya.

Eight photos, each one showing me, side on, unaware that I'm being captured on film, each in a different place, at a different time. And, chillingly, Kolya, there in every one of them, looking on, the suggestion of a smile on his cruel lips.

I meet Schnorr's eyes, frightened despite myself.

'We think he's closing in. This suggests you've been targeted by him.'

'Then why not kill me and have done with it?'

Because he wants to remind me that he can . . . at any moment.

Old Schnorr looks down. 'Was I wrong, Otto?'

'Showing me these? No. But what do we do with them? I don't know . . . burn them, maybe?'

'Burn them?'

'As I see it, it's no more than a trick. A means of making us over-estimate the man. I mean, if he could do this for real, then why aren't I dead already?'

'Maybe . . .'

'No, no maybes. If he could get *that* close *that* often, I'd be dead. I've seen the hatred in his eyes. He longs to kill me. So why not just kill me? Why play these games?'

'Unless these predate the reason for his hatred? Unless . . .'

Only there isn't an 'unless' that makes any sense. So this has to be a cheat. A way of fraying my nerves.

I notice Old Schnorr studying me, a deep concern in his face.

'Tannenberg?'

His concern becomes a smile. 'Tannenberg. But for Urd's sake be patient with them, Otto. It's hard enough making this change.'

349

'It is agreed,' the Russian woman, Alina Tupayeva, says, smiling at me, leaving me half-lowered into my seat.

I look about me, trying to make sense of what she's said.

'*Agreed?*'

'Yes,' she says. 'We've talked it through and Gehlen's right. We need an edge, and what better than the Great Men. Besides, Gehlen is right, we must have done *something*, otherwise we'd have been beaten already!'

That kind of makes sense, and besides, it gets me what I want.

'So when's it to start?'

'It's begun already,' Ernst says. 'Galileo Galilei is being debriefed as we speak, and teams are in the field, attempting to bring back Einstein.'

'Oh,' Zarah interrupts, 'and we've recorded it all.'

'Good . . .'

Only this meeting is clearly not meant to be, for right then Svetov appears in the air beside me, and, with apologies to the *veche*, takes me aside into the farmhouse.

Inside he closes the door, then turns to me, his face solemn. 'Forgive me, Otto, only I am the bearer of bad news, I'm afraid. About Katerina . . .'

I groan, my legs going, fearing the worst.

Svetov reaches out to steady me. 'We've sent in more than a dozen teams so far, each one of them following up some clue or other, and three times now we've come close. Very close. But each time we've tried to snatch them away *he* was in there before us.'

'*He?*'

'Kolya.'

'Then they're . . .?'

'Alive, yes. At least . . . as far as we know.'

I look down, unable to speak, and the big Russian squeezes my arm gently again, as one might comfort a child.

For a moment there I'd thought them dead.

My words are barely a whisper. 'What am I to do, Arkadi?'

'I don't know, dear friend. I really don't. But we won't give up. I promise you that. Until the very last, we'll keep on looking.'

When he's gone, I stand there, knowing that I can't go back, can't face the *veche*. Not yet, anyway. And so I jump, back to Four-Oh, back to Hecht's room and seal the door, lying there in the half-dark, waiting for the medication to kick in, tears rolling down my cheeks.

'Gods of my father's father, help me now,' I whisper. 'Make me strong, Father Odin. And keep my sweet girls safe until we meet again.'

Only the gods surely aren't listening. If anything, it feels like they've abandoned me. That here, in my hour of need, they've turned their backs on me and mine. And, wiping away the tears, I turn and, sitting on the edge of the bed, curse the two men who have spoiled my life, and vow, there and then, that I will one day slit their throats. For all they've done.

And all they're yet to do.

350

I shower and dress, then go to the observation room, where I find Ernst and Old Schnorr, seated on the far side of the one-way glass, taking notes.

'Galileo?' I ask, staring at the man seated in the room beyond, impressed by the aura that he gives out.

Ernst looks across at me and smiles. 'The same.'

I turn my attention to the man, knowing that in our time he's been dead thirteen and a half centuries.

Galileo is in his early forties subjectively, and has already faced the kind of adversity no scientist should ever have to face, his theories attacked and ridiculed, his ideas on heliocentrism banned by the Catholic Church as heretical.

And now he sits there, dressed as he was on the day he was picked up by our team back in 1620, not quite sure where he is or why, his expression a mixture of bemusement and frank annoyance. He looks very much like the figure in Giusto Sustermans' portrait, wearing the same black cloak with a frilled white collar, his beard and moustache well groomed, his hair receding.

He looks tired, soul-weary and beaten.

I take a seat next to Old Schnorr, and watch.

'What's that language he's speaking?'

'Italian. A very old dialect of it, from Pisa, where he was born.'

'Ah . . . and what are we telling him?'

'The truth.'

'All of it?'

'All of it.'

'No wonder he looks bemused. You think he's going to believe it?'

'He'll have to,' Ernst says, and laughs.

'We've made him a book,' Schnorr says. 'A history of astronomy from our perspective, here at the tail end of the third millennium. I've had it translated into Latin.'

'And has he seen that?'

'Not yet. Kurt and Maxim are trying to explain things to him first. Just the basics. More than that and he'd probably have a stroke . . .'

'Or think he's bewitched . . .'

I study our two de-briefers a moment. Kurt Muller I know. I taught him, several years back, but Maxim is new to me, a young Russian agent from Up River. Both seem to be taking a gentle attitude towards their captive, but alarm bells sound in my head just watching it.

'Can you imagine,' I say, 'how much this must be like being interrogated again, by the Inquisition?'

'There might be similarities . . .' Schnorr begins, but I cut him off.

'No. Let's stop it right there. We're going about this in totally the wrong way. Let's back off and give him that book of yours, Master Schnorr. He's got an imagination – yes? – so let's feed that. Let's make him ask *us* questions. Then give him one of our slates. Nothing special. Just a standard machine, like our students use, and let him play with it. *Then* tell him where he is and why.'

Old Schnorr looks to Ernst, who nods, then touches a panel in front of him.

'Kurt . . . Maxim . . . come out of there for now. We'll take this up in a while, but Otto wants to try something first.'

The two figures turn and nod their acknowledgement, then, their chairs scraping back, come out of there, leaving Galileo alone in that plain, undecorated cell.

'The book?' I ask, putting my hand out to Master Schnorr.

'I'll have it brought. We were going to leave it in his room. We've been ferrying some of his stuff here, you understand. DNA copies from his rooms in Tuscany, including the desk he works at. I was going to leave it there, for him to find—'

'Which would have been good. Only we need to convince him from the start. And what better than to give him another fourteen centuries of astronomical speculation?'

'What if he doesn't believe it?' Ernst asks.

'Then we'll have kidnapped the wrong man. No. The real Galileo will digest this like the finest caviar. He'll lap it all up and ask for more, I bet you.'

'You *bet* me?'

'No. This is our way in, Master Schnorr. Can you have other such books made up for each of our . . . helpers? Not necessarily in Latin, but in accessible linguistic form for each of them.'

'It can be done.'

'Then do so. And let's make the first room they experience in Four-Oh a bit more *comfortable*, eh? A bit more welcoming. Because that's what it reminds me of. The Inquisition.'

Ernst looks to Old Schnorr and then back to me. 'I'll do what I can.'

'Good. Then give me the book and I'll start again. Do we have a translation device for a form of Italian he'll understand?'

'We should have,' Ernst says, standing now, keen to get to work.

'Then bring me that, too . . . and a slate. Oh . . . and maybe we can get someone to sketch out a working notion of what Four-Oh actually is, with diagrams . . . and without relying on Gehlen's equations. Not yet, anyway.'

'It shall be done,' Old Schnorr answers me, then, chuckling to himself, he hurries away, an eagerness in his ancient eyes that hasn't been there for years.

351

Galileo Galilei is a soft-spoken man, but his words have an authority I've rarely come across. He is that rarest of birds, a man who *believes* despite the whole age he lives in being against him. It is why most scientists revere him, because to them he represents the scientific spirit in its purest form. Like all of those we propose to extract from Time, he is a rationalist. And in that past age, where the Catholic Church reigned supreme, to be a rationalist was equivalent to being a God-denier, and therefore a worshipper of the devil.

'What is this?' he asks, touching the large-format book as if it were unclean.

I wait a second for the translation to whisper in my ear, then answer him, the Italian translation following only moments later. 'Why don't you look inside?'

He starts, like someone has just pricked him with a needle, his eyes staring at my own, as if I were about to change my form.

'Seriously,' I say, the Italian like an echo. 'I think you'll find it interesting.'

He hesitates, then reaches out and slowly lifts the cover. Inside, I know, is the title page, and the date of publication . . .

He reads those words, then looks up at me again, his eyes much fiercer than before.

'Are you mocking me?'

'Not at all,' I answer. 'Look through it. You of all people will understand.'

'Understand?'

'The truth of what's written there. It's all built upon your work. Or rather, on the foundations that you built.'

There's the slightest change in his expression, a look of doubt mixed with hope, and then he looks back at it, hesitates once more, and then plunges in, turning to a page almost halfway through the book, hefting the thick weight of it over and down, then studying the pages – strewn with diagrams and photos that can be accessed at the touch of a fingertip.

'Lord Jesus Christ preserve us!' he says, staring at it like it's the devil's own writing. 'Who are you people?'

I lean forward, trying to see what he's looking at, and smile. He's looking at the Galilean moons.

'You are here,' I tell him. 'Now. In the last days of the third millennium. We are from the future, and that's where you are, at our platform, which is called Four-Oh, and . . .'

'Stop,' he says quietly, but with immense authority. 'Four-Oh? Like 0 and 0 and 0 and 0.'

Once more I smile. 'Precisely that. Like a coordinate . . .'

And I see that he's seen what I mean, and that even if he hasn't taken everything I've just said on board, he's taken the first step towards understanding it all.

'And these . . . on the page here?'

'Are Jupiter's moons . . . named the Galilean moons, after you.'

He nods, almost as if he hasn't heard that last part, then reaches out to touch one of the panels, and jerks his finger back as it comes alive beneath his touch.

And then, unexpectedly, he laughs, and then bursts into tears. 'This is . . . Heaven, is it not?'

It is not, I want to say, recalling my own situation, but instead I nod and smile, watching in wonder as he turns the pages of the hefty book, his eyes as wide as a child's, as one after another new fact touches and connects with his mind.

352

I don't look or feel much like an angel, yet that is what he takes me for. I try to explain what it is I've spent most of my life doing, fighting wars throughout Time, but he seems not to connect with that part of it. As he sees it, he has been gathered up by one of God's angels and brought to Heaven itself. And nothing I can do or say will alter that for him.

Even so, I am encouraged. Perhaps our scheme might work. That is, if Kolya doesn't act to spoil it all. And maybe, from wherever he is right now in Time, he is planning just that. Only this time I'm not going to let him. We are going to make this work, see if we don't!

Two more have arrived in the past hour. One – Einstein – I know. I've met him in the past. The other – Leibniz – I've never met before today.

Wherever 'today' actually is.

I've read the two-page 'prompt' on Leibniz, and understand from that just how important he was in the field of mathematics, not to speak of his role as a philosopher, but from first impressions he's a somewhat vain man, given to moods. A rationalist, but also a professional diplomat; a man much dependent on patronage. Oh, and I know that that was how it was, in his time, his era, but I can't help but see him as a creature of compromise, not another Galileo.

And there's also the matter of his wig. In the struggle to extract him, Leibniz lost his wig – and what a creation it was! Look at any picture of the man and you'll see what I mean. Without it, he seems a much less imposing fellow. His shaved and powdered head is almost comically unimpressive. So we have promised him a wig to match his own. Oh, we have them in our stores, for use by our agents, but the man is incredibly fussy, and, after having tried on more than twenty different models, tempers – both his and ours – are close to fraying.

'Send him back,' Ernst says, watching the man storm across the room for the dozenth time.

'I would,' I say. 'Only Gehlen was insistent. Leibniz was his idol when he was young, and he must be part of the team.'

Ernst grimaces. 'More trouble than he's worth,' he murmurs, and I have to agree. There's no humility to the man. No give and take. He is full of his own self-importance. But what Gehlen wants . . .

Einstein, by comparison, is charm itself. He takes his new situation in in an instant and, accepting where he is and why, is a font of enthusiasm for our project.

That said, of all these great men, he is the one we are most familiar with, and so, hearing that he's been extracted, a small crowd gathers in the corridors nearby to greet him.

Anyone who has ever travelled in Time will know of Einstein. It was his challenging of classic Newtonian physics that was the first step on the road to Gehlen's equations; his thinking that, via the general theory of relativity, allowed all this to happen.

Like Galileo, he is revered.

Big men and little men, I think, as the three men meet each other for the first time in their awkward fashion, their first exchanges stiltedly translated.

Which, I can see already, is going to be a problem. We are going to have to choose a *lingua franca* for these men to use, if they're to be of any use at all.

Even as they make to bring the next of them – Wolfgang Pauli – through, so the three who are already here are taken to their quarters.

It's all been rather hastily prepared. Rooms have been created for each of them around a central hub; beds and desks and chairs and shelves installed, brought in from our stores.

The hub itself is a large lecture theatre with desks and computers and screens. Commonplace stuff for us, but for them this is something else entirely.

The best moment of them all is when Ernst gives Galileo a slate. It's a standard-issue machine, the kind our young trainees use. But to Galileo . . .

He presses the pad at the foot of the page, as he's told to, and then gasps and almost drops the thing as it lights up, his eyes staring out of his head.

'Satan's balls!'

There's a gust of laughter at that.

Even as he says that, he's drawn to the machine that's in his hands. It fascinates him, and his whole being craves to know more. And I know there and then that this will work, for there is not one of them who won't react the way he is reacting now. Who won't be sucked in by this. Knowledge. It's what they live for. More than sex or power or money. They long to *know* new things.

Both Einstein and Leibniz look to me, as if to ask where *their* magic boxes are, and, smiling, I hand each of them one of the wafer-thin machines, then let them get on with it. If they've questions I'm sure they'll ask.

Only they don't ask me. No, for I'm still their enemy in some fashion, still the one who had them abducted from Time, and quickly – very quickly, and despite the language difficulties – the three men form a bond, using their slates to make their way about this strange world they've found themselves in, sharing their discoveries, until, with a laugh that slowly changes to something more serious, all three of them look to me.

'We're in the future, yes?' Einstein asks, speaking for all three of them. 'We're actually deep into the future.'

And then the three men laugh again, looking to each other, sharing a delight at this magical transformation of their lives.

353

Only there are snags.

Old Schnorr sits there, going through the figures for the third time, then looks up at me and shakes his head.

'It won't work, Otto. We're putting too great a strain on things. The sheer amount of manpower we're having to divert to service this project and look after our "guests" . . . the cooks and cleaners and the like, the linguists, the copyists and the service staff to give them whatever books or resources they need . . . all of that alone makes it difficult.'

'But we can do this, no?'

'Well, yes, but it stretches us thin.'

There's a knock. A moment later, Ernst steps into the shadowed room.

'Gentlemen,' he says. 'We have a problem.'

'Leibniz?' Schnorr asks, but Ernst shakes his head. 'It's the women. They're up in arms about Gehlen's selection. Six men and not a single woman.'

'So what are we supposed to do?'

Ernst grins, then hands me a list he's taken from the pocket of his tunic. I study it a while then hand it to Master Schnorr, who snorts, then shakes his head again.

'Two more?' he groans. 'How will we ever cope?'

'Well, for a start we could make them cook for themselves. Yes, and clean up after themselves, too.'

Schnorr looks dubious. He looks back at the list and frowns. 'It's not even as if they're that well known . . .'

'It's a man's world,' Ernst says.

Only I can see the women's point. If we're really going to build this new world we've been talking of, then they ought to be represented on a project like this. They've been our brood cows far too long.

'Agree to it,' I say. Then, curious, I look to Ernst. 'Who drafted this?'

'Zarah, and Urte . . .'

'Then give *them* the job of extracting these from history. If they want them, they can bring them in. But as far as Gehlen's list is concerned . . . I'll go see him again. See if some of these can't prove . . . dispensable. Feynman, for instance . . . Oh, and there's one here I don't even know. Moseley. Does anyone know him?'

Ernst shrugs. 'Well, there's one off the list.'

'If Gehlen will agree.'

'He'll still have five names . . . seven if we include the women's choices.'

'Okay. Get moving on it.'

Ernst nods. 'I shall. Oh, and just to let you know. Two more were brought through about half an hour back. I thought you might want to go and welcome them.'

I raise an eyebrow in query.

'Pauli . . . and da Vinci.'

'Da Vinci... ? You've *seen* him, Ernst?'

'Not yet. But it rather gives you goose bumps, no? To think just what we're doing here. Gathering them all in one place at one time.'

354

We finish off what we were doing, then hurry across to the Welcoming Suite. To find the Great Man himself – dressed in the flowing robes of his time – holding court, everyone hanging on his translated words.

Even Wolfgang Pauli, considered by many to be the father of quantum physics, looks in awe, unable to quite believe he's there in da Vinci's presence. Mind you, physically there's a quantum leap between da Vinci's godlike aura and Pauli's movie-villain looks. No. Pauli looks like an ordinary Jewish man of his time and place, complete with shabby suit, whereas da Vinci . . .

Da Vinci looks eternal.

Seeing me, noting how the others look to me, saluting me with the slightest bowing of the head, da Vinci meets my eyes.

'Are you their prince?' he asks, the fifteenth-century Italian followed an instant later by the translated words.

'Their master,' I say and smile, for I have never felt so undeserving of the title.

'And this is?' He gestures to the room about him. A very Italian gesture, part shrug, part expression of his contempt.

'A room,' I answer, and realise how inadequate that sounds. 'A room existent in the future.'

And he laughs, as if he's in a conversation with a madman. A madman who amuses him. 'And you can prove that?'

'Do I need to?'

He's silent a moment, then changes the subject. 'Why exactly am I here? You want me to work for you? Is that it?'

'In a fashion . . .'

And surely the fact that we are talking – that our words are being translated even as we utter them, forming a whisper in the air – ought to convince him that something's happening, something very odd indeed. But the Great Man plays it all very cool.

I note that Old Schnorr has followed me into the room, and turn and take his slate from him, then hand it to da Vinci.

'Here,' I say. 'Just touch the surface.'

He takes it. Touches. Then studies it a while, a sudden intensity to him that was not there just an instant before. And then he looks to me again.

'A room . . . in the future, yes?'

I nod.

'How far into the future?'

'Fifteen hundred years.'

If I expect him to be surprised, I'm disappointed. He considers it a moment, then looks back at the slate, touching it gently, then looking to me.

'You draw it across with your fingertips,' I say, and, taking the slate from him, show him.

'Ah . . .' he says, then, for the next ten minutes, he is silent, his hand moving over the surface of the lit-up screen, summoning things then sending them away. *Getting it* immediately.

'Interesting,' he says, handing it back.

'This is Pauli,' I say, introducing his companion. 'Wolfgang Pauli. He was a great *scientist* in his time.' Only I can see the word means nothing to da Vinci.

Pauli smiles uncertainly, then nods to me in gratitude for making the attempt.

'Can I try one of those things?' he asks, putting out a hand.

I give him the slate, then watch as he too toys with it a while. And then he looks up at me and grins.

'The future, huh?'

'And we're fighting a war,' I say. 'In Time. And we need your help . . .'

And I see how both men look to me, taking that in, before turning to meet each other's eyes.

'A war, eh?' da Vinci says, and nods as if he suddenly understands. 'A war against whom?'

355

All of this, I'll admit, has taken my mind off other things. Tracking down Reichenau is my number one priority, and the *veche* have given me – their Master, summoned to attend their meeting again – permission to go back to 2343 and pursue him at any cost.

But there's one thing I need to do before I leave. I have to go and see Gehlen again. To try to persuade him – against his wishes – to cut Moseley from the list.

And so I go, back to that room with its gaseous presence. Back among the living dead.

'No,' Gehlen says as I step inside, the cold air wreathing me, making me shiver.

'No?' For, of course, he has access to every small exchange throughout Four-Oh. 'But Master Schnorr says . . .'

'Bugger Master Schnorr,' he says. 'I need every name on that list. And six more . . .'

'Six more!'

'Yes, and especially Moseley. Oh, and tell Master Schnorr that we've resources enough, and that far from stretching us thin, this will make us much stronger, much more capable of carrying out our campaign against that abomination, the *doppelgehirn*.'

I make to open my mouth to speak, but he makes a tutting sound, like I should know better.

'Enough, Otto. Now go and do something useful, like sending out agents to bring back the new additions. And Moseley. Make sure you get Moseley.'

And that's it. I am dismissed.

Back in Hecht's rooms, I summon Ernst and Master Schnorr, and tell them what Gehlen said. How insistent he was. Only when I come to the question of additions, they are up in arms.

'Like whom?' Ernst asks.

And, reading from Gehlen's new list, I answer. 'Max Planck . . . and Thomas Edison . . . and Aristotle . . .'

At which both men look to each other and make a face as if to imply Gehlen must have taken leave of his senses.

'Aristotle?'

'Yes. And Moseley . . .'

That draws a complete blank.

'Henry Moseley,' I say, meaning to look him up at some point.

'Ah . . .'

There's an awkward pause, then:

'Newton arrived, while you were gone,' Ernst says. 'And Rutherford's next to be extracted. Urd preserve us, Otto, there won't be a single bona fide genius left in the timestream if this goes on!'

'No.' And the thought of it amazes and amuses me. Simply to see who works best with whom, what friendships will be formed, and what this group of exceptional men will come up with. Maybe Gehlen was right after all. And besides, if he said we had sufficient resources, who was I to challenge that? Who knew better than Gehlen?

I look to Old Schnorr. 'Do whatever's necessary to make them comfortable. Never mind the resources.'

And I turn to Ernst. 'You've heard, yes? About 2343. About us going in again. The *veche* have agreed it.'

'Yes?' But I can see he is unhappy about this. He fears I'll be out of my depth, going in among the Mechanists. More than that, he fears for my life.

'I'm to leave within the hour,' I say. 'Just as soon as I've got my stuff ready.'

'Otto?'

'Yes, Ernst?'

'Don't let what you feel lead you to make mistakes.'

356

And so I jump back to 2343, into the toilet compartment of a high-speed monorail, heading east toward Neu Berlin.

Outside, the rain is falling heavily. I stand there a moment, hands pressed against the cold glass, feeling the powerful movement of the train, looking out at the long chain of gun-emplacements that shadow the track and, further off, a kilometre or so to the north, the redoubts – black anti-missile silos – which form a defensive 'wall', symbols of a deeply paranoid age. Here and there their line is broken by massive factories, their chimneys piercing the clouds, their energy-taps deep-rooted in the earth, dark smoke and blood-red flame giving them a satanic look.

The papers in my document case say that I'm a senior geneticist from the institute in Cologne, and as I go back out to the carriage, so one of the *do-hu* – the domesticated humans – helps me find a seat and stow my case.

I smile at the three men seated about the table, then sit, knowing better than to introduce myself. This time I am thoroughly prepared. Unlike the last time I visited the Akademie, on this visit I am to go to the very heart of things. In my jacket pocket is a letter inviting me to a special gathering of all the leading geneticists, in the Reichstag. The event is to be hosted by the president himself. It is, as I know all too well, a critical conference. Laws will be discussed here; laws that, in the coming years, will be passed – laws that have their basis in this grand meeting of geneticists.

My real purpose, however, is to meet some of these men – the leading experimental geneticists of this age. To get as close as I can to them. For one of them, I'm sure, will know about Reichenau. Why, they might even have operated on him and made him into the *doppelgehirn* he became. And this conference – the most famous of its time – is my best chance of getting that information.

Nor is my presence – on *this* train, at *this* table, in *this* carriage – un-planned, for sharing this table are three others who are going to that conference, including one of my prime targets, Theoretician Fischer.

Fischer sits across from me now, his eyes closed, listening to the plug-in that coils from out of his neck and re-enters his head just behind his left ear. In his seventies now, his great shock of grey hair swept back neatly, he looks serene, *controlled*. But while he is possessed of a vast intellect, he is also a somewhat pompous man.

More Leibniz than Galileo.

That said, like almost everyone in a senior position in this future state, Fischer is a fanatical adherent of genetics. A member of the Weimar Institute – the leading academic and experimental college of its time – Fischer has made numerous trips to the Akademie to give lectures, and it is quite likely that he was involved in the *doppelgehirn* experiments. I say *quite* likely, for while we have sent back agents to watch him, it hasn't been possible to ascertain exactly what he was involved in on the numerous times he was here. Whatever was done was done within a veil of strict secrecy, and so his participation in such experiments remains conjecture.

But if I can get close to the man – if I can win his confidence and his trust – then maybe I might coax it from him in casual conversation.

It's a long shot, but worth trying.

Time passes, and then the old man opens his eyes. He catches me staring at him and – somewhat annoyed at being exposed to my eyes – stares directly and disdainfully past me, as if dismissing me.

It's a bad start, I realise, and there's only one way to put it right.

I lower my head and avert my eyes, then utter an apology.

'Forgive me, Theoretician Fischer. I was lost in my thoughts just then. I didn't mean . . .'

He raises a hand to curtail me.

'It's fine,' he says, though I can see it's not.

I say no more. Make no attempt to communicate further with the man. I've blown the one chance I had of gaining his trust, maybe his friendship. Oh, I could jump back in and start again, only that might draw attention from just those we don't want attending.

I sigh, and for a moment there is only the smooth, powerful movement of the train, that and the distant murmur of conversation from further down the carriage.

'You are?'

I look up, surprised to find Fischer addressing me.

I give him the fake name I've adopted for this incursion, then take the falsified letter from my jacket pocket and hand it across.

'Ah,' he says. 'I see . . .' And hands it back. 'I've never heard of you before, Meister Kroos. What's your specialty?'

I make to answer him, noting the hardness behind his smile. He doesn't like me. Has still not forgiven me for finding him so open. So this sudden interest in me is . . . what? Political, I'd say. An exercise in making good. In not creating potential enemies. Which, until he knows more about me, I clearly am.

His pleasantry is a pretence. But then, so is mine.

'My work has none of the grand sweep of your own, Theoretician,' I say, making no attempt to be subtle in my flattery. 'It is, I'd argue, of the very narrowest range.'

'Go on . . .'

I glance at the fellow seated at Fischer's side, then meet Fischer's eyes once more.

'My work is on the hox genes. On the ramifications of making slight adjustments to their function.'

'The hox genes, eh?' And Fischer unexpectedly laughs. 'It could not be narrower, neh? And that is your . . . area of study?'

I smile. 'It could not, and yes it is.'

Fischer laughs again. 'And you are to give a paper on this . . . *expertise*?'

'I am.'

That is, if I have to. If they ask me. But I hope they don't, because what I know about the hox genes is as basic as it comes.

Nor does it take too long before I find myself at the very edge of my knowledge, left staring over the abyss as Fischer asks me about 'transcription factor cascade'.

I hesitate, then sigh with relief as a steward approaches us, to ask what we would like to eat. I smile as Fischer takes the menu from the man and scans it, his recent presbyopia suddenly revealed by the way he holds it slightly away from him.

Which is interesting, because it would be very easy to correct his eyesight, and yet he hasn't had it done.

Meaning?

I'm not sure what it means. Whether he's afraid to have surgery, maybe?

'The pork dish,' he says to the steward, and hands the menu to me. Then, lowering his voice. 'Did you know that Hausmann is giving a speech at the conference? Nothing official, and by invitation only, but . . . you know Hausmann?'

The fact is, I do, but I am shocked to learn this. It isn't in the history books. Yet it explains a lot. Particularly his spectacular rise to power in the late 2340s. If he had the ear of such influential men as Fischer . . .

'The pork for me, too,' I say, handing the menu on to the fellow next to me.

Turning to Fischer again, I smile. 'I read his *Against Random Chance* just a month back. The man expresses himself well.'

'Doesn't he.' And this time the warmth in Fischer's eyes is genuine. 'You would like to come, then?'

I feign delight, but the truth is, I am more than happy at the way this has suddenly developed. Germany in the Mechanist Age is a crypto-fascist state, but Hausmann would take things even further. He is the leading exponent of what he calls a 'sculpted society' – the results of which can be seen in Manfred's

Germany, several centuries on. His theory of 'social health' is nothing less than a 'purification' programme, a cleverly worded justification for taking whatever actions he might deem necessary to take. That, or an advanced and extreme form of eugenics. To hear the man in person and possibly even speak to him, that would be an insight into what's happening here. Only . . . it's not why I'm here. I'm here to find Reichenau. To track him down through one of these men.

But meeting Hausmann *in camera*, so to speak . . . that might be one way in.

'I'd be most grateful,' I say. 'Most grateful indeed, Theoretician.' And bow my head, as the monorail powers its way on to Neu Berlin.

357

We part company at the Potsdamer Bahnhof, Theoretician Fischer whipped off in a limousine to attend some important function while I seek out a cab to take me to the Akademie. But even as I try and locate the taxi rank, so I find myself aware that I'm being shadowed. Or think I am. Then I glimpse one of our agents and, finding an empty stall in the public toilets, leave my case, jumping right out of there, back to Four-Oh.

Svetov and Ernst are there at the platform when I come through, both men looking somewhat sheepish. They are contrite, but I'm really angry.

'What the fuck do you think you're doing? Even if the enemy weren't looking for me, surrounding me with half a dozen of our agents would alert them, don't you think?'

'We thought . . .' Ernst begins, but I shut him up.

'Well don't! I've made a really good contact with Theoretician Fischer, and I don't want that spoiled. So call off the bodyguards.

If I'm in trouble, I'll jump straight out of there. Otherwise leave me to do what I'm good at. Okay?'

The two of them look to each other, unhappy, then Svetov shrugs. 'Okay. But don't take any unnecessary chances—'

Only I barely hear them. I'm out of there, back to the cubicle in Potsdamer Bahnhof.

358

Where, gathering up my case, I leave the toilets . . .

. . .and walk straight into two security guards, dressed head to toe in black leather. They grab hold of me and arrest me on the spot, on suspicion of being a spy.

I can't imagine how they got on to me so quickly, but I have to go along with them. Despite what I said to Ernst and Svetov, I can't just jump out of there – not in so public a fashion – because that *would* blow the whole operation.

I'm taken to the police fortress in Potsdam, a very different Potsdam from the one I knew back in the eighteenth century, all high rises and soaring towers. There, beneath the arc lights, in an unfurnished cell, a senior member of the *Schutzstaffel*, Ulrich Gress, greets me cordially.

'Meister Kroos . . .'

Gress is a pleasant, well-mannered man, who apologises profusely for having arrested me, but says that there's been a tip-off and that they simply have to make sure.

As I sit there, facing him across the desk, he studies my ID – again, a perfect fake – then hands it back to me, telling me he needs to make some calls.

He leaves, but he's back in minutes, apologising once more for my inconvenience.

'I'm sorry, Meister. It's not how we'd like it, but we can't afford to ignore *anything* these days. Why, there was an attempt on the president's life, only two nights back.'

That much I knew, it was in my briefing, but I act as if I'm shocked, and who knows whether he's fooled or not, but he tells me I'm free to leave, and that he will fly me to the Akademie if that helps.

I'd be churlish, of course, to refuse, but all the way across he subtly questions me, under the guise of being interested in who I am and what I'm doing here.

I play along with his little game. Only something about the man makes me suspicious in a different way.

What if he's one of Reichenau's men?

It's unlikely. Then again, what better guise could he have than as an SS officer? What better way of having constant access to me and my doings here?

As we're flying, I try to glimpse whether Gress has a pendant about his neck, but it's impossible to see beneath the collar of his uniform.

'If you need anything,' he says, as I make to disembark in the forecourt of the Gast Gebaud, the 'Guest Building'. And he hands me a slip of plastic which holds all his details.

'Thank you, Oberlieutenant.'

And in a moment he is gone, leaving me alone.

I turn full circle, taking it all in. Other fliers are descending onto the massive pad, dropping like great black lozenges through the darkness between the monolithic buildings, their lamps cutting great swathes of light through that blackness. I move away, heading towards the brightly lit entrance to the Gast Gebaud.

What if he is? I ask myself, thinking of Gress. *What if he does work for Reichenau?* But if so, why wouldn't he keep me? Why let me go?

It's a good question, only I have a possible answer. To find out what I was up to, and, at the same time, to keep an eye on me and make sure I was no threat.

I go inside and ride the lift to reception, twenty floors down, deep in the earth, where another of the *do-hu* serves me, giving me my electronic key and a sealed letter.

The letter intrigues me. Who, apart from Ernst and Svetov, knows I'm here? And why would they write me a letter?

Back in my room, I lock the door then slit the letter open with my thumbnail.

And laugh. It's a note from Theoretician Fischer, saying how much he enjoyed my company and would I be his guest at dinner tomorrow evening?

It seems I've talked my way inside.

I stretch out on the massive bed, hoping for a good night's sleep, but it's less than five minutes before I have a visitor, Svetov appearing out of the air.

'Otto . . .'

I sit up. 'What is it now?'

Svetov looks about the room, taking in its opulence. 'Are you all right, Otto? Your movements . . .'

'I got picked up. By the local SS. A man by the name of Gress. Here's his details . . .'

And I hand Svetov a handwritten copy, based on the plastic card Gress gave me.

'He might be worth looking at. There was something about him that was odd. I even wondered whether he might be one of Reichenau's men.'

Svetov looks up, interested. 'Okay. I'll check him out. But I came because we've had some news.'

'News?'

'From Hecht's brother, Albrecht. He's finally turned up.'

'And?'

'He's got news of what happened to Hecht.'

359

Albrecht is sitting with Master Schnorr, in Schnorr's private rooms, when I arrive. I embrace him briefly, then sit, facing him, listening as he briefly tells his tale.

Hecht did, it seems, return to the Haven for his final days, and it was there that he met his death.

'Who killed him?'

Albrecht hesitates, then, softly, 'You did.'

His words stun me. But Albrecht explains.

'It was Reichenau. He managed to place a mind-brace on him.'

'A mind-brace?'

'It controls the cerebellum by means of pulsed signals. Hecht thought at first that it could be removed, but that wasn't so. It's semi-organic, you see, and as it slowly infiltrated his mind, so it slowly took him over. Eventually it would have controlled him totally. My brother would have been Reichenau's tool, and Reichenau would have had full access to Four-Oh. Hecht could not allow that to happen.'

'Okay. I see that. But why me?'

'Because you were the only one he trusted. Even at the end, even after all you'd done, he knew he could count on you.'

'And the ash-leaf pendant?'

'Reichenau left that. Hecht said you would know what it meant.'

I look down. This, surely, is proof that Reichenau and Kolya have been working together, for how else would Reichenau have obtained it?

'How did Reichenau locate the Haven?'

'I don't know. But my brother thought that Reichenau must somehow have "tagged" him with something like the patch he used to take Gehlen from his age. There is no other way.'

'And the Haven?'

'Is safe again. We've changed the jump coordinates. They always did involve two small jumps rather than a single one.'

'And now?'

'You must go there, Otto. You have to kill him.'

Which is what I knew he would say. Only how can I?

'It is done,' I say. 'And yet it remains to be done.'

'So it is,' Old Schnorr says, tears welling in his eyes. 'So it is.'

360

Albrecht and I stand there on the platform of Four-Oh, waiting to jump back to the Haven, back in the Deep Past, where all of our records are kept. Svetov, looking on, has been left with strict instructions to seal it off if, for some reason, we don't come back within the hour.

'Imagine,' I say to Albrecht, in the moment before we depart, 'Kolya in charge of all that valuable information.'

'Or that two-headed bastard,' Albrecht answers. 'It's unthinkable.'

I nod, and back we jump, Four-Oh throwing us in effect a micro-second to the right, and then a huge, long way – like a catapult shot – back into the distant past.

We appear from the air, our senses alarmed, an immediate sense of wrongness making us turn and look and see . . .

. . . the Neanderthal village, burning. No sign of any of the creatures.

Albrecht looks thoroughly confused. Unlike us, he is not used to change. 'This didn't happen before . . .'

No. Nor is there any sign of Master Hecht himself. We go to the door in the mountain face and find it untouched.

'Thank Urd,' Albrecht murmurs, then taps in the code to give us access. But inside there's still no sign of Hecht.

'Has Reichenau out-guessed us?' I ask. 'Is he here still, somewhere in the Haven, waiting to kill us?'

It is a possibility, after all.

I go outside, gun at the ready, my skin crawling now, expecting Reichenau to come at any moment. Only when someone does come, it's Hecht. It's he, it seems, who set fire to the Neanderthal village, he who chased the tribe away, firing gunshots into the air to frighten them.

'Why?' I ask.

'So that *he* couldn't hurt them.'

'He?'

'Reichenau.'

And now Albrecht emerges and, seeing his brother, hugs him to him, tears coursing down his face.

'This is it,' Hecht says, breaking from his embrace and turning to me. 'You know what you must do, Otto.'

I shake my head, denying him.

'How can I?' I ask, torn apart by what he's asking of me. '*How*?'

Only his eyes are filled with the certainty of someone who has come to terms with what faces him. Even in his final moments he is still the Master.

'Because you must,' he says. 'For all of us.'

I shake my head once more. I cannot, *will not*, do this. Only Hecht has strength enough for us both.

'It's okay, Otto. I do not fear death. Only life as a slave.'

Hecht takes a step toward me, smiling at me, his *Eizelkind*, all disagreements behind us. Then, his voice filling the air, he repeats the words that I know are engraved on the base of the Tree of Worlds that's in his rooms.

'*Tok, Ick, jraule nicht vor Dir!* ... Death, fear thee not!'

And I nod and raise the gun.

361

Back at Four-Oh, I sit on the edge of my bed, staring at my hands and at the ash-leaf pendant I hold between my fingers.

It is done, the worst of it behind me, and yet I cannot push on. It is as if I've been turned to stone. Trapped, like Ernst was once trapped, every living breath a torment.

And it is Ernst they send to me. Ernst who crouches by me, kneeling to face me, a limitless sympathy in his eyes.

'I know how you feel, dear friend,' he says quietly, gently holding my hands in his own. 'I know the agony of it. But it's done now. You must move on.'

'*Move on?*' My voice is filled with anger and frustration and hurt. 'How can I move on? He *has* her. Reichenau. He and Kolya. And they're toying with me. Making me their puppet, making me kill one of the few men I've ever loved. I don't know how I can live with that, Ernst. I . . .' I swallow, then. 'I keep seeing it. His face . . .'

Ernst is quiet, then. 'Are you ready now?'

'Ready?'

'To go back in. To see the job through.' He pauses, then: 'The simple truth is, we need you, Otto. You're the Master now.'

'To the death,' I say, and Ernst almost smiles. Only he doesn't, because he *does* know how this feels. He alone of them.

119

362

And so, feeling angry and hurt, I return to 2343 and to the Gast Gebaud where I am staying for the conference.

I have been back there only minutes when one of the *do-hu* knocks on the door and announces that dinner is about to be served in the main dining hall.

I go down to the big banqueting hall on the eighteenth floor and join my fellow geneticists, and there, at my table, is the second of my 'targets', one of the King's own private surgeons and, in actuality, one of the King's creators, Hans Klug.

Klug is a very jovial, effusive man in his mid-fifties, a very different kind of man to Theoretician Fischer. But Klug is also highly political, and no fool, and on being introduced to the man, I find his eyes trying to penetrate my own – to work out what kind of man I am. Whether I'm a threat or a potential ally.

For so it is, in this state at this time.

Drinks in hand, we talk, and it's clear Klug warms to me, for, less than ten minutes after we have first met, he offers me a job.

'Why?' I ask him, surprised by the offer. 'Forgive me, Meister, but you don't even know my work!'

Klug smiles. 'No. But I know it must be good for you to be here. Besides, it's the *man* I always go for. Good brains are ten-a-pfennig these days, but a good man . . .'

And he reaches out and holds my bicep for the briefest moment, squeezing it, as if testing a horse's withers.

'You're good Aryan stock, Meister Kroos, and I like that!'

I agree to meet with him later, to formalise our new arrangement, but I suspect his interest in me is as much sexual as it is political, and in the mood I'm in I'm quite ready to hit the man should he over-step the line.

The dinner is long and tedious, but eventually I get back to my room. Ernst is already there. He tells me that there's been a change of plan. One of the rebels they've captured was based in the Mechanist Age. What's more, he has vital information.

And so we jump. This time back to Moscow Central.

363

Zarah meets me at the platform and, before I go on to interrogate our captive, asks me if I'll spare the time to let her update me as regards the 'Great Men' project.

'We've only two more to bring through,' she says, handing me a slender folder, in which is a printout of her thoughts on the usefulness or otherwise of each of the 'extracted'. I glance at one, then look to her.

'You're not convinced, are you?'

'I'm not a convert, no. But they've not really started yet. We're letting them get accustomed to things. It's a tough assimilation process, but most of them are up to it. The women, however . . .'

'Yes?'

She hesitates, then. 'It's just that they're finding it particularly hard. The men . . . they can't help it, I guess, but they were raised in another ethos, for the main part. They consider the two women a waste of time. There to get the food ready. Marie Curie is having none of it, of course – she's a match for most of them – but the other, Rosalind Franklin, is finding it particularly hard.'

'So what do you propose?'

'That you have a word with them, Otto. Make it clear that it's an equal partnership.'

'But what if it isn't?'

Zarah looks at me, disappointed. 'Is that really what you think?'

'I don't know. It's just . . .'

I don't say it, but just look at the list. Galileo, Newton, Einstein, da Vinci, and Aristotle, for a start! Those five alone ought to come up with a few ideas. Then again, I've read about Rosalind Franklin's work – how she went up to Cambridge to meet Crick and Watson, the winners of the Nobel Prize for their work on the double helix structure of DNA, and took their 'model' of the double helix and there and then reconstructed it. Only a truly great scientist could have done that. And, of course, when it came to giving out prizes, she was overlooked, time and again. So maybe Zarah has a point.

'I'll talk to them,' I say. 'Knock a few heads together. But right now . . .'

Right now I have a rebel to question.

364

He's standing with his back to me as I step into the room. Even so, there's something really familiar about him, something that makes the hairs on my neck bristle. And when he turns . . .

Dankevich! Fedor Ivanovich Dankevich!

I almost laugh, only I'm not in a good humour, and, drawing my knife, I cross the room swiftly and grab him, slamming him again the wall and putting the blade to his throat.

'Talk, you bastard! Everything you fucking know!'

But Dankevich just smiles and, slimy as ever, tells me he wants a pardon before he says another word.

Svetov and Ernst have come into the room, but neither interferes. They know well enough what I think of Dankevich, and now that he's been proved to be a traitor, they're as dismissive of the man as I.

To think he was a member of the veche.

I tighten my grip on the man and prick him with the knife's sharp tip.

'Listen, you weasel. I have absolutely nothing to lose. Whether you live or die is nothing to me. I would just as soon slit your throat as learn a single fucking thing from you. So the only way you can possibly persuade me not to gut you like a pig is for you to tell me everything.'

And again I prick him. Harder this time. Drawing a trickle of blood. Not sporting, I know. But then the bastard deserves it.

Dankevich swallows, then nods.

I look to the others, then, easing the blade from his throat, sheathe my knife and push Dankevich away.

We sit, he on the far side of the desk, Ernst and I with our backs to the door. A door 'guarded' by Svetov, who knows Dankevich all too well.

'So?' I ask. And Dankevich launches into his tale.

'It began six years ago, subjective. I was there, in Neu Berlin, in the Mechanist Age. We'd heard something . . . about some new experiments that had taken place. Something that was affecting the timeline. I was put in charge of a team of five to investigate . . .'

'Go on . . .'

'Your Master, Hecht . . . he must have had the same idea, because he sent in a team of your agents to take a look around. Krauss was in charge. Phillipe Krauss. We crossed paths a few times, had a few small skirmishes, before we realised what was going on.'

'And?'

'Something changed. One moment there was no trace of it, the next—'

'You mean Reichenau, yes?'

'No. Not at first. Reichenau came later. No. I mean the experiments . . . into making a functional *doppelgehirn*. The academicians had this idea, you understand. They wanted to force an evolutionary leap. As it turned out, the experiments proved something of a failure. Less than ten per cent proved functional. The rest, well, the rest simply went mad.'

'But Reichenau . . .?'

'As I said, he came later. No. What happened next was that I got captured. By Krauss. I thought I was dead, but he surprised me. Told me about how he'd built this little sect among the German agents. How they were operating as a rogue unit. I didn't see how they could, because they, like we, were being tracked every moment we were in the field. That's when he showed me the pendant. I didn't believe him at first. But we arranged to meet up again, and this time he handed some of the pendants over. He never said how he got them, or from whom, but it wasn't Reichenau. Not at first, anyway.'

He looks down a moment, as if recollecting events.

'That's when it began for me. Like Krauss I started recruiting. Fellow agents who weren't entirely happy with how things were being run. Malcontents, you might call us. Only we saw ourselves as revolutionaries. *Undrehungar*. And what we did, far from being traitorous, was visionary.'

'And then?'

'Then, suddenly, he was there. I jumped back one day and there he was, bang in the centre of the Akademie, walking about like he owned the place, that big head of his turning this way and that, as if to take in his domain. Only I'd never seen him before that moment. In effect, he had never existed. Only suddenly he did. Suddenly he was laced in tightly to it all. As real as you and I. But where he'd come from . . . that I never found out.'

'So he was to blame?'

'To blame?' Dankevich shrugs. 'If you want to call it that. He certainly took over. Planning it all. Sending us in here, there and everywhere. Rattling the cage, as he liked to call it.'

'Meddling.'

'Oh, he certainly did that. He went back years to change things. Each tiny event prolonging the War. Keeping it going, long after its natural term. Making change after change until we couldn't remember how it had been to begin with.'

'And you *wanted* that?'

For the first time there's the slightest shadow of doubt in his eyes. 'I don't know. I guess it becomes automatic after a while. You must remember that. How we did what we were told? And then you met *her*.'

Her? But I say nothing. Only note the tone of contempt in his voice when saying the word.

'He hated that. Hated the way they protected you. Hated you being happy, I guess. He's like that, though. He thinks he's Loki . . .' Dankevich smiles at that, like at a fond memory. 'That's where you got it wrong, Otto. Thinking he had some kind of plan, when all he wanted to do was to cause mischief between you.'

'So where does Kolya fit in?'

'Kolya?' Dankevich looks genuinely puzzled. 'Who the fuck is Kolya?'

I stare at him a moment longer, then draw my gun and, before either Ernst or Svetov can stop me, blow a hole in the fucker's head, watching him slump lifeless to the floor.

For *her*.

365

Svetov isn't happy.

'Dankevich may have been a traitor, but—'

'But what? You believe any of that crap he was talking? The man's a liar. I mean . . . did we experience any of those changes he said happened? No. Reichenau was there from his creation on. Not before and not after. There was nothing sudden . . . No. I'm not taking any of that shit off him. I've had to kill Hecht. And as for Katerina, that bastard still has her—'

'And Dankevich may have known where,' Ernst says quietly.

'Dankevich knew nothing! Reichenau didn't even tell him about Kolya, so why should he know where Katerina's being kept?'

Svetov looks down, calming himself, trying to ignore the corpse just across from us. 'You'd better get back, Otto.'

'Back? Do you really think I'm going to find anything back there?' And I shake my head. 'He's toying with us, Arkadi. Yes, and pissing himself laughing.'

'No,' Svetov says. 'You'll find something. You just have to keep looking.'

Only, again, I don't believe that. Meeting with Dankevich again, knowing that my gut instinct was right and he was a traitor . . .

The thought of it makes me stop dead, wondering what other mischief he's been up to. I mean, for the past few weeks he's had access to every single debate, every single decision that we've made. Oh, he might be dead now, but I guarantee he's still making trouble, somewhere out there in Time.

'Get men on it,' I say, looking back at Svetov. 'Get them to track down everywhere he's been these past few days. Who he met. What he did. And when you've found all that out, come and tell me. Till then I'll go back. See what I can find in 2343.'

And I jump . . .

366

Back in my room at the Gast Gebaud, I shower and change and, within the hour, go down to meet Hans Klug at the bar and, by chance as it happens, notice yet another of my 'targets', August Eichel.

The vivacious, silver-haired Eichel is surrounded by young men, and at first I am reduced to the role of observer, but then Klug comes up alongside me and engages me in conversation.

'How are you, Meister Kroos?'

'Call me Otto,' I say, using the name that I've chosen for this Age. My own, true, but then what more natural?

I ask him, with all reverence, just what he's been working on recently, and he smiles and leans in and whispers, 'You should come and see. It's very interesting.' But that's all he'll say, and we change the subject.

I look about me. The décor here is extravagant. This bar, the biggest of the hotel's five, is called The City Of The Dead, and as if to emphasise that, there are pictures of living skeletons wherever one looks. Why, even at the bottom of your glass a skull smiles back at you.

For they are obsessed with death, here in this Age. Though nothing like as much as they'll be four centuries hence.

'Otto,' Klug says, coming back to me, 'let me introduce you to an old friend of mine. Otto, this is Augst Eichel . . .'

I take the great man's hand and smile. In return he holds mine firmly, giving it a real man's shake, all strength and challenge, his cobalt blue eyes staring very intently at my own as he does.

It's rather like looking at a machine, but that's maybe to be expected. Much of Eichel's work is in the field of human enhancement and his basic foundation work will allow the development of the Guildsmen.

Indeed, here at the bar, to either side of me, are the two main architects of the world I've witnessed Up River in the twenty-eighth century. Manfred's world. And Gehlen's.

'I hear you're working on adapting the hox genes,' Eichel says, and I feign embarrassment and delight that the great man should have noticed me at all.

'Mine's a very small area of research,' I say. 'Then again, it is the oldest shared genetic material. Why, the hox genes of the chicken and the fly have a common ancestor that's over 670 million years old . . .'

And so it goes on . . . a long, interminably long evening turning to morning at the bar.

Later, back in my room, showered and ready for bed, there is a knock on my door. If it's Klug, I'll have to tell him I'm not interested, but it proves to be a bi-sex *do hu* sent by Klug for my use: a stunningly attractive model that is both masculine and feminine at the same time.

It's a kind thought, even if slightly perverse, and I pen a thank-you note to him, but I seriously can't face what is essentially a sex-toy, and send it away.

But whatever the cause, lying there in bed I can't sleep, and when Ernst jumps into the room to warn me that Gress is on his way to my room with an armed squad, I have to hide my arousal from him.

'You can't jump,' Ernst says quickly, in case I should try. 'They've a man just outside, watching the room, making sure you don't escape.'

'So what's the plan?'

'I don't know,' Ernst answers. 'But I'll go back now. Get us working on something.'

'Okay . . .'

But he's gone. And, as if a veil has been pulled aside, I realise that while I can't jump out to avoid them, I can go back, just so long as I return here in a moment or two, objectively.

I look about me at the room, wondering if it was part of someone's plan to catch me fucking a *do hu* in my room, then jump, back to Four-Oh.

367

To find Ernst and Old Schnorr waiting for me, a pack of special equipment in Schnorr's hands. What he calls 'products of the new thinking'.

Our great men – and women – have been busy. There's a design for a protective under-jacket that can withstand the blast of bullets, grenades and laser-fire, and there's another for a device that will allow me to listen to what's being said at Four-Oh wherever I am in Time.

Last, but far from least, there are diagrams for a couple of 'weapons' that look totally innocuous but are, in fact, highly deadly.

I am surprised by these, because from what I'd heard our Great Men didn't want to get involved with anything that would harm someone. I say this to Ernst and he grins.

'It's a well-known fact that scientists don't always grasp the full implications of their discoveries. Da Vinci, particularly. The man has a whole future armoury in his head and doesn't realise it.'

'I see. And how soon will this stuff be ready?'

'A week? Maybe two?'

I find that encouraging. 'I ought to go see them,' I say. 'I promised Zarah.'

But Ernst shakes his head. 'The situation is resolved. We took them all back a week and did some intense brainstorming. The women held their own, so now they're accepted. We even have a romance, of a kind. Young Moseley and the knowledgeable Miss Franklin.'

I know neither of them, but now's not the time for questions on that score. Now I need to get back, to face Gress.

I jump in just a second or so before the hammering starts on my door.

'Meister Kroos! Open the door, *now!*'

'Who is it?' I demand.

'It's internal security! Open up or we'll kick our way in!'

I count to five and, a moment before they start shouting again, undo the latch and pull the door open. At once they're on me, turning me about and cuffing me.

'What *is* this?' I protest, fake indignation in my voice. 'I demand to know why I am being treated in this manner!'

Gress pushes past me, looking about him at the room.

'Oberlieutenant Gress,' I say. 'I demand to know what the charges are against me!'

At which Gress comes over and, in a sombre voice I've not heard from him before, tells me that I'm a spy, working for the Russians. That the entries in the records about me have been falsified, and that no one that they've spoken to at the Cologne Institute has ever heard of me. All of which is true.

'Ridiculous!' I say. 'Someone has been having a game with you, Oberlieutenant. Or, more likely, spreading vicious lies to discredit me.'

Gress is about to say something more, when Klug himself appears at my door, clearly hoping to find me alone and willing, for my room is fourteen floors below his own penthouse suite.

'What in Urd's name is going on here?' he demands, putting on his most pompous and authoritarian air. 'Don't you realise who this is?'

'Meister Klug, I—'

'This man is with me,' he says, ignoring the SS man. 'He is a brilliant geneticist and is here on the invitation of the president himself. Now on your way, man, before I decide to take offence!'

It is marvellously and effectively done, for Gress and his men leave smartly, Gress making no attempt to argue with this particular Great Man. Knowing that to do so might mean the end of his career.

Alone with him, Klug turns to me and, not unkindly, asks me what's going on.

'A jealous colleague, perhaps. You know how they are.'

'Oh, I know,' Klug says, and turns to close the door, before turning back to me, his expression changed, an uncertain smile on his face.

'You know, Otto, I've grown very fond of you . . .'

But even as Klug takes a step towards me, Ernst appears in the air behind him, stun gun in hand, and fires off a charge, felling Klug like a tree.

368

I sit on the edge of Klug's bed, in his room on the top floor of the hotel, watching as the physician gives Klug a thorough examination. Klug himself is groggy. He doesn't know quite where he is, or what day of the week it is. Finally, the physician looks up and declares that the great man must have had a seizure of some kind.

When the physician is gone, I move closer, looking down at him attentively.

Klug is grateful. He genuinely believes that he had a stroke or heart attack of some kind, even though his heart is healthy.

'Is there anything I can do for you, Meister?'

Klug looks away, moved. 'There is one thing . . .'

'By all means. Name it.'

'My speech . . . I'm due to give the keynote speech, tomorrow . . . If you could give it for me, Otto.'

'It would be my pleasure,' I say, squeezing his hand. And he directs me to his case, in which the text of the speech is kept. I take it out and flick through the pages, then realise what it is. It's nothing less than a history of Klug's research activities for these past twenty-five years, and there, as a footnote near the very end of the document, are details of the *doppelgehirn* experiments.

I look up from the folder, meeting his eyes. 'You do me a very great honour, Meister Klug. A very great honour indeed.'

369

'So?' I ask, looking about me at the others gathered about the big farmhouse table. 'What do you think?'

Behind them, out beyond the hills, the sky is dark with cloud.

Zarah looks about her, then speaks up. 'Well, at least we know now who he is – *both* of him.'

'And where he comes from,' Svetov adds.

That had been the shock. To discover that Reichenau – at least, *part* of Reichenau – was Kolya's illegitimate son, given over to the

Akademie by Kolya for experimental purposes. It showed there was no love between them. But beyond that?

Ernst is shaking his head. 'I don't know. My gut instinct is against this. We got this information far too easily. It was just too much of a coincidence that we should stumble on this by accident. This feels . . . *planted*.'

'I agree,' I say. 'It has the feel of someone meddling again. Planting false information to throw us off the real trail. Reichenau would have known of Klug's speech. He would have taken measures to prevent it, surely? To allow it to fall into our hands like this . . . No. I don't think he's that inept!'

There's a rumble of distant thunder. The guards at the bottom of the field, spaced out every thirty metres or so, look up, expecting the storm at any minute.

Tannenberg looks bleak for once. Abandoned.

'Well, I disagree,' Old Schnorr says. 'The man is vain. He might even have enjoyed the idea of being in Klug's keynote speech. And there's no doubting that he has a presence, there in 2343, and there must be a reason for that. So let's find out.'

Svetov speaks up, as another great rumble of thunder fills the valley, closer this time, the slightest hint of lightning in the far distance.

'What I want to know is how the little monster keeps on anticipating our every move. He and Kolya. It's like they've got the inside track to things.'

'A traitor, you think?'

Ernst shakes his head. 'We had one traitor and he's dead. Remember? No. It seems to me that the only way to deal with Reichenau is to take him out, right now. Go for him direct at all the places we know he frequents and see just how fast he can jump out of there each time.'

'We know where he's been in the past,' Zarah chips in. 'So let's start with those. In Werkstatt 9, back in the twenty-eighth century. At Gehlen's research establishment on the day that the bombs fell. And at Baturin, back in 1708. Let's send in a crack squad to each of those and attack him. It surely can't do any harm.'

There's a growl of agreement from the others, but not from me. I share the scepticism Ernst expressed earlier. It *was* too easy. And, talking of gut instinct, mine is to let be. We haven't yet caught him off guard, and if he were to hit us back . . .

Yet that's the *veche's* decision. To go for his throat.

The rain begins, big drops of it falling from the heavens, forming dark spots on the wooden deck. And as it does, so we jump out of there, one after another, until only Ernst and I are left, the heavy rain soaking us in seconds.

'We'll take him alive if we can,' Ernst says, as the rain becomes a downpour. 'I promise. Find out where they are, and—'

But I am gone.

Promises, I think, as I make my way through to Hecht's rooms, water dripping from me. *What fucking good are promises?*

370

I'm told to take a back-seat role, which is why, as we materialise in the air just inside of Werkstatt 9, I find myself as an observer as our team blast their way up the stairs and across the walkway to get to the supervisor's office.

The firefight is intense, but then suddenly we're inside and my men come down to me, holding a struggling man between them.

'Who's this?'

'He's the supervisor, Master. He says he's never heard of Reichenau. You want us to question him?'

Perhaps I ought, but I half expected this and know – without a shadow of a doubt – that torture would achieve nothing. No. Reichenau has made changes here, erasing himself from time.

I leave four of them to search the place and see what they can find, then get the rest of the team out of there, linking up with Ernst at Four-Oh.

'You should see this,' he says, and grabbing my arm, jumps back . . . to Erfurt in the twenty-eighth century, only, instead of a castle, there's a ruin and no sign whatsoever of Gehlen's research facility.

We jump again, to Baturin this time, and to the back street where I once glimpsed him, only that too is a ruin, the house demolished by fire.

Reichenau has destroyed everything in his wake.

Scorched earth, I think, recognising his touch in all of this.

And finally we jump back to the Kolya house in Berkeley, California, in January 1952, to find . . . not even a house, just a vacant lot with a For Sale sign posted on a tree.

How? I ask myself. *How does he know?*

371

Which is precisely what I ask Ernst when he comes to see me later.

Only Ernst has no answers either. Reichenau seems to have vanished from Time. Meanwhile, the *veche*, it seems, have met again, this time without me.

Ernst?'

'It's nothing,' he says, reassuringly. 'They simply want you to go back in. Back to the original plan. To infiltrate 2343 – make friends with the big, important men – and see what we can find out.'

'So you want me to read Klug's speech?'

'That and the rest of it. The socialising and the lectures and . . .'

In other words, all of the dull stuff, the stuff I really hate. Academics! Urd help us, who in the gods' names would be an academic?

372

And so I return.

'Meister Kroos!' Theoretician Fischer booms, seeing me across the crowded room and gesturing to me to join him. 'What *have* you been up to?'

For word has got around about me 'saving' Klug's life. The academicians look at me now with guarded smiles, as if I'm the man to know.

Which is not quite what we'd planned. To draw attention like this . . .

I present myself to Fischer, who takes the opportunity to put his arm about my shoulders and speak to me quietly, almost intimately, his breath, smelling of mint, in my face, far closer than is decent.

'I missed you last night, Otto. You should have come and seen me.'

And then, much louder, for all to hear, 'Have you heard, gentlemen? Meister Kroos is to present the keynote speech tomorrow! It is an honour he well deserves!'

And he gently squeezes my right shoulder before saying, quietly and to my ear once more, 'I look forward to seeing you later on, Otto. We should become closer, you and I, yes?'

But Fischer knows not to overplay things and moves away, 'working' his way around the big reception room.

The president is to be here soon, along with several of his ministers. And the prince, though he's too frail to stay long. But before either arrive, my new patron, Meister Klug, makes an appearance in a luxurious healing couch, the big wheelchair pushed by an attendant, the old man smiling and gesturing, positively beaming when he sees me, his 'saviour', as he calls me. Which makes me think of Ernst, stunning him like a prize bull as he rushed across the room to ravish me.

'How are you, Meister?' I say, crouching to address him face to face. 'Are you feeling any better?'

Klug grins back at me and clasps my hands, clearly delighted to see me. 'Much better, Otto, thanks to you. Have you read it through?'

He means his speech, and I have, a good six times, until I was word perfect.

'I have it by heart,' I say, and he grins even more and squeezes my hands.

'That's good, Meister Kroos. Very good.'

But there are things I need to know. Like when and where all this happened. Because the speech he's written doesn't give such facts. And so I gently, subtly coax these from him, under the guise of natural interest. And, reassured by the fact that these are his fellow geneticists, he speaks about it, and the first thing I discover is that this was done a good ten years ago, when the two men who together *form* the creature we call Reichenau were barely in their twenties.

'I almost chose differently,' he says. 'At first the Francke body was to be the host. It was fitter, stronger than the other. But when it came to the week before the operations, I changed my mind. There was something about Reichenau that convinced me he should be the host. Some *psychological* quality, you might call it. And so it was that it was the Reichenau half that was the host.

We removed Francke's head and then reconnected, attaching the spinal brace, and . . . ah, but you know all that, Otto. I am pre-empting your speech, no?'

'*Your* speech, Meister,' I say, and everyone listening to us laughs, delighted by our exchange.

But now I have more detailed information and if I can find a moment I will jump back and have Ernst investigate that time period.

It is two hours, however, before I get the chance.

Ernst is there at the platform. For him the wait has been brief. A matter of seconds.

'Autumn,' I say, '2323. There at the Akademie. He was there at least two weeks, maybe longer.'

'Good,' Ernst says, beaming. 'I'll get on to it at once.'

And he hurries from the platform, leaving me to jump back again, into that hot and crowded room, just in time to see the president make his entrance.

Adelbert Schafer is a tall, elegant man. He has been president these past six years, replacing the unfortunate President Koch, who, some say, was killed at Schafer's orders. Whatever the truth, Schafer has ruled Greater Germany with an iron fist, and if anyone is responsible for setting Gress and his SS dogs on me, it's him.

Eventually I meet him and shake his hand. It seems he too has heard of how I'd 'saved' Meister Klug.

'You did the State a great service, Meister Kroos,' he says, his steely eyes fixing me. 'If there is any favour I can do you in return . . .'

It's unexpected.

'Thank you, Herr President,' I answer him, and bow respectfully. And he moves across to greet Klug himself, in his wheelchair, crouching to Klug's level to speak to him, the two men talking for a moment before they both turn to me, then roar with laughter and chink glasses.

It's a strangely disconcerting moment, for it seems almost as if they're mocking me. That all the rest – all of the praise and laughter – is but an act.

And if it is?

It is a warning for me to be more careful. A reminder that I don't really fit in around these people. That, like the sword brothers I was once among, these men would kill me were they to know the truth.

And so the evening passes and I find myself back in my huge room, fifteen floors down from the likes of Klug and Fischer, the chain on my door, hoping that Fischer won't come visiting, that he's found younger and more willing flesh to try.

I sleep, and wake to find myself bathed in sweat, gripping the bedclothes like I am about to fall, the dream I woke from making me gasp. My girls, but not my girls. My girls transformed, their flesh as pale as bleached ivory, their eyes like pearls, unseeing, each of them walking past me in that ruined, twilit landscape, my darling Katerina last of all.

Like the dead, their feet making no prints. As if they never were.

I lie there for a time, trembling like a frightened child, then go through and shower. What does it mean? That Kolya has disposed of them? Or is it *just* a dream? Am I wrong to give it meaning?

I go to the window and stand there, watching the sun rise over Neu Berlin, filled with dark forebodings, then turn and go to the wardrobe, where the *do hu* have hung my suit for the ceremony and, not bothering to call them, begin to dress.

373

The anteroom of the ancient Reichstag building is packed. More than a hundred academicians are there, with their servants and bodyguards, making their last-minute preparations. Only I, waiting in the wings of the great auditorium, Klug's speech in hand, am unmoved. Like an island of calm in the midst of it all.

I have seen Klug already, in his palatial penthouse suite, to make the final small changes to his speech. Now there is nothing else to do but wait for the ceremony to begin.

That dream, that awful dream, has been on my mind all morning. Much as I've tried to draw a veil over it, the thing simply will not go away, fuelling my fear that something has changed; that Kolya has somehow made his move.

And if he has?

I don't know. For once I am totally at a loss. Nor do I want to think it through. Not now, anyway. Not before this is done.

'Otto!' someone calls, and I see it is Theoretician Fischer. 'Good luck with the speech!' he says. 'We'll meet up later, yes?'

I nod, then turn back. All manner of dignitaries are on that massive stage now, taking their places before the ceremony begins, including the King, President Schafer and the Grand Master of the Guilds, Kurt Hammill, whose role within this State is far less influential than it will be in centuries to come.

And as I watch, so Klug is brought onstage, in a healing couch, to be placed between the King and the president, the great man beaming across at me, his protégé.

The main hall of that massive auditorium was packed already, but now the balconies begin to fill, the great men hurrying to their places, even as the room behind me empties, leaving me the last man standing.

I watch as a huge screen moves on its tracks overhead, while the projectors – there to give all the relevant illustrations to my talk – come to glowing life.

It is almost time.

A tall man in a dark cloak crosses the stage, stopping at the microphone, to turn and bow at the great dignitaries seated there. This is Meister Schwab, the Speaker of the Reichstag, and Schafer's Chancellor. A powerful and charming man.

I stay where I am, waiting for his summons as he introduces me to the host. And as I do, I am aware just what a historical moment this is. This great gathering of the German hierarchy. Why, it's like Nuremberg again. All that's missing are the flags and banners, the torches burning up the darkness.

Finally, I hear my name, see Chancellor Schwab turn and summon me, and go across to a great storm of applause. And, as it falls quiet again, so I face them and begin.

Their enemy. The fake among them.

But that's by the by. I am aware now of the massed ranks in the Reichstag below me, their eyes drawn to the things that are being projected into the air above me – pages of statistics and diagrams, still images of the procedure. It all goes well, yet as I come to the part about Reichenau and how he came to be, so that great audience gasp.

I half turn, still speaking, wondering what's going on and realising as I do that the crowd is not looking at the images *above* me, but at something just *beyond* me.

And there, smiling at me, laser-gun in hand, is the unmistakable figure of Reichenau himself.

I fall silent.

And even as I do, so his voice sounds clear in that great, echoing space.

'I hear you were looking for me, Otto. Only I'm very hard to find. Unless I want to be found.'

'How do you do that?' I ask him, narrowing my eyes, trying to guess what his next move will be, ignoring the great crowd that is witnessing our exchange. 'How do you anticipate each move we make? Are you up there ahead of us in Time, looking back, or . . .?'

Only Reichenau is not listening. His smile has gone, his face is harder now. There is hatred in his eyes and on his small, narrow lips. Hatred and madness.

'Time to die,' he says, and pulls the trigger.

Part Thirteen
Pretzel Logic

'We are stillborn, and for generations past have been begotten not by living fathers, and that suits us better and better. We are developing a taste for it. Soon we shall contrive to be born somehow from an idea.'

– Fyodor Dostoevsky, *Notes from the Underground*

I wake. To silence and stillness.

Someone is holding my hand. For the briefest moment I don't recognise them, and then I smile. It's Urte. I look up at her in wonder.

'Why aren't I dead?'

She smiles. A tender, anguished smile. 'Who said you weren't?'

'Then . . . you brought me back?'

'No. We kept you alive, then patched you up. You're lucky to be here at all. He burned the focus out of your chest before you could react. We think he meant to take you with him, but we got to you first.'

I pull back the cover and look at my chest. There is discoloration but the skin is fine. They've done a good repair job on me.

'How long have I been out?'

'A month. But we sent you back. You haven't missed anything.'

'No? I—'

I look past her, sensing movement in the doorway on the far side of the room. It's Ernst and Zarah, and, just behind them, Svetov. They all have a look of relief to them, and from that I realise how close I must have been to death. Proper end-of-it-all death.

'Are you all right?' Ernst asks. And I nod and smile and take his hands. Only one thing is eating away at me. One question that, it almost seems, I have been asking myself all the time I've been unconscious.

How does Reichenau know what we're going to do every time?

If we could answer that, we'd surely have him.

But I say nothing of that yet. Instinct tells me I ought to let things stew a while. That an answer *will* come. But not until it's time.

'Otto?'

'Yes, Urte?'

'Do you feel up to visitors?'

I smile. 'So you four aren't visitors?'

'No. I mean . . . it's young Moseley. He wants to come and see you.'

'Moseley?' And for the briefest while I don't recall who he means. But then it clicks. '*Moseley*? The one Gehlen was so insistent about?'

'And for good reason,' Ernst says. 'The man's a genius.'

'As are they all—'

'Yes, but . . .' Ernst laughs, a sharp, strange sound. 'Well, you'll see.'

And so, an hour later, Moseley comes to visit, the young man – in his mid-twenties at most – dressed in Edwardian clothes, his dark hair cut short, his black boots highly polished.

He looks the very picture of his age.

'Meister,' he begins, bowing to me, but I'm having none of that.

'It's Otto,' I say, and, from where I sit propped up among my cushions, I indicate the chair nearby.

He takes the seat, then clears his throat, his whole manner awkward. 'Thank you for seeing me,' he says. 'And thank you for bringing me here, to Four-Oh. I . . .'

'It wasn't me,' I say, before he gets too effusive. 'Gehlen wanted you. He was insistent.'

'Maybe, but . . . I was dead. In my world, I mean. Or my timeline, should I say. Shot dead at Gallipoli. My best work ahead

of me. But here . . .' He looks down. 'I've never felt so free. So . . .
happy, I guess. And to be in such company . . . I keep thinking
I'm dreaming all of this . . . that some time soon I'll find myself
awake again, back in the trenches at Gallipoli, thick layers of flies
covering everything. Or maybe that was the dream. A bad dream,
but a dream all the same. Because I feel alive here. Truly alive.'

I smile. 'You're welcome. But look, why are you here? What
do you want?'

'Want? No, Meister. I don't want anything. Not for myself. But
I've heard what's been happening, and I thought . . . Well, I
wondered if I could help. If you ran things past me, I . . . Look,
I know it seems immodest but, it's what I do. What my mind
does, rather. It connects things. Comes up with answers. It always
has done, since I was a boy. And I thought . . .'

'Then you thought right,' I say, knowing instinctively that this
is what was needed. For someone to come along and look at it all
from a fresh viewpoint.

And so we begin. Randomly. Me pulling things from the air
and him asking questions. Until, suddenly, he lifts a hand to stop
me.

'Okay. I think I see what it is.'

'You do?'

He nods. 'Our friend, Reichenau . . . imagine if you looked
like him – if you had to suffer that other brain in your head, there
all the time? What would you do?'

I shrug. What *would* I do?

Moseley leans toward me. 'I'd go back and change it, wouldn't
you?'

'Maybe . . .'

'No. No maybes about it. You would. So why doesn't he? Why
can't he?'

'I don't know. I . . .'

'What if Meister Klug's footnotes were true, and Kolya did give over his illegitimate child to become a *doppelgehirn*? And what if he wants it to remain that way? What if Kolya is *preventing* Reichenau from making that change, possibly even protecting that section of Time against Reichenau?'

I consider that, realising, even as I do, that I am excited by the idea. Kolya and Reichenau, not friends at all, but enemies! All this time I have been wrongly assuming that they have been working together, when in truth . . .

'Schikaneder,' I say. 'That's who we need to see.' And though Moseley does not follow me, I see it clearly. Yes, it's time to pay our artist friend another visit. To ask him a few more questions. By knife-point if necessary.

And, throwing the sheet back, I swing my legs round. 'Come,' I say to Moseley. 'There's not a moment to be lost.'

375

But first I go to see Old Schnorr.

'Master Schnorr,' I say, looking across at him from the doorway. 'I need some information about Herr Schikaneder.'

'Come on in, Otto,' the old man says, gesturing towards the empty chair just across from where he's working, his thick-lensed glasses on. 'It's good to see you well.'

I turn, meaning to introduce Moseley to him, but Schnorr anticipates me.

'Henry . . . how is it going?'

'Well, Master Schnoor. Very well. But Otto needs some information urgently.'

'About Schikaneder?' And he puts down whatever it is he seems to be mending and looks at me. 'What kind of thing, Otto?'

'His real name, for a start.'

Schnorr seems to freeze. His eyes fix mine. 'No, I—'

'I need to know,' I insist. 'And all else you know about him.'

The silence between us stretches. Breaks.

'Hecht,' he says. 'His given name was Hecht, Klaus Hecht.'

'No,' I say. 'I don't believe it. He's nothing like Master Hecht. He *looks* nothing like him.'

'No,' he concedes, 'but he shares the same mother.'

'So he's a half-brother?'

'Yes. but look, there's little else to say. He didn't fit, so we exiled him. End of story.'

'And yet Kolya contacted him. He was the only one. And that must mean something.' I shake my head, trying to figure this. 'Did Hecht – our Hecht – ever get to see him? In Prague, I mean?'

'Not as far as I know.'

'But he might have?'

'You'd have to ask the women. They'd know for certain. Or Albrecht. *If* he'll tell you details of his brother's life.'

I turn and look to Moseley. 'Henry, will you look into that?'

He nods and is gone. I turn back, looking to Old Schnorr again. 'It has to be him. He's the piece that doesn't fit the puzzle.'

376

And so, just an hour later, I find myself back in Prague, on the fifth of December, 1892, the day after I visited Schikaneder for the first time.

As I make my way across the Charles Bridge towards Schikaneder's house, it's snowing once more. My gun is tucked into the pocket of my long coat, my knife sheathed at my belt.

And, in a folder in my hand, I have a picture of Reichenau that I drew from memory.

The hour is late, the roads almost empty. As I make my way through the Jewish Quarter, I find myself whistling an old folk tune. A Russian song, I realise and laugh. *Korobuska* . . .

And find myself facing a smallish figure in a cloak.

My hand goes to my knife.

'Good evening,' the figure says in perfect Russian, and as they throw back the hood, I see it is a woman. A very young and very pretty woman.

'You're not from here, are you?' she says, and smiles.

A whore? I wonder. She looks too sweet, far too well dressed, to be a whore. But why else would she be out here at such an hour? And why approach a stranger such as I, unless . . .?

I draw my knife a moment after she's drawn hers, and as she lunges, targeting my heart, so I quickly jerk aside and, tugging the gun from my pocket, strike out, using the handle as a club.

I can feel the bone crack. Hear her strange little croak as she tumbles and lies still, the knife clattering away on the icy paving.

Urd protect me! I think, crouching to feel for a pulse, knowing that she is dead. Then, knowing I need to hide her, I take her by the feet and pull her across the street, rolling her beneath a bush that serves as the boundary to the garden of one of the nearby houses.

I cross back. There's little blood, luckily for me, and, picking up her knife, I look about me, then hurry on. Only I'm rattled now. Does this mean that Kolya knows I'm here? And if so, will there be other assassins on my way, waiting to jump out and ambush me?

I take two paces then stop dead, realising that I've not been thinking, that I ought to be jumping back to Four-Oh to let them know what has just happened. Only I know that if I do, he'll jump back in – if it *is* Kolya – and bring her back to life. Then try again.

I start to run, trying not to slip, looking this way and that, listening out for pursuing feet, or for some sudden movement in the shadows.

And suddenly I'm there, the house Schikaneder lives in looming up ahead of me, its windows dark. Quickly, knowing I must be bold, I force the door and, inside, in the hallway, count to ten, getting my breath back before I climb the stairs.

If I was Kolya, what would I do?

If I was Kolya. But what if it wasn't him? What if she was just a thieving whore? Because if he knew that I was coming here . . .

If he knew, then he'd have struck again . . . and again . . .

I go up. Past the first two floors and on, up to the very top where Schikaneder lives. And force the door there, waiting outside, listening to hear movement from the rooms below, or from the apartment in front of me.

Silence. Or the nearest thing to silence. I can hear Schikaneder in his room, snoring away.

Unless that's a recording, left for me by Kolya . . .

Only now I *am* being paranoid. Suspecting every little sound, every tiny movement.

I step inside, scanning the darkened room. Nothing. Or nothing I can make out. The room itself is warm, however, and as I get closer, I see that he has set a fire in the grate. I take the poker from where it hangs and dig into the ashes, and for a moment there's a faint glow of embers. In its half-light I see that he has left clearing up until the morning, for there's a dirty plate and a half-drunk glass of wine on the table, and, on the floor nearby, a newspaper.

I straighten up, forcing myself to relax, telling myself I'm a fool to think Kolya could be here ahead of me, when I didn't even know what I was going to do myself. The man is not a mind-reader, after all.

As the glow from the embers dies, I cross the room, checking on Schikaneder. He's sleeping soundly, and, pulling the door closed behind me, I go across and light an oil lamp.

In the wavering light, I begin my search. It's here somewhere. It has to be here. Some mark of Kolya's presence, that is. And, because where one of them is one usually finds traces of the other, of Reichenau.

It's the best part of an hour before I find something. Schikaneder's notebook, hidden away in a folder on a shelf in the corner of the room. I flick through quickly, then flick back, a line in one of the entries catching my eye. I'm about to write it down, when I hear a floorboard creak just behind me.

I spin round, to find Schikaneder there, pointing a gun at my head. If it were anyone else I'd have taken a chance and jumped him, but Schikaneder, for all he now is, was once *Reisende*. He's been trained, and the simple manner in which he holds the gun is a reminder of that. He's not forgotten everything.

'*You!*' he says, genuine annoyance in his voice. 'What the fuck do you think you're doing?'

I jump out, then jump back in directly behind him, my laser trained on the back of his head.

'Drop the gun!'

Only Schikander doesn't. He half turns, meaning to take me out, only he's far too slow. Forced to fire, I aim for his gun hand and squeeze the trigger, a great charge of ionised air leaping from my hand to his.

He screams, his hand suddenly on fire, flesh melting like marzipan, a hideous stink filling the room.

'You bastard!' he groans, dropping the gun, trying to beat out the flames. 'You heartless fucking bastard!'

Only it doesn't matter what he calls me, and, pocketing the laser, I grab a wrap and throw it to him, then stoop to pick the gun up, just in case he grows forgetful and tries to use it again.

377

I bind him and bandage him and tie him down in a chair, then I inject him with a drug to make him answer me truthfully.

I stand above him, between him and the wavering oil lamp on the mantelpiece.

'Who is Reichenau?'

Schikaneder makes to answer, then winces painfully, as if he's receiving a shock to the head. He grits his teeth and forces an answer out.

'I . . . only met him . . . once. He . . .'

And he slumps, unconscious.

I leave him a moment, jumping back to Four-Oh to discuss the situation. Ernst meets me there.

'What is it?'

'I'm not sure, but I'd say he's got some kind of mental block about Reichenau. Something that prevents him talking about him.'

'Okay. Then we'd best get Diedrich.'

Diedrich is officially Four-Oh's physics expert, but he's had experience of working with blocked states, Ernst's among them.

He and Ernst jump back with me, and while Ernst checks on the flats beneath, Diedrich opens up his case of phials and gets to work, injecting Schikaneder with a cocktail of drugs, then wiring him up to a monitoring device.

'Okay,' he says finally. 'That ought to work to block the blocker. But it's only temporary. Try not to stress him too much. You could lose him altogether.'

Just then Ernst returns. He's been jumping into the other apartments in the house and has discovered something strange.

'There's nothing. Nothing at all in any of the apartments. Not a single tenant. But more than that, there's not a shred of carpet or a stick of furniture. All there is are the curtains, and they're drawn. Maybe that's how it was arranged when they exiled him here, but it's spooky, like this is some kind of theatrical set.'

No wonder no one heard his screams.

I make to speak again, only suddenly there are shouts and whistles blowing in the streets below. My guess is that they've found the corpse I left beneath the bushes.

I go to the window and look down, and sure enough, there are policemen hurrying by down there, their torches flickering in the dark.

Ernst asks me if I know what's going on down there, and I tell him.

'Kolya – is that what you're thinking?'

'One of the two,' I say. 'Either that or it's just some kind of weird coincidence.'

But neither Ernst nor I believe in coincidence. Because in our line it usually means trouble. And this place – which has known Kolya's past presence – seems ripe for trouble.

We wait for Schikaneder to regain consciousness, then begin again, Ernst and Diedrich keeping out of sight as I start question-ing him.

'So you met him only once, is that right?'

'Who do you mean?'

'Reichenau. Is this what he looks like?'

I hold up my pencil portrait of the *doppelgehirn.*

Schikaneder stares at the drawing grimly, like he can't look away, then forces his eyes down and nods.

Feeling sorry for the man, I soften my tone. 'What did he do to you?'

'Heeeeh . . .'

'No,' I say, interceding quickly before he passes out again. 'It's okay. You don't have to answer that.'

Schikaneder deflates with relief.

I stare at him a moment, understanding. This isn't just mental conditioning. In all likelihood he was physically tortured by Reichenau, and perhaps for precisely the same reason: *to get information about Kolya.*

'You told him about Kolya?' I ask, making it as gentle a query as possible, but even so, he really struggles to get an answer back to me – a single nod of his head.

'Things you didn't tell me last time?' I ask, and he nods again.

But before I can ask anything more, Diedrich stops me. The stress levels are way too high.

Which is frustrating, but then I do feel for the man.

'Give him something,' I say, turning to Diedrich. 'Let him rest a while, then we'll try again.'

Diedrich looks dubious, which isn't a good sign, but he does what's asked of him, giving our exile a strong shot of something to make him sleep.

'There,' he says. 'I'm going back. Call me if and when you need me again.'

And he's gone, leaving me with Ernst.

'So?' Ernst asks.

'The journal,' I say, going across to the table where I placed it earlier. 'There was a line . . .'

I flick through, looking for the passage that caught my eye earlier. One line leaps out at me:

'It's all there in the paintings.'

I'm not quite sure just why this caught my attention, because the paintings of his I've seen weren't exactly filled with clues about anything. It's just the agitation in the handwriting at that point that alerted me – as if it really cost Schikaneder even to write such an indirect direction.

Setting the journal aside, I begin my search. Most of the paintings are like the one I first saw – simple, bleak landscapes. But then I open a cupboard and there they are – paintings of Reichenau and, unmistakably, of Kolya. But it's not just that those two are in them, it's the backdrops, full of minutiae and details.

Clues, I think, and smile for the first time.

378

Talianov studies the painting for a long, long time, then looks up at us, nodding decisively.

'Schikaneder put all he knew about those two into these paintings,' he says. 'It's clear he let his unconscious speak here, silently uttering all of those things that he couldn't say aloud . . . all of those things that he was programmed not to say . . . it's all here!'

Talianov is the Russians' psyche expert. A master interpreter of others' indirection. If anyone can interpret these symbolic landscapes, then it's him.

'The trees in this one . . . look at how he distorts their forms. Nothing's truly as it is, but everything has meaning. It's all . . . *translated.*'

Svetov, seated next to me, grunts his agreement, even as Talianov gestures towards the bigger of the two dual portraits, the one in which Kolya's back is turned to Reichenau.

'Here . . . just beyond the figure of Kolya . . . there's what looks at first glance to be a pond and a school of tiny white fish, only the pond is the socket of an eye, and the school of fish . . .'

Spermatozoa . . . each of them bearing the slightly altered face of Kolya.

There are more than a dozen of these special paintings, and each one of them forms a symbolic landscape. Real yet not real. Their purpose entirely revelatory. A way of 'getting around the fence', as Talianov calls it.

A whole richness of clues. Like the two felled trees that, in the painting, are bound together with rusting iron bands. What could that be but Reichenau himself? The *doppelgehirn* busy, always busy. Whereas Kolya – drawn often in these studies – is always a lonely figure. Always isolate. Schikaneder paints him always with a space between him and the rest of things, as if his presence there has burned a hole in the canvas.

And that, we've quickly come to realise, is how to read these. Not singularly, but as a whole, taking in the repeated nature of the symbolism. Recognising that Schikaneder could only do this in fits and starts, fighting all the time against the pains in his head, the deep reluctance of his conscious self. Repeating because in repetition the meaning of the symbol can emerge.

But most important of all is what is not symbolic. Some of the backdrops . . .

'I'd say that that's a real place,' Talianov says, tapping the very realistic-looking monastery which dominates at least three of the paintings. 'St Petersburg, do you think?'

Svetov shakes his head. 'No. Not St Petersburg. But it is Russian. And old. Very old. I'll circulate copies of this to all our agents, see if anyone comes up with anything.'

'Good,' I say. Then, looking to Talianov again, 'Sergei, give me a report on each of these . . . that and your overall impressions.'

'I shall.'

'Then let's meet later on.'

And I jump, back to Prague, to join up with Diedrich again.

379

Diedrich doses Schikaneder up again and, when he's ready, we present him with the first – and strangest – of the canvases.

The painting has an interstellar backdrop. Everything in that canvas suggests a searing coldness and vast distances, even the two small but solid central figures, which seem coated with a kind of jewel-like permafrost, their eyes burning with a star-like intensity.

It is an apocalyptic vision and, seeing it, Schikaneder gives a choked gasp, as if it's suddenly impossible to breathe, and passes out.

'Urd save us!' Diedrich mutters, getting to his feet. 'The conditioning must be strong. There must be some kind of implant.

'Let me,' I say, and examining Schikaneder's neck and the back of his head, I find a slightly raised patch, not too dissimilar from that which Ernst had on his flank that time, when he was trapped in the clearing. Yet even as my fingers close on it, Schikaneder vanishes.

380

Back at Four-Oh, Svetov is waiting for us. One of the Russian time agents has recognised the scene in Schikaneder's painting. It's the 'Troitsky' Monastery – the Troitskaya Sergeeva – just thirty-five miles or so north of Moscow. The question now is when. But

Svetov has an idea about that. He tells us about Peter the Great and the revolt of the Kremlin guard, the Streltsy, in August 1689, at the very start of his reign. It was to the Troitsky Monastery that Peter fled, resting up there before returning to Moscow to deal harshly with his rebellious forces.

I tell Svetov to organise a team and go in, to scout about and see what can be seen. But he's had an idea of his own. He wants to try to locate Reichenau's 'daughter', Gudrun. That is, if she hasn't just ceased to exist when Reichenau made his changes to Time.

And so we jump in, to Neu Berlin in 2747, to Burckel's apartment once more.

Burckel is surprised to see me – weeks earlier than I was scheduled to arrive – but he's shocked to the core by Svetov's appearance – all furs and beard – there at my side. We quickly talk him round, however, explaining what's been happening and what we need to do, and in no time at all he's helping us, arranging stuff like he did first time round. Putting out feelers and asking favours of his 'friends'.

Only locating Gudrun isn't easy. She's not at the Werkstatte when we visit it, nor does anyone remember her. But we know that there was a register of all the *doppelgehirn* at the Akademie, and if we can get access to that . . .

At this impasse, it's Burckel who comes good once more, recruiting a hacker from among his associates. He's good and finds us the details we've been looking for – in fact, there's only one there could be, and that's a Gudrun born in 2722. Noting the surname Jensen, we begin to trawl the public records again, until we finally locate her, in a northern suburb of Neu Berlin. An hour away by public transport.

I decide to go in alone. She's home and lets me in, a lot shyer than she was before. And, as before, I find myself staring at her overlarge double skull with what is almost aversion. I'm not sure whether she'll know anything, but she clearly knows who I am, and when I show her the etched portrait of Reichenau she smiles and nods.

'He was the eldest of us. Our mentor.' For the first time I get a glimpse of Reichenau's personal life and how he was raised in the Akademie. Her view of him is, I feel, sugar-coated, only then she surprises me.

'He's a thief,' she says thoughtfully. 'There's absolutely nothing he won't steal. Black holes, identities. Even souls.'

'Is that what the picture album was?' I ask. 'Just something he'd stolen?'

She smiles, her tiny mouth stretching. 'He has it, you know. I've seen it. It's quite some document. Looking through it, I felt I knew everything about you, Otto. Your woman . . . she was very beautiful.'

I go cold at her words. 'Does Kolya have her?'

'Kolya?' And there's a note of query in her voice that makes me feel that she genuinely doesn't know who I'm talking about.

'Kolya was his father,' I explain. 'He gave Reichenau to the Akademie.'

Gudrun looks puzzled. 'He never mentioned it.'

'So where is Reichenau now?'

She shrugs. 'He visits me when he wants to. But not often. I think he likes my company. I'm one of the few who isn't repulsed by the sight of him. I've even let him . . . you know? . . . before now. But I don't think he needs that as much as other men.'

I think of that. Imagine them in bed together and feel sick at the thought. But I also feel somewhat sad at her fate. To be a *doppelgehirn*. It must be dreadful.

'Thanks,' I say, deciding there and then to put a watcher here, just in case Reichenau comes calling. And then I jump. Back to Four-Oh.

Back to exciting news. Reichenau has been spotted, close by the Troitsky Monastery!

'It looks like he's meddling again,' Svetov says, reporting to me. 'But Peter's safe. We've put a crack squad in place to protect him.'

Which is all well and good, only I have a very strong feeling about this. I want to see how things are for myself. And so we jump, back to Russia, and to the Troitsky Monastery, late on the night of the seventeenth of August, 1689.

Seeing it for myself, I reassess what I'd previously been thinking.

The Troitsky Monastery – the Laurel of St Sergius Under the Blessing of the Holy Trinity, as it's more fully known – is Perhaps the holiest of sites in the whole of Russia. More than a monastery, it is effectively a fortress, its thick, fifty-foot-high walls circling the monastery for a full mile, its strongly constructed buildings impregnable, that strength bolstered by the fact that a thousand men of the Sukharev Regiment of the Streltsy arrived here only an hour back, to man its walls and protect the young Tsar.

Even without Reichenau's presence, this is a cusp moment in Russian history, for forty-five miles to the south-west, Peter's elder sister, the Regent Sophia, has just had news of this and is considering what she ought to do.

All summer this confrontation has been brewing, but things are swiftly coming to a head.

Earlier, Peter was woken by one of his servants, to be given the news that the Streltsy were on their way to where he was, in the royal hunting lodge at Preobrazhenskoe, meaning to kill him and put his sister on the throne in his place.

His panicked flight, thirty-five miles on horseback to the monastery, might seem like an over-reaction. Only Peter has good reason to fear the Streltsy – even those who claim to be supporting him. Seven years ago, after his father's death, false rumours of the murder of his young brother, Ivan, brought the Streltsy to the gates of the Kremlin, seeking 'justice' and bloody vengeance.

What followed over the next three days was unlike anything Moscow had witnessed before or since. Three days of rampage and brutal bloodlust, the Streltsy searching for their victims in the corridors and hidey-holes of the royal palace, then hurling them from the balustrade of the Red Stairs onto the spears of their fellows, before finally hacking them to pieces, the good and gentle Matveev among them.

Scenes that Peter, clutching his mother's fearful, trembling hand, was forced to witness. Nightmare moments for a ten-year-old to experience. And now they'd come again.

'So what's he up to?' I ask Svetov, hoping he has some clearer idea than I have as to just how Reichenau means to affect the situation here.

But Svetov makes no more sense of it than I. Only Reichenau is most definitely here – our agents have spotted him on three separate occasions in the last few hours – and why would he be here if all he meant to do was look on?

No. He's up to something. He has to be.

We jump back, then summon Ernst and Zarah and Old Man Schnorr, and Makarov, our expert for this period in Russian history. Gathered about a table in one of the seminar rooms, we throw ideas at each other, but nothing more profound occurs to any of us other than that if Peter dies on this night, then Sophia becomes Tsarina and Russia's history changes dramatically. Under Sophia, and without Peter's obsessive drive to make Russia a sea power, Russia will become a third-rate, landlocked country, picked upon by Poland to the west and the Turks and Tatars to the south. A country with no future. Another Lithuania.

Only, even as we're talking, one of our agents reports back that Reichenau has been seen again, this time with Golitsyn, Sophia's lover and 'Keeper of the Great Seal'. Golitsyn, whose two disastrous campaigns to take the Crimea have led to this tense state of things.

'Why Golitsyn?' Svetov asks. 'In the context of history he's a total nonentity.'

'Like Kravchuk,' I say quietly. 'And yet without him . . . Look,' I say, aware that I'm on the edge of something here. 'Is there something Golitsyn might do that would change things? That might, even, tip the scales in his favour?'

'His two campaigns,' Makarov, our expert, chips in. 'They each failed for the same reason. The adoption by the Tatars of a scorched earth policy.'

'Scorched earth?'

'Yes,' Makarov says. 'The Tatars burned the steppe in front of Golitsyn's Russians. It's said that the whole of the horizon was on fire. And without forage for their horses and cattle, it was impossible to continue. Golitsyn *had* to turn back.'

I look to Ernst, whose eyes have also widened at the mention of those two words.

Scorched earth, eh?

'What if he had moved faster?' I say. 'What if, say, using his cavalry alone, he had swept in before they knew he was coming, then secured the forage for the main body of his army, coming along behind. Could that have worked?'

'It could,' Makarov answers uncertainly.

'Only victory – triumph over the Tatars and their allies, the Turks – would have changed the whole situation back in Moscow. Sophia could justifiably have claimed the throne as Autocrat, with Golitsyn as her consort, ruling alongside her.'

'It's not *entirely* impossible,' Makarov says, 'but unlikely, no? The Cossack forces – their cavalry particularly would have made such a scheme a very dangerous proposition.'

'I agree,' Svetov says. 'I've seen them in battle. They're savages, Otto. Fearless, too. They would have cut Golitsyn's cavalry to pieces!'

'Yes, but . . .'

Only I can see that no one about the table thinks my scheme would work.

'Okay. So why did Reichenau target Golitsyn? Why not Fedor Shaklovity? He seems a far more likely candidate for working with if he wants to get rid of Peter. He's a much more ruthless man.'

'If getting rid of Peter *is* what Reichenau wants . . .'

Only the fact is that we really *don't* know what he's doing or why, and until we do, well . . . all we can do is make sure Peter comes out of this unscathed.

The air blurs suddenly and two men – agents of ours – appear from the air.

'Meister,' they both say, conscious of the slightest echo in their voices.

'You first,' I say, pointing to one of them, seeing the concern in his face.

'Reichenau has made his move. He's infiltrated the monastery. Sent his men in to stir things up. He's got them wearing Streltsy uniforms, but they're carrying lasers. The Sukharev Regiment are terrified. They think a team of shape-changing sorcerers has descended on them!'

'And Peter?'

'We've smuggled him out. But how safe he is . . .'

'And you,' I say, turning in my seat to indicate the other. 'Anything to add?'

He takes a breath. 'Reichenau's men are in Moscow, in the Streltsy Quarter. They've been firing the Streltsy up with stories of Peter's atrocities, claiming that he's taken Sophia captive and that his men have been torturing her. Also that Peter has made a deal with the Poles, and that a Polish army will be in Moscow within the week.'

'And they believe that?'

But I know they will, because the Streltsy are an ignorant and superstitious mob when it comes right down to it.

'So what do we do?' I say, speaking to my fellow *veche* members.

'We hit back,' Svetov says. 'Take back the Troitsky and . . .'

And what? Get into the biggest ever firefight? Is *that* going to help us?

I shake my head. 'You know what? I think this once we do nothing. Let things burn themselves out. Keep Peter safe, sure, but the rest of it . . .'

And as I say it, I know it's the truth. Reichenau *doesn't* have a plan. Wasn't that what Gudrun told us? And Schikaneder, too. But he likes to see us skittering about, wasting our time and energies. Like ants. So let's not give him the satisfaction this time.

After I've given them my decision, we sit there for a time, silent, contemplating what has been happening, and then the first of the two messengers returns.

'They've gone, Meister. Just like that!' And he snaps his fingers. 'The Sukharev are terrified. They're claiming that they faced a regiment of demons. Mind, half of their number simply ran, and they're probably still running, down the long road to Moscow.'

I smile at the thought. But my smile quickly becomes a frown, as the other messenger appears, in a dishevelled state, like he's been in a fist fight.

'Meister, I . . .'

He reaches into his jacket pocket and takes out an envelope, then hands it to me. I hesitate, but Ernst urges me on. 'Go on, Otto. Open it. It'll be from him.'

I meet Ernst's eyes and nod, then tear the letter open.

I read it then hand it across.

Svetov grunts. 'All those deaths. It means absolutely nothing to him, does it? It's all just a game. A simple amusement. Something to fill Time.'

But I find myself asking another question. Has he been making mischief elsewhere? Distracting us with this while . . .

While what? I mean . . . just what *is* the significance of the monastery? Why was it in the photos and the paintings? Or is Reichenau simply giving us false clues to follow?

While he does what?

I feel once more that I'm on the very edge of understanding it . . . but then it's gone, leaving just a tingle at the nerves' ends. There is an answer to all of this . . . somewhere. Some explanation for events.

I take the handwritten letter back from Zarah and read it again. It's short and to the point.

You're learning, Otto, while I remain in two minds.
Your friend. Reichenau.

My friend?

Ridiculous. But it makes me remember the time I've spent with the man. Before I knew what he was. In Neu Berlin in the last days before the bombs fell.

Among the *undrehungar*, and at Werkstatte 9.

My friend. And now my enemy's enemy.

166

I try to hold that thought. That Reichenau, my enemy, is also my enemy Kolya's enemy. And so, by dubious logic, Reichenau considers me his friend.

Or is that, too, just mischief?

Of course it is. But even as I begin to pick at the knot, so I am summoned. Gehlen wants me. No. Put that accurately. Gehlen demands that I come, and at once!

'What does Gehlen want?' I ask. But no one seems to know, and so I ask around, unwilling to go in unprepared, feeling the slightest bit irritated – and surprised – by the *genewart*'s behaviour.

And find that there's been some kind of verbal brawl between Gehlen and his 'guests', the Great Men. According to Newton, their spokesman, Gehlen has been uncooperative. Their feeling is that they're very close to solving the problem of the mobile foci, even, perhaps, of producing a working model, only they're being hampered by Gehlen, who has been holding back vital information.

I tell Newton I'll speak to Gehlen, but our exchange suggests to me what's been happening. Gehlen considers time travel to be *his* child, the equations *his* equations, and he clearly doesn't like the Great Minds tinkering with it. It's all a matter of ego. Of scientific jealousy.

Or so I'd guess. I go see the *genewart*, stepping inside, into that cool blue space, the door hissing shut behind me.

Its voice fills the empty room. 'Otto. You must do something. Those scientists . . .'

'What's the problem?' I say soothingly, hoping that this is something that can be solved with a bit of diplomacy and ego massage. That said, I remember just how spiky he was when he was still fully alive.

'Their arrogance!' Gehlen says, his colourful presence in the blue flaring up, as if he's angry.

'How do you mean? Have they been . . . *disrespectful?*'

To which Gehlen laughs caustically. 'They think they know everything.'

'I see. And you're unhappy with the situation?'

There's a pause, several billion nanoseconds passing as Gehlen considers his response.

'I think we should send them back.'

'Send them back? But *you* asked for them, You said . . .'

'I know what I said. But it hasn't worked. All they do is bicker and squabble.'

I'm not sure that's the truth, not from the reports I've had, but that then asks the question – can an artificial intelligence lie? It seems it can.

'Isn't there some way we can try and make it work?'

'Are you doubting my judgement, Otto?'

'No, I just . . .'

And I shrug, searching for something conciliatory to say, only Gehlen has other gripes as well. The Russians, for one.

'I'm not happy with this, Otto. To have Russians walking about, unchallenged in Four-Oh. That surely must be wrong. For two hundred years—'

'Are you *suspicious* of them?'

But it's something of a rhetorical question, because even as I say it, I realise that he is. Suspicious with an extended lifetime's worth of suspicion. And what's to be done about that, without us giving up what we've been trying to do here – to end the bitter race war and find a better way of governing ourselves? Yes. But will Gehlen accept that?

Come to that, does it *matter* if he's uneasy? After all, who's he to call the shots?

'We must find new ways,' I say, 'new paths—'

But his voice booms over mine. 'I cannot tolerate it, Otto. Neither the Great Men nor the Russians. All this . . . It's just a step too far.'

'It's difficult, I know, changing our ways of thinking and behaving, but . . .'

'But nothing, Otto. They must go. The experiment has failed.'

'Failed?'

Only I know it has hardly begun. That Gehlen is not giving it a chance. And he's wrong, because nothing is achieved overnight. Things take time. And Time is something we have lots of, here at Four-Oh.

'I'll have to discuss this,' I say. 'With the *veche*.'

Only I know what they will say. And so, it seems, does Gehlen.

'You've been running about in circles these past few weeks, Otto. Can't you see that? Can't you *see* what's been happening?'

'That's not fair.'

'No? So what have you achieved? Have you found Katerina and the girls? No. Nor shall you while this situation persists. Their absence makes you weak, Otto. Vulnerable. And they know that.'

They?

Gehlen specifies. 'The Russians.'

I swallow bitterly, realising we have come to an impasse.

'The *veche*,' it says. 'that's just a way of controlling you. You are the Meister, no? Then act like the Meister. Throw off the *veche* and act!'

That silences me. Because something of what he says is true. The *veche* is like a halter, controlling me, keeping me chomping at the bit. Even so . . .

'I'll talk to them, and come back to you.'

I wait, expecting an answer, but nothing comes. And I realise after a moment that Gehlen is no longer talking to me. That he's gone incommunicado.

'Hans . . .?' I ask, addressing him by his familiar name. 'Are you there?'

He doesn't seem to be. Or is he just being moody?

'Hans . . .?'

With a suddenness that shocks me, the room dims, all background noise ceasing as the whole of Four-Oh goes on to emergency lighting.

'Oh fuck . . .' I say, turning and, going across to the hatch, which, thank Urd, still functions, slip out into the corridor, heading back to the platform.

383

'What's happening?' I ask, as I step out by the platform.

'You tell me,' Ernst answers from where he stands with Zarah, staring down at the main control screen. 'What in Urd's name did you say to him?'

'I said nothing. I . . .' I let out a shivering breath. 'I didn't think he could do this. Can we still use the platform?'

Zarah nods, but she looks gravely concerned. 'It's on reduced power, but it's still operational. I've never seen the like. We've known all along that the AI controls Four-Oh, but I guess we've always believed that *we* controlled the AI. As for Gehlen . . . well, he's certainly never used it this way before now. It's like he's flexing his muscles. Threatening us.'

'How serious is this?'

'Serious enough. I can try over-riding the system, but it's not even as if we've got any wires we can pull out. All we have is the gaseous core, controlling it all. And besides, who knows what effect it would have on our agents out in Time?'

'Okay. Then we stall. See what Gehlen comes back with. Zarah, you take charge here. Ernst and I will go to Moscow Central and consult. But if anything happens, let us know.'

And with that we clamber up onto the platform and, hoping Gehlen won't spread our atoms over some distant star system, jump . . . to Moscow Central, where Svetov and Saratov are waiting.

384

Seated with them in one of the anterooms, I get straight to the point.

'The trouble is, he doesn't trust you.'

'Doesn't . . .' Svetov laughs. 'That dead thing doesn't trust *us*?'

'Not entirely dead.'

Saratov raises a hand to interrupt. 'Okay. Okay. But the question is how do we deal with the situation? We've no problem here at Moscow Central, but can we survive without Four-Oh?'

'Theoretically,' I say, not liking the drift of this. 'But you're talking about action way down the line. No. What we need to find out is *why* Gehlen's suddenly so touchy. What's happened to make him start behaving this way? For over two hundred years he's been fine – doing our bidding, you might call it. That's why this is so strange. It's not even as if Gehlen was giving out any warning signals. One moment he was fine, the next . . .'

Svetov looks down and shakes his head slowly. 'I've a very bad feeling about this. You remember what you told me that time, about Gehlen's "history", and particularly about how – while he was still a living, breathing man – he was taken by Reichenau and held captive by him for an indeterminate time. Time enough, possibly, to implant some kind of controlling programme into his mind?'

'And then wait to use it for two hundred years? Is that even vaguely likely?'

'Maybe it's Reichenau's ultimate fall-back,' Saratov says. 'His last throw of the dice, if you like.'

'I don't know,' I say, doubting very much that Reichenau could be as patient as that. 'But it might explain how Reichenau – and Kolya, too – know so much about our movements. I mean . . . has Gehlen been feeding information to our enemies somehow?'

'I can't see that,' Svetov says. 'We'd have noticed that, surely? Or you at Four-Oh would have, should I say.'

'If I'm honest, I can't see it, either,' I say. 'I think Zarah and the women would have noticed even the slightest "leak" or signal out.'

'Maybe so,' Saratov says. 'But I'd say it's worth checking up on. Jump back, Otto, and get Zarah to question the women as to any anomalies in the feed. Anything that didn't quite make sense at the time.'

'And in the meantime?'

'In the meantime we channel as much as we can through Moscow Central . . . away from Gehlen and any influence he has on things.'

'Okay.' And it's agreed, there and then. And I jump . . .

385

. . . into a state of utter chaos.

The situation at Four-Oh has deteriorated in the short time I've been gone. The lighting is almost spectral now, while the air itself is thin and stale. Eighty per cent of our functional capacity has been shut down, deliberately, it seems, a bit at a time, and it's only because we have the most rudimentary of backup systems – put in as an afterthought – that we can function at all.

More worrying than that, the platform's range has been seriously reduced, resulting in many of our agents being trapped out there, in danger, unable to jump home to Four-Oh. But Zarah, bless her, has everything in hand in that regard. She's been getting their locations and time coordinates and sending them, by messenger, to Moscow Central for Svetov to act upon.

But in those few minutes, as Zarah briefs me, I have an idea. Gehlen doesn't like his 'guests', eh? Then let's see if those guests he's so keen to get rid of can resolve the problem of Gehlen and the controlling AI.

Only when I go to visit them, in their special quarters, it's to find that Gehlen has incarcerated them in one of the conference rooms and refuses to release them.

Things are slipping away from us, moment by moment. And if something isn't done . . .

I stop dead, knowing what I have to do. Enough's enough. We can't have Gehlen lecturing us and threatening us in this fashion. What he's doing is a hostile act, and in doing so he has become our enemy. And there is only one way to deal with your enemies. To confront them. And destroy them if you must.

Only the hatchway is locked, and there's no other way of getting to the AI.

Which is where Zarah and Urte come into things, for between them they manage to over-ride the *genewart* for just long enough for me to open the hatchway and slip inside.

It slams shut behind me.

I walk across, facing the glowing presence in the wall, realising as I do that Gehlen is slowly chilling the air, thinning it at the same time, making it hard for me to breathe, let alone talk. Only he can't shut me up entirely.

'You have to stop this, Hans. We are your friends. And you . . . you swore to protect us . . .'

My head hurts and my throat is burning now, but I keep on talking.

'It's Reichenau, isn't it? He's corrupted you. Fed you false data. Lied to you. He's our enemy, Hans. He's always been our enemy. Ours and yours. I . . .'

I have to stop. My head is swimming now, my vision distorting.

'Reichenau was my friend,' Gehlen says, finally. 'He—'

'Reichenau was *never* your friend. He—'

I fall to my knees, knowing suddenly that I will die, here in this room, on a fool's mission to persuade an insane operating system to act more humanely.

My voice is hoarse now. *'Hans . . . please . . .'*

And slump, my forehead pressed against the ice-cold wall.

Is he watching? He must be, for while he does not restore things to their normal state, he responds to my suffering, making the air less chill, less thin. Enough to let me speak.

'You mustn't do this, Hans. You kept us safe. For two centuries and more you kept us safe. You let the volk *live. You can't turn against them, now. You can't.'*

'You *betrayed* me, Otto.'

The words chill me as much as the air. It seems so final.

'It wasn't me,' I answer, my voice almost a whisper. *'It was Reichenau. He's been dripping poison into your ear for years now. Feeding you lies.'*

I am at the edge now. Barely conscious. A minute more and I'll be dead.

'Disconnect,' I say, as my eyes close, perhaps for the last time. *'Order the AI to shut down. Now, Hans . . . before it's all destroyed.'*

It has been like talking an errant child down off a ledge. Only I have no more to give. I am exhausted, close to death. As I take a breath so the air seems to rattle in my throat.

Goodbye . . .

And even as I give my last farewell, so I sense, rather than see, the presence that is Gehlen brighten intensely against the blue, like it's giving off a sequence of coded instructions, then fade to nothing.

Gone. Only the blueness remaining.

Ten seconds pass. Fifteen. And then, at twenty it all comes on again, in a great wash of colour and sound that floods Four-Oh.

Only I too am gone.

386

How many times can you die and be reborn?

I picture myself, dead on that cart in Krasnogorsk, Katerina's corpse laid beside my own, the two of us dead for all time, and wonder if that must be, if all of this misguided struggle against fate is really worth the effort.

Zarah and Urte saved me. Jumped in and brought me out between them, placing my corpse-cold form into a resurrector and throwing the switch, hoping against hope that I'd revive.

Dead, I was. Dead for the best part of three minutes. And then back. Back like I'd jumped from somewhere deep inside myself. Somewhere deep and usually impenetrable.

Except for the dead. And the resurrected.

Only I am ill, badly ill, the gaseous presence of the *genewart* having leaked into the room and poisoned me.

For a time I linger, halfway between life and death, in a state of constant hallucination.

My dreams are strange and wild, yet amid them are small nuggets of truth. In one of them, a blinded Reichenau stumbles about in a huge and empty room, searching for something, while Kolya crawls around the walls, a cruel smile on his lips. In another a white horse and her five white foals flee from a dark stallion that has Kolya's madly staring eyes. Kolya again is in the third, his mouth hinged back as he floats in space, swallowing whole planets.

And when, finally, I come around, it is to find myself strangely at peace with myself, finding, for the first time since Kolya dumped me in that alternate timeline, that I have clarity of thought.

Reichenau, I know, is 'blind' now, his source in Four-Oh shut down. And maybe that's true for Kolya as well.

I decide it is time to go on the offensive. To go out and finish Reichenau off. Only where should I look? 2343? 1952?

No. I must trust once more to instinct.

To Baturin . . .

387

And arrive there on the evening of the second of November, 1708. Menshikov's troops are to the north of the ancient Cossack capital as I walk its crowded streets again, heading for the quayside inn, The Goat of Marmaris.

Nearer the inn, I move back into the shadows of a doorway, watching as I leave the woman's room. Then, when my earlier self has gone, I slip inside.

'What, back again?' she asks. 'Changed your mind, mister married man?'

I draw my needle-gun and aim it at her, and watch her eyes open with understanding. She stands and begins to dress.

'So you know.'

'Yes,' I say.

'If I wanted to I could jump. You couldn't fire that thing fast enough.'

'Perhaps. But I want answers. Like who you are working for.'

'You know who I'm working for. Or will be working for, that is.'

That puzzles me. 'What do you mean?'

'That I'm not even born yet, where you come from. I'm one of the Angels.'

'Angels?'

She smiles. 'You'll understand it soon, Otto. Once you've been through the loop. Once you've seen and done it all.'

I watch her pull her top on then tie the silken sash. 'One thing . . .'

'Go on?'

'If you're not working for Reichenau, then why is he here in Baturin?'

She comes closer. 'You guessed it correctly when you were last here. He's recruiting the dead. Whole armies of the dead. Or people who *would* have been, if he'd not removed them from time. It's a trick he learned from his father. But whatever Kolya does, Michael does bigger. It's how he is. Like Loki. He likes to meddle. To set brother against brother and bring down the gods.'

'How do you know so much about him?'

'Because I was his lover . . . for a time.'

'Did he know . . .?'

'That I was an agent? No. Because you didn't ever reveal it to Gehlen.'

That surprises me. 'You know about that?'

She smiles, then reaches for a brush to do her lustrous black hair.

'Of course I know. I've read the histories. I know what happens. And now you get one wish, Otto. One . . . *request*. I already know what it is, but you still have to say it.'

I hesitate, then ask. 'Where is he? Reichenau? Where will I find him?'

'Think snail and shell,' she says. 'Think of two huge soap-bubbles joined by a single surface, surrounded by nothing. Think of a man, his ear to the floorboards, listening to his neighbour down below.'

I mean to ask what she means, to clarify, but in that instant she is gone. I sniff in her perfume, then jump back to Four-Oh.

388

Over the next few days I have all but a skeleton staff moved out of Four-Oh and into Moscow Central. It's there, in front of every-one, that I explain just where Reichenau is, 'riding on the back of Four-Oh', tapped in directly to its power source, the black hole.

My plan is simple and direct. We close down Four-Oh com-pletely and move our operations wholesale to Moscow Central, which will effectively become Four-Oh.

Leaving Reichenau without a power source to run his platforms.

And Kolya too?

The answer is . . . I don't know.

As for the move, that proves more difficult than I imagined, mainly because a huge number of new quarters have to be created within Moscow Central, and while there's no problem as far as creating new 'no space' rooms to replace those lost from Four-Oh, this settling in of the two ancient enemies at close quarters – almost literally shoulder to shoulder – is bound to cause us more than a few problems.

With everything ferried across, the hour finally comes for us to switch things off, and as I pull the switch, so some of the older and more prominent agents – those who have known no other home – raise their glasses to 'Time Passed', caught up in the emotion of the moment. There are hugs and tears, but Svetov, representing our allies, raises his glass, sounding a new tone of determination.

'Brothers . . . sisters . . . it's time to go hunting!'

389

The trouble is, where?

With all of Time and Space to comb, it's like looking for a needle in a haystack. Then again, Reichenau and Kolya are only mortal and, with no power source, they're more vulnerable than they've ever been. Clever as each is, they have to rely on others to do their bidding, and it is through these associates that I mean to track them down.

Not to mention Katerina and my girls.

I decide to look at every place we know Reichenau has been, and then – one after another – to hit the historical 'cusp-points', such as major battles, as well as times and places that we know he might be tempted to tinker.

I call an emergency meeting of all of our leading agents, where a list of targets is drawn up, fascinated to see just how similar a view of history the Russians have to us. Indeed, there's such an understanding between the two sides it's difficult to believe that we were ever enemies. Yet we are conscious that there are still rebels, out there in Time – and not just Russians.

Which is when Svetov gives me the news.

A handful of German agents have vanished. Gone, possibly dead. There's certainly no signal coming back from them. But

I think it's far more likely that they have joined up with Reichenau, convinced by his honeyed words to keep the great war going.

We decide to sweep Time, looking for signs, focusing first on all those places where our agents have gone missing. And while we wait for answers, I sit with Svetov in Hecht's room and talk, sharing our experiences – the places we've been, the things we've done – and wonder why we haven't done this before.

'Rumour is you killed him,' Svetov says.

'Who do you mean?'

'Kravchuk.'

'Ah . . .' and I look away, remembering what he did to my darling girl. The way the light had winked on the blade of his knife before he pulled it across her throat.

'Yes, and I'd do it again, a thousand times.'

'I never met the man, but . . . was he really so odious?'

'Not one redeeming quality.'

'I can't imagine it,' Svetov says. 'To have my fate in another's hands.'

'And not just any "other". You can't imagine how it felt. As if Time itself were against our happiness.'

'Do you think Hecht knew what you were going through?'

'Not in the least. But the women did. And understood. You might say that it was the first act in their little revolution.'

Svetov falls silent a moment, then looks at me again, a deep sorrow in his dark brown eyes.

'And now?'

'Now? I'd say it's the only thing that keeps me going – knowing that the loop will bring me back to them eventually. And before you ask, I *have* to believe that. If I didn't . . .'

'It must be difficult.'

'It's more than that.' Only I don't say what it is.

'We're all behind you,' Svetov says, squeezing my arm. 'You know that, Otto.'

I almost smile. Only I feel too great a weight on me. To think they're out there somewhere, alone and suffering, maybe dead. The mere thought of it is awful. If I start imagining it, I'll fall apart.

I jump up and cross the room, then take a book down from the shelves.

'Look,' I say, opening it to the title page and handing it to him. 'Have you ever seen this sign before?'

He studies it then looks to me again. 'Aside from it being the very shape of the foci Reichenau uses?' He shrugs. 'It's the symbol for infinity, isn't it?'

'It is. But it's more than that. As a mathematical symbol it goes back to 1655, when the mathematician John Wallis first used it. Some say it's based on the Roman numeral for a thousand – indicating many, or a lot. Others say it's based on omega, the last letter of the Greek alphabet, but in modern times it has come to mean other things, like the worm Ouroboros, always swallowing its own tail, or, in its most physical form, the Möbius strip.'

'And you, Otto . . . what does it represent to you?'

'Time itself . . .'

Svetov considers that, then nods. 'Time itself, huh?'

'In all its forms. We talk of loops, right? Well, this is the form I think of when I think of loops. Not a simple circle but this, this lazy eight, with its suggested movement – out and back. And I'm not sure why, but it's almost like it's been imprinted on my brain.'

'I see.' Svetov sniffs in deeply, like he's been wondering whether he ought to tell me something.

'Go on . . .'

He smiles, then is serious again. 'It's just . . . towards the end, in those last few months . . . while Master Yastryeb was still with us . . . Well, he seemed to have changed. Nothing I could fully identify, only . . . he *was* different. There was a secret meeting that he went to. He wouldn't say where he went, or who he met, but I think he went to see Hecht. What was said or argued between them, no one knows. Yastryeb wrote nothing down, nor spoke to anyone about it. Yet I think some agreement was made between the two men. I think . . .'

'Yes?'

'I think that's when they realised that it wasn't just Us and Them and *Rassenkampf*, but something much more complex. I'm not even sure they knew quite what it was. Only that someone else was muddying the waters of the timestream.'

'And you think their deaths were somehow "triggered" by them knowing?'

'It's possible, no?'

'Possible, yes, but then . . . why wouldn't they have said something? And why didn't they look into it?'

'I don't know. Maybe they'd begun to do that . . . before they died.'

'I would have known.'

'You think? Just as Hecht knew about you and Katerina?'

There's a knock. 'Meister?'

'Come in!'

It's young Tomas, fresh from the platform. 'Forgive me for interrupting you, Meister, but you did ask us to keep you informed.'

'And?'

'All six teams are back, and not one of them have made any sightings. Not the smallest trace. It's like they've vanished completely.'

I'm surprised. I expected *something*. But what if their vanishing act has to do with Four-Oh coming offline? And what if – dare I even think it – we may have actually *erased* our enemies from Time?

I voice this, even though it's not a thought I want to entertain. Since abandoning Four-Oh, I have been growing more and more worried about Katerina and the girls. It's been so long now that I am beginning to give up hope. No matter what I've said to Svetov about the loop, I am close to losing myself to despair. Would Kolya have kept them unharmed for this long? I almost don't dare to think about it. At the same time, I cannot help myself.

The truth is it would be better if I knew that they were dead, for then my rage – my vengeful anger – might fill Time itself.

Only Tomas proves to be wrong. Even as I make to dismiss him, so another of the Russian agents, Alina Tupayeva, reports to me with news.

'We've taken two of them,' she says. 'Kabanov and Postovsky. The two agents that Seydlitz and Kramer thought they'd killed back in the thirteenth century.'

'While I was in Christburg with the Brothers?'

'The same.'

'And you say captured?' Svetov asks. 'All in one piece and breathing?'

'With all working parts . . . except for their time pendants. Those we took.'

'Time pendants?'

'Reichenau . . .' Svetov says quietly. 'They've been working for Reichenau all along.'

'Yes, but now we have them,' I say, getting up. 'So let's ask a few questions.'

'Meister . . .' Tupaveya says, bowing her head, her dark hair swaying. 'We had to leave them in situ. Without the time pendants we couldn't get them back here. And we couldn't leave them on them, so . . . they're still there. My team are keeping a watch on them and awaiting orders.'

'I see. And where's there?'

'Nomonhan, Meister, in June 1939. They were advising the Japanese army.'

Which interests me a lot, because Nomonhan is another of those historical cusps. Had the Japanese succeeded with their massed assault on the Soviet Union, the war could very easily have ended differently, with the Russians defeated in a long war on two fronts.

Just the kind of thing Reichenau would get involved in.

'Okay,' I say, looking to Svetov. 'Let's go there now. Before he can vanish them away!'

390

Little men. That's what they turn out to be. Worker bees in the great Time War, lacking even a single thing of interest to tell us about their Master.

We drug them, question them again, but there's nothing new. Reichenau never confided in these men, and that tells us something about him. Something we didn't know before that moment.

He's a trickster, yes, but also a cautious man as far as whom he chooses to trust.

Oh, and when I say we learn nothing, that's not entirely true. We know now where this pair have been in Time – and when – and, knowing that, we can draw up a chart of their movements and, from that, get some idea of the pattern of Reichenau's meddling.

If pattern there is.

I leave Tupayeva in charge and jump out of there, Svetov hot on my toes.

'What now?' the big Russian asks.

I look to him, then climb down from the platform. 'I don't know about you, Arkadi, but I need some sleep.'

Indeed, I'm feeling quite exhausted. Let the *veche* deal with things for a time. Only I need something to keep those dreams I've been having at bay.

Urte gives me something which, she says, will knock me out cold, but before I've had the chance to take it, more news comes in from Nomonhan.

A third agent has been taken, this time one of Reichenau's lieutenants, in overall charge of their operations on the Russian–Japanese border. Svetov says he'll deal with it, but I'm curious to find out just what this new agent knows that Kabanov and Postovsky don't. It's likely that he'd have much greater contact with Reichenau, and at least some small inkling of what his overall scheme is. So Svetov and I go back together, to find that the agent they've taken is an old colleague of Svetov's.

'Nikita!' Svetov exclaims, as we meet the man. 'What is this?'

Only the man won't meet his old friend's eyes. Nor answer his question, it seems. He sits there at the desk, his hands and feet chained together, and says nothing.

Oh, he knows we'll get the truth from him, but he's not going to betray his Master easily.

Svetov turns to me. 'This is Nikita Kaminski, Otto. I've worked with him back in the time of Catherine the Great, and in the Mechanist Age. He was a good man. Reliable. *This* . . .'

And he throws his hands up expressively, as if to say he can't understand what his old friend is doing here, working for our enemy.

'Did he have one of the pendants?' I ask, and Tupayeva, who's standing at the back of the tent, confirms that he did, and that they've taken it from him, as from the other two.

I look to her. 'Have you begun the interrogation?'

'No, Meister. I thought you'd want to do that. I thought this one might just know something about your girls. And maybe . . .'

I turn to Kaminski, who still won't look at us. 'Well, Nikita? *Do* you know anything?'

His shoulders seem to set more stubbornly. He'll talk – even he knows that – but not until he's forced to.

'Okay,' I say, tired of all of this, not in the least hopeful that he will have information about Katerina. 'Get Diedrich here. Let's see what this one knows.'

While we wait, I sit, facing Kaminski, looking directly into his face. He's a tall, rather emaciated man with the look of a peasant about him, but right now he's trying to seem remote from things, defiant. Only I'll break him if I have to. Make him babble like a baby.

Svetov stands behind me, putting his hand on my shoulders. 'What do you think we should do with him, when we've finished with him, Meister?'

'I'd feed him to the wolves,' Tupayeva says from the shadows.

'That would be a blessing,' Diedrich says, appearing suddenly in the air to one side of the desk. He puts his case down on the desk and, getting straight to work, sorts through endless ampoules until he finds what he's been looking for. 'I'd keep him alive,' Diedrich says, never for a moment looking at Kaminski. 'Keep him in torment every waking second.'

'He can do it,' I say, speaking to Kaminski. 'He can make your life hell, Nikita. I only have to authorise it.'

'And he would,' Svetov says. 'If it meant you were hiding Katerina from him.'

If I expected him to react to that, I was wrong, and – even before we begin the interrogation – I know that there's one thing that he doesn't know, and that's where Katerina is.

And maybe none of Reichenau's men – no, nor Reichenau himself – know where she and my other darlings are. Maybe only Kolya knows that. If Kolya's still operating in Time after we'd shut down Four-Oh.

I raise a hand. 'Okay. Let's stop it there.'

Diedrich looks to me, puzzled. 'Meister?'

'Let's put him in a cage. Guard him day and night, and see who his Master sends to rescue him. That's if he does.'

'But Meister . . .'

I turn back to our prisoner. 'Nikita. Why didn't you jump out of there when you knew your fellow agents had been taken? Why didn't you go and report the fact to your Master, Reichenau? And why were my people able to take you so easily?'

Stubborn, he says nothing, but I can see – can read in his body language – that I've struck close to the gold. I lean closer, a sudden certainty in my voice.

'We've shut you down, haven't we? When we closed down Four-Oh, we cut you off from him, didn't we? Trapped you where you were, in the timelines.'

He wants to say no. To tell me where to stick my theory. Only I'm right. Kaminski, and all the rest of the rebels who form Reichenau's rag-bag army, are trapped in the worlds they're operating in. If we can find out where they are then we can take them, team by team. Maybe even Reichenau himself.

'Svetov . . .'

'Yes, Meister?'

'Get this one back to Moscow Central, then question him thoroughly. Tell him if he gives me what I want then we'll be easy on him. If not . . .'

I can see just how much that irritates Kaminski, talking about him as if he's not there in the room with me, but I know what I'm doing.

'I'll leave it to you.'

And I jump.

Back to Moscow Central . . . to find that it's partly true. News has come. Our shutting down of Four-Oh *has* brought Reichenau's activities to a grinding halt. Or so it seems from the handful of rebels we've captured.

And among those captives is one I've met before. One I should, I guess, have known would be working for Reichenau in the field. Heinrich.

Yes, Heinrich, Reichenau's right-hand man from the twenty-eighth century.

Telling Svetov to put the others in the cells, I decide to question Heinrich alone.

391

'Do you know me?'

Heinrich looks up, meeting my eyes. It's a lazy gesture, as if he need not bother to answer, only he does. 'I know you, Otto Behr.'

It's unexpected, but I continue.

'You have two choices,' I say. 'You can talk freely or we can drug you and torture you. I don't mind which, to be honest.'

He looks down at his shackled hands, then back at me. 'What do you want?'

'Everything you know.'

'About what?'

'About your Master. About Reichenau.'

'You want a lot.'

'Yes, and I've all the time in the world to listen.'

He considers that, then nods. 'So what specifically?'

'About the kidnappings . . .'

I'm watching him very closely as I ask, hoping for some small reaction, something I can latch on to. Only his puzzlement is genuine and I feel a stomach-wrenching sense of hopelessness wash through me.

I would have sworn that he would know.

'Your Master had no involvement, is that what you're saying? That he didn't *help* Kolya in any way?'

'Help him? No. My Master would have nothing to do with him.'

'You're sure about that?'

'Absolutely. He hates him. You can't imagine just how much he hates him.'

As Kolya hates me, I think. But this is interesting. 'Hates?'

'For what Kolya did to him, partly. For making him share a body with a total stranger. But there was an element of envy in there, too.'

'And Kolya? Did he hate him back?'

Heinrich laughs. 'Kolya? No, but that's it, you see. That's what Reichenau hated the most. His father's complete indifference to him. That's what irks him most . . . that he doesn't care.'

I sit back, shocked by the revelation. If it's true, that is. Only why shouldn't it be? It would explain a lot, after all.

I change tack.

'Is it true, then, that Kolya is defending certain parts of Time against Reichenau's attempts to change them? Segments of Time where he's got a . . . let's call it a personal investment.'

'Where his "brothers" are, you mean?'

He nods. 'You can't imagine how many times he's tried to penetrate Kolya's defences. And do you know how many times he's managed to succeed? Not once. Not a single fucking time.'

'Then you don't know where he is?'

'Oh, we know where he is, all right. It's getting there that's difficult. Go in and he changes it. Instantly.'

I pause, my heart thudding in my chest. 'Do you have the time coordinates?'

'You want them?'

I nod, chilled suddenly. For this is the closest we have come. But Heinrich isn't finished.

'I can give you them. All of them we know, that is. Only it won't help you. Not unless he *wants* you to meet him.'

And maybe I should leave it at that. Only I have one last question.

'Does Kolya have his own power source?'

Heinrich sits back, relaxed now. 'As for power sources, I don't properly know, though I'd guess that he does. He certainly has his own platform. We tried to infiltrate it, you know, like we did Four-Oh, only he knew what we were up to. It's his paranoia, so Reichenau says. It makes him wise to such tricks.'

392

'Well?'

There are four of us sat in the lecture theatre, having watched the recording of my interview with Heinrich – Ernst, Master Schnorr, Zarah and, of course, myself – and we all have differing opinions on how much we should trust what Heinrich's said.

Ernst is cynical. 'It's a tissue of misinformation,' he says, 'designed to lead us astray while Reichenau slips away, his schemes intact. No, Otto . . . Heinrich was Reichenau's man without a doubt – obedient to the letter – and why should that have changed? Why should he be giving away his Master's secrets so cheaply?'

'Because the situation has changed and our friend Heinrich's a pragmatist?' Zarah answers him, keen to get on with things and end the debate.

'Master Schnorr?' I ask. 'What do you think?'

Old Schnorr pulls at his beard, considering matters, then shakes his head. 'I don't know. I simply don't know. Reichenau hating Kolya . . . well, that makes a lot of sense . . . Only . . . well, Ernst has a point. It all felt too easy. Heinrich answered everything like he'd been rehearsed. And we all know how much Reichenau likes to play games and set traps and create mazes. So . . .'

'So he was lying,' Ernst chips in, and I have to admit, watching it a second – and third – time it seemed more and more artificial. Like he was playing a role. Reichenau's man to the last. Only . . .

'I think there's an element of truth in there,' I say. 'That bit about Reichenau hating Kolya. I can imagine that. And it fits with other information we've received. Which is why I think we should use the information Master Schnorr has obtained about Kolya and go after him. Forget Reichenau a moment. Let's go for the greater threat.'

Ernst starts forward, as if he's about to challenge me, then stops, lowering his eyes.

'You have something you want to say, Ernst?'

Only Ernst knows what's going through my head. He knows, from long experience, from being close to me all these years, that going after Kolya is only an excuse. What I really want is...

But then you know that.

Zarah looks to me, her eyes sympathetic. 'Otto's right. Reichenau can wait. We've disempowered him. Locked him up and thrown away the key. So what better time to go after Kolya?'

There's a moment's silence, then Old Schnorr speaks up. 'What Heinrich said, about how difficult it is to get to Kolya. Do you think that's true?'

'I don't know. All we have is Heinrich's word.'

'The word of a liar.'

'True, but . . .' I hesitate, then lay out my plan. 'As I said, we use the information Master Schnorr has compiled on Kolya and make a series of concerted attacks on Kolya's ancestors throughout Time. We keep hitting them and hitting them, slowly wearing them down, using up Kolya's forces until he's forced to confront us directly.'

'And then?' Ernst asks.

I smile. 'And then we crush him like a bug.'

Only even as I say it, even as I smile, imagining killing the bastard, the shadow of their absence falls over me once more.

But what if he kills them, Otto? What if he waits until the last and then kills them anyway?

But no one asks that question. No one but the dark voice in my head.

393

Svetov, when he hears there's to be an operation, smiles broadly, showing his strong white teeth. 'Okay! Let's get the bastard!' Only it's not the bastard he really wants to go after. For some reason – and it seems fairly general – the majority of our people would rather be finishing off Reichenau than going after Kolya. Maybe it's just that awful, fear-inspiring double head of his, but . . .

As far as our people are concerned, Reichenau is Number One on the wanted list, with Kolya a distant, unthreatening Two. They don't like him, sure – after all, didn't Kolya steal Katerina and the girls? – but there's no heat in their dislike, no passion. Their hatred is almost entirely impersonal.

Maybe that's because – quite literally – Kolya keeps himself to himself. He doesn't *meddle*, after all, and when it comes right down to it, it's hard to hate what you never confront.

Put simply: Kolya provokes a cold, abstract revulsion; Reichenau a dark, emotional hatred.

Only I've seen behind Kolya's eyes. Seen the bitterness and paranoia there, the intense and spiteful hatred that's like molten magma welling up in him. Oh, he seems rational enough, only he's not. No, he's far more dangerous than Reichenau. Far more deadly. Why, if what Heinrich says is true, and Reichenau can't touch him, then maybe we would do well not to take him on.

Only I must.

Ernst comes to me late in the evening and says what he couldn't say earlier, in the presence of Zarah and Old Schnorr, his voice gentle but firm.

'I know how much it must hurt, Otto, but you can't use your girls as an excuse to formulate policy,' he says. 'You did that once before and look where it got us!'

'It got me Katerina.'

'And lost her. Not to speak of the girls. Besides . . . were we to throw every last man – and woman – against Kolya, my guess is that he'd simply slip aside, outflank us and maybe attack the platform itself. And then where would we be?'

I look down, trying to control my feelings. Ernst should not have come. He might be right, but what does that mean, faced, as I am, by such potential loss? No, I'm right, as I was right at the very beginning, to let my heart guide me in these matters.

I mean, isn't that why Time is shaped the way it now is? Because of she and I? Because we risked everything for love?

Well, then . . . enough of caution. Enough of waiting for someone to give me the yes to go ahead.

Enough . . .

'Otto, I—'

'No,' I say, ocean depths of feeling shaping the word. 'Go away now, Ernst and leave me be. It's my choice now, not yours.'

'But Otto, I—'

'*Go*,' I say. And, faced with the finality of the word, he goes.

394

And returns, a mere two hours later, bringing bad news.

There has been a brawl in one of the bars of Moscow Central, between German and Russian agents, and while no one has been badly hurt, feelings are running high. Idleness, it seems, is as great a threat to us as any of our enemies.

The news depresses me, and, alone in Yastryeb's rooms, I feel at my lowest ebb. More than that, I find I have changed my mind again about what to do.

I pace the room anxiously. Ernst is right. We can't just throw all of our forces against Kolya. To do so would be to forget everything we've ever learned from the Game. Oh, it might be that the Game will one day fade from collective memory and be forgotten, but while we still have enemies to fight . . .

Until then we must use what we know. It isn't just a case of attacking our enemies where they're weak, but anticipating where *they* might attack *us*.

I stop, facing Master Yastryeb's shelves, then gasp, astonished, for there, directly in front of me, is the photo album, the one I first glimpsed in Reichenau's room in Werkstatte 9.

I take it down, surprised to find it here in this room. How in Urd's name did it get here? Who brought it? Did one of the agents find it and bring it back for Yastryeb?

I sit down and, my hands trembling, open it.

And catch my breath, for there, in that first photograph, is Katerina, beside me, outside our house – *our dacha* – there in Cherdiechnost. She is dressed in a long white cotton dress, her hand in mine, one of our baby daughters – Martha – just behind us, to our right.

And then there's me.

Gods, I look so Russian in that shot, dressed in my white full-length linen *Tolstovka* shirt, my features hidden behind a full growth of beard, my skin burned dark by the sun.

I sigh, moved deeply by the sight. I have no memory of that day. For all I know that day is yet to come, and that thought ought to bring me joy, only . . .

Only I can't believe it. If the loop is broken, will all of this be gone?

I turn the page.

And there we are again, inside this time, hand in hand as ever, our fingers interlocked, Razumovsky – my darling's father – sat in a chair, tankard in hand, beer froth on his beard, laughing, drunk no doubt, as we lean towards him, glasses raised, celebrating.

Celebrating what? A good harvest? A birthday? A new child?

Again, this is yet to come. Is in some other life. A life I've yet to live. Only is that really so?

Seeing these images ought to bring me comfort. Ought to make me feel that Fate is on my side. On *my* team. Only there's Kolya, and we have died once already at his hands. So who's to say?

Unravel one tiny part of it and what follows? Will it all come undone? Will these images fade on the page? Will they simply vanish, along with us? Or are they locked in tight?

I close the book.

This scares me. Is this some game of his to destabilise me? To kick my legs away from under me and make me fall? Are these images *designed* to trouble me? Because there are more questions than answers here. I mean, why not be more direct? Why *this*?

Yes, and who took these? Who, out of all of those we knew, could have got this close to us, this intimate, yet not been seen? Not anyone from the thirteenth century, that's for certain. The technology alone says no. So who?

My mind casts about for answers, only there are none.

Mischief . . . it's all mischief.

Which, on the surface of it, seems like one of Reichenau's japes. The man loves to be cruel, and what better way of being so than to show us what he plans to take away? Our lives, our love, and all that we hold dear.

I summon Svetov and ask him if any among the Russians know how the album got there. If one of them found it maybe and brought it back to Yastryeb. He takes it from me a moment, flicking through, amazed by it as much as I, then hands it back.

'I'll see what I can find out.'

He leaves, and is back in moments. 'Nothing,' he says. 'No one's got a clue how it got there. Yastryeb himself must have found it.'

I thank him and, once he's gone, settle with the book, working through the photos methodically. There are a quite a few I can put a place and time to, especially those set in Cherdiechnost, of which there are many, but there are half a dozen or more that I can't place. And as for the final picture, that is strange indeed, for it shows Katerina in militaristic garb, standing before an ancient *schloss*, a massive needle-gun clutched to her chest.

I don't recognise the background, but then that is what my experts are good at – Russian and German – and, making a copy of the picture, I get them to work on locating just where and when it was taken.

And in the meantime I decide to go in after Kolya.

395

Saratov comes to see me at my summons. He listens while I spell out what I want, then beams a smile back at me. 'I've just the team.'

And within half an hour they're there, stood in Yastryeb's old rooms, attendant to my every word.

Five young Russians, all of them women, all of them totally unknown to me before that moment. But Saratov promises that they're the best. And so he introduces them – Izolda, who is lean and tall with ash-blonde hair; Darya, who is small and dark with arms like a wrestler; Klara, who blushes when I give her my hand; Anzhelika, who could quite easily be Izolda's sister; and Sofia, clearly the eldest of them and the leader, for it's she the others look to. All five wear furs and carry heavy weaponry. They're not, any of them, the world's most beautiful women. No, they're peasant stock to the bone, and, like their menfolk, they seem unfazed by whatever lies ahead. *Volunteers*, Saratov confides, speaking quietly to my ear. Volunteers and utterly reliable.

'Where have you been serving?' I ask, looking to Sofia.

'Here and there,' she says vaguely, her face set like stone. 'Why? Where do you plan to go?'

I like that. Like her defiant spirit. 'Mantua,' I answer.

'Why Mantua? And when?'

'Why? Because *he's* there. Or was. As to when . . . sometime in the early fifteenth century. You know the place?'

I see how they look to each other, then all shake their heads. A team. Clearly a long-established team.

'Don't worry,' I quickly say. 'We're going to go in beforehand. Get acclimatised. But discreetly. We don't want to tip him off.'

'And then?'

'And then we kill him. If we can.'

'Him?'

'Kolya.' And I hand her the drawing I've made of the man and see how they pass it, one to another, then look to me again.

'What did he do?' Klara asks.

'The bastard killed me. Me and Katerina.'

396

Mantua, before the great war that destroyed it all, was a small north Italian town, east of Milan and west of Venice, and, at the time we're talking of, it was ruled by a single family, the Gonzagas. In 1459, Pope Pius the Second convened the Council of Mantua where he proclaimed a new crusade against the Turks. It's at this time that Kolya was there – or rather, one of his 'brothers'. From what we know, he's there as part of the Pope's entourage, but with Kolya the detail is always vague. Look too closely and the man tends to vanish, along with anyone related to him.

We jump in, one after another, after dark, meeting up to the south of the town, on the far side of the three lakes that form Mantua's defences. Built in the twelfth century, they're Mantua's special feature, but they're not going to stop us. We wait there while Darya inflates the raft, looking across at the town, which, reflected in the water, is more beautiful than ever. We're dressed for the age, in woollen knee-length tunics. The women, having had their hair cut short, ape the look of men, of common peasants from this age. It's a style that has changed little since the late Roman era and it's easy to blend into the background, but we're taking no chances.

The raft inflated, we climb in and paddle slowly, silently across the Lago di Mezzo, disembarking on the far shore, beneath the high wall.

'Okay,' I say quietly. 'You all know what to do, yes?'

There are nods. We've rehearsed this several times in the past two weeks, but this is the first live run; the first time we've been *here*, in Mantua itself.

'Okay,' I say again. 'Then let's have a look about. If you're challenged, come away at once, and if you really, really have to, jump out of there. Otherwise, the point is to acclimatise. To get us used to Mantua. And to try and find out where that bastard's holed up. Because next time we're here . . .'

Only I don't have to say. They know. Next time out it'll be kill or be killed.

As it is, they're carrying weapons. Just in case. Crossbows and swords and daggers. Things that don't make a noise. That won't start alarm bells sounding in Kolya's camp – wherever that might be.

I watch them turn away and vanish, blending into the night. It's dark – moonless – but that doesn't matter. We're all wearing adaptable night-sight lenses.

I stand there a moment longer, wondering where the bastard is, what he's doing at that moment, and whether *they* are here with him. Prisoners. Chained to some dank wall in a lightless dungeon.

Just the thought of it's too much. For a moment I stand there, swaying. Then, knowing what I must do, I move on, heading after them, down through the narrow backstreets of this ancient, medieval town, looking for the man who holds my future happiness in his hands, knowing that if we meet it will be he or I.

397

I stand, in the entrance to the great square, looking across at the Palazzo Ducale. Even this late there are still stalls out and people, drinking and talking and laughing. I look across and see Sofia and

Izolda on the far side of that great, cobbled space, watching as they slip inside the palace building, Sofia taking one last glance around before she's gone.

Klara and Anzhelika are over to my left, in the far corner. Like the others, their shadowed forms are marked with a glowing circle that only we can see. A precaution, just so that we don't shoot our own.

And Darya is . . .

I look about me, trying to locate her. Only there's no sign. Has she been delayed somehow? Has some over-zealous guard stopped her?

Only there's no way I can communicate with her. For these live runs we're 'radio silent', and have to be. What's more likely to tip Kolya off, after all, than to have the medieval airwaves filled with communications chatter?

I head towards where she is supposed to be, hurrying now, then slow as she emerges from one of the side-alleys, two men – locals, presumably – following her a step or two, gesturing threateningly, then falling back as they see me approach.

'*You okay?*' I ask in a whisper.

'Nothing I can't handle.'

We hurry on, counting the entrances to our left before ducking quickly inside, into the musty, lamp-lit corridors of the Gonzagas' palace.

There are guards everywhere, but this late they're inattentive, or simply dozing. Mantua is sleepy, its guardians – at least on this lowest level – less than watchful. Even so, we need to take care.

Upstairs, behind locked doors, is the Gonzaga family's wealth. Paintings mainly, but gold, too, and jewels. But we're not interested in any of that. We're looking for the Pope's guest suite.

We have ten minutes to locate it, and then we're out of here, hopefully unseen.

We stop at a kind of crossroads, one broad corridor leading away, another leading on. There are voices up ahead and drunken, raucous laughter. I send Darya on, then follow at a small distance, knife drawn, but the revellers, sat about a table in the room to our left, pay no attention.

'Mantuans,' Darya says, when I've caught up with her again.

I nod and hurry on, hearing her steady breathing behind me, then slow. There are guards, at the next turn of the corridor. Two men in papal silks.

I look to Darya and nod. This is one way in. Only as we turn to leave, one of the men steps forward and calls out to us.

'You . . . What are you doing here?'

I step forward, my body folded into a cringing bow, answering him in the local dialect of Italian I have practised. 'Master, forgive me, but we were sent for.'

'Sent for?'

My eyes study the man. There's no trace of Kolya in this one. No resemblance whatsoever.

'We were told there was an accident. Some plates . . .'

'Come here,' he says. 'Beneath the lamp where I can see you properly.'

I do as I'm told, my right hand on the hilt of my knife as the guard thrusts his face into my own. 'Peasants,' he says, turning away and waving us through dismissively.

We bow once more, then hurry on. There are stairs, at the top of which are more guards, and this time . . .

There's a bright flash, and the smell of burning ozone fills the air. Darya cries out and stumbles forward, then vanishes.

I turn, seeing the figure on the turn of the stairs, behind the carved marble of the balustrade. A tall, gaunt figure, his left hand raised, holding a needle-gun.

Fuck!

The two guards on my level are shrieking now, terrified, certain that they're witnessing some major sorcery, but I'm not waiting for the bastard to fire again. I'm out of there . . .

And back in an instant, wearing a laser-shield, a heavy duty laser aimed at where Kolya's 'brother' was only a moment before. Only he's gone.

Klara jumps in, then Sofia, and suddenly there are a group of agents up above us on the turn of the stairs, firing down at us, even as we fill the air with burning threads.

Fuck!

There's an awful smell of burning flesh, and shrieks and—

'Out of here!' I yell. And just like that we're back, in Moscow Central.

Or four of us are.

I look to Saratov. *Dead*, he mouths. And even as he says it, so I see our agents jumping back, to bring the bodies home.

Darya, I realise. And who else? Klara is here and Sofia and . . .
Anzhelika . . .

I groan, seeing the sorrow in those young women's eyes. It was just a dry-run. Things weren't supposed to kick off in that fashion. And how did that fucker know? Because he was on to us immediately, like we'd tripped some kind of alarm.

How does the bastard do it? How is it that he's always a step ahead?

We send a team back to Mantua the day before the firefight and find it changed, the Pope and his entourage nowhere to be seen. Kolya and his brothers gone.

And it's not just Mantua. Wherever there's been a trace of Kolya – wherever he's set up his defenders to protect the genetic line – there's now no sign of him. As if he's been erased from history. Only I'm pretty sure that isn't so.

Master Schnorr reports to me, only hours later, to tell me that gaps have begun to appear in his record of Kolya's ancestry. Kolya, it seems, is moving his ancestors about, resettling them in new towns, making it harder to trace them and track them down.

Or at least, that's what Old Schnorr *thinks* he's doing.

For myself I think that maybe our tactics are beginning to work. With our recently combined forces of Russians and Germans I know we have a numerical superiority over Kolya, and that it's only a question of time until we make that count. Only before I can go back in and make a new attempt to cut his ancestral lines, I get news from Svetov, about the photograph. The one of Katerina.

They've traced the location and narrowed down the time to within fifteen years. The place? Wewelsburg, in old Westphalia. The time? Sometime in late 1942.

'You want to go in?' Svetov asks.

Do I want to go in? I almost laugh, only my mouth is dry and my hands are trembling now.

'Why so vague?' I ask.

'About the time?' Svetov shrugs. 'Because it's her. Katerina. We felt, well, that you'd want to take the last few steps.'

I nod. It's sensitive on their part. 'Organise it,' I say, and Svetov nods, then leaves the room.

398

Waiting for my agents to come back with the precise timing of the photograph seems the longest time of my life.

Why?

I reason it thus. If I can only get to her I can find out where Kolya took her and then go back and rescue her. That is, unless the picture itself is faked. But then, why should it be? And if it is real, then I really do have a chance of finding and saving her.

As I look back through the pages of the album, I realise that the pictures have been changing in subtle ways. Or is that my imagination? For a while I think that must be so, only then I see it. I actually see one of the images change, right before my eyes – not by much, admittedly, but enough to let me know I'd not imagined it.

And then, finally, they come – to advise me that they have made a sighting of a woman approximating to Katerina's description.

'They couldn't get close enough, but . . .'

I go in. To Wewelsburg in April 1942, and find myself on a wooded hillside, watching as an assault is launched on the ancient *schloss* by a group of men and women dressed in black. Slipping among them, I finally confront her.

Katerina. My love.

She takes me aside, unsurprised to find me there, then tells me what I need to know.

'Only you must be careful,' she says. 'Take one wrong step and it will all collapse. Act rashly and the loop will fold in upon itself.'

'How do you know that?' I ask, and she tells me to ask young Moseley.

'Moseley knows,' she says. 'He's worked it all out. Or will do. They even have a diagram. But there are two paths and you must choose wisely. One leads here. The other . . .'

And she smiles her beautiful smile and holds me briefly, letting me kiss her, the simple warmth of her – her scent – enough to drive me mad.

'Now go,' she says, her fingers lingering on my arm. 'Find me. Save me. But be very careful. It's all very fragile from this point on. Make no assumptions, Otto. It can jump either way. That's the beauty of it. And the danger. But be of brave heart, my love, and I'll see you here again. When it all comes round.'

And she turns and is gone.

399

I jump back, then summon Moseley, who *does* explain it all. Time, it seems, operates much as the rest of the universe, only 'with negative values'. Even so, it is ruled – like the smallest particles of the physical universe – by the uncertainty principle.

'The loop you're in, Otto, might indeed – as Katerina warned – collapse in upon itself, and everything dissolve like smoke. It is up to you now, by your actions, to make that loop real.'

'Have you seen this?' I ask, handing him the album. 'It's changing all the while.'

'Changing?' Only as he opens it, his eyes widen with delight. 'Changing . . . ah . . .'

'You'll look at it, yes? See what sense you can make of it?'

'I'll try my best . . .'

400

And then it comes. A note, sent through time, from Katerina, telling me where she and my daughters are being held.

It is in *her* writing, *her* hand, elseways I'd not believe it. And so the four of us – Ernst, Svetov, Urte and myself – jump back to see what we can find.

It is late evening when we go in. The place? The Teutoburg Forest in northern Germany. The time? The late summer of AD 9. It is the day before the great battle in the forest between the

German tribal leader Arminius and Publius Quinctilius Varus' three great Roman legions – a battle which the Germans won, utterly destroying the pride of Rome's army and ending the Emperor Augustus' expansion into the northern wilderness.

I do not know why Kolya could possibly be here, for unlike Reichenau, he seems indifferent to history, focused as he is on his own personal timeline. But this is where Katerina told me to be.

We scout around, noting all manner of anomalies with the history that we're familiar with. The Roman forces, for a start, are far larger than they were, with whole phalanxes of auxiliaries that weren't there originally. Some, I note, are Cossacks, 'survivors' of the burning of Baturin, I would guess. And that, more than anything, convinces me that this isn't Kolya's work at all. This has Reichenau's thumbprint all over it. And then, as if to confirm that, we spot the unmistakable figure of the man himself, there in Publius Quinctilius Varus' tent.

Svetov wants to go in at once and take Reichenau out, only I stop him. Finding Katerina and my girls is my number one priority, killing Reichenau a distant second. Besides, Reichenau isn't going anywhere without a power source for his focus.

Leaving Svetov to keep an eye on Reichenau, Ernst and I begin a search of the encampment, jumping in and out of time to keep from being seen.

I am beginning to despair of ever finding anything, when Urte joins me to tell me that they have located Katerina. Urte takes my hand and jumps, to where she is, there among the slaves in the Romans' baggage train.

Seeing me there, my darling's face crumbles and she begins to sob. As I take her in my arms I close my eyes, for this moment is too wonderful to be real. To find her finally, even in this fashion, unwashed and chained to a wagon, twelve centuries before her time, is a kind of ecstasy. Yet it also breaks my heart. What suffering she must have undergone. What torment.

And yet she's here, unharmed – or so it seems.

'Otto . . .'

I hold her to me fiercely, kissing her brow. 'I'm here, my love.'

Only the news she gives me breaks my heart again, for they have been taken from her. Our girls. Taken by Reichenau and secreted away, somewhere in time.

I stand back, letting Urte cut the chains from her, then hold her again while she sobs, letting her grieve. But what I feel now is a cold anger. That and a need to kill the bastard.

'And Kolya?' I ask quietly.

Katerina looks at me, meeting my eyes, her own eyes red, her face blotched, her hair like a rat's nest. But still beautiful. Still my darling girl.

'Reichenau stole us from him. He—'

Only she cannot say any more. It is just too painful. I squeeze her gently, kissing her cheek, aware more moment by moment of the smell of her. It must be weeks since she last washed and the humiliation of that is clearly getting to her.

I call Urte to me. 'Heat up some water. Or steal some, if not. She can't . . .'

But Urte's hand on my arm stops me. 'We'll see to her, Otto. Make sure she's fine.'

I smile my gratitude, then turn back to Katerina.

'We'll find them,' I say. 'I promise you we will.'

But there's a more pressing matter. We can't let the Romans take her back again, so I organise for a team of agents to come and guard where we are, dressed in the cloaks of the praetorian guard. They are there in an instant, forming an armed circle about us fifty metres across.

Urte brings water and scented soap and shampoo for Katerina's hair, and while she washes away the grime, I gently ask her what transpired, knowing how much it hurts her to repeat this tale.

'Where he took us I can't say. A wilderness, it seemed. There we were guarded by what he called "his brothers". I don't know how long we stayed there. Weeks. At first we were treated all right. Only then he began to take them from me. Natalya first, then Irina and Anna. Losing Martha was the worst, for I was not given the chance to say goodbye. I woke one morning to find her gone, leaving only baby Zarah.'

She takes a long, shivering breath, then starts again, a faint tremor to her voice.

'They let me keep Zarah . . . for a while, I think as a way of making me behave. But when Kolya started moving me through time, Zarah was taken from me – she was quite literally torn from me. I fought to keep her. But it was no good. He's much too strong . . . emotionally.'

I go to speak, but she gently puts a finger to my lips.

'And that was it. The last I saw of them. Maybe . . . a year, eighteen months ago? Since then . . .'

Only she doesn't say what. Saying as much as she has has drained her emotionally. She turns to me, then pulls the smock up over her head.

'Wash me, Otto. Make me clean again.'

401

Back in Moscow Central, I sit at her bedside as she sleeps, my hand in hers, listening to the soft sound of her breathing, watching those lovely breasts of hers rise and fall beneath the cloth, drinking in the sight of her.

Now that she's been returned to me, I feel even more acutely just how much I'm missing them. My *kinder*, my darling daughters. If I had *known* what had happened to them . . .

If I had known – if I had seen it with these eyes – I would have moved heaven and earth, and all alternative earths, to get them back. Or tried. Only it's not that simple. Hecht would not have allowed it for a start.

Does Kolya still have them? Or are they dead?

Maybe. Only I'm not to think of it.

Back in the Teutoberg Forest, Ernst is trying to find out where Reichenau has gone, and what he's doing right now. Still meddling, no doubt, but even he must know he can't go on like this. No, thinking about it I realise that he needs to make some bold move if he's to survive. To grab what isn't his and change the game. To give him back the edge he had.

For a trapped man is a dangerous man. And Reichenau, without his platform, is trapped.

Urte joins me, taking a seat across from me. She's quiet for a while, then—

'I didn't understand at first . . .'

'No?'

'Not until I saw you with her. She . . . means the world to you, doesn't she?'

'It didn't make sense. Not until I met her. It was Us and Them. *Rassenkampf.* Aryan versus Slav. And then, suddenly, it was just Us. Me and . . . well, and her.' I'm quiet for a second or two, staring down at her, then meet Urte's eyes again. 'Hecht didn't understand, but you did. The women. Without you . . .'

'We had no choice,' she says, speaking over me. 'We . . . talked about it. Out of Hecht's hearing, naturally. Zarah and the rest of us. For you to lose her . . . we couldn't let that happen. You forced our hand, Otto. It was betray Hecht or let what you had die. And we couldn't let that happen. Only then . . . well, you lost her. And there was nothing we could do. Kolya . . . he's not on any of our charts. He exists, yes, but isolated from it all. Or so it seems. Even when he went to see Schikaneder . . . well, it just didn't register. He knows how, you see. We talked about that too. What, in all likelihood, it meant.'

'And?'

Urte shrugs. 'And we're still guessing. All we know is that he has his own power source. The rest of it . . . well, it's like he's some kind of magician. His ability to predict our moves. That simply isn't normal. I mean . . . he shouldn't be able.'

'No.'

And yet he does.

We sit there in silence for a time, lost in our thoughts. And then Katerina wakes.

'Better?' I ask, squeezing her hand.

She squeezes back, and smiles. The prettiest smile I've ever seen.

'Urte's here.'

She half turns, then nods. 'Otto, I . . .'

I see the inner struggle in her face. Her emotions are stretched taut and thin, like wires about to snap. To have got me back but still to have them missing . . .

'We're going after him,' I say.

'Him?'

'Reichenau. And when I have him I'm going to squeeze it out of him.'

'About Kolya?'

'Yes. He has to know something.'

Only she doesn't seem to believe that. She squeezes my hand again. 'You should be careful, Otto. You know what he's capable of.'

I do. But I don't wish to dwell on that right now. The best strategy right now is to take one step at a time. Reichenau first. Just in case he knows where my darlings are being kept.

'Otto?'

'Yes?'

'Can I come with you?'

'*With* me?' Only I can't tease her. Not so soon after I've got her back. And so I hand her the copper ash-leaf pendant that Hecht left for me. The same that I had made for her on our long journey upriver. Half a lifetime ago, it seems.

'Come,' I say. 'Let's get some clothes on you, then we'll join Ernst. He's been keeping an eye on Reichenau while you slept.'

'You know where he is, then?'

'We do.'

'Then bring me some clothes. It's time we gave that bastard a taste of his own medicine.'

402

My darling girl is a great deal harder than she was when last I saw her. There is an edge to her now that wasn't there. That same hardness only mothers know, especially those who have been deprived of their children.

Not that she wasn't always a fighter. But now, as I say, there's an edge. Place Kolya before her now and she wouldn't hesitate to slit his throat for what he's done. After torturing him first, of course. For to find them is the only thing that matters. Which is why she goes back. To get strong again. And to be trained up. That done, she joins me again and, taking the big laser gun Urte offers her, climbs up onto the platform.

'Ready?' she asks, looking back at us, like some warrior queen.

'Ready,' I answer her, jumping up onto the platform beside her, then turning to give Urte a hand up.

And we jump, back to the Teutoburg Forest, where Ernst and Svetov are waiting, both of them carrying big laser rifles – the kind that can pick off a target at fifty yards. The same make as the one Katerina carries.

'Any sign?' I ask, looking about me, aware that where we are is deep inside the Roman camp, our presence hidden by a clump of pines.

'He's in there, somewhere,' Ernst says, gesturing towards the camp.

'So why are we all the way over here?'

'Because this is where he came. An hour or so back. We followed him . . . and then suddenly he wasn't there, like he'd jumped. We looked around, but nothing. And then, suddenly, he was back. Like he'd stepped out of thin air.'

'But I thought . . .'

I pause. Maybe we've misread the situation. Maybe he *has* got access to a platform. One of Kolya's even.

Only I don't get a chance to rehearse any arguments, for right then trumpets begin to sound all around the Roman camp as preparations begin for the great battle that will decide the Germans' fate.

'Can we get closer?' I ask, and Ernst organises us into a huddle . . . and then jumps.

We emerge in a clearing not two hundred yards from Varus' tent.

'There,' Svetov says, handing me his field glasses. 'There's the big-headed bastard.'

And so it is. Along with Publius Quinctilius Varus and a dozen or so Roman commanders. Only we're far too vulnerable where we are. Oh, we could jump up close and kill him, only how would that help us find where our children are? No. We must take him cleanly. Pluck his pendant from him and get him somewhere safe. Somewhere his agents couldn't get him back from. Somewhere bleak and dark that stinks of hopelessness.

Which is all he deserves.

'What now?' Ernst asks.

'Follow him,' I say. 'Stick as close as you can without being seen.'

The trumpets sound again. There's the sound of horses neighing nervously, of swords being drawn from sheaths, to be stropped one last time. Yes, and of great phalanxes drawing up. Thousands of men who are fated by history to die. The battle will commence two hours from now, in the pouring rain, the terrain having forced the Romans to stretch their forces across almost ten miles. It will be then, when they're at their most vulnerable, that the Germans will attack them, several miles from here and, if history rings true, will slaughter them to the last man.

Only I don't think that that's what Reichenau has in his doubled mind this time around. He means the Romans to win.

And what if they do?

Then there'll be no German nation, nor, it seems from Svetov's comments, no Russian nation either, for according to our projections, the Romans will go on to conquer not only the whole of northern Europe but the Ukraine as well. Germany and Rus will never exist. Which is why, I guess, the Russians have never attempted to meddle with this portion of time.

'Okay,' I say, realising that something must be done to prevent that, 'Ernst, stay where you are. The rest of you follow me.'

And so we jump out of there. Only not to anywhere in the forest. No. I take my team back to Moscow Central, where, recruiting Zarah and young Saratov, I have all of us dressed up in the costumes of the time, only with brilliant golden capes, trimmed with emeralds. Then, getting the heaviest modern armaments we can find, we all jump back, only this time into the middle of Arminius' camp.

Our appearance out of the air causes great consternation and fear. Even so, the brave Arminius steps out from the press of savage warriors by his tent, sword in hand, to confront us.

'Who are you?' he demands, and I answer him.

'We are the gods of the forest!' And to make my point I fire off my weapon, making a great pine tree leap into the air in flames. 'We have come to fight alongside you,' I say, meeting Arminius' eyes.

Arminius stares at me in wonder for a moment, then bows low, grinning broadly. His warriors, surrounding him, do the same.

'Then you are most welcome!'

403

This tale begins long before today, and I know some of it.

As a youth, Armin – Hermann, to us, son of Segimer, chief of the Cherusci – was taken captive by the Romans and brought up in Rome as a hostage, along with his brother Flavus. Given the very best military education, Arminius rose to the status of Equestrian, a petty noble and servant of the empire. It was in this role, serving beneath Publius Quinctilius Varus, a minor member of the royal family, that the twenty-five-year-old took his revenge on his father's enemies.

Two years before this day, the Balkan territories had risen against the empire. Thirteen legions – a full half of the empire's military strength – were sent in to put the rebellion down. Which they did, only Rome, for the first time in many years, was vulnerable, and when news came of rebellion among the German tribes,

Varus was given the job of putting that rebellion down. However, owing to the troubles in the Balkans, he was given only three legions to accomplish this.

Unknown to Varus, rumours of a German rebellion were false; were, in fact, the product of Arminius' fertile imagination. There was indeed unrest among the German tribes, but no actual rebellion. This, it appears, was Arminius' scheme. As trusted advisor to Varus he would lead the Roman army into unfamiliar territory and, deep in the Teutoburg Forest, fall on it and destroy it. It was a scheme he had worked on for years, secretly making peace between the German tribes, unifying them, and now – today – it would come to pass.

And his opponent, Publius Quinctilius Varus? Varus was a cruel, unforgiving man, a hated man, known principally for his use of crucifixion to punish his enemies. But he was also a vain man who, in this instance, took the wrong advice.

And so twenty thousand men – the pride of Rome – were marching into a trap, unaware of what they were about to face.

Or so it was, until two days ago.

I jumped back. Located where Reichenau made his entrance on this scene, and then watched. Saw how Varus greeted the abomination. How they roughed the *doppelgehirn* up, and just how close Reichenau came to being nailed up on a cross. Yes, and then saw how Varus' disgust changed to sudden astonishment as Reichenau's 'legions' – Cossacks and Russians, Turks and Vikings, and many others from the rag-bag of time – appeared among the trees surrounding the great man's camp. A force equal to Varus' own, there to aid him against the rebellious German tribes.

Which was when he learned of his trusted advisor's plan to lead them all to the slaughter. Learned and, sending in scouts to verify the facts, confirmed Arminius' treachery.

As for Arminius, he fled, before Varus could lay hands on him, knowing that he faced not twenty but forty thousand, all surprise lost.

And so it hangs. Ahead lies Kalkriese Hill, the historical site of the battle, here in Osnabruck county in what will one day be Lower Saxony. Here to witness . . . what? Another great Roman victory? Or can the Germans, having lost the element of surprise, having lost numerical superiority, still carry the day?

We are there to help them. Only will six of us – even with our high-tech weaponry – be enough?

I'm guessing that we shall. But we're in totally uncharted territory here. What if Reichenau's forces are enough to swing the balance? What then? Should we jump back again – and again and once more again – to change things in our favour? Or is that part of Reichenau's scheme – to draw more and yet more of us into this one desperate fight and, by that means, cripple us?

The truth is, this once I do not know.

I jump back. Ernst, Urte, Katerina, Zarah and Svetov are waiting for me.

'Well?' Ernst asks. 'Is it enough?'

The rain has begun to fall. The same rain that did such damage to the Romans when they first fought this battle.

'I think so,' I say. Only I'm not one hundred per cent sure. Should I get reinforcements? Should I throw a force of our agents in on the Germans' side, just to be sure? Or is that what Reichenau is counting on? For surely he must know we are here. Surely – having planned this much – he looked and *saw* us here.

Only again I don't know.

And – the thought strikes me suddenly – what if this isn't Reichenau's scheme after all? What if another's hand lies behind all this?

After all, for Katerina to be here . . . that remains unexplained.

'Okay,' I say, as the rain gets heavier. 'Let's get into position.'

404

What if? I think. *What if?*

But it's too late to change things. We are committed now.

I stand among the German warriors, watching the thick press of armoured legions come on along the muddy swamp that lies below us, their chest armour seeming to form an impenetrable wall of polished metal. Only, unlike before, this time we cannot get to them, for flanking that flooded path, on the banks of it, defending them against our tribesmen, are Reichenau's forces, jeering and laughing, happy, it seems, to be risking their lives.

The rain is coming down in torrents now, and in the historical version of this battle, the Roman archers were unable to use their bows, the legionnaires' shields heavy, soaked by the rainfall. Only Reichenau has done something about that, issuing them with waterproof versions of their weaponry.

Yes, and not only that. Some of his men have guns. Needle-guns, and lasers, stun grenades and rocket-launchers and . . .

I realise I have underestimated Reichenau, for he has thought to play the same trick as us and bring in weapons from the future.

We are not only outnumbered, we are out-gunned.

So what if we *do* go back and bring in reinforcements? Armed with the latest weaponry. I've come this far, after all. Surely I have to take the next step?

The two armies clash, with a noise like a train wreck, and as they do, so the air is filled with the stench of ozone and burning flesh. There are screams and explosions and gunfire and . . . well, all hell breaks loose, and mainly against our forces.

Historically, the Roman army was stretched thin, surrounded, forced by press of arms and the incessant rain to follow a single course – one that led to their own destruction.

Only history has been rewritten. Ten minutes of this and we'll have lost.

I look across the line to Ernst and Svetov and make a hand gesture that they know means to jump. But jump where? '*Moscow Central*' I mouth exaggeratedly, turning to my left to repeat the gesture and the mouthing to our women – Katerina and Zarah and Urte – and in an instant we're out of there, the six of us steaming, standing there in the silence of the platform.

'We're losing,' Ernst says, saying it for us all. 'We've got to go back to before the battle began and go in early with some heavy-duty weapons. What we've got—'

Zarah, I note, is bleeding. 'Are you okay?' I ask, concerned.

She nods. But I can see she isn't good.

'Go and get that fixed,' I say, then, looking about me, I shake my head.

'That's it,' I say, understanding coming to me. 'We've been thinking much too small. We've been approaching this in completely the wrong way.'

405

The Germans are losing. They're stumbling back before the joint onslaught of the Roman infantry and the Cossack cavalry. Some of them even turn and run. And then . . .

It flashes overhead, huge and black, like some enormous flying creature, and as it does, so it lays a carpet of burning, golden light among the Roman ranks that roils up twenty, thirty feet into the air, burning everything it touches.

I am there as it banks over the main Roman force and drops what seem like eggs – huge black eggs with the shape of giant grains of rice – among their ranks.

Trees splinter and the earth heaves and lifts into the air, once, and then again and again, the sound of it hurting our ears.

They are fleeing now, Russians and Romans, Cossacks and Vikings, our own men – defeated only a moment before – turning back to pursue the escaping armies, blades and axes flashing in the sudden sunlight, cutting down any they can catch, a sudden glee replacing the abject fear of moments earlier.

Yes. I have cheated. Gone back in time and set up a factory and an airfield in this age, using endless quantities of our DNA – tanks of the stuff – to build these craft and bring them through, piece by piece, assembling them here in this godforsaken, godless time.

Showing off, I guess you'd call it. Or overkill. Only anything Reichenau can do, I can do ten times better.

Talking of whom . . .

The Germans find him hiding beneath a pile of bodies in a ditch, well away from the incinerated part of the battlefield. They think he's a demon of some kind and want to boil him alive, but Arminius persuades them otherwise, knowing that we want him for our own purposes.

Which is good, only . . . one moment he is there, the next . . . *gone*! As if he'd stepped through an invisible door. Or so the two guards claim.

It's the kind of thing that could easily make you paranoid. Make you mistrust your fellow men, only their utter bemusement – their conviction that some form of witchcraft must have happened – convinces me they haven't been bought by our friend.

'Where?' I ask them. 'Show me precisely *where* he vanished.'

And, hesitantly, each in turn enacts the route Reichenau took, mimicking his steps.

'Was there anything . . . *unusual* about the way he vanished. Did he . . .?'

I don't know quite what I was going to ask, but it clearly rings a bell in the mind of one of the guards.

'That was it . . .' the man says. 'He seemed to reach out with his right hand, and then . . . well, he gave what was like a little skip and . . . *jumped*.'

'Ahh . . .'

I have them mark the place with stones and set one of my own agents to guard it, then turn to where Svetov and Ernst are waiting for me.

'Well?' Svetov asks. 'What now?'

'We trace him back,' I say, knowing in my head what's to be done. 'Go to the last time we saw him, in Varus' tent, and trace where he subsequently went. Ernst, you tracked him for a while . . .'

We go there. Watch him in Varus' tent, then see him leave there, hurrying away, as if there's something urgent to be done.

'Not a happy man,' Svetov observes. And that's true. Through the field glasses, I can see that something's troubling our friend. And I wonder for a moment if he knows what lies up ahead in time? Only if he does, then he must still be able to travel *through* time. Which might explain how he vanished just now.

Only something doesn't seem quite right.

We jump to the far side of the encampment, once more among the trees, in time to see him emerge from among the rows of tents and make a beeline for what seems like a stone outcrop, not two hundred metres from where we're crouching, watching him with our field glasses.

'There he is,' Svetov says, and even as the words are out of his mouth, Reichenau vanishes again.

'Where the fuck . . .?'

We make our way carefully across to where we last glimpsed him and search around, only he's not there. There's no sign of any doors or plates or . . .

From the camp beyond us the trumpets sound.

'Come,' I say, knowing that there's only one thing remaining to be done. 'Let's go back.'

Back to where the guards had him and lost him. Back to where he jumped into the air, through the invisible door we've marked with stones. Because that's where the bastard is. Right there, and nowhere else.

406

'What if he's waiting for you, Otto? What if he's standing there, needle-gun in hand, waiting for you to step through?'

I shrug. Either I go through or I don't. And if I don't?

It's the same dilemma that I had with Kolya, when he took my girls. Take his hand and step through, or . . .

Or lose all chance to get them back.

'What worries me . . .' I begin. 'What really troubles me, is that maybe Reichenau is up to his old tricks. Stealing things again. That this portal isn't his at all, but Kolya's. And if it's Kolya's . . .'

'*Otto!*'

I look up the slope to where Zarah is standing amid a copse of trees. 'What?'

'It's Arminius,' she answers, in fluent Russian, trying to keep her voice as low as possible yet audible. 'He and all his chieftains. Coming to thank you, no doubt.'

Yes, and to seek explanations for all the wizardry.

We stand there, waiting, as Arminius appears over the crest, striding slowly through the tall grass, his cloak flowing out behind him, a dozen warrior chieftains following him closely, a mixture of awe and fear in their eyes. The first Germans, and almost, today, the last.

From their hesitancy, I can tell that they're deeply disturbed by all of this, Arminius particularly, and while he feigns confidence, he's really not too sure. What if we were to turn our weapons on his people?

Oh, he's incredibly uncomfortable about what we did, and I wish it were all a lot simpler, but I'm afraid he's going to have to live with that, because I'm not going to make the first attempt to explain who we are or what we're doing. He's a good man, but such knowledge might really fuck him up. I know too much about the man's future, and if he knows that we can travel in time he might want to know how and when he died, and then I'd have to tell him how he'll be assassinated by these self-same chieftains twelve years from now on the orders of the Emperor Tiberius.

And then what would transpire? A bloodbath, probably.

Only that's not going to happen. No. What Arminius plans is something far simpler, far more in keeping with the traditions of his people. We are to be thrown a feast. Even now his men are building a feasting hall, their craftsmen cutting down trees and constructing the frame of the great hall while their fellow warriors are out there on the battlefield, retrieving the bodies of their fallen comrades and slitting the throats of the injured Romans and their allies.

You might think this all an unnecessary diversion from our main task – which is to find and capture Reichenau – but then we have all the time in the world to do that. All we have to do is jump back to the moment before Reichenau jumped through, and enter the portal that he used to get there before him – waiting on the other side to watch him come through and see where he went.

Until then, our time's our own.

'Forgive me, Great Lord,' Arminius says, 'but who is he? That monster . . .' And he makes a gesture, tracing the bulky shape of the doubled-skull.

'An enemy,' I say. 'Why, what did he call himself?'

'Before he betrayed me to Varus? Before I had to flee for my life?' The young warrior king shudders with indignation. 'He claimed he was the bastard son of the gods. He said . . .'

'Go on . . .' I coax him. 'What did he say?'

'He claimed he had seen the end of it all. Ragnarok. The Twilight of the Gods. He said he'd been there, watching, when it happened.'

'And what did Varus make of that?'

'I don't think he believed any of it. All Varus wanted was his troops. Bloodthirsty bastards that they were. If you had not intervened . . .'

I play that down, but sense that Arminius wants answers, if only to placate his tribal chiefs. Not that he's going to force us to speak of it – we *are* gods, after all – yet he burns to know what has really been going on.

'That craft . . .' he says, looking at me as if to gauge how far he might push things. 'What in the gods' names *was* that?'

Yes, and where did it come from? That's what you want to ask.

Only I'm not going to tell him. Let them believe that this was a battle between the gods. Let this remain one of those stories that their great-great-grandchildren will tell. Now is not the time to tell the truth. No. We've meddled with things far too much already.

'Later,' I say, and watch him bow his head obediently. And realise, as I do, that I've overlooked something – that we need to gather up all of the future weaponry that might remain on the battlefield, if only to prevent future archaeologists from unearthing such anachronisms. Not to speak of what might happen if they fell into the wrong hands here.

'Ernst,' I say, turning to him, then, in Russian, *'Get a team in here, right now. As many as can be spared. I want every last piece of weaponry that shouldn't be here found and removed. We may have to body search some of the German warriors, in case they've tried to smuggle them out, but . . .'*

'We'll get a team working on it,' Ernst answers, pre-empting me.

'And Ernst . . . Have them dressed in black. As nondescript as we can make it.'

And he turns and leaves, heading towards a clump of the forest that wasn't affected by the fire-bombing – so that he can jump out of here without any witnesses – emerging only seconds later, facing us this time, returning at the head of a host of black figures, who spread out and, in silence, begin their work, combing the corpse-piled battlefield.

I turn back, facing Arminius. 'Come,' I say, beckoning him to follow me, away from the part-blackened scene of carnage. He follows, his chieftains falling in behind him, hands on their sword hilts, fearing that at any moment I will turn into a demon.

407

As darkness falls, we go inside, into the freshly constructed hall, our hosts greeting us, bowing low as we step through, into the torch-lit interior.

Looking about me, I see that Arminius' craftsmen have done an excellent job, and as we climb up onto the high table, so I deign to give my host a gracious smile.

But Arminius' eyes are focused elsewhere, looking past me at my darling Katerina, whom Ernst escorts. And who can blame the man? For in the intervening hours, she has changed her golden cloak for a dress of the purest blue, and had her hair combed out and . . .

As I turn, she smiles at me. An angel's smile. She looks stunning. More beautiful, perhaps, than I have ever seen her, for the weight she has lost has given her beauty a sharper edge. Has honed her features, like a sword's blade, to a finer point. And as she turns, taking her seat beside me, I see that every eye in the hall is on her.

I wait, still standing as the others take their places, then, as total silence falls, look to Arminius – simple 'Hermann' now – and gesture to him to begin the festivities.

For the next four hours, we drink, and sing, and listen to the poets of these crude and ancient peoples, feigning intoxication – not drawing attention to the alcohol filters we carry in our stomachs – and avoiding all explanations.

Gods. Isn't that enough of an explanation for them? Only I can see it isn't. No, there are some there that would kill to know our secrets. Only we *are* gods, and when one – a lesser chieftain of the Sicambri – drunkenly challenges Svetov, it is Urte, the smallest of us, who, pushing Svetov back into his chair, takes up the challenge, to the great delight of all.

Katerina makes to intervene, but I cover her hand with my own and smile.

'Just watch,' I whisper in her ear, then sit back, aware of Arminius' eyes on me, a query in that look.

The Sicambri – Baetorix – is a brute of a man. He stands, drawing his sword, but Arminius is having none of that. 'No weapons,' he says, his voice brooking no opposition. 'You settle this hand to hand.'

At which Baetorix scowls. But then, looking at his opponent, who, at Arminius' words has shed her weapons belt, he grins ferociously. God or no god, how could this slip of girl defeat him?

There is tumult in the Hall. Wagers are being made. Two warriors, seated at one of the lower tables, throw beer over each other and are pulled apart by friends and brothers, before embracing like old friends.

'He'll kill her,' Katerina says to my ear, deeply worried now. 'I mean . . . look at the size of him!'

Oh, he is indeed a monster of a man, and as he throws off his cloak and takes his place in the space between the tables, I have just the slightest doubt. If Baetorix is thrice her size, that's not exaggerating. His arms alone are monstrously muscled. Like pines. And as Urte steps down, into the wavering shadows of the combat space, so I remind myself of all the workouts Urte and I have done together, and smile.

As she takes her place before him, so the big man laughs. 'Goddess Urte,' he says, his deep voice making the hall fall silent. 'I promise not to hurt you.'

'You *promise?*' she answers, a mischievous twinkle in her eyes. And, crouching in her familiar way, she beckons him on.

He moves like a great bear, stretching his arms out, as if, in closing them, he will crush her. But she's far too swift, far too agile for his strong yet ponderous movements, and as he seeks to close on her, so she rolls and turns and springs high, and is suddenly behind him, clinging to his back, her hands reaching over his shoulders to tug at his beard.

And as he bellows, reaching up to grab her, so she swings back and, using her hands, flips and slides between his legs, her head connecting sharply with his balls.

Baetorix's bellow goes up an octave, becoming almost a shriek. He reaches down to clutch himself, and as he does, to the great merriment of the watching warriors, Urte punches him in the nose, once, twice, blood spraying, the crack of the breaking bone sounding clearly over the sudden silence.

Baetorix grunts, then stares at her, bemused, swaying suddenly, putting one hand out before him, which Urte knocks away contemptuously. Then, jumping high, she kicks out at the big man's chin, using restraint at the last, such that the otherwise killing blow merely disables him.

I watch as Baetorix staggers and then falls, like a great tree falling, straight and heavy, the weight of him spread across three of his fellow chieftains, his great bulk pinning them down and flattening one of the great wooden tables.

And as the dust settles, so a thunderous cheer goes up. All are on their feet, cheering and stamping, raising their beer mugs to the slender slip of a woman who has defeated their champion. And as it swells and fills the Great Hall, so Urte stands there, beaming, looking down at her flattened adversary, then, accepting the heavy jug of beer she's offered, downs it in one – just to make a point – lifting the empty vessel to Arminius in salute, his own saluting her back before, along with every other man in the hall, he tilts his own jug back and drains it at a go.

408

In a break between songs and story-tellings, I venture out, into the dark, cool night, the scent of death far stronger out here between the pines.

But it is not the smell of carnage that makes me stop and look about me. It's something far stranger. Birdsong.

Taking a torch from one of the guards, I go out and, following the sound, trying to place it, I make my way back over the crest to where, but a few hours earlier, we had stood, after the battle. And there, near the line of stones we laid, some two or three yards in the air, is a sight I've never seen before.

Birds, endless birds, appearing and disappearing in the air, their solid forms lit by the wavering flame of my torch.

A portal. A doorway between two worlds. Reichenau's escape route.

Yes, but more than that. Much more than that.

I go back to the hall, then bring Katerina back with me, watching the golden features of her face as she takes it in. 'Is that . . .?'

'A doorway, yes. To a different world.'

'And Reichenau used this?'

I hesitate, then nod. He must have. The two guards swore he had. But all's not always as it seems.

'*What are you going to do?*' she asks quietly, in Russian, conscious that someone might be listening.

'I'm going back through,' I answer. 'When the feasting's done. I'll jump back, then go through before Reichenau. That way . . .'

But I can see she's unhappy with that for some reason.

'*We,*' she says. '*Not you, Otto. We.*'

I make to argue with her, but she shakes her head and frowns.

'*You're going nowhere, Otto Behr. Not without me there by your side.*'

And so, after the feasting, we slip out past the dozing guards and snoring warriors, then gather at the portal, just the six of us, our flickering torches lighting the scene.

All's been decided. We know what each has to do.

But first back, to Moscow Central, to make up the packs that we're to carry and to run through things again. Then back here, earlier than now, an hour before our *doppelgehirn* friend arrives.

Oh, we know what we must do. We know our only chance now is to follow – at a distance – and find out where he goes and where this leads. If it leads anywhere.

Only surely it must? Such bolt-holes always have a back door. Why trap oneself, after all? And if this is Kolya's work, as I am heavily convinced it is, then maybe more than one.

The man has a devious mind, after all.

Only bear this in mind. We are not used to portals. Not of this kind. All of our lives have been spent operating off of platforms. Of being tracked and thus of being relatively safe. This has an air of danger to it, the possibility of being lost.

Lost in Time. There's little that is worse.

And is that where they are now? My girls? Lost in Time? Trapped in one of these back-door universes?

If so, then we shall never find them.

'Otto?'

I look to her.

'Your face just then . . .'

'It's fine,' I answer. 'Just a trick of the light.' I reach across and take her hand, my voice softer, gentler than before. 'But come. We have demons to pursue.'

409

We step through, into an open-air temple, on an island in a lake, the moon shining down from a blue-black sky, its silver shield reflected in the water.

Where or when we are I could not say, only that, with its warm breezes and Mediterranean-looking trees, this has a familiar feel to it, and when Katerina joins me, stepping from the air like a ballet dancer, I ask her if she knows this place.

She shakes her head.

'So how did you get among the slaves?'

Katerina shrugs. 'I don't know. He must have drugged me. One moment I was in the cell, the next . . .'

'Cell? What cell?'

'The place he kept me. I don't know where . . . or when. Just that one moment I was there, locked into that foul and lightless space, the next I was chained to a cartwheel in the Roman encampment. And that's where I was until you found me, weeks later.'

'I don't understand . . .'

And I don't. Unless Reichenau was hiding away what he'd stolen. Keeping Katerina from being taken back by Kolya.

I look about me, then look to her again.

'Was it hard?'

'*Hard*?' Her laugh is pained. 'Being *his* prisoner? You don't know, Otto. You just don't know. When he took us . . . from Cherdiechnost . . .'

She takes a deep breath, as if mentally steadying herself, then continues. 'I was about to tell you, Otto. I'd pictured it in my head. Do you know that? Imagined me telling you; imagined how your face would have lit up; imagined your joy at my words. Only . . . only I never got to tell you. And then . . .'

'Tell me.'

She hesitates, her eyes searching mine, then places her hand flat against the curve of her stomach. 'That I was pregnant. Pregnant with your child.'

The words shock me. 'So what . . .?'

'I lost it,' she says, quieter than before. 'Or rather, he made me lose it. It was a boy, Otto. A boy.'

'It was Kolya, yes, who made you do this?'

She nods, her eyes reliving the grief of it.

I go to her, folding her in my arms, feeling her warmth pressed against me, and let her cry for the child she never had. He and his five lost sisters. And I add that to the growing list of reasons why I will kill Kolya.

'Come, my love,' I say, after a while, drying her eyes, knowing that there is business still to do, here in this uncharted place. And so we get hidden, up there at the top of the slope above the temple, there among the Mediterranean-looking trees.

Waiting for Reichenau to come through.

410

I'm beginning to think that we had somehow got things wrong, when finally he steps through.

I see how he looks about him, his eyes searching the shadows for movement, paranoid to the last. Only he's right to be this once, for we are there, watching his every move, following him.

He circles the temple, then seems to sniff the air – it's hard to tell exactly through the field glasses – and then, as if satisfied he's alone, he makes his way across.

For a moment I think that maybe the temple is another portal, only he moves round it, past it, heading down the slope.

To what?

As Katerina strains to go after him, I hold her back.

'*Give him a moment,*' I whisper. '*We don't want him to see us, do we?*'

No. But the terrain here is difficult for such a pursuit. It's far too open. Follow him directly and he'll only have to turn about to see us. Yet if we stay within the border of trees . . .

'Come,' I say, deciding to risk it. 'But keep crouched down, and if he turns, fall flat.'

And so we go after him, crouched down, half-running, half-scuttling like crabs, trying to make no noise, sensitive to his every move, and as the slope climbs and then falls again, so we see his destination.

It's a small village, tucked in between two rocky outcrops, its lower levels overlooking the sea, forming a harbour.

Medieval, I think. *Yes, and archetypically Italian by the look of it.* There is another, smaller outcrop to our left.

'*There,*' I say, nudging her, indicating the raised hump of rock and earth.

We go across, crouching down, getting our breath.

And not before time, because just then Reichenau turns abruptly, looking back up the slope, as if to catch us out. I duck down smartly and stay there, rigidly still, holding Katerina against me, counting to twenty before popping up once more . . . only to see his unmistakable figure much further on, down the slope, almost at the village, hurrying now.

'*Come,*' I say, my whisper urgent. '*We mustn't lose him.*'

But even as I say it I realise that it doesn't really matter. Now that we know where he's heading we can jump back and place ourselves down there, among the buildings, and watch from there where he goes.

Only suddenly he's not there.

Katerina looks puzzled. 'Otto?'

We walk down, Katerina following me, a few metres behind, her gun drawn.

For the next half hour we search those narrow, deserted lanes and find . . .

Nothing.

Katerina looks to me. '*Well?*'

It's late. The houses are shuttered, the church and the seafront inn closed, the latter padlocked. If there's anyone living here, then they'll be safe in their beds right now. Only I'm not going to let that stop me.

I burn out the lock on the quayside inn, then kick the door open.

And nothing. Not at first, anyway. Then, from somewhere at the back of the building, I hear a door creak open. There's a vague muttering. Medieval Italian, I'm sure of it, and then a figure appears in the bar where we're standing – a sleepy middle-aged man, a balding fellow with a huge cushion of a belly, an unlit candle in one hand.

'Where is he?' I ask, in the only strain of Italian I know. 'The monstrosity . . . Where does he go?'

The man feigns ignorance, until I draw a knife and, slamming him down in a chair, threaten to gut him unless he gives me an answer.

Frightened now, he stammers a reply. I can't make it out at first, but then I understand. The ruin. That's where he goes. And that, too, it seems, is where he comes from.

Another portal, more like. The back door I was thinking had to exist.

'Take me there,' I say.

Only he's scared to. 'That thing . . .' he says, pleading with his eyes for me to understand. 'He kill me if I help—'

'And *I'll* kill you if you don't!'

And I press the knifepoint into his neck enough to make him yelp.

'Okay . . . okay!' he says. 'I take you . . . yes?'

And so we go out, into those moonlit streets, heading towards the harbour, going down the narrow steps, and there, beneath a ledge of rock, overlooked by us first time out, is what seems some kind of ruin, its cracked white columns and broken piles of rock rising just above the waves.

'Here?'

'Here,' he says, clearly wanting to get as far from that place as he can now that he's delivered us.

'So where is he?' I ask, and the poor man shrugs.

'All right,' I say. 'You can go.'

And he backs away, bowing as he does, his face a picture of gratitude.

I turn, looking out across the ruin. It's ancient, Greek, or Roman, or maybe even Etruscan. Whichever, it looks like it's been built into a cave. There's a white stone wall to our left and a set of narrow steps leading down, but in the underhang, it's difficult to make out any detail, it's so dark.

The only way we're going to find out is to go down.

But not now. No. We need to return to the portal by the temple and jump back, then come in again, earlier this time.

Which is exactly what we do, and we are there this time, hiding behind a low wall on the far side of the ruin when he makes his appearance.

We hear him come down, into the ruin, his torch briefly lighting up the ceiling overhead before he focuses the beam on the inner darkness.

I give him a ten count then follow, slipping through the gap, taking great care, my fingers finding handholds, Katerina just behind me, the two of us following the torchlight.

We've not gone very far when we hear voices – low, masculine voices – even as a second torch beam illuminates that ruined space.

Finding a vantage point, we see Reichenau's silhouetted figure, facing what is clearly one of Kolya's ancestors – one of his 'brothers'. The latter is holding what looks like a very mean piece of weaponry, keeping Reichenau at bay. But Reichenau is pleading with him now, offering all manner of things if he'll only let him jump up.

Things are sketchy in the wavering torchlight, but my guess is that there's another portal here, or something like that thing in the desert, some kind of massive focus. Whatever, it looks like Kolya is guarding all of the entrances to his time realm.

If that's what it is.

Reichenau's pleas don't seem to be getting him anywhere, but then nature lends a hand. There's a sudden noise as a small animal – a rat, maybe – scuttles across the floor of the ruin. For the briefest moment the 'brother' is distracted, and in that instant Reichenau springs, launching himself, letting fly with a knife that pierces the other's throat.

Clambering up onto the platform, he quickly finishes the job, then, with an almost cursory glance about him . . . vanishes.

411

Katerina wants to go back and bring reinforcements, but for once I'm loath to. I want to follow while we yet can, to find out where this leads. And this time I have my way, Katerina joining me on the platform as, not knowing where we are going, we jump.

Into a scene of total desolation, refugees everywhere, buildings on fire, aircraft thundering overhead, and there, across from us, half a kilometre away at most, making his way towards a huge building with a shining golden dome, is Reichenau.

We start to run.

Getting to the dome is harder than I thought. Whatever's going on here, the fighting is intense, and more than once we have to stop and shelter, but eventually we get there and slip inside.

The building displays signs of a fierce firefight. Bodies are strewn everywhere. Kolya, I realise, has fashioned a real rabbit's warren through Time, and every gateway is defended by his 'brothers'. Only here – as we can see from the corpses piled up around the platform – Kolya's ancestors have died in some numbers defending it.

But there's no sign of Reichenau. We can only assume that he's jumped through yet again . . . and so, again, we follow.

Is this foolishness? This slavish following of him? Maybe. Only my gut instinct is that this is the quickest way out, and besides, we're not fated to die here nor in any of these places. We've still got to complete the loop. To come full circle and emerge wherever it is that we are fated to emerge.

But not here. It doesn't end here.

We jump up, onto the platform, and, hand in hand, step through, into a scene we know very well.

Cherdiechnost!

It's early morning and a heavy dew is on the long grass. Bird call fills the air, yet one single look reveals how different it is.

What was once a flourishing estate has been transformed into a work camp, with long barracks, high fences with barbed wire and guard towers. Where we have jumped to, we are inside the fence, and, glimpsing Reichenau making his way across the fields, we quickly follow.

Only now we are spotted by one of the guards. A call goes up for us to halt. We hurry on, but laser fire now burns a blackening line just ahead.

I turn, aiming my weapon, and open fire. There is a shriek and an awful screaming as the guard, in flames now, tumbles from the tower.

And as he does, so Reichenau turns, looking back, and sees us . . . and begins to run, heading for the church with its white walls and blue cupola.

It's there, in that ancient, wooden church, the scene of so many pleasant gatherings across the years, that we finally corner him.

He's standing there, before the altar, snarling, cursing the air, frustrated that there is no time portal here, no way of jumping out, where he's clearly expected one. And my guess is that Kolya, warned that someone was penetrating his defences, has finally taken action and closed down one of the gateways.

Or that's my guess.

I make to hail him, only, before I can say a word, Katerina pushes past me and confronts him, her gun aimed at his exaggerated skull.

'Where are they? Where did you put them?'

He turns slowly, as if in a daze, seeming only then to take in the fact that we are there.

'Oh,' he says, almost dismissively. 'You.'

He has near on killed me once before, and I would happily blow the man away, except that he knows things, and his fixed smile registers that fact.

We need him, and he knows it.

'Help me and I might help you,' he says.

And that word 'might', which suggests he's doing *us* a favour, riles me beyond all belief.

'Are they unharmed?' Katerina asks.

The bastard can see that she's afraid for her daughters and he uses that. He looks back at me, no sign of any human warmth or kindness in that expression, just calculation. 'Do you seriously think I would harm such a valuable commodity?'

The words make me go cold. Facing him, I begin to understand what he is. Not really human at all. An experiment, with all the warped thinking of an experiment.

Yes. I doubt it no longer. Reichenau is capable of anything, from the pettiest theft to the vilest murder, and I wonder what he has done to my girls that will make me want to kill him. For I'm sure there must be something. Something unimaginably vile.

The thought of it makes me hesitate. Can I *really* make any kind of bargain with this creature? He is a liar, after all, and not just any liar, but a liar through and through – as if it's been imprinted in his DNA.

No, I realise. I can't. Which leaves me with only one course of action: to take him back and, via the Russians' platform, physically take him there. Wherever 'there' is.

I go to Reichenau and place the barrel of my laser against his bulbous head.

'Okay,' I say. 'Let's go.'

412

A small crowd has gathered at the Russian platform as I bring Reichenau through, his hands bound, a thick cloth blindfold about that grotesquely large head.

This is their enemy and there are many – like Freisler – who feel he should be killed, his threat extinguished at once. Only he still holds my daughters, and until they're returned to us I'll not consider harming the man.

We place him in a cell, the doors heavily guarded, then convene a meeting of the *veche*. It's there that I explain my plan, which is to use him as the means of getting back my girls. Then, if he satisfies us in that regard, we'll do what Kolya attempted to do: exile Reichenau in a cut-off timeline, like Bonaparte on Elba.

But Freisler still isn't happy, and he isn't alone. Even my good friend Svetov is uneasy.

'What if they're dead already, Otto? What if this is just another trap? Or some trick to get his freedom?'

'Maybe,' I concede, and it's a huge concession. 'Only I have to risk that. All I know is that I'm not even thinking of leaving them captive. Not for an instant.'

And so it is. Only, sympathetic as they are, they have grown weary of this pursuit, and now that we have him in our grasp, it would make more sense to 'deal' with him at once, before, Loki-like, he tricks his way out of things once again.

As it is, I win the vote – if only by the most slender of majori-ties – and, while Reichenau is kept in his cell, agents are sent out to prepare the 'exile' world.

Katerina, meanwhile, has taken to her bed. 'Exhaustion,' Old Schnorr says, looking up from her bedside. 'She overdid it, Otto. You can't blame her, I'd have done the same, but it was too much, too soon. There's nothing intrinsically wrong with her, but she needs to rest. Those months as a slave depleted her. The last few days she's been running on empty.'

I sit there, across from Schnorr, and place my hand over hers. She's sleeping – drugged up to the eyeballs, so Meister Schnorr says.

It's while I'm sitting there, alone with her, watching her chest gently rise and fall in the dim light of the room, that young Saratov comes, bringing news.

It's bad. The very worst. And when he's gone, I sit there, stunned, staring down at the document he brought.

I'm still there when she wakes. She squeezes my hand and smiles.

'Otto. How long . . .?'

'Oh, a long while.'

She seems surprised. She's about to say something more, but I stop her.

'Listen,' I say, putting a finger gently to her lips. 'Word has come.'

'Word?' The smile has gone from her lips.

'Reichenau is dead. Murdered in his cell. And Freisler has fled.'

I look up, seeing the pain in her eyes. Knowing that she knows what this means. That we might never see our girls again.

'What's to be done?' she asks, her voice a whisper, the first tear rolling down her face. Only then it hits her. There *might* actually be a way. She starts forward, gripping my hands.

'But we can jump back, surely, Otto? Go back in time and prevent it?'

'Normally, yes. Only . . .'

'*Only?*'

'Only Moseley's document says this is all part of the greater loop. A crucial part. Change it and certain things will not happen.'

Katerina stares at me. '*What?*'

And I realise that she knows nothing about Moseley and the Great Men project, nor even the greater loop. I might just as well have spoken in *ge'not* for all she understands.

And so I begin at the beginning, with the scheme to create the think tank to end all think tanks, and our kidnap of history's greatest thinkers. Which in itself is difficult, because the whole notion of great men – of men who are philosophers and mathematicians and little else – is totally alien to a young woman from thirteenth-century Novgorod, where trade and naked power is all they understand.

'So what's actually *in* that?' she asks, pointing to the document in my lap.

'Loose ends,' I say.

And that's pretty much the truth. Because what they've done – and with no consultation with me – is to go back to the Haven and trawl through everything and anything that had to do with Katerina and me . . . alongside anything relating to Reichenau and Kolya – looking for those things that have not been tied up. Those parts where the loop seems to have been broken.

Quite literally, for loose ends.

It was in the process of doing this that they discovered that Reichenau was no longer active in Time. That the fewer and fewer 'new' appearances he made were all linked to the past. Nothing new was happening to him. Not only that, but the more they looked, the more they saw how intricately he was tied-in to the loop Katerina and I had begun, like the cement between the bricks.

And, having stumbled upon that notion, they took it further and started making a chart – something far more ambitious than the one I'd sketched out on that big sheet of paper – to include all of this, whether it was tied-in tightly or just existed separately, *loosely* you might say.

Moseley had explained it to me. How they had started with the very simplest of charts. With all the familiar stuff. The stuff they knew connected. And how, day by day, they had added more, making the thing more complex, more subtle, more . . . *alive*.

Reichenau, it seemed, was dead, and he was going to stay dead. *Time-dead*, as we're accustomed to calling it. Resurrect him and – so our experts claimed, and who was I to contradict them? – it would all unravel. Imagine rope bridges falling slowly into endless chasms and you get a rough idea of it.

And Kolya? Of him there wasn't a trace. Not beyond what we already had. And since Reichenau's death there was no way of tracing him, except . . .

Except through that part of the loop that went to Krasnogorsk.

To follow or to break the loop. Those, it seemed, were our only options.

And if we broke it?

Then chaos would descend. Complications the like of which we could scarce imagine.

'Like what?' I asked young Saratov.

'Imagine a hall of mirrors, only with each image slightly different, slightly askew from the rest. Imagine realities mixing and merging, the great branches of the tree fusing into one big, broad trunk, within which nothing made sense. Imagine, well, madness itself. Madness as the reality we're inhabiting. Nothing making any sense at all.'

'And how do they know this?'

Saratov hesitated, then, in a tremulous voice: 'Because we've glimpsed it. Because we've seen the faintest shadows of it, like an after-image on a giant retina.'

'So what's the answer?' Katerina asks, as I look to her again. 'Are we to do nothing, Otto? Are you seriously happy with that?'

And I want to say no. That I *am* doing something, and that if we follow the loop it must lead us somewhere. Only the loop at some point runs through Krasnogorsk, and if there's a path that leads on from there, then it's a path that leads through Death itself, for nothing yet has changed the fact that it is she and I who lay there, dead on the cart.

But that lies ahead. Right now it's a question of deciding what to do with Reichenau. As if there really is a choice.

No. The battle of the Teutoburg Forest was his last great throw of the dice. That's what they're saying. And Old Schnorr agrees. The man is dead for good, his head smashed open and no one to put Humpty back together again.

'What if they're wrong, Otto? What if . . .?'

Only I know they're not. To have no new sightings of him in Time . . . that's as clear an indication as we can get.

I reach out, holding her to me. Only it feels like I've betrayed her. That I've failed somehow in my duty as a father. And so I have. And, realising that, I feel a sudden hollowness.

What could I do?

Only I don't say that, because I know how she would answer it. She would ask me to defy them, even as I've defied them many times before. Only this time it would be futile. One man searching Time, for a needle in a thousand billion haystacks.

Which is true. Only holding her, listening to her cry, I feel diminished, because I am the one who left his children as hostages to Time.

Sweet darling girls forgive me.
But no one hears.

Part Fourteen
Loose Ends

413

Loose ends. That's what we're chasing now. Loose ends.

Meanwhile, here I am once more, seated in the darkness of Yastryeb's room, the Tree of Worlds glowing in the space before me as I ponder the strange nature of Time.

For Time is many things.

Time is like the surface of a pond, or a river, flowing downhill. Time is an abrader, the force that grounds mountains into dust. Time is an elevator moving between the years. Time is an arrow, a hunter, a thief, a storm in which we're lost.

Time is . . .

Time has a thousand qualities, but mostly it's the thread that holds the universe together. Without it there is no movement in the universe, no birth and no death. Take Time away and the universe would halt, become a single frozen frame.

Which makes me wonder if what that poor bastard Burckel said, so long ago, has now become the truth of it.

'We act like policemen, Otto. Time cops, when we really ought to be acting like revolutionaries. Undrehungar. *We could change things. Really change things. Not piss about meddling in historical events – what good does that do ultimately? The Russians only change it back! No. We need to get to grips with the underlying phenomena, with the infrastructure of history, not the surface froth.'*

How dismissive I was back then. How lacking in insight. Yes, and who would believe that I would one day embrace that madman's philosophy? None of my past selves, anyway.

Katerina is in the next room, sleeping the sleep of the deeply hurt, the drained and the despairing. The gods know how hurt, for she has truly cried herself out. Close as I am to her, it's hard for me to imagine just how much she is hurting; how deep that emotional connection goes. A man might kill for his daughters, but only a mother can love them in the way Katerina loves her girls, with the ferocity of a wild beast.

And me? Oh, I have shed tears enough these past few months. It has been hard – incredibly hard – living life without them. But then I have always been alone; always one short step away from death.

Old Schnorr comes to me, but what he has to say is of little help. Kind as he tries to be, how could that old man give me advice? How could he understand what I am going through?

As for the women – Zarah, Urte and the rest – they have left me alone, convinced, I'm sure, that I would only see their sympathy as another form of meddling in my life. That's not true, of course, but I can see why they've kept their distance. And maybe they're right to. I'm on something of a short fuse just now, as Ernst found out when he made an appearance as representative of the *veche*.

And I'd apologise, only it *isn't* his business, and it *isn't* for the best.

Which leaves me here, now, seated before the Tree of Worlds, its many branches pulsing slowly in the darkness. This, until it changes, is reality. This, for good or evil, is the state of things right now.

Or is it?

Where, after all, are Kolya's worlds? Where are the realities to which his time portals connect?

The truth is we don't know. Even the one we travelled through, from the Teutoburg Forest to Cherdiechnost, is gone – as if it never was.

Erased, no doubt, by that pale, ghost-like figure and his 'brothers'.

What I *do* know, however, is that he has access to our worlds. I don't know how, or where, or when, but simply for him to be in the loop – for him to be there at Krasnogorsk, our pale, lifeless bodies there on his cart – argues for him owning other time-gates, other portals, connecting him to the worlds we operate in.

I stand and stretch and yawn, then climb, up out of the pit.

I need to be doing something. To be chasing him down. Only how do I do that when I don't know where he is?

There's Krasnogorsk, of course, but no one wants to go there, me least of all, for fear that we'll break the loop and it'll all go collapsing in upon itself. No. Krasnogorsk's no option. At least, not yet. Not until we've exhausted all other possibilities.

Then what?

Young Moseley takes the decision out of my hands. 'Otto,' he says, coming into the room. 'We need to consult you.'

'We?'

'The *manus*,' he says, as if I know what he's talking about. But he quickly explains. 'We've put a team on it, Otto – a *manus*, looking into time-phenomena. Aristotle and da Vinci are the main contributors, but Pauli and Planck have given up a lot of their time, if you'll excuse the pun, and a lot of the weirder stuff has come from them. And then there's Rosalind . . .'

'Rosalind?'

'Rosalind Franklin, our DNA specialist. Without her . . . well, she's a ruddy marvel at identifying the obvious.'

'Yes?'

'Yes. They're waiting for you right now.'

'Waiting where?'

'Up ahead.'

And so we jump. Ahead. To a place I've never been before, a full millennium into the future, a place of manicured lawns and high, soaring temples, with a perfect blue sky above. There are no signs of any people, however, not a single one, and when Moseley tells me what year this is, I'm shocked.

'How in Urd's name?'

Moseley smiles. 'We did a little tampering with Gehlen's equations. They weren't quite right. That's why there was a ceiling to your time travelling. That might have been deliberate or not, we don't know, but . . . well, come . . . the others are waiting inside.'

Inside? Only there doesn't seem to be an inside. We're in an open space. And then, a moment, later, we aren't. Suddenly we're seated at a big table, Moseley and I and the others, Moseley's colleagues facing us across the smooth oak tabletop, a view of grassy slopes and snow-capped mountains through a window to our right.

Aristotle and da Vinci are still dressed in the clothes of their own times, long, flowing silks that make the pair of them look like Grecian gods, but Pauli and Planck are wearing simple black cotton one-pieces, like they're members of some futuristic club, which I guess is very much the truth of it: the Great Men – and Women – club. As for Rosalind Franklin she too is dressed in black, only her ankle-length dress is made of silk. She's slender with deep brown eyes and a vaguely aristocratic look about her.

'Gentlemen . . . Rosalind . . .' I say, greeting them, conscious as I do that I've barely spent any time with them; that it's possible that they're feeling just a tiny bit neglected.

'Otto,' da Vinci says, in his newly acquired English, the language they've chosen for their discussions. 'We have been looking at the records and . . . well, there's a lot that makes no sense. A lot of gaps.'

'Gaps? What, in the loop?'

'In Time itself,' Aristotle says, his voice stronger, deeper than da Vinci's, his deeply blue eyes piercing me. 'Where you and your Russian friends meddled with the event landscape.' He shakes his head, as if he's disappointed in me. 'All these years you've been treating Time as if it were indestructible, something robust and resilient, as if it could heal itself, no problem. But that isn't so. Time is a fragile thing, Otto. Just how fragile we're only now beginning to understand.'

'That's true,' Pauli interjects, before I can object to what's just been said. He's a strange little man, Wolfgang Pauli, with the look of a down-at-heel mafia boss, not an expert in quantum physics and spin theory. Black doesn't suit him, either, and the one-piece merely acts to show up his paunch.

'Looking through the loose ends document,' he says, 'we came across numerous instances where damage to the fabric of Time, brought about by deliberate changes in historical events, have caused deeper, longer-term damage.'

'Such as?'

It's Rosalind Franklin who takes it up. 'There are parts of time that have faded, Otto, just as if the fabric of reality has been worn away. Others have *stiffened*, for want of a better word, grown less elastic, and there's parts of it that have . . . well, I don't know how you'd describe it . . . but it's as if reality itself has crumbled and flaked away. And then there are the time winds.'

'Time winds?'

'It's a new phenomenon. We noticed it first in the photo album you handed on to Moseley,' da Vinci says, and the modern words seem strange coming from his mouth – anachronistic. 'You know, the one of you and Katerina travelling in Time. They're gone, Otto. All of those wonderful images faded almost to nothing, blown away by the winds of time.'

'Gone . . .?' I feel a twinge of regret, and alarm, thinking of those images. Did that mean that those parts of the loop had also gone? Had my access to them, my connection *with* them, faded just as the photos had faded?

I ask them directly, and see, from the way they look at each other, that this is something they don't know. Not yet, anyway.

'We're re-evaluating things,' Moseley says. 'But one thing we're convinced about is that we need to end this soon. To find Kolya and trap him and . . . well . . . end it.'

To make things right again, I think. *To make it stable.*

Only where would Katerina and I be if Time were repaired and made good again? We'd be erased from time, surely? My darling would have been dead a thousand years before I never met her. Not to speak of our five non-existent daughters. And surely they know that? Surely they have discussed these things among them?

I'm afraid to ask. Because to heal Time they must take my life from me.

Later, alone with Moseley, he turns to me. 'We should dispose of him,' he says, and for the briefest moment I'm uncertain who he means. But then I get his drift.

'Reichenau?'

'Yes. We can't just leave his body in the morgue.'

I consider that a moment then nod. While he's there, in the morgue, there's always the temptation to bring him back. But there's an answer to that. A way we can make sure he doesn't come back to haunt us. And that's to eject his corpse into the void, into the space between the universes, a space he sure as hell won't return from.

Which is what we do, a dozen or more of us – Russians and Germans – gathering to witness the disposal of our old enemy.

Gone.

And there's part of me that's delighted that the bastard's dead; that would kill him again a thousand times for all he's done. But it's like I've said before: without Reichenau, how do we get at Kolya? For there's no doubting that Reichenau knew *something*.

I look to Saratov again. 'So how do we get at him?'

'Kolya?' He shrugs. 'I honestly don't know. Yet he must make his move, yes? To capture you. To be there in the loop. If we just wait . . .'

Only how can I just wait, with my girls out there still?

'I'm going after him,' I say. 'He must have his portals somewhere. If we can find those . . .'

Which seems desperate, only my instinct tells me that something has changed. That our actions have had some effect after all, and that, though it might seem that he's evaded us, we have caused him considerable inconvenience. After all, it can't be easy shutting down portals and opening up new ones.

And, now that I think of it, things *have* changed. Whereas before Kolya's set-up – or what we've glimpsed of it – has been incredibly flexible, his approach to Time plastic, as embodied in his willingness to destroy everything and start again at will in a scorched-earth fashion, this strategy of using a complex, interconnected rabbit-warren of gates and portals through Time signals a complete change in his approach, because the more complex those set-ups are, the less flexible they become.

Meaning what? That Kolya has finally lost his edge? If so, then there must be a way we might take advantage of this new inflexibility of his. Only it's still as young Saratov says: to get at him, we need to wait for Kolya to show himself. As he surely must.

Only I'm not going to wait. Thanking Saratov, I jump away from there, back to Moscow Central in the last days of 2999, and, wasting no time, I go to see my beloved and tell her what I've been thinking, and she listens to me and smiles and then pulls me down onto the bed with her, and we make love, for the first time since I found her again. And suddenly I know, know without a single shade of doubt, that following the path of logic will only get us so far. No. It is the other path – the path of the heart – that we must follow now. What use are Great Men and their schemes if what they advise me to do is against my strongest instincts? What bloody use?

414

The tiny lecture theatre is packed as I take the rostrum, the meeting attended by more than sixty of our number; once enemies, now friends and allies.

Katerina is there, of course, seated in the front row with the other women, but every face I see is one I'd trust with my life.

I give a little speech, telling them what it is I have to do. How I cannot be Meister any longer and feel the way I feel. How logic can only take us so far, and . . .

And then that huge bear of a man, Svetov, stands, interrupting me, telling me not to apologise for what I'm feeling and that if the fate of our sons and daughters is not a good enough reason for taking action, then what is? And suddenly everyone is on their feet, cheering and yelling encouragement.

And there and then a great scheme is devised, to scour space and time, however long that takes. For, as Svetov rightly argues, if anyone can do it, we can.

The fact is that Reichenau could have hidden the girls anywhere and at any time, and from the hints he gave to Katerina, they are probably being held separately, and even if we find one, that won't necessarily lead to the others.

What makes it difficult is that Reichenau is dead. 'Or was,' I say, realising that once again I have overlooked the most basic of Time's properties. 'But he wasn't always dead, and if I can find him again . . .'

415

And so it begins. I return to the Teutoburg Forest, a week earlier than before, tracking the Roman army as it pushes north into the wilderness.

I don't know exactly when or where Reichenau contacted Varus, but from what I see of the Roman legions, I know that Reichenau's forces have yet to link with them.

I have one big problem here. If I intervene directly then I'll probably break the sequence that leads to Reichenau's death, and – before that – our victory over him.

The question is, do I want to do that? I decide that I don't. Now that Freisler has done it, I want Reichenau *kept* dead.

So how do I find out what I need to know?

That one's easy. I observe him at a distance and then follow him. Find out who he talks to and what *they* know. Get at his secrets through his underlings, for it's almost certain that Reichenau hasn't acted alone – not on the scale on which he's operating.

I stay *in situ*, following the legions north, living off the land and off my wits until, finally, I spy Reichenau, and witness the first meeting between Varus and the *doppelgehirn*, seeing how Varus wanted to crucify or burn the man as a demon, and how Reichenau persuaded him otherwise.

That evening, I follow Reichenau back to the invisible portal in the forest and then on, through the Medieval Italian village and down to the ruins again, where – this time – there is no sign of a guard. I follow Reichenau through, taking the same route as last time, on through the 'changed' Cherdiechnost and into the church, where, behind the altar, there is one final time gate.

I hesitate, then go through after him.

Out, into the Akademie in Neu Berlin in 2343. Full circle, or so it seems.

But why here?

I wonder whether this might not be some kind of psychological imprinting and decide to have a good look around. I go to the room where, last time, I spoke to the 'brother' and to young Kolya himself, but the room is empty. Nor is there any sign of Reichenau or where he's gone. I'm ready to admit defeat and jump back to Moscow Central when I decide to follow a hunch.

I make my way to the laboratories, cutting through the locks with my laser one by one, knowing that my presence there will almost certainly bring security guards running.

And there, in the big room where the political prisoners are kept for experiments, among the other young prisoners, I find what I had almost given up on finding, my daughter Irina, the nine-year-old in a piteous state, half-starved and shackled inside one of the pens.

An alarm is sounding now, its klaxon filling the air. Running feet are hurrying toward me.

I stoop and, kissing her brow, swear to her that I will be straight back to get her.

And jump . . .

416

Back at Moscow Central I find that I'm trembling, anxious to get back there and secure her freedom. And while I know it will be almost simultaneous from her point of view, the preparations at my end seem to take ages.

To get her out of there, they have decided to make a special mobile focus for Irina, and an agent has been sent off to Cherdiechnost, in happier times, to get a DNA sample for that. At the same time, to cover our tracks, it is decided that it might be a good idea to set off a few explosions, somewhere else in the Akademie, to distract the guards.

All this agreed and everything prepared, I jump back in . . .

Only, in that briefest of instances between jumping out and back again, someone else has entered that huge room.

It's one of Kolya's 'brothers' and he's barring the way between me and my darling Irina. The sight of him makes my blood go cold, because this once again shows a frightening prescience on Kolya's part. How in Urd's name does he keep doing this? Just how does he anticipate my every move?

This fellow has the jump on me and, somewhat nervously, I feel, he orders me to throw my gun down. He is keen to stop me, only this once I will not be stopped. Throwing my gun away, I leap at him and knock him aside, then struggle with him. For one brief moment I have the bastard – can feel the life ebbing from him as my hands close about his windpipe – only right then another of them suddenly appears, his hands gripping my throat.

A blackness overcomes me as I struggle for breath. It's like a vice is being tightened about the top of my skull. And then I stagger back, gasping hoarsely as I take in a lungful of air.

For a moment I haven't a clue what's happening. There are shouts and screams, explosions and the smell of burning flesh, and as my vision returns, I see that I'm no longer alone. Svetov is there, and Saratov, and Ernst, and between them they have killed the brothers.

'Otto,' Ernst says, turning a full 360, his eyes searching the air, as if more of them might yet appear. 'Are you all right?'

Only it doesn't matter about me. Gasping, I look about me for the big cutters I brought back with me and, picking them up, go over to where she's still held, in the cage.

I cut it open, then lean in to sever her shackles. Then, throwing them aside, I reach in and, tears in my eyes, lift her out, shocked by how light she is, how frail.

Slipping the pendant about her neck, I jump back to Moscow Central, leaving the others there, guarding the air, waiting for Kolya to make his counter-move.

417

Katerina is waiting there and, as I step through, Irina in my arms, so she gives a little cry, then jumps up, onto the platform.

'Oh, Irina . . . oh my darling girl.'

I hand her to her mother, then stand there with them, hugging them both to me, the three of us gripping each other tightly, trembling, tears streaming down our faces.

'Take her,' I say. 'Clean her up and let her get some sleep. I'll see you later, yes?'

And, kissing them both once more, I jump back, to join Ernst and the others.

'What happened?' I ask. 'Why didn't they hit us in force? Why only two of them?'

'That's precisely what we've been asking,' Svetov says, shifting his bulky figure uncomfortably. 'My guess is that that series of attacks we launched has stretched them thin.'

'Maybe,' I say. 'But just two? To guard one of my daughters? You'd have thought . . .'

Only I don't quite know what I expected. None or a lot.

I look to Ernst. 'Where are the guards?'

'We dealt with them, before we came in here.'

'Ahh . . .' But I have the feeling that we've missed something. Something important. Though Urd knows what it is. Maybe the ease with which we gained our victory. Because before now his brothers have given as good as they got – and maybe better. But this time . . .

Stretched thin *might* explain it.

'Okay,' I say. 'Let's leave it for now. We can always send a couple of agents in to look for clues.'

'Clues and loose ends,' Ernst says. 'I'll organise it.'

'Good. Then let's get back.'

418

I leave them to it, returning to my girls, who have barely been separated since being reunited. As Irina sleeps, freshly bathed and cuddled up in her mother's arms, Katerina tells me what she has discovered from our daughter, much of it overheard from Reichenau's guards and lackeys.

Some of it she isn't clear about, having been deeply traumatised by it all. But what *is* clear is that Kolya meant to keep them hostage and his temporary loss of them to his 'son', Reichenau, enraged him. Irina believed that Kolya was working to steal them all back, and had succeeded with some of them. Why? Because the 'brother' who was in the room with her when I jumped back, spoke of 'coming to see your sisters'.

That's interesting. It suggests that we might yet track them down. But the Akademie wasn't the only place Irina was kept. There was a fortress, it seems. By the sea. Very cold, like in Russia, only everyone there spoke fluent German. Which makes me think of what Schikaneder said to me that time. Makes me wonder whether this might not be Kolya's St Petersburg fortress.

It's a long shot, but it seems like something I ought to follow up on, and soon, before Kolya erases it, as he's wont to.

And so I go back to St Petersburg, at the time of Catherine the Great, in late July 1771, and begin to look around. I hire a boat and go out to where Schikaneder said that Kolya had built his fortress. There's no sign of it from the water, but I want a closer look and go ashore, digging about among the scrubland. And there, embedded in the earth, part hidden by the overgrown grass and weeds, I find a series of metre-long metal grids from which warm air drifts up.

This is it. It has to be.

I decide to get help.

419

Ernst straightens, then looks across at me, a smile lighting his features.

'It's here.'

We go across, Svetov and Saratov and I, even as Ernst draws the nettles and long grass back with his arm to reveal a huge metallic trapdoor.

'This is it,' Svetov says, deeply pleased. 'It must be.'

I nod. Kolya's fortress. Only how do we get in?

We bring in tools – shovels and pitchforks, which fit in with the age – and start to excavate the place, only we've not got very far, exposing maybe a quarter of the big, circular opening, when we get visitors. Local fishermen have seen us, and soldiers from the nearby fort have been sent out to question us. They hail us from their boat, which is maybe twenty metres out from the shore, but come no closer. It's a time of plague in St Petersburg and everyone is jumpy.

Svetov, an expert on this age, goes across and greets them. We have anticipated this, and have prepared two 'corpses' – long, padded parcels of just the right weight, wrapped up in dirty sheets – which are visible in the boat. Our story is that they've died of the plague and that we're burying them, but the young lieutenant isn't satisfied. He asks Svetov who we are and where we're staying. We've anticipated this, too. Svetov tells him we've been working upriver, building a *dacha* for our master – a man whose name the young lieutenant clearly recognises but could not consult, even if he wanted to, because the man's a thousand miles away in Moscow.

'You want to look?' Svetov says, gesturing toward the 'corpses' in the boat, but the young man shakes his head. You can see that he's still unhappy, which means he's likely to come back, and so Svetov switches to 'Plan B'.

'Look,' he says, as if the young officer has caught him out. 'I know how it looks, but our Master has instructed us to be very discreet. He's looking to build a hospital – to service the great city – and we've been looking at the wasteland here as a possible site. He's worried that if the wrong ears get to hear about it, then they might charge over the odds for purchasing the land.'

At this the young lieutenant nods. Such deals he can understand. He gets his men to manoeuvre the boat closer to the shore.

Svetov turns and signals to young Saratov, who goes to the boat and brings out the leather purse that's there in the box and hands it to Svetov, who takes it and turns back to face the young officer again.

This, as Svetov knows, must be done with great delicacy.

'Forgive us,' he begins. 'I should have come to you directly, I know, only . . .' Svetov smiles. 'Your time is valuable . . . I recognise that. To have made you come all the way out here . . . we ought to recompense you for that. You and your men, that is.'

And he weighs the purse in his hand for a moment, before throwing it across the narrow stretch of water that now separates Svetov and the boat.

The young man catches it, like that's all he ever does, then opens the drawstrings and peeks inside. And is clearly pleased, from the nod he gives.

'Well,' he says, in a very businesslike manner. 'That makes things clear. We'll bother you no longer, gentlemen. I hope your searches don't prove to be in vain. A new hospital, eh?' And he turns, signalling to his men to come away, his expression as much as to say he doesn't believe a word.

I let out a long breath. We'll not be hearing from that direction again. Only the diversion has destroyed any attempt at secrecy. If Kolya is inside he will know now that we're out here, trying to get in. Even so, we decide to carry on, and when more than half the door is exposed, Svetov and Ernst draw their lasers and, setting up screens to shield the operation from common sight, start to cut out the lock to the trapdoor.

It's solid steel and takes a while, and we're not sure that we're still being watched or not from the trees on the far side of the river. If we are, then questions will be asked. The bright flare of the lasers, the smell . . . neither bears much explanation.

But suddenly we're there. The trapdoor sags, then falls away.

We aim our torches into the darkness below. Inside there's a tunnel leading down, with a ladder leading down to some steps.

Saratov, the youngest, goes first, slowly and silently. At the bottom he lifts his torch, looking about, then signals the all-clear.

We follow, down to the bottom of the steps where Saratov is to be found, standing in a massive doorway, staring inside with astonishment.

I stand beside him, then whistle, amazed by the sight that meets my eyes.

It's one massive space, like a giant hangar, and at its centre . . .

A massive transport. Some kind of spaceship by the look of it!

'The gods preserve us,' Svetov murmurs, shaking his head in disbelief. 'Is that what I think it is?'

Ernst merely laughs.

We go down the steps, then walk across, looking about us, expecting trouble at any moment – agents jumping in and lasers firing, only . . . the place is deserted, with only the sound of our boots ringing against the metallic floor breaching the silence. The wall cameras don't seem to be tracking us and the lighting seems to be emergency lighting.

Which can't be right, surely? I mean, why would Kolya have gone to all of this trouble merely to abandon it?

Or is it simply awaiting his return?

Or maybe we've already won. Maybe Kolya is dead, in another part of Time, and all of this is now abandoned. Anything is possible. Only I don't want to assume anything. And besides, I want to find Kolya alive so I can find out what he's done with my other daughters.

Doors lead off the massive hangar, and, in rooms surrounding it, we find all manner of things. There are supplies here for a small army, but there's no sign of life. Not anywhere. All of the high-tech communication technology is switched off and, it seems, has been for some while. When we try to get it running again, it shows no sign of being functional. Which is strange. Then again, all of the life-support systems are on automatic.

And all of this, of course, is one huge anachronism, for this is 1771, and there were no spaceships back in 1771. Not according to the history books. And that must mean something. Kolya must have had plans to use all of this for some purpose.

But what? Was he looking to get off-planet, where we couldn't possibly find him? Is that it?

The answer is, we simply don't know.

'Okay,' I say. 'Let's go back. See what the others make of this.'

And in my mind I'm thinking that maybe they could set the Great Men on this. See what they come up with. Only why should they make more sense of this than us? For I'm beginning to think that their greatness isn't as useful as we thought it might be. That maybe our field experience – in Time – might be worth one hell of a lot more than all their philosophy and physics. But I keep my thoughts to myself . . . as yet. Because maybe I'm wrong. Maybe they *will* come up with a solution or two. Only Time, as they say, will tell.

420

Only when we get back to Moscow Central, it's to find that Katerina has gone, following up on something an agent brought back for her. And that fazes me temporarily, because why should *she* be getting things from Time?

I ask Zarah to send me in after her at once, and find myself in a place I recognise, in Belyj, a town I once visited with Katerina on my long journey overland. This is where the smithy was – where I got the ash-leaf pendant for Katerina. But I sense that this is much later than that occasion, for things feel a lot different.

It's not a big place, but I can find no trace of Katerina, even though she jumped through only a minute before me. I go to the waterfront. There are slaves there, sleeping in the shade of one of the huts. There are also three boats moored there, their contents covered in crude tarpaulins. I'm about to climb on-board the first of them to search it, when three men emerge from one of the huts and confront me.

I can see from their attire and their weaponry that these are slavers. That wouldn't normally bother me, only I notice that one of them has one of the 'lazy-eight' pendants about his neck – those worn by Kolya's followers – and I wonder whether the man's a time traveller.

Whether they all are.

If so, then I'd have no advantage if it comes to a fight, not without me jumping out and jumping back with help. Only I want to know where Katerina has gone – whether, maybe, they've taken her – and so for once I'm direct, asking them in the local Russian dialect if they know where she is.

Only these, one of them tells me, are Thuringians, and when I ask again, in their tongue, where she is, they just laugh.

'She dead,' one of them says, in halting English. 'She *very* dead.'

Which I don't believe. I mean, why should they kill her?

No. I think that maybe they've ambushed her. Taken her hostage.

I make to jump out of there and jump back in a moment earlier, when someone – a child? – calls my name.

I turn sharply, to find – to my great shock – not just one of my daughters, but two, Natalya and Anna, slouched there, chained up with the slaves, clearly slaves themselves. Appalled, I take a step toward them, putting out my hand, as if to comfort them, even as one of the men brings a rock down on my head.

And wake, my head pounding, to find that I'm lying in the bottom of a boat, heading upriver.

I try to put my right hand to my chest, only both my hands are bound to a pole which runs beneath me. In fact, I'm trussed up like a turkey. I move my head the little that I can, trying to see who else is in the boat with me, only I can't. All I can see is the dirty sheet that's pulled taut above me.

I can hear the sound of the oars, however; feel the movement of the boat in the water, and know that there's someone just behind me. I can also smell tobacco, an anachronism in this age.

I lie back, relaxing, for a moment forgetting what I saw. And then it comes back to me.

I groan, in sudden agony, and as I do, a shadow falls over me, an upside-down face peering down at me. Bearded. Russian.

No, Thuringian, I remember.

'Not dead, then?' he says, and laughs.

I'd answer him, but my throat is too dry. The stranger speaks again, clearly amused.

'You want to know where you are and who we are, don't you?'

I manage something. A pained croak.

'Where is she?'

'Dead,' he says. 'We told you that. She stepped out, directly into the beam. Exactly as he said she would.'

I close my eyes, pained by it, *seeing* it in my mind's eye.

Kolya, I think. *It has to be. And now we both die, without any second chances.*

'Where are you taking me?'

'Upriver,' he answers me. And chuckles.

421

Two of them carry me ashore and place me in a dark, insanitary hut. Lying there, in the midst of that squalor, I wonder why no one has jumped in to check up on me, or why Zarah hasn't simply pulled me out of there. That'd be the normal process. So maybe my focus isn't functioning. Maybe it's been damaged or destroyed.

A long time passes. Voices come and go outside. Flies buzz about me.

This is the lowest I have ever sunk, and for perhaps the first time ever I wonder if I've been defeated. Only suddenly there are shouts and gunfire and screams. As silence falls, the door creaks open and, in the moonlight, someone crosses the hut and looks down at me.

With the light behind him and his face in shadow, I can't see who it is, but when I hear the voice, relief floods through me.

Ernst.

422

Outside, laid out like so many haunches of meat on the ground, are the strangers who kidnapped me, dead now, their lazy-eight pendants taken from them.

Ernst is quite distraught. He can't stop apologising to me for leaving things so long and cutting it so fine, but what he tells me makes good sense.

'Once we knew you were taken we followed closely, hoping to snare Kolya when he made his appearance. Only Kolya didn't show, and when we overheard those three discussing whether they should wait for the man or simply cut your throat, we decided to move in fast.'

And Katerina?

Katerina, it seems, is safe. She too was part of their plan to get Kolya and was wearing protective clothing against the laser. That and the shot she took to feign death fooled them totally.

'So you *used* me!' I say, not knowing whether to be pleased or angry with them.

Ernst grins. 'We knew you'd go in after her. In fact, that part of it was *her* suggestion.'

That stops me in my tracks. And then suddenly she's there, holding me, kissing my face and grinning, as ever making me feel that I'm the luckiest man in Time. I'm so relieved I forget to be angry with her. But then, suddenly, I remember something else.

'I saw them!' I say, my face a hand's breadth from hers. 'Natalya and Anna! We have to go back and get them!'

Katerina is shocked. 'They're here?'

'No. Back at Belyj, among the slaves.'

'Then what are we waiting for?'

And we jump. Katerina and I. Back to Moscow Central, then to Belyj. Back to the waterfront.

Only this time we jump back to a moment just before we last jumped in, so that we see, from our hidden viewpoint, an earlier Katerina jump in, directly into the laser cross-fire.

Stunned – they think dead – she drops to the ground and is quickly dragged into a nearby hut by one of the men, the others following a moment later.

We wait, and a minute later I jump in – or an earlier me – and we watch events unfold, from the emergence of the three men from the hut, to the sudden arrival of a fourth slaver, who creeps up on me while I'm distracted.

The sight of him bringing that rock down on my head makes me wince. They, meanwhile, bind me up and carry me onto the boat.

Three of them climb on board, leaving just one of them to guard the slaves.

When the boat has gone from view, Katerina and I make our way quickly across to where the slaves are. Creeping up on him,

I knock the guard unconscious, and as he falls Katerina jumps onto his back and lifts his head by the hair, meaning to slit his throat. But before she can, Natalya cries out to us – 'No, Mama! Not him! He was good to us. Made sure we ate. Kept us from being beaten.'

Katerina turns, staring at them, almost not recognising the two girls, in whose eyes tears are welling. They are dishevelled and dirty and underfed, and Katerina goes to them now, holding them to her, even as I start carefully laser-cutting their shackles from them. And then they're all free and we huddle together in a moment of purest joy and relief. My girls!

Grinning like a madman, I take two pendants from my pocket and slip them over my daughters' necks. Only, before they jump, Natalya stops them. 'No, Papa. We have to come back for them. For all the others. We can't leave them here.'

I want to object, to tell her that we can't be responsible for everyone, only a look in her eyes cuts me short.

'Promise me, Daddy,' she says, gripping my hands tightly. 'Promise me you'll return for them.'

I nod, and a smile appears on her face, like the sun coming out from behind the clouds, and we jump, back to Moscow Central, and a reunion with Irina.

423

Fresh from showering, I listen as Ernst and Svetov discuss the situation at Moscow Central.

There have been fresh and much more serious troubles between the two sets of time agents. It seems that a fight over a Russian woman has ended in the death of one of the German agents, the three Russians who killed him having fled into Time.

'We have traces on them,' Svetov says, 'if you want us to go in and take them captive.'

'Let me think about it, Arkadi.'

This is a major set-back. Not only has it caused fresh tensions, but it means, in all probability that Kolya has three new recruits. Up till now we've tracked down most of the rebel agents, accounting for all but eleven of the rebel Russians and six of the Germans. It isn't many, but with three more additions, that little core of resistance could prove a real thorn in our side, especially as so much manpower is being taken up searching Time for my daughters, as well as trying to track down Kolya himself.

Ernst lowers his head in that habitual way he has when he's about to suggest something awkward, then meets my eyes.

'You won't like this, Otto, but I want to make a suggestion . . .'

'Go on.'

'Well, it's just . . . now that three of your girls have been found – and praise be for that – we might just ease off a little and reallocate some of our manpower towards dealing with the rebels.'

'Wind it down, you mean?'

I don't mean to be hard on him. He's my best friend, after all. But I'm not about to ease off, not while two of my girls are still missing.

'No,' I say, and before Ernst can say another word, Svetov takes his arm and pulls him over to the corner of the room.

'You don't have children, do you, Ernst?'

'Not that I know of.'

'Then listen to one who has. If only one of my children remained missing, as Otto's girls are missing, then I would scour Time and Space to try and find them, using as many agents as I needed for the task. Which is to say, once we have located Martha and Zarah we'll deal with the rebels. But until then finding the girls remains our priority. Do you understand, dear friend?'

Ernst nods, but I can see there's still part of him that wants to contest the decision. But that's how Ernst is. Tactical.

When Ernst is gone, I thank my Russian friend. 'You speak as if you have experience,' I say, and notice how a cloud crosses Svetov's face. 'You say you had children.'

'I did . . .'

'And?'

'You Germans took them.'

I stare at him, stunned.

'Oh, I'm not blaming you, Otto. That was how it was. But that's why I'm doing what I'm doing now. To change things.'

I study the big man a moment, seeing him in a totally different light. 'Would you like to share a beer, Arkadi?'

And he smiles. Back to the man I've come to know. My enemy turned friend.

'That would be good, Otto. That would be very good indeed.'

424

I wake with a start, from a dream I do not want to remember. The room is dark, and as I lie there, letting my pulse cease racing, I hear it.

Katerina is to my right in the darkness, a warm presence there beside me, the sound of her breathing soft yet strong, and, just beyond her, softer still, I can hear the breathing of my daughters.

I lie there a while, my eyes closed, listening to the gentle symphony of their intermingled breaths, the sound of them, alive and safe, there in the dark, close by, then let out a long sigh, as the topic of my talk with Svetov last night comes back to me.

Finding Katerina and the first three of my girls has been all too easy. And it's not just me who thinks that. Svetov thinks it too. And others. Like me, they think that Kolya would not have discarded such valuable 'cards', such precious hostages, unless he had some greater, nastier scheme.

Svetov thinks that the very manner in which Kolya has distributed them, as prisoners and slaves, suggests that he wants to play on my imagination and, perhaps, draw me further in – into a trap of some kind. But that's mere hypothesis. Who knows what's in Kolya's twisted mind?

Quietly, careful not to wake them, I get up and slip from the room, pausing briefly, allowing myself to glimpse them, their sleeping forms framed in the narrow rectangle of light from the corridor, before going to join the others for breakfast.

Ernst is there already, seated at the breakfast table, which comfortably holds ten, along with Zarah and Saratov. There's no sign of Svetov, but that's unsurprising. My guess is that he's sleeping it off. And no surprise there, for he must have drunk three times what I consumed last night.

'How's your head?' Zarah asks, a faint, understanding smile on her lips.

'Fine,' I say, reaching for the coffee jug.

'I would have joined you,' Ernst says, looking at me from over his steaming cup, 'only something came up. I thought I should deal with it.'

I wait, expecting more, but Ernst, it seems, is done. Nor does Zarah – who, as platform controller, must know what it was – take the matter up.

I let it pass. 'Have you thought any more about our friends? The think tank, I mean . . . Is that producing anything worthwhile?

And, more to the point, is it causing any damage back there in the past?'

Zarah looks to Ernst, as if something's already been said between them on this matter, then shrugs.

'It's hard to say. Some of the things they've come up with are pure genius. But there do seem to be side effects.'

'Yes?'

Ernst sets his cup down. 'We've only just started investigating the matter, but . . . it does look like there's some kind of universal balancing act going on. Being here, in the future, has undeniably resulted in some real scientific breakthroughs, but probably not as many – or as great – as we hoped for. At the same time, there's no doubting that the fact that their absence from the past – in their specific places in Time – has slowed down scientific and social progress. Almost to a halt in some of the worlds we've studied.'

'But that's reversible, yes?'

Zarah answers me. 'It is. Providing that we slip them back into the timestream at precisely the point where we took them from. Which we can, in the blink of an eye.'

Yes, I think. *And they'll not recall a moment of their little adventure.*

Ernst looks to me. 'Are you beginning to question what we did, then, Otto?'

'It's been playing on my mind, yes. Just that the idea for this was wholly Gehlen's. That he was the one who set the rules and chose who was to be taken from the timestream. And then, what with what he did next . . . trying to suffocate us all . . .'

'D'you think Reichenau was behind it, Otto?'

'It's possible, don't you think? Or even Kolya . . .'

I'm about to say why I think that's possible, when Saratov comes into the room, holding young Natalya by the hand. Seeing me, she runs across and hugs me, spilling my coffee.

'She was wandering the corridors,' Saratov explains, 'looking for you.'

'Well, now she's found me,' I say, and, grinning from ear to ear, I pull her up onto my lap.

She's clean now and wearing fresh clothes, and for a moment she presses in against me as if she'll never ever let go again. But then she looks at me.

'I wanted to remind you, Dada.'

'Remind me?'

'Of your promise. You said you'd free them.'

'I did, didn't I?' I look to Zarah. 'I promised her . . .'

'I know,' Zarah says, getting to her feet, even as one of the kitchen staff comes over to wipe the spillage. 'It's all organised. As soon as you're ready you can go in.'

'And Katerina and the girls? Can they witness this?'

'They'd best wait here, by the platform, where we can protect them. Just that bringing five bodies through might prove problematic, what with Kolya's possible intervention.'

'You think that's likely?'

'They were wearing lazy-eight pendants, remember? As to whether that makes them Reichenau's men, or Kolya's, we don't rightly know, only that it's possibly the latter, and we need to make sure it's not a trap of some kind or that they don't penetrate our defences.'

I give a little bow to her, impressed as ever by her preparedness, then look to my daughter. 'Natalya. Go fetch Mummy and the girls. Uncle Saratov will take you there, and then we'll bring your friends back here.'

She kisses me. A big wet sloppy kiss, then jumps off my lap, going to Saratov and taking his hand. He nods to me and smiles, and then they've gone.

I turn back to Zarah.

'What precautions are you taking at the platform?'

'We'll have a dozen of our best sharpshooters in position. That's separate from the team we're sending in.'

It makes sense. Even if we're over-reacting, the fact that Kolya had men in there should make us extra careful. Because from what we're learning of him, Kolya is never predictable.

I allow fifteen minutes, then go to the platform, where Katerina and the girls meet me. Our men are already in position, the team ready to go through, and I lead the way, jumping through onto the waterfront, expecting . . .?

Expecting it all to be gone, frankly. Because that's Kolya's way. He's a regular vanishing act. Only it's exactly as it was, and, having dealt with the solitary remaining guard (gently, because Natalya insisted) I free the five remaining slaves and, once they've all got time pendants about their necks, jump back.

The slaves are all Danes, two young boys aged eleven and thirteen, a young woman of twenty and two men in their mid-twenties. None of them are related, though the woman and one of the men hail from the same village. They're clearly bemused by what has happened and consider me a great sorcerer. They kneel before me, bowing their heads almost to the ground, but I tell them, haltingly, in their own tongue, that they are free now and that rooms and clothes and food will be provided.

Meeting them, seeing their all-too-human reactions, I am moved, more than I care to admit. Freeing them makes me feel that I have done something good, something *positive* in the world.

Sitting Natalya down, I ask her about her experiences, and learn that she and Anna were captive for two whole months. The simple thought of it appals me and makes me want to change it, only Natalya won't let me.

'It's part of me now,' she says. 'It made me grow up, Papa. Don't change it. What good is experience if you can change it at will? I want to remember how it felt. No, more than that . . . I *need* to remember.'

I am awed by her words. It makes me challenge everything I have ever done in my life.

What good is experience if you can change it at will?

It's a big question for someone like me who *can*. Aside from which, I am used to solving problems with a gun. So this . . .

This is a revelation to me. An epiphany. An opening of eyes.

425

But there is still Kolya to contend with, and, just as we think we might have lost him for ever, one of our agents comes back, dishevelled and breathless, to report that he has seen Kolya, or, if not, one of his ancestors who looks very much like Kolya. Only Katerina and I would know for sure. Katerina is keen to pursue him, but I am not so sure. I don't intend to dash in madly after my adversary. Not this once. No. I am convinced that this is a trap. And besides, I have another plan.

I am going to send in Schikaneder.

We bring the exiled agent back from his bolt-hole in nineteenth-century Prague, to Moscow Central. Schikaneder is shocked that peace has been made between Germany and Russia. Shocked yet delighted, because this is what he's wanted all along.

Alone with him in Yastreyeb's old rooms, I offer him a 'deal'. Either he goes in and reports back or he'll be incarcerated permanently.

Schikaneder really doesn't want to go. He trembles at the thought of encountering Kolya again. But he has no option. For once I am intractable. If he ever wants to see his cosy rooms in Prague again, then he has to help us.

He begs and pleads, but finally he agrees. Only what he doesn't know is that I am giving him just two days to find Kolya and confirm it's him. After two days we'll pull him out of there, whatever happens.

426

While Schikaneder is inside, I decide to jump back and visit Albrecht Hecht in the Haven. With a little time on my side, I have decided to see whether there *are* any records of Kolya's activities in Time.

Only it's a very sombre Albrecht that greets me on the mountain slope, and it is very quickly obvious to me that, now that his brother is dead and the Neanderthal community dispersed, he is finding his solitary life in the deep past very hard to take. Duty alone is keeping him here.

'You shouldn't have let them come here,' he says, as he taps in the password and stands back.

He means the Great Men, their '*manus*', but I tell him that had nothing to do with me.

'But you're the Meister, Otto. One word from you . . .'

'It's not like that,' I interrupt, 'it's all *veche* and committees and . . . the days of the Meister deciding everything have gone. They died with your brother's death, and Yastryeb's.'

'I see.'

We go inside, into that massive storeroom of alternatives.

'So what do you want, Otto?'

'I want to find Kolya,' I say. 'He must be somewhere here. He can't have erased all traces of himself from everywhere. It isn't possible.'

'Maybe not,' Albrecht answers. But he has a thoughtful look about him, as if there might be a way.

For the next ten hours we pursue the man, starting with what we know and making guesses as to where he might have gone. Only it's heavy-going and even after a full day's work, we've made no progress whatsoever.

I want to bring in help, but Albrecht is against that. He's almost paranoid about keeping the Haven's secrets – especially its location – to as few people as possible. He doesn't like the idea of its existence becoming common knowledge, and, after a heated discussion, I agree that I will return alone, then jump back to Moscow Central.

427

In the brief time that I've been gone – in what's less than half an hour subjective – a great deal has happened.

Poor Schikaneder has been 'returned' to the platform, dead, stripped naked, his body bearing identical scars to those inflicted on the young Teuton knight, Brother Werner, his corpse laid out like a star, his fingers and his feet cut off, his chest opened up with an axe. His eyes have been gouged out and his ears cut off, his tongue cut from his mouth. Finally, they have carved the sign of the cross into his crudely shaven skull.

There is no mistaking Kolya's message. He means to wipe out Moscow Central, the same way he destroyed the Teuton Knights' fort.

Or so I believe. Only how will Kolya manage that?

Moscow Central can 'filter' anything coming through to the platform – preventing bombs and other, similar threats – and, if our calculations are correct, we outnumber Kolya and his brothers by a factor of eight to one. Even if Kolya has 'access' to the platform, which isn't a certainty, he can only jump a few men through at a time.

I'm taking this very seriously. Responding to his threat, I summon Zarah and have her bring all of our agents home to Moscow Central. Then, while some of them guard the platform – here and in the recent past – I address the rest, outlining my fears.

Only Svetov isn't convinced, and when our agents have been sent back, he takes me aside.

'I think you're wrong, Otto. I think you might be showing Kolya far too much respect. If he *is* spread thin, then what better than to use our fear *against* us. He is a master of misinformation, after all, and it would suit his purpose, surely, to make us think he knows more than he does or is more capable than he actually is? He's only a single man, after all.'

I tell him that might be so; that I might, indeed, be attributing too much to the man, only in my own mind I'm fairly certain As much as I loathe the bastard, he deserves respect. In my estimation, Kolya, much more than me, is the true Master of Time.

428

Leaving Svetov in charge, and with strict instructions to maintain only a defensive strategy, I jump back to the Haven.

Albrecht greets me, in a much better mood than last time, announcing that he's found something.

Though I've been gone, subjectively, only an hour, two weeks have passed here in the Haven and Albrecht has barely slept in his quest to unearth some small clue to Kolya's history.

He takes me inside and shows me what he's found – several entries in the history of a close-matched alternative world. The very same world, it turns out, that I was trapped inside. The world where Phil Dick became president. Either that or a world very much like it.

I read the entries, then nod to myself.

Of course . . .

And, thanking Albrecht, I jump . . . back to Moscow Central.

Back there, nothing's happened, and the very fact that nothing's happened is fraying our agents' nerves. Those guarding the platform are getting jumpy, and many of them are deeply unhappy with my passive stance. They want to get out there in Time and do what they're good at – locating Kolya. Only I know that we'd never find him.

Yes, and I also know that Kolya will have to come to us – eventually. He won't be able not to.

Only what finally comes back is quite horrifying. I'm there when it happens, the platform shimmering briefly as something arrives.

It's a child's hand, severed at the wrist and clutching a hand-written note. As before, I send an agent back at once to the time-coordinates from which it came, but we find nothing. Drawn on the note is a map and four words, in Kolya's handwriting.

'*Come and get me.*'

We quickly run DNA tests on the hand and, to our horror, find it belongs to baby Zarah.

Katerina, deeply anxious, wants to go in at once and find her, only I know this will be a trap, and for once everyone agrees. If Katerina and I go in, we'll die.

I begin to say this to Svetov, only as I do so I stop dead, realising what I've said, knowing that I *must* have died – that it's all part of the greater loop we're in.

'This is it!' I say. 'This is where we do it, Katerina and I!'

Svetov doesn't know what I'm talking about, but I turn to Katerina and, taking her hands, ask her the most difficult question I've ever had to ask.

'Are you ready to die, my love? To die so we might live?'

429

And so, four hours later, we are back at the platform, preparing to go in, the platform crowded with well-wishers, everyone conscious of the huge significance of this moment.

Kolya's hand-drawn map has been analysed and, together with an analysis of the coordinates from which it came, we now know when and where we are jumping to – to the winter of 1239 and to a small village just to the north-west of Moscow called Himki, eleven miles from . . .

. . . Krasnogorsk.

I know this and am nervous and afraid. What lies ahead is like every last bad dream you could possibly have had. If we fail then we really will be dead, for Katerina and I have both seen this. Leaving strict instructions, we jump in six hours earlier than the moment that the note was sent through, and, taking up a hidden position, we settle in and wait.

Sure enough, six hours later, a figure appears briefly in the clearing, holding something. There's a distortion of light surrounding the stranger's hand, as if all of the photons are being sucked into a tiny black hole, and then the figure vanishes. A moment later our agent jumps through, looks about him, then jumps out again.

A full two minutes pass, and then Katerina and I jump into the clearing and move across to crouch beneath the trees, looking back and waiting.

Thirty seconds later another Otto and Katerina jump in and, joining the others, turn away, following the path beneath the trees.

We wait, watching our counterparts move out of sight, then jump out of there, back to Moscow Central. The team there – Svetov and Ernst, Master Schnorr, Zarah, Urte and Saratov – look concerned, but I am grinning.

'It worked! It *must* have! Otherwise how did the second couple get there?'

But none of the others share my confidence.

'We can still withdraw,' Master Schnorr says. 'Pull them out and abandon this.'

But I'm determined. 'No,' I say. 'You can't. Not until we've gone in there, *twice*.'

And, looking to Katerina, taking her hands, we jump back in, becoming the first pair that we saw jumping through earlier.

It's from that new position that we now witness the second couple of Katerina and I jump in, not ten metres from where we stand. And as they do, so I feel my stomach tighten. Because they are the ones who will live. That's right. *We* are the ones who will die, this 'version' of ourselves. *We* are the ones who we have already seen, our naked corpses lain on their backs on that monster's cart, and as we make our silent way along the path that leads to Himki, I can't help but feel afraid, both for me and for my darling Katerina. For it has begun. From this moment on, Fate has us in its vice-like grip. Here, on the path to Krasnogorsk.

Like a madman with a razor in his hand . . .

Make no mistake. Both she and I are terrified. For even if we survive this duplication in Time, we will still have died, will still have suffered the pain and awful finality of death. Yes, and it's the not knowing how or in what circumstances that really frightens me. It's the fact that he – Kolya – is in control here, and not me.

Walking along beside myself I feel a prisoner in my own body. I am, quite literally, beside myself; a puppet in the hands of a puppet master.

The village is close by now. Stopping, we turn to face each other, embracing one last time, then watch as our other selves hasten away, to secrete themselves and see what happens next.

Through my eyes but not through my eyes.

And so, alone and unarmed, we walk into the centre of Himki.

It's a small, shabby town, and as we enter the central square, a wasteland of dust and animal droppings, so people come out to stare, their expressions sullen, mocking, as if they know what is about to happen here.

I grip Katerina's hand tightly, talking to her quietly all the while, reassuring her, only she seems less afraid than me. As we stop, so she turns and looks to me, her beautiful dark eyes smiling at me one last time, and I feel both blessed and cursed.

'If I must die to win them back, then so be it. But *he* will never have them.'

It is a brave utterance. But how true it is, I fear to discover.

Across from us is an old, Orthodox church, a big wooden building with a rudimentary cupola, the blue paint flaking from the tiles. The big double doors are closed, yet, as we stand before it, the old bell begins to sound and people gather, as if for an execution.

As yet there is no sign of Kolya or his helpers, nor of the cart. For a time we wait, then I push the doors wide open and step inside. I look around in the intense gloom, then focus on what lies there beneath the altar . . .

And cry out, my heart torn from me, for there is my darling Zarah, as pale as death, spread out in that familiar star shape before the cold stone altarpiece, a bloodied axe beside her.

Until that moment I had been content to die, simply to fulfil the circumstances of the loop, but now I want revenge. To tear Kolya limb from limb.

Katerina, coming alongside, sees it too and falls to her knees. 'Oh, dear God . . .'

The bell still rings. With a start I realise that if it's ringing, then someone must be sounding it.

I run across and am almost halfway up the stairs when the church doors are pushed open wider. Two seconds pass, three . . . and then a figure steps out into the light, and even in silhouette, I know who it is.

Kolya!

With a bellow of rage, I hurl myself down the stairs, jumping them three at a time, snarling, desperate to get to him, yet even as I'm jumping through the air, my hands grasping for him, he shimmers and is gone.

430

I reappear, sprawled on my face at Moscow Central, Katerina on her knees beside me, gasping.

Scrambling up, I look about me for answers. It's Svetov who provides them.

'We had to pull you out.'

Remembering the sight of baby Zarah, lying there dead beneath the altar, I groan.

'Why?'

'Because you were wrong. We had Moseley and his team look at it and they all agreed. Your second selves could survive, yes, but only at the price of staying in the loop. They'd be trapped there, because as soon as they came out, they'd have to go straight back in, simply to be there – to be alive at all.'

'But now?'

'Two of you are still in there. They'll jump out and jump back in, and this time they *will* die.'

'But surely they have to survive so that they can jump back in again and be there in the first place?'

Moseley, who's there in the crowd, answers me.

'That's true, and after a while the physics of it break down. The timeline stretches to its limit and ends and – bang! – it's erased, to the point where they jump in in the first place and act merely as observers.'

'But how can that be?'

'Because of the nature of the universe. Because both states exist alongside one another – them dying and them jumping in – the two states perpetually alternating, one after another for eternity.'

'But we see ourselves, dead on the cart.'

'That's right. You do. Just before that timeline ends. Before it's erased. Remember what happened? You were pulled out of there, remember?'

'And Katerina? The Katerina I left there, at Krasnogorsk?'

'She must have vanished, along with the rest of it.'

'And us?' Katerina asks. 'Us *now*, I mean.'

'You two are safe now. Outside the loop. Alive. But we almost had the wrong two killed, Otto. We almost messed up!'

431

Alone, I brood on what has happened. I feel numb, devastated by Zarah's fate. Her death has shocked me profoundly. Katerina, unable to cope, has taken to her bed, leaving me to tell the other girls – if I can. Only I don't think I *can*.

I ought to feel rage, only I don't. It's as if all of my anger has been replaced by a sense of utter futility. I can't even cry, I feel so numb. Only suddenly I realise something. If I'm out of the loop, then I can go back in. Not to save myself, but maybe to save my baby daughter.

To change things.

I run to the platform, arriving breathless, even as Alena – Zarah's Russian counterpart – comes across.

'Otto? What is it?'

'I have to go back in. Back to Himki.'

'But you can't—'

'I have to. I can save her. Little Zarah. I can get her back.'

Alena wants to call the others and discuss it, only I'm sick to death of discussing things. In the end I order her to send me back two days earlier than before.

Sighing, Alena shakes her head, then, gesturing for me to get onto the platform, sends me back.

432

I stay off the path, making my way around that godforsaken town, keeping among the trees that surround it, then come in from the north, using all of my skills not to be seen. There's a hill to the east of the town and I position myself there, looking down on all the comings and goings. I wait throughout the long day and, eventually, just before nightfall, my patience pays off. I see Kolya walk into town along the path, his two young assistants pulling an empty cart.

While I've been waiting, I've been trying to work out what to do. The Otto and Katerina who are in this timeline have to die, because I have to see them at Krasnogorsk, on the cart. But what about baby Zarah?

Asking that question direct, it makes me realise something. Something we've overlooked. There was no sign of Zarah in the cart. Katerina, yes, me, yes, but no sign of *her*. Kolya doesn't seem to have her with him. Is she therefore in the church already?

I jump back to Moscow Central, then get Alena to send me back in, this time *inside* the church, an hour earlier. And back in I go, to find the church in almost total darkness, the windows barred, the big front doors locked. Confident that I won't be seen from outside, I light a lamp and walk over to the altar.

And there she is.

I kneel beside her, my heart breaking once again, yet when I lift her severed wrist to see how it's been cauterised I realise she isn't cold; that she's drugged, in fact, not dead! And with that, hope blossoms inside me. I jump out, then jump back in, almost immediately, clutching one of the time pendants on a necklace. Gently lifting her head I slip it on, then tuck it within the collar of her smock dress to keep it from sight.

For a moment longer I kneel there, drinking in the sight of her, then, bending close, I gently kiss her brow.

'*Daddy will come for you.*'

And then I'm gone. Vanished from the air.

433

Only this time there is a welcoming committee awaiting me when I get back: Saratov and Ernst, Zarah and Urte and Katerina, Svetov and Master Schnorr, among others. They are angry with me for having acted unilaterally once again.

I try and explain why I did it, and Katerina, having heard about baby Zarah, is placated, but the others want me to stick to my word and consult them in future.

I say I will, then spell out what *I* think we should do.

To begin with, we need to keep watch – see what we can see – then jump in and rescue Zarah. That's our number-one priority. But that's not all. I need to know *how* I die, and what Kolya says and does, because that will give us a clue to his behaviour, and that, I feel, is vital.

'But we know why,' Katerina says. 'You lost him an empire.'

'No,' I say. 'We all did that. It was our job. But why hate *me* for it?'

Only there's no answer to that. His hatred seems irrational, the product of some imbalance in his nature, some mental instability, like a black cloud blowing from the arctic north.

Or so it seems.

Yes, and one thing more. We need to find out where Martha's being kept. Because I won't rest until I have her back. Until we're a family again, complete and whole.

But first Zarah. First Krasnogorsk and all that follows on.

434

I make my brief preparations then go to the platform, keen to jump back in. Only Alena is there again, in charge of the platform, and this time she will not budge. I'm going nowhere without the permission of the *veche*. She even has written orders to that effect!

Furious, I go and confront them, finding them in the main conference hall, looking at charts and maps.

'What in Urd's name is happening?'

'We're going to make another push, Otto,' Svetov says, coming across, his whole manner conciliatory. 'Against Kolya.'

'But I'm Master. Why wasn't I told?'

Svetov puts a hand on my arm. 'We were going to, Otto. We were just working out the details before presenting it to you.'

'And what if I said no?'

Svetov looks about him, then shrugs. 'Then of course we'd take no action. But that won't happen. These are measures *you* suggested, Otto. We're merely putting flesh on the bones.'

Flesh on bones. I shake my head angrily. First they harass me at the platform, then they meet behind my back to formulate policy!

'For Urd's sake, Arkadi! Who's Meister here?'

Svetov huffs, exasperated now. 'Why do you make it so difficult, Otto? You're Master, fine . . . only you don't *act* like you're Master! You act like you're still only an agent, and an irresponsible one at that! Kolya is running rings about us, and why? Because you react to everything he does. And the one time you didn't react – when he sent back Schikaneder's corpse – was the one time you *should* have acted!'

'And what ought I to have done?' I ask, squaring up to him.

'You should have hit him hard,' Ernst says, pushing in between us. 'At every point along his ancestral line. You should have made the bastard sweat. Made him move his pieces 'round the board!'

'And what if that failed? What if, in the meantime, he hit back at us, right here at Moscow Central? What then?'

'It looks like he could do that anyway,' Zarah says. 'Any time he wants.'

I'm silent a moment. Then: 'Is that what you think? What you *really* think? Then let's surrender to him right now. Let's make *him* Master!' I pause. 'The way I see it, I'm alive. I've come through the loop and, though I died, I'm still here, fighting back. And my little girl is there, in that church, a time pendant about her neck, ready to be carried out of there. But first I want to find out what he's thinking. What he's got planned . . . yes, and why he hates me so much. If I can get answers there, then, well, maybe we can formulate some coherent plan of action. But now's not the moment for what you're suggesting.'

They turn away from me, debating what I've said, their voices low, for their ears only. And then Svetov turns to me again.

'Okay. But this is the last time, Otto. The very last time. If you mess up this time we do it our way. Agreed?'

'Agreed.'

And so I'm there again, hidden from sight on the wooded hillside overlooking Himki, even as Kolya and his two assistants walk into view with their empty cart.

My mouth is dry. It's these three and that cart – only with my and Katerina's bodies on it – that I first saw, long ago, in Krasnogorsk, when I was a prisoner of Nevsky's. Yes, and what I am finally about to witness is mine and Katerina's deaths.

Only . . . Svetov has pulled me out of there, and my other self (and Katerina's, too) are not in the church but are looking on. I don't even know where they are at that moment, only that they, like me, are watching as events unfold below us.

And suddenly I get a very wrong feeling about everything. I know that the Otto and Katerina that are watching are not expecting to die, merely to observe, and if they're threatened they might just jump straight out of there.

So just how is Kolya going to kill them?

The thought has just entered my head when I see another Otto and Katerina approaching the church, not a hundred yards from where I am. They go inside and, though I cannot hear the groan of their discovery – of little Zarah lying there 'dead' on the altar stone – I know what's happening.

The old, discordant bell starts ringing loudly, but I am watching Kolya closely as he walks across to the church and, after a moment's dramatic pause, throws the doors wide open.

As Kolya steps inside, there is a bellow of rage . . . and then silence. And I know – because it's in the loop – that the Otto and Katerina who were in the church have been pulled back to Moscow Central.

And all the while the old bell rings.

I wait, wondering what will happen next, then see Kolya emerge from within, carrying Zarah limply in his arms. As the two young men bring up the cart, Kolya throws her down onto the sacking like she's barely worth considering.

The sight of it inflames me. I want to kill the man, and could, only I know we must wait and watch.

I cannot act. Not yet.

Craning my head, I look for a sight of my other self, and suddenly see him slipping between the houses stealthily, making his way over to the church. And even as Kolya is busy giving his assistants instructions, my other self slips into the darkness of the church.

Kolya straightens, as if somebody has spoken into his ear, then nods.

He turns, smiling now, and walks back across.

I am about to go down, to try and get a better view of things and maybe even overhear what's happening in there, when Katerina suddenly appears beside me.

'I thought it was you,' she says and smiles at me, taking my hands.

I'm confused. 'Were you here already?'

She nods, and again my mouth goes dry. How do I tell her that she has to join my other self in the church? That she *has* to die?

'What happened?' she asks. 'What was it he threw on the cart?'

Only I can't answer her.

'Look,' I say. 'You have to go down there. There's been a change of plan.'

'Down there? But . . .'

I pull her to me, kissing her gently. 'They pulled us out,' I explain. 'We . . . weren't the ones.'

Katerina's lips part, as if she's about to say something, then she stops, her eyes shocked.

'Then it's *us*?'

'I'm sorry . . .'

For a moment I close my eyes, savouring her touch, the warm, sweet scent of her. And for that moment it seems impossible that I will ever let her go. Only I must.

I release her.

Her eyes hold mine for an instant longer. Those same eyes I fell in love with, half a lifetime ago.

'I love you, Otto. I always will.'

And then she's gone.

In agony now, I follow, making my way down through the trees and out among the shabby-looking houses. And there, suddenly, before me is the church.

The bell stops, the sudden silence haunting. I count the seconds and then there's a gunshot, and then a second. My heart is in my mouth.

Is that it? Are we dead? For an instant I think I'm going to vanish, to shimmer into nothingness, only I'm still here. Still in the loop.

Carefully, I peer round the side of the building, toward the doorway. The crowd of villagers is still there, surrounding the empty cart.

For a moment there is nothing. A moment that becomes a full minute, and then Kolya steps out into the daylight.

'Ilyusha! Malya!' he calls. 'Come! Get them onto the cart!'

At his order the two young men come into view, hurrying to do Kolya's bidding. I watch them drag my corpse by the legs, out of the church and through the dirt, swinging me up onto the cart beside Zarah's infant figure. I swallow drily as they go back, then reappear, dragging my darling girl between them, swinging her as before, once, twice and third time up onto the cart, grunting with the effort.

It's a sight I can barely face, and yet I force myself to look.

And all the while this is happening, Kolya has his back to me. He stands there, watching, relaxed, or so it seems, smoking a thin cigar.

Now that the bodies are on the cart, Kolya is ready to leave. He stubs out his cigar, then walks across and, with an insolence that almost breaks my resolve, he leans over Katerina and plants a kiss upon her cold, dead lips.

435

I slump against the wall of the church, my back to it, my eyes closed.

Kolya has gone, and I too should have gone – back to Moscow Central – only there's one last thing to do. I have to get Zarah back.

Only I keep seeing, in my mind's eye, the two bodies being dragged through the dirt . . . and that final, awful kiss.

Staggering up, I lean forward and am violently sick. I know I ought to go back and rest before returning – that time is on my side in that regard – only I don't think I could face anyone just yet.

And besides, there's Zarah to bring home.

Some of the locals have noticed me by now. They come closer, staring and pointing at me, but I ignore them. Wiping my mouth, I push through them aggressively, hurrying to catch up with Kolya.

I know where he's heading – west to Krasnogorsk – but I know I'll simply get lost unless I follow close, keeping them in sight. They can't travel fast, not with the cart slowing them down, and it's only minutes before I spot them, directly ahead of me, through the trees. Keeping well back, I trail them, using all of my skill not to be seen. But what's strange is Kolya's coolness, his apparent lack of concern that he might be being followed. Or is that part of his scheme? Does he *know* I'm following him?

All that I know is this. That when the cart arrives at Krasnogorsk, only two bodies – mine and Katerina's – will be on it. There was no sign of a child's body on the cart first time out. But then, from nowhere, another thought strikes me. If I was wrong about baby Zarah, then maybe I was wrong about the other bodies. Maybe they *weren't* corpses, after all, but were drugged the same way Zarah was drugged.

Only why would Kolya do that?

Besides, I heard the shots and saw the bodies. And there was not enough time between the shots and the appearance of the bodies for drugs to have taken effect. Not only that but Kolya wanted me dead. I've seen the hatred in the man's eyes.

For the next three hours I keep my distance, looking about me from time to time, fearing an ambush. Then Kolya stops and the tiny group have a rest.

I decide that it's time to make my move.

Only when I get closer I am dismayed to see no sign of Zarah's tiny body on the cart. Has Kolya discarded her on the way? He must have, and yet I would have seen that, surely? I work my way closer, until I've got a clear view of the cart.

No. There's no sign of her at all.

Swallowing hard, hoping I've not lost her for good, I jump back to Moscow Central.

436

Katerina and the others are waiting for me. They want to know what happened, but I'm insistent that they send me straight back in. To Zarah, wherever she might be.

Alena doesn't want to. There are risks. I look to Svetov pleadingly and he nods, and so in I go again, to find myself among the trees, just outside of Himki, beside a tiny stream, in which my darling baby girl lies, face down.

I cry out, then stumble across, kneeling to lift her up. Cradling her to me, my heart is rent by how cold she is. She's blue around her lips and her body's still, no sign of life in her. I groan, then, knowing what I must do, set her tiny body down and jump to Moscow Central.

And in an instant I am back, only two hours earlier this time, hidden from watching eyes, there on the turn of the path, beside the stream, even as we hear the cart trundling closer down the path to my right.

I duck down, watching as Kolya stops the cart, then, picking up Zarah's body by one arm, throws her, like a piece of rubbish, into the stream, where she lies perfectly still.

Watching from hiding, I am filled with anxiety. Anxiety and a profound hatred. I want to kill Kolya there and then, to tear the cunt apart limb from limb. But I also want to save my child and know I have only a minute or so to do so.

Only I can't.

Kolya stands there, then lights up one of his small cigars and takes a long draw from it, a self-satisfied smile on his lips, almost as if he knows I'm out there looking on. And maybe he does.

The waiting is almost too much for me to endure, but then Kolya flicks away the partly smoked cigar and, turning his back, walks off into the trees.

I wait for a twenty count, fearing that he'll turn back, then rush across, lifting her up out of the water, and jump, knowing her best hope is back at Moscow Central.

437

There is a long, agonising wait, and then news comes. Zarah will live.

The relief I feel outweighs all else. Yet there is still one of my girls – Martha, at five the second youngest – missing. Is she, as Zarah was, back in Kolya's un-tender care? Or did Reichenau still have her? Whichever, I sense that getting her back will be the hardest task of all.

But I have other things to attend to. Svetov and the others have finalised the details of their planned campaign against Kolya, and they want to present me with the scheme.

'Why these points?' I ask, intrigued by the specifics of it.

'Because those are where he's weakest,' Old Schnorr answers, leaning toward me as he does. 'Elsewhere his ancestors are surrounded by family. They're a big, strong, healthy clan for the main part. But in places the genetic connection is slender. In places the family almost dies out. Single children to elderly parents and things like that.'

'Go on . . .'

'One other thing,' the old man says, grinning now. 'We've charted the bastard's DNA.'

Knowing how careful Kolya is, how he tends to recover every 'brother' that he loses, I'm shocked by this news.

'*How?*'

'We took samples from a whole range of his relatives, both distant and otherwise. Brothers and cousins. Partners from outside the central core.'

'And?'

'And we filled in the blanks – worked out what ought to be there – and then ran a computer reconstruct. Have a look.'

And Master Schnorr gives me an almost photograph-quality picture of a man who is undoubtedly Kolya, especially the eyes.

'Okay. That's great. But what use is it?'

It's young Moseley who answers. 'We're working on special antibodies. What you might term bacteriological toxins. Things that are harmless to us, but would be deadly to him.'

'And how do we pass these on?'

Ernst smiles. 'That's where you come in, Otto. We're sending you to Krasnogorsk, Otto. All you have to do is breathe on him.'

Only I know, instinctively, that it's never going to be that easy.

438

While they're busy preparing things, I see my girls who are 'camped out' in the care-room where baby Zarah is being kept.

The 'room' is kept isolated from the rest of Moscow Central, two full-sized air-locks making sure that no harmful bacteria spread through the *nichtraum*.

Inside is a room I know well. I have been here often, over the years. It is always as big as it needs to be: never too large, never too small, constantly adapting to its usage.

Urte is in charge of the nurses, and I see at a glance that she's set up a big king-sized double bed for Katerina and the girls, right up alongside Zarah's cot.

They don't notice me at first, but then Anna does. She squeals with excitement. 'Daddy!'

It's the signal for the three girls to rush across and cling on to me, giving me hugs and kisses, encouraging each other in their enthusiasm. I laugh, delighted, and look past them towards Katerina, who looks on, a loving kindness in her eyes.

Despite showering and their new clothes, my girls look a ragamuffin crew, far too thin, all of them hardened by their experiences. *Changed*.

A regular wolf pack, they've become. Fierce and wild.

The three of them clinging to me, I carry them across and plump myself down on the bed beside Katerina, my arm about her shoulders, kissing her tenderly, even as the girls cling ever closer to the two of us.

'How is she?' I ask.

'Okay . . . they say she'll live.'

Young Zarah looks deathly pale still, lying there in her cot. For now they are keeping her in an induced coma until the toxins have cleared themselves from her system, which could be days yet.

As if on cue, Consultant Bauer comes over. He's a tall, studious-looking man of fifty-plus years, with a patch over his left eye. It's something he could easily have repaired, but he's rather proud of it.

Standing beside the cot, he puts a hand down to feel young Zarah's brow.

I know Kurt Bauer well. He was a good time agent in his day, and an even better surgeon. He has brought me back from the dead three times, not to speak of the dozen or so times he has put me back together again.

298

'She's doing very well, considering,' he says, smiling down at the pale shape of my daughter. 'She was very weak. I don't think she was fed for six or seven days, not to speak of the scars.'

'Scars?' I look to Katerina, who looks down, then back to Bauer.

'I'd not say this, Otto, not in front of the girls, but they already know. It was Natalya who noticed it first.' He pauses, then, 'She was tortured, Otto. Things separate from the severed hand . . . oh, and we can grow that back, don't worry.'

'Tortured?' He nods, the smile gone. 'Burns and cuts. Small things but . . . well, I should imagine it was terrifying. That man . . .'

I nod. But I am shocked by this latest news. Tortured. How the fuck could you torture a child of three?

I turn to face my girls, and now that I look at them I see how different they are. Very different. Now, when I look in their eyes, I see shadows there, shadows and scars.

Katerina leans forward. 'Girls? Go and get something to eat. Consultant Bauer will take you. I . . . I need to speak with your father.'

I wait until they're gone, then turn to face her, taking both of her hands in mine.

'So?'

'You need to know,' she says. 'The things that happened to them. That were *done* to them. We've been talking about it. As far as we could, anyway.'

I stare at her, astonished, wanting both to know and not to know.

'Irina started it. Last night. She had been dreaming. Having nightmares. She woke the others and they woke me. And then we talked. Reluctantly, at first, but then . . .'

Katerina takes a long, shuddering breath, then begins, and by the time she's done I am gripping her fingers tightly in my own. My darlings. My poor, poor darlings.

'And that's it,' she says.

But now that I know these things I cannot settle. I want to kill him, of course I do, but it's much more than that. Once he's dead there will be others. Similar-minded bastards who enjoy tormenting others. And am I to kill them all?

'I was hoping to take them home, back to Cherdiechnost, but Ernst says they can't guarantee our safety. Not while Kolya is still alive. So here we stay.'

'It won't be long,' I say, trying to reassure her. But we've been fighting our corner of Time for near on three hundred years now, so who's to say?

'I need to go,' I say, kissing her and holding her tight against me. 'There are things to attend to. But I'll be back. I promise you, my love.'

And so I leave her there, in safe hands. Only as I make my way back to the platform, I wonder why it is that I feel quite so desolate. After all, I have five of my girls back. Five more than I had hoped for, and surely that's something to thank the gods for? Only it isn't. I want it all. I want my darling Martha back, and that not-knowing-where-she-is is like a small death. That's why I'm going to do what I have to do. That's why I need to summon the *veche* for a special meeting.

Because I'm not fit to be Master. Not fit at all.

439

Dawn finds me pacing the deck outside the big farmhouse in Tannenberg, the great sloping field of waist-length grass running down to meet the darkness of the Prussian forest.

It is from there – from the new platform we have built – that they will come.

And when will this happen?

I look about me, taking in the cloudless blue of the sky, the freshness of the day. It is the eighth of October, AD 783.

Turning, I can smell the strong scent of paint and resin, of glue and freshly sawn wood, and that same faint, burning smell I loved as a youngster in 'the Garden'. Everything freshly made, all of it built anew to try to throw that demon Kolya off our scent.

And all of it planned, designed and constructed while I was gone, visiting my girls. All of it decided on without consultation. By the *veche*. Who now come at my bidding.

If anything, that convinces me of my course.

I am not needed here.

Young Saratov comes first, whistling to himself as he makes his way up through the heavy swathe of grass, his hands pushing the weight of green away from him. Halfway up the slope he sees me and raises a hand in greeting. I raise mine back at him. Here, at least, is an ally. A man who would do my bidding without question.

Only why should he? Those days are gone for ever, along with Hecht and Yastryeb and 'the Game'. Nor can we return to them; not if we're to organise things differently. Only . . . it annoys me. Irritates like an itch under the skin, where no scratching can locate it.

As he comes closer, he calls to me.

'Otto! How are the girls?'

'Fine,' I say, trying to smile. Only Martha's shadow lies over everything I say and do. Her absence shapes my mood. And my mood is very dark.

'Good,' he says, jumping up onto the deck, then coming over to embrace me. 'It must be good to have them back.'

'It is. It really is . . .'

Only...

Only I don't say that. Instead I turn and, with my right arm, indicate the new building. 'When was this decided?'

'Two weeks from now. It was your idea, Otto. But I guess you've not come to that part yet.'

I search his eyes briefly, then shake my head and smile. 'And there was I thinking . . .'

'That you were left out of the decision-making?' Saratov shakes his head. 'Never. We would never allow that.'

'And yet the *veche* is divided, no?'

He hesitates then nods, his whole mood suddenly serious. 'I'll tell you everything later, Otto. But for now remember this. Everything you're about to say this morning has already been said. Said and agreed upon. And tomorrow, back at Moscow Central, Old Schnorr will come to you to try to argue you out of it.'

'And what will I say to that?'

'Oh, of that I've no idea. Only that he visits you. But hey . . . here are more of our guests. Alina is the one in the big bearskin, Vasilisa the smaller one, in the Mechanist overalls. She's our best marksman. She can put a hole through a man's eye from two hundred yards.'

I watch them approach. I've met Alina several times now, but the other?

I lean closer to Saratov, keeping my voice low. 'I don't understand. This Vasilisa. Has she been voted in to replace someone?'

Saratov frowns. 'What do you mean?'

'The other one . . . Alina . . . I remember. She was sitting at the far end of the table. But this one. I've never seen her before this moment. A marksman, you say?'

'Markswoman,' he answers quietly. 'But about the other . . . are you serious, Otto?'

I am. Only I say no more, for the two of them are upon us.

Alina hugs me, asks about my girls, but the other – Vasilisa – is more reserved. She gives me her hand, then stands back, letting Alina speak for them both.

'It's gone very quiet, Meister. It feels like they're waiting for something, gathering their strength. We've had dozens of agents reporting in and they all say the same thing. That it's gone quiet. And no sign of our enemies.'

I turn to Saratov. 'What do our friends in the think tank say?'

I see how he looks to the other two, and realise I've asked an awkward question. It's Saratov who answers me.

'They've gone.'

'Gone?'

'A week past. All, that is, except for Moseley. It was he who told us . . . eventually.'

'Do we know why? I mean . . . they weren't *taken*, were they?'

And I shudder to think of them in Kolya's hands, working for *him*. Only then I register what Saratov actually said. 'A week?'

'Yes. They tampered with our cameras. Made it seem like they were there, in their quarters, when they weren't.'

'I see. But gone where?'

'Home, I'd guess. Seems like the novelty wore off.'

Only that doesn't ring true. I can't imagine them getting bored of this. No. There's some other explanation.

'Did we manage to track them? I mean . . . has anyone looked into that aspect of things.'

'We have,' Alina answers. 'In fact, I did it personally, and there's no trace of them having left Moscow Central.'

'Then they're still there.'

Saratov laughs. 'How could they be? There's no trace of them, and we've searched the station from one end to the other.'

Yes, I'm thinking, but this is a *nichtraum*, a 'no-space'. Consequently it does not obey the same set of physical rules as the rest of the universe. And if anyone could work out how to exist in a *nichtraum* without being traced, then Galileo and his friends would certainly be capable.

'They're here,' I say. 'In the same way Reichenau was there, in Four-Oh. The question is, how are they feeding themselves, and how are they tapping into our power and water and air supplies?'

Saratov is nodding now. Only I'm asking other questions suddenly. Like . . . *why?* And to what end? And is that end helpful or harmful? And if harmful . . . then why? What have we done to them to make them turn against us?

If that *is* what they've done.

Zarah and Urte have arrived by now, along with Svetov. And then Ernst finally comes, along with Master Schnorr, the old man supported on Ernst's arm.

Eight in all, I realise, and ask what's happened to the rest. And am told that they are far too busy to attend, especially as they know already what I'm about to say.

Which, again, irritates me. Is no one to be relied on?

I begin to protest, only Ernst cuts me short, drawing me aside on the pretext that he has something really important to tell me.

'What is it?' I ask impatiently when we are back indoors and out of earshot of the others.

'There's been a development,' he says. 'Reichenau's people have been trying to get him back. So far without success, but we've doubled our watch on those timelines that lead to earlier sightings of him.'

'And?'

Ernst shrugs. 'I'm assuming that that's enough. The way we reason it is that if something were going to happen in that regard, it would already have happened. That monster would be back, causing trouble, and he isn't, so . . .'

'Okay,' I say. 'But keep on this, moment by moment. Assign a team.'

'It's done,' Ernst says, smiling.

'Good. Then let's get back and get this over with.'

440

It's all done in no time. Half an hour, at most. I have my say and they listen. And then they're gone, leaving me there, alone, no decision made, my dilemma unresolved.

Family man or not, and changed as I've been by events, I am still, at core, a lone wolf, and it's that that prevents me now from acting effectively. For how can I be Master of all when I am scarcely master of myself?

And there are many who agree with that. Who feel I am the wrong choice. And who am I to argue with them?

But for now I remain as Master.

I return to Moscow Central, conscious as I climb down from the platform, that there's a heightened sense of alertness. Armed guards are everywhere.

Katerina and the girls are sleeping when I go to see them. For a while I just sit there, watching them, getting some sense of ease from the simple sight of them. Only this is far from done with. The worst of it lies ahead, within the loop.

As I make to leave, so one of the nurses, a big Russian woman called Ludmilla, who I've not met before, calls me back and hands me something – a large envelope, containing papers.

'What's this?'

'Katerina asked me to hand it to you. If you returned.'

Back in my rooms, I sit in Hecht's chair, in the glow of the World Tree, feeling strangely apprehensive. It's not like Katerina to do this kind of thing.

I slit the envelope open. Inside are four small letters – handwritten, the writing on each quite distinct. I know those hands.

I take the first of them – Natalya's – and unfold it. 'Daddy,' it begins.

It's relatively brief. Six pages, front and back, ending with her love. But between . . .

I shudder, then wipe the tears away. My darling. My poor, poor darling. And now that I know, I wish I didn't. For here, written in her child-like hand, is everything that happened to her while in that monster's charge. The whole of it, condensed into a howl of pain. Things she couldn't say to me, face to face. Things that need a distance to be said.

I set it aside, trembling as I pick up the second of them – Irina's – her hand quite different from her elder sister's. Much neater, and somehow more adult. But I remind myself, she's only nine. 'The things I've seen' she says, and once more I wish I didn't know, for she has seen what infant eyes should never witness. Experiments and the like. Abominable cruelty. Oh, and not only what she saw, but what she suffered, too.

And, reading this, I feel a numbing impotence. An awful sense of helplessness. Protecting her – that was my job. That was what I was meant to do. And that's the worst of it. To think of her, hopelessly longing for me to come and save her, day after day, month after month. And nothing. Nothing but that awful feeling of abandonment she speaks of here, that led her to despair of ever seeing any of us again. What torments she must have suffered, my poor dear, chained in that awful cage, lost and, it seemed, un-loved.

Trembling, I put Irina's account aside, then stare at the next of them, written in Anna's rounded but shaky hand. I'm not sure I can read another word of this, for this is killing me. Each word is like a drop of acid on my soul. Only I must. This is my duty. To know and understand and maybe help prevent it ever happening again.

Only how can I guarantee that?

I take a long, shivering breath, then unfold it. 'Daddy,' it begins.

Oh gods, and this really is the worst. For this alone I would kill the man. Kill him and then bring him back to life and kill him a thousand times again. A slow, tormenting death.

Oh darling Anna, did he really do that to you?

And more. Saying the unsayable. Each word a prayer for forgiveness. For surely she must have done something terribly bad to deserve such punishment. Only I know my darling Anna. There's not a single bad atom in her, and certainly nothing to make her deserve such hideous treatment.

'You cunt. You fucking cunt,' I say, addressing the air, as if Kolya can hear me. 'For this alone I'll have you. I swear it.'

And so to Zarah's letter. Words whispered to her mother's ear and set down. Words that finally make me understand what evil resides in that man. For no one could have done to her what he did – not if they had the smallest trace of goodness in them. Of empathy.

No. I understand it wholly now. Kolya is a man without a spark of human decency in him. A man who can do the unthinkable and sleep soundly afterwards.

And as I think that, so I wince with pain, recalling how he plucked her from the cart and threw her into the stream, like a discarded doll.

A demon. I'm convinced of it now. A creature of sulphur fumes and malice.

I turn to the last page of Zarah's tale and find, to my astonishment, her account of where she was briefly kept, before Himki and the cart. A big, hangar-like place, at one end of which was a strange, silver vehicle with stubby wings.

The fortress! It *has* to be. Upriver from St Petersburg

It was there that Kolya gave a talk to several hundred of his 'brothers' who had gathered to hear what he had to say. And while she, exhausted, had had no memory of anything he said, Zarah did see something of significance.

Shortly after Kolya had addressed the gathering, when the hangar was empty and silent once again, the silver vehicle had started to glow. For a moment it had flickered faintly, as if appearing and disappearing, then grew still again, solidifying, like when the river froze over in winter.

I reread that passage then sit there, wondering how I can use it. Oh, I know now *where* it was. But what use is that without knowing *when*? Or is that really a problem? I mean, what if I sent back dozens of agents, each to one segment of time, each waiting there, weeks, maybe even months, for Kolya to show up? After all, we know roughly when it was built, during Catherine's rule, in the mid-eighteenth century, which narrows it a little. Only . . .

Only wouldn't that tip him off?

He's too clever to be got at so directly. No. We've seen how he does things. How he changes things. How – before we can jump right in and grab him – he is gone, no sign of him remaining.

Like he knows what we're about to do. And not just once but every time.

My eyes return to the bottom of the page. 'Love you, Daddy' it reads, written in a spider-like scrawl with her left hand.

I take a long, shivering breath, then place the letter on top of the others.

Reasons, I think. Good reasons to stay on and see the job through. Only I've made my mind up in that regard. I can't be Master.

441

Which seems to be the general consensus.

The next morning, when I meet with them again, the *veche* vote to accept my resignation. Oh, there's disappointment, but it's no surprise to any of them and no one really fights to keep me. Which knocks me back a little. Was I that poor a Meister?

I say they accept my decision, but at the last moment Ernst persuades me to think it over for a day or two, and I agree to do that – only it's almost certain now.

Afterwards, however, Old Schnorr comes to me and asks to speak with me alone. He tells me that it was only the fact that both Hecht and Yastryeb had wanted me as Master that had persuaded them to appoint me in the first place.

'You were never made to be Master, Otto. At least, not in the old way of doing things. But "the Game" is over now. The War has ended, and when we've seen to Kolya—'

'If . . .' I say quietly.

'Well . . . we may need a new kind of Master for a new age.'

'Then find one.'

'I think we have. Only the others don't realise it yet. *You* don't realise it. A new age needs new thinking, new ways, not the old ones. And you, Otto, you're flexible enough mentally for that task. More than that, you're *morally* competent.'

Schnorr's words surprise me. 'Morally?'

'Yes, morally. Take Cherdiechnost, for instance. That was a start. A whole new approach to things. And the slaves you freed. Only you must go further. You need to reforge things. Especially how we act in Time.'

Surprise has given way now to astonishment.

'Don't act so hastily, Otto,' he says, placing his hand on my arm. 'Stay a while longer. At least until we've hunted the bastard down.'

'And then?'

'Then we'll reconsider things. But Kolya first. You won't be safe, Otto, not until he's dealt with. You want to retire, no? And spend your remaining days at Cherdiechnost?'

'I do.'

'Then see this through.'

442

Ernst finds me in the fight school, in one of the small gyms at the far end of the central corridor, working out with knives and swords.

It's late evening and, as he changes into a combat suit then joins me in the fight-pit, it's clear he wants to talk.

'Are you afraid of him?'

'Of Kolya?' I laugh dismissively. 'No. I've beaten him once, even if I don't remember it. And I'll beat him again.'

Our swords clash. Ernst takes a step backward.

'I've been thinking . . .'

'Thinking?'

He circles to the right. 'About when you changed. And why.'

I turn slowly, keeping face on to him, my body shadowing his every movement, my sword making shapes about the tip of his. 'Is that important?'

'Oh, crucial.'

He taps my sword tip with his own, feints, then resumes his circling.

'You've changed,' he says, his blue eyes meeting mine. 'When it first happened, I didn't understand. I just thought you'd lost it. I didn't think you . . . *capable* of love.'

'No?' I laugh. 'Nor I. That whole part of me . . . I really didn't think it possible. Love . . . it seemed such a trivial thing. So unimportant.'

'And now?'

He feints left, right, then lunges, even as I move aside, brushing my sword tip against his right shoulder. In battle I'd have drawn blood.

'I'm getting old,' Ernst laughs, moving his upper arm to ease the pain. 'Back in the day you'd never have got close.'

'No.' And it's true. Ernst was always the better swordsman.

'But my question . . .'

'Now?' He looks at me, then lifts his sword again, shadowing mine. 'I think it suits you, Otto. To have a softer side, I mean. All of this . . . it's brought out what was always latent in you, from childhood. You were always kind, you see. Yes, and you always did what was fair. Only you had to look really hard to see it. You were so cold to those who didn't know you. Indifferent. Or so it seemed.'

Ernst is circling again, to the left this time. He lunges once more. There's a sudden flurry of movement, ending in Ernst crying out in delight. '*There!*'

I step back, feeling the painful stinging of the bruise, there in the middle of my chest, just above where my heart is.

'Dead,' he says, and laughs.

'One less I owe you,' I answer, and suddenly, for no reason, we're smiling.

'Old Schnorr came to me earlier on,' I say. 'Said I should stay on.'

'Is *that* what he said?' He lowers his sword a little, as if taking that in. 'Well, he's right. Only not in the old way. You need to come up with some new ideas, Otto. Ideas of your own. *Constructive* ideas.'

'New ideas?'

I lower my sword. I can't fight *and* concentrate.

'Precisely,' I say. 'Look . . . since the War between us ended, a lot of agents – German as well as Russian – have been sitting on their hands, wool-gathering, waiting for something useful to do, and they don't like that. That's why we've had so much tension. They've been drinking too much and getting into fights, and that's not good. They need something to do. Something to keep them busy.'

'So what do you suggest?'

I put the practice sword away, then sit on the long bench, facing him.

'We all know the problem. You and I especially so. It's to do with how we've been bred. From children on, we've learned how to fight for our survival . . . to wage war without compromise, without mercy. But now we're expected to respond to things entirely differently; to embrace those we were previously trained to kill. So the question is this – how can you possibly recondition people who have been soldiers all their lives? How can you give them greater satisfactions than they had? For there's no doubting it, being a *Reisende* – a time agent – is the biggest high of all. And to give that up! No wonder there's been trouble. We're having to deal with people whose natural instinct is to kill rather than conciliate. To eradicate their enemy. And what can you give them in place of that? What emotion could get close to matching it?'

'And yet we must.'

I nod, but I can see Ernst agrees with me one hundred per cent. For he, remember, knows what it is like to have lost the freedom of operating in Time, of being one of the chosen ones who could step between the worlds. That was no small thing to give up.

What, then, is the answer? To become time police? To use our powers to regulate the worlds we travel to? The truth is, I don't know. Not yet. But something new must be attempted. Before we slip back into old habits and start with *Rassenkampf* again . . .

Ernst pulls off his combat suit and walks over to the shower on the far side of the gym. 'And Kolya?' he asks.

'Kolya will summon us, when he's ready. That's his way. It makes him seem commanding, like he's in charge of things, but really it just shows how insecure he is.'

'Insecure?'

'Yes. That's his weakness.'

'And Martha?'

I take a deep breath and then say it. 'Martha's lost.'

'*Lost?*' Ernst looks horrified.

'I'm almost certain of it now. Why, I've been lucky as it is. But I keep thinking, what would I do if I were Kolya? What would I make certain of? And I think I know. I'd destroy something – or someone – my enemy loved. Just one of those he loves, not all of them. Not enough to make me rage like a man who has nothing left to lose, but enough to damage me. To make me ache inside. Just one would do the trick. Just one.'

Ernst stares at me, not knowing what to say. He comes across and holds my arm, but I shake it off, my whole mood suddenly cold and distant.

'That's why I need to kill him this time, Ernst. Not with a breath, like Old Schnorr wants me to, but with cold steel. I can't help it. I need to see his eyes go out – to see the spark of life die in him. For what he's done. For *all* the things he'd done.'

443

Svetov looks up from behind his desk, surprised. 'What *is* this, Otto?'

'A list,' I say. 'Things to keep our agents busy.'

'But these . . .' Svetov shrugs. 'The changes . . .'

'Will be good ones.'

Svetov hesitates. 'Then you've changed your mind?'

'About not wanting to be Master? No. But if it must be, then I think we ought to start doing things my way, not Hecht's. And not, with due respect, Yastryeb's.'

Svetov looks back at the list, then points out an item. 'But this is—'

'Madness?' I smile faintly. 'Hecht would have thought so, certainly, but who are we fighting? Ourselves? Or those who would have us fight? No, Arkadi . . . we have a chance here. A chance to make *real* changes.'

But I can see that the big man thinks I am taking things too far and much too fast. He wants to take my list and discuss it with the others.

'By all means,' I say, when he suggests this, 'only don't take too long about it. Idleness breeds trouble.'

To which Svetov gives me a curious glance before hurrying off to discuss things – and no doubt to debate whether their appointed Master has totally lost the plot.

They come to me an hour later, in Yastryeb's old rooms.

Svetov, as ever, is their spokesperson. He hesitates a moment, then taps the sheet of paper on which I've written out my 'list'.

'On what basis did you compile this list, Otto? It's rather . . . hit and miss, don't you think?'

'Things I felt bad about,' I answer, not getting up from where I sit in Yastryeb's chair. 'Things I could never quite square with my conscience.'

'But you have Frederick on the list. Frederick!'

I am unfazed. 'Think of how many he had killed. How much his people suffered for his grandiose ideas!'

'Yes, but they loved him! He was their hero!'

'Then let's have done with heroes, eh? Let's shoot them all between the eyes.'

Some of them find this shocking, blasphemous almost, but I'm feeling in an uncompromising mood.

Zarah interrupts. 'Even if we accept what you're saying, the fact is that if Frederick dies, then we surely cease to be as a people. I mean . . . kill Frederick and do we even exist?'

I smile, amused for once by the idea. 'Then let's find out. Let's see if we really needed him, or whether it wasn't just vainglory.'

'And if we *do* need him?'

'Then I'm wrong and we can't change a damn thing. Nothing *worth* changing, anyway.'

'You sound like Burckel,' Ernst says.

'And is that so bad? You said yourself that I should come up with some new ideas. So what do you say now? Do you approve?'

'Of all of it? No. But most of it . . . well, I say let's try, only . . . *slowly*, bit by bit. See if it works. Let's not rush into things. Besides, there's still a war on, of sorts. We've yet to deal with Kolya.'

And, as if to illustrate that fact, we are attacked within the hour, Kolya making several abortive attacks on Moscow Central, testing out our defences before withdrawing, the whole thing becoming a game of cat and mouse, with our agents chasing Kolya's brothers back into the timelines from which they've come. Only

Kolya is very good at covering his tracks and really adept at turning the tables and ambushing any agent of ours who goes through after Kolya's.

Keen to begin my own ventures, I find this new phase of the War frustrating as sin, and – to make some kind of meaningful response – agree to endorse others' plans to hit out at what they've identified as Kolya's weak points.

Experienced in such ventures, I am to lead a team of two dozen heavily armed agents, while Svetov leads another team of equivalent size, while Ernst, Schnorr, Zarah, Katerina and others remain behind to 'hold the fort'.

But we are swiftly disillusioned.

Within moments of jumping through, both forces are under intense fire, heavily outnumbered. Regrouped back at Moscow Central – and with seven agents missing – Svetov concedes that I might have been right after all. Maybe he *has* underestimated Kolya.

444

With things gone quiet again at Moscow Central, Zarah has arranged for Katerina and I to go back – far back – to somewhere no one, not even Kolya, could pursue us.

Back to the Haven.

Katerina has brought the girls, but they are sleeping now, under canvas, exhausted from an afternoon exploring this distant Eden, of inhaling this rich, sweet, wholesome air. No better playground in the known universe.

And so it is that we spend the evening with Albrecht, beneath those ancient stars, the peaks of the Alps catching the last of the sun as it sets in the far west, painting the treetops crimson.

We are up on the great stone platform, overlooking the valley where the Neanderthal settlement once was. Albrecht has built a fire and brought food to cook, and for the first time in months I relax, knowing I am safe. And the thought of that makes me wonder if this – much more than Cherdiechnost – might not be a final resting place for Katerina and me. A place to live out our days and raise our girls. Only I'm loath to ask Albrecht; loath to spoil his idyll. And in any case, it could never be, for to introduce such a powerful alternate timeline, with the intelligence and knowledge my girls and their mates are certain to possess, and which, with equal certainty, they'd pass on down the generations, would, in all likelihood, change destiny's course. So I don't raise the issue. Don't spoil this perfect day.

We talk, and as the hours pass and the wine flows, so I have the sense that Albrecht is keeping something from us. There's a light-heartedness, almost a playfulness about him that I haven't seen since before the death of his brother.

Eventually I ask. 'So what's new? What have your researches thrown up?'

'*New?*' Only he's smiling now, and I know he must have been researching *something*, because that's what he does. That's how he spends his days. He warms his hands in the fire's flames, then looks up at me. 'I've been looking at all the different strands, Otto. All of those worlds you two brought into being.'

'And?' Katerina asks, reaching out to take my hand.

'And in over ninety-seven per cent of them you married Kravchuk. Like it was fated.'

Just the mention of that name makes me bristle. 'Then how did we get to this?'

'Because you wanted it so,' my darling girl answers, and Albrecht nods.

'Katerina's right. We're here because you willed us to be here. There's no other explanation for it. Time and again you came back to tackle the problem.'

'Problem?'

'Yes, of how to keep the woman you loved while at the same time being loyal to your Master, my brother.'

'Only the universe, surely, doesn't work that way?'

'No.'

'Then . . .?'

'Kravchuk's the key,' he says. 'A man largely unknown to history, yet whose existence or non-existence was of central importance. There must be others like him, only this was the first one we'd encountered. He's there, in every world we looked at, like some great over-ride switch. Kill him and the map turns red. Let him live . . .'

Albrecht is silent a moment, then. 'I've been looking at something else, too. Something much more personal.'

He reaches back, into the darkness just behind him, then turns back, holding out a bulky file to me.

'Handwritten,' he says, before I can comment on it. 'Just in case the computer file got hacked somehow.'

I meet his eyes. 'What is this?'

'It's the story of your life, Otto. And of all the other lives you might have lived. Oh, and I made up a small album with photos from the different timelines, only . . .'

'Only it went missing, no?'

Albrecht nods, a flicker of uncertainty in his eyes. 'How did you know that?'

'How was it you *didn't* know?'

'Those images . . . they wouldn't have been stable outside of the Haven. They would have slowly faded. Or disintegrated. They wouldn't have lasted long, anyway.'

'They didn't.' And I tell him what I know about the album and its history, and see from his expression that he's puzzled. He doesn't know who could have taken it from there, far less how it got into Reichenau's hands.

Hecht, I think. It had to be the Master himself who took the album from here. Only why? To show me? Then why didn't he? Why was it in Reichenau's hands first time I saw it?

I look away a moment, out into the darkness that surrounds our bonfire. The warm, Palaeolithic darkness.

'Did they never come back?' I ask.

'Who do you mean?'

'The Neanderthals.'

'Ah . . .' And he too stares out into that blackness. 'One or two. But not to settle. I think they lost trust in us, after what my brother did. It was for their safety, only he never got to explain that to them. They only saw what he did, not why.'

I look down at the file in my hands, reluctant – deeply reluctant – to open it. But Katerina is having none of that.

'Open it, Otto. For the gods' sake, put yourself out of your misery and open it.'

445

And so, for the first time ever, I learn of my parentage and, through Albrecht's meticulously detailed chart, see who I am related to and how intricately interwoven the web of lives was at Four-Oh.

Family, I think. *True family*.

Only then Albrecht shows me something else – the Russian charts he got from Svetov, and while there are differences, there are also distinct similarities genetically, to within less than half of a percentile.

We are one people and always have been. This proves it beyond a doubt.

'Then the War . . .?'

'Was pure mischief. The whole notion of race is a nonsense. A dangerous illusion.'

'But your brother—'

'Never knew it. It would have . . . *undermined* him. Destroyed what he was. And maybe that makes me culpable . . .' Albrecht stops, then looks to me again. 'That's why you need to change it, Otto. To stop all that redundant tribalism and put an end to it all.'

He's right, of course. Which is why I'm there, six hours subjective later, facing the *veche* and outlining my scheme to get at Kolya.

As I see it, what we need to focus upon is what Kolya wants.

And what does Kolya want?

Two things. To protect himself in Time, and to kill me.

'I know now where we have to go,' I say. 'Or at least, I think I do. But first I need to salve my conscience. To set a few things right. If you think that's indulgence, fine, I'll abide by the council's wishes, but I really think we should try this. See what happens, and how it makes us feel about ourselves.'

Some of them look puzzled at that, but I get my majority.

'Good. Then I want six volunteers. Six agents who are willing to die for the cause. Because we're going right to the heart of things, and we're going in an hour from now.'

446

The heart of things? It all depends, I guess, on how you see this.

They see themselves as the peak of a long, evolutionary process that began with the Germanic tribes, was honed and refined by the Brotherhood in the northern crusades, and was finally perfected with themselves: these blond-haired Aryans, chosen by the gods themselves.

They, of course, don't know just how far they are to fall, no, nor how far they'll climb above what they ever aspired to be. Only we, from our perspective in Time, can witness that. But here, in the years of the Third Reich, they believe themselves to be at the very height of their powers.

The *Schutzstaffel*, better known to us as the SS. The elite of the National Sozialistische party. The so-called Master Race, and they the masters of it.

Yes, and our one-time allies in the War in Time.

We have jumped through into Wewelsburg, in Westphalia, on the seventh day of April, 1942, the spring sun beating down on the high battlements of the great *schloss*, from a sky as blue as Dresden china.

This is the epicentre of the Nazi dream, the high temple of the *Schutzstaffel*, rebuilt from the ruin it was at vast expense. Three million dollars American, a huge sum in that time, and that excluding all the free labour. Workers provided by the camps.

We jump in, then jump again, into the Hall of the Supreme Leaders, where, partially naked, nine of the leading members of Hitler's SS, together with a dozen or more subordinates, are carrying out one of their mystic ceremonies.

Before they know what is happening, my team – Katerina among them – are wreaking bloody havoc, strafing them with bullets and killing, among others, Felix Steiner, Reinhard Heydrich, Karl Frank, Walther Darré, Heinrich Müller, Franz Huber, the Commandant of Dachau, Theodor Eicke and Himmler himself. The shooting over, we pile them up in the massive central basin of that big, circular room and set fire to their corpses.

At one swoop almost the entire command of the SS has been destroyed. Only we don't stop there. Jumping in and out of time, we set charges and destroy the place – along with its Aryan library of twelve thousand volumes and its training grounds.

Pausing from my bloody work, I look down from the battlements and see, just as I knew I would, Katerina's meeting with my younger self. I watch us kiss, then part, and, as they vanish from the scene, so too do I.

It is done. Another segment of the loop fixed firm and unassailable, like setts in a strong stone wall. Yes, and more of the murdering scum executed. Bad men, punished for what they did.

But it isn't enough. Standing there on the platform of Moscow Central, I realise that. No matter how many of the bastards I kill, I will never feel clean. Never feel *absolved*.

We jump in again, this time to the Prussian wilderness in the summer of 1236, where, in the moonlit darkness, a group of Teuton knights, including my younger self, are approaching a native village.

My stomach clenches, knowing what is to come. May the gods help me now, for this is nightmare territory.

As we step out from under the trees, I can see how terrified the villagers are at our sudden appearance. Breaking off their festivities, some of them turn to run. I call them back, speaking in their native tongue, promising them that they won't be hurt.

'Go to your huts!' I cry. 'And wait until I summon you again!'

They go, some of them reluctantly, even as the knights of the brotherhood enter the clearing, stepping out from between the trees, swords raised. Men I know well. My comrades in the timeline they inhabit.

Turning, I confront them, raising the heavy stun-gun I have brought with me this time.

As the others slow their pace, Meister Dietrich steps out before them. As yet his sword is sheathed.

'Brother Otto. What *is* this? And why are you dressed like that?'

The brothers are confused now, for I am both here and there, among them. They look from one to another and exchange gruff words. Is this devilry of some kind?

In truth, I guess it is. As for my younger self, he seems just as confused as the rest of them, and when I raise my voice, ordering them to turn about and return to their homelands or feel the wrath of God, there are growls of anger. Only they're not really sure what they should do. As a body, they look to the Meister for guidance.

'Onward!' the old man calls, finally unsheathing his own mighty broadsword. 'Leave none of them alive!'

Only before he can take a pace, he falls to his knees, his chest on fire.

There's a great howl of fear. Even so, some of the men press on, beginning to run. Only now we pick them off, the air criss-crossed with the traces of our lasers. And then, suddenly, the knights break and turn and run, fleeing for their lives, shrieking with fear.

Wizards . . . they have surely fought wizards here today.

And maybe they have. Only once more I don't feel good about this. It wasn't in any sense a fair fight. But then, even as the villagers emerge, wide-eyed with astonishment, but also gratitude, so I remind myself what my brothers did here in that previous timeline. How they slaughtered the innocents . . . and for what? For God and Christ and Christ's mother, Mary?

No. This is an unholy place, a place that stinks of charred flesh. An awful smell that fills your nostrils and makes you want to retch. An unclean smell.

I put my booted foot on Meister Dietrich's chest and stare down into his lifeless face. Dead, and deservedly so.

I walk across to where the fight was fiercest, looking for what I know I'll never find.

Myself.

And turn full circle, taking in the carnage, seeing how my comrades, standing here and there among the dead, are uneasy with this.

'Did anybody . . .?'

They shake their heads, mumble 'not a thing' or 'he must have jumped straight out', but they all know what I'm asking. I mean, what did he make of that? And has it changed a damn thing, back in the past?

Supposedly not. Else we would know, surely?

All I know for sure is that there are paradoxes at work here.

We jump back to Moscow Central, and jump straight out again, to Velikie Luki in northern Russia in the spring of 1942.

And a scene that makes my stomach turn.

It is a cold, clear morning, and in a clearing a kilometre outside Velikie Luki, four hundred souls – gypsies, communists and Jews – have been stripped bare and lined up along a ridge, facing a line of machine-gun posts, a great trench between the two. And, at a nearby table, Dr Walter Stahlecker and his men from Einsatzgruppen A look at a map, here to do Hitler's bidding and eradicate all 'undesirables' they come upon.

Oh, I have been here once before, a long time ago, and seen the cold absence in those eyes, the faint amusement as the guns go off and the bodies dance and fall. Such wickedness.

Make no mistake. Stahlecker is an evil man. Only we're here to change all of that. Or make a beginning, anyway. Because today the rules change. Today the victims will escape, unharmed, while Stahlecker and his men . . .

As I watch, our agents jump in. There is a brief struggle at each post as the soldiers try to escape their fate, their fingers reaching up to try to tear the garrotting wire from their throats, kicking out and struggling as the life drains from them.

Stahlecker looks up, startled by the sudden noise, and whirls about, drawing his luger from its holster. Only he too is too late, for as he turns, so Katerina shimmers into being in front of him and fires a single bullet, dead centre in his forehead.

It's over in less than a minute, the executioners executed, the naked men on the ridge – cold, trembling men, dead already in their own imaginations – call out in the sudden silence.

'Help us! For God's sake, help us!'

Even as Ernst appears with his assistants, pulling carts on which are new and comfortable clothes. Enough for all. Yes, and food and medical equipment, and . . .

Guns. And rocket launchers and grenades, and flamethrowers, and everything they'd need to make this war a bit more even, a bit more 'fair'.

Ernst's idea, not mine.

I step over Stahlecker and spit full in his damaged face. And then jump, back to Moscow Central, back to another change of clothes, and then in once more, this time to Neu Berlin, on the sixth day of June, 2747.

Only this time we jump directly into the centre of the maelstrom, materialising inside the great fortress of the *Konigsturm*.

And while Ernst and Svetov and the rest target the lesser members of the great family that live here at the centre of Greater Germany, so I am to go for the head itself.

Manfred. Tenth of his genetic line, more than two centuries old and a good three times my height. Not to speak of body weight.

I find him in the same room where first I met him, sprawled out on his giant throne, his legs stretched out like fallen pines, the same great fur draped about his shoulders, making him seem like he's Lord of the Primeval Forest. Yes, very like the first time, only one day later. The day of the feast and his aunt's assassination. The day when he was tipped over the edge.

He frowns at me, clearly puzzled by my presence there.

'Otto . . . what are you doing here?'

'I came to see you, Meister,' I said. 'Before certain things happened.'

That puzzles him even more. 'You *know* something?'

Nothing that Time will not reveal. Only I don't say that. What I do is draw my laser and point it at him.

'I'm sorry, Meister, because I liked you very much. But what I've seen . . .'

He stares at the needle-gun as if I'm insane, then laughs. 'You wouldn't dare . . .'

Only those are his final words. If screams are not to be counted as words.

I burn out one eye, then burn the other, jumping back to avoid being kicked by one of those massive legs, then close on him to finish the job, setting his fur on fire before drilling a hole deep into his chest, blood bubbling and boiling up from the big, charred hole I have exposed, there beneath his massive ribcage.

He kicks out, once, twice, then falls still, his huge mouth fallen open, as if to swallow me.

I swallow bile. That was awful. I liked Manfred a great deal. Even at the last, when madness overcame him, he was . . .

Magnificent.

Katerina joins me after a moment, clearly in awe of all she's seen here; the sheer scale they have built to, these Germans of the twenty-eighth century.

'Now what?' she asks. 'Will it not happen? Will Gehlen never finish his equations?'

Only he must, for we are still here, locked into the loop. If he hadn't, then surely we'd have all vanished, like a puff of smoke.

We jump back, to Moscow Central, to find our comrades in a heated debate as to where all of this is leading. Ernst and Svetov are certainly at loggerheads over the morality of our actions.

'Tell him *why*, Otto,' Ernst says, turning to me. 'Tell him what you said to me.'

'That it's necessary? Arkadi knows that. He knows we must take such actions to free us from the past. From all of those firing squads and hangings, the bombing and the gassing, and all that talk of blood and iron. Loving kindness, tolerance – these simply won't do to free us from such behaviour. It's as I said: we must execute the executioners. There is no other way. To tolerate them for a moment, to let them glimpse the least weakness in us . . . No, dear friend. There must be no more piracy and plunder, no more deals with bad men. We must eradicate their cruelty and rid the world – the worlds, dare I say it? – of their evil.'

Only it doesn't feel right. Not entirely. And besides, I have one last 'visit' to make. Perhaps the hardest of them all.

447

It is the twelfth of August, 1759, and I am on the battlefield at Kunersdorf. Below us, the slaughter rages on, but here, on this small, grassy platform, raised up above the battling armies, we can see how the tide has turned.

Less than an hour ago, it seemed as if the Russians had been routed, but now it is our turn to flee the carnage of the battle. The day is lost. Not that Frederick will see that or acknowledge it.

As I walk across to him, so Frederick turns his horse and smiles at me, patting the tiny snuff box in his pocket. It was my gift to him, the means by which his life was saved earlier in the day. Only things have changed.

'Otto?'

Steeling myself, I aim my gun and fire, the musket ball flying straight and true, boring a hole between his eyes and taking off the back of his skull.

He slumps then topples from his horse. Dead.

I watch his staff turn and look, horrified. And jump . . .

. . . back to Moscow Central where, it seems, all hell has broken loose. The Tree of Worlds is roaring with a fiery red light, like it has, at one and the same time, caught fire and is being tossed about by a great storm.

I watch it a while, until it grows calm, its natural colour returning, the roar diminishing to a gentle susurration. And I know, without being told, that killing Frederick was the cause of that great disturbance. That I was within a whisker of changing it all in some great 'time change', some *Zeitverandern*. It did not succeed. And part of me is pleased that things remain as they were. Yet a further part of me feels purged. It felt good to kill the old bugger, to give him a taste of death, even if the changes won't stand.

Old Schnorr speaks from the shadows in the corner of the big room.

'Time heals itself, Otto. Even so, you must not try too much. Too much change and it will all come undone. Too much and the connections break.'

'Then it's as I thought,' I say. 'We can't change it after all. It's all been for nothing.'

He heaves himself up from the chair he's in, his face poking out into the light.

'No, Otto. Some of it you can't change. The paradoxes thrown up do not permit it. They revert almost immediately. And some changes are just too great. The river must flow, Otto. You cannot dam it up.'

'Then there are things that *must* be? Evils that *must* stand?'

'So it seems. Even a peaceful man – why, even Marcus Aurelius himself – had to fight his enemies.'

'Then what can I do that is different?'

'Make smaller changes. Subtler ones. Stop thinking of great men and great battles. Tackle evil at its roots. You need to change the *climate* of Time, Otto. Killing Frederick, that's still thinking in the old way.'

Once again I am reminded of Burckel's words, even as, exhausted, I stagger and hands reach up to hold me and help me down.

'We need to get to grips with the underlying phenomena, with the infrastructure *of history, not the surface froth.'*

448

And so, with a little help, I come up with something new.

My first experiment is with Hitler.

We save the three children that his mother lost before Hitler was born, and then, after his birth, arrange for his father to have a fatal accident, saving young Adolf all those years of his father's bullying. As a result, Hitler grows up in a stable environment, unbullied and in fact *loved* by his elder sisters, the young child – lacking the character deficiencies of old and looking up to his big brother, Hans, becoming a stretcher bearer in the war where he wins an Iron Cross for his bravery.

Not that it ameliorates *everything*. The war still ends badly – Hitler cannot affect that – and Germany sinks into depression and division. Yet the fact that Hitler is not there to take the helm of the National Socialists changes things. Without his guiding force they fail to gain power and when the crisis comes it is revolution and not war, with the communists taking brief charge of Germany before things settle. The Second War, when it comes, is in Asia, between the Japanese and the Americans – a brief spat over oil and rubber that is quickly over.

The *veche* are delighted. But I am far from happy. For none of this fills the void in me that is caused by the loss of my daughter Martha. Important as such changes are, I cannot settle until I have tracked Kolya down and found out my daughter's fate.

I have been putting this off, but now I have to face it. I have delayed too long. Krasnogorsk beckons me – that one place where I know for certain Kolya is – even if it is at the risk of being trapped for ever in that timeline.

Yes, and I must go alone.

449

And so to Krasnogorsk, on that dreary afternoon in the winter of 1239.

I hide in the wood, well away from the treelined riverbank and wait for events to unfold, witnessing Nevsky arrive with Katerina and I, tied up like slaves and led on ropes, staggering, exhausted from the long journey, the four Russian agents who were posing as Nevsky's *druzhina* – his bodyguard – following on horseback.

I watch the exchange between Nevsky and myself, then follow at a distance as they go to make their arranged meeting.

And there, in the flesh, is Kolya, waiting beside one of the huts, his two assistants and the cart nearby, on which there are two corpses.

And so the wheel turns once more and I see Kolya purchase Katerina and I from that cunt, Prince fucking Nevsky. I hear Kolya's triumphant laughter peal out, and as he turns, witness the sheer malice in his eyes, and then the shock in mine as – for the first time – I see my own body on the cart, Katerina dead beside me.

It is an awful, awful feeling. Yet even as Nevsky hands the ends of the ropes to Kolya, I can see how the Russian agents look to each other, as if ashamed. And sudden understanding comes to me. They *know*. They know I am their Master now. So this . . .

This is betrayal.

Only even as I work this out, my other self has gone down on his knees before Katerina. 'This is it,' he says, his voice breaking. 'Do you understand? This is the end, my love. They've won.'

And he vanishes, pulled back to Four-Oh by Zarah and Hecht.

And Kolya . . .? Kolya lets out an angry bellow and rushes towards Katerina.

But before he can travel half the distance to her, Zasyekin and Rakitin, two of the Russian agents, step out in front of her, swords drawn.

Kolya hesitates, uncertain suddenly just what is going on, and as he does, so another of the Russians, Pavlusha, turns and, taking a gun from his belt – a *staritskii*, I note – orders Nevsky to get down from his horse.

There is a sudden flicker in the sky, like lightning, only the sky is clear and blue. A moment later there is a great crackling noise, like over-amplified static. It seems almost natural, but the hairs on my neck bristle, knowing what it is. The timeline is drawing to its close. It is, in a very real sense, beginning to break up.

Nevsky, not recognising what Pavlusha is pointing at him, asks angrily what the fuck they think they are doing.

'Get off your horse!' Pavlusha repeats threateningly, and to let Nevsky know what the power of the weapon in his hand is, lets off a bolt past his ear, setting the pines behind him on fire.

Nevsky yelps with fear, his face changing almost comically at this demonstration. Panicked, he scrambles down off his horse.

But Kolya isn't done. 'Give me the woman!' he orders, making to push past Zasyekin, but Zasyekin isn't having any of it. He pushes Kolya away, then places the point of his sword against his chest.

'Back off, old man!'

Thus far I have held back, waiting to see what happens, but now I step out, drawing my own laser – a *spica* – as I come into view.

'You took your time,' Zasyekin says, with a weary familiarity. 'Put the pendant on her and let's get out of here. Can't you see what's happening?'

And as he says this, so, suddenly, there are two of me, our words just slightly out of phase. In fact, there seems to be two of everyone at that moment with just the slightest differences in their movements and their positions, showing how this timeline is splitting into two very distinct possible alternatives.

I glance to my side and see myself looking back at me. But in the very next instant I am singular again, the whole scene back to normal.

Nevsky looks petrified. Even Kolya looks worried.

'Come on!' Zasyekin yells, only there is a distinct echo to his words, and, at the same time there are whispers of other words, sudden ghostly images of other movements – of Kolya attacking Zasyekin and being skewered, of Nevsky running from the clearing, and of Katerina turning toward me. And yet no one has moved.

Where the river was is suddenly a dry earth gulley. The trees are suddenly bare of leaves and blackened. Ash covers the floor of the forest. And then that vision is gone and four of each of them stand there, faintly overlapping, that slight difference in words and movements more exaggerated this time. It's like four separate realities are running at one time, and then, as before, it snaps back to normal . . . or almost so, because now there are small, black, three-dimensional patches floating in the air, like parts of it have been erased. And at the edges of those small black holes, reality is fraying, turning slowly to mist and darkness.

Seeing me, Kolya shrieks and, moving back a pace, draws a big, snub-nosed state-of-the-art stun gun. It's clear he means business. He knocks Zasyekin aside with a blow that fells the agent, then aims the gun at me, but even as the charge leaps from the mouth of the gun towards me, so I sense someone flicker briefly into existence just at the corner of my eye. I can't make out who it is, but their warning cry comes a moment too late as the charge strikes me full in the chest.

There's an instant of excruciating pain, and then Time seems to jump backwards, so that, unharmed, I see Kolya draw the big snub-nosed gun from his belt. But this time, even as Kolya knocks Zasyekin aside with his free hand, another person jumps into the clearing. It's young Saratov, and while all the rest of us are hesitating, he takes action, firing his handgun three times, blowing Kolya clean off his feet!

I'm horrified. I wanted to capture Kolya alive, but now, it seems, he's dead.

I turn to Saratov. 'What the fuck are you doing?'

'Getting you out of there. All of you.'

He throws Zasyekin a time pendant for Katerina, then turns back to me and throws two more to me. 'Come on!' he yells. 'We've got less than two minutes . . .'

And, even as he says it, so the whole scene seems to twist weirdly, like it's all been pulled inside-out through a huge, three-dimensional lens. The very air shudders, like it's the skin of a drum that's been struck. Our images duplicate briefly, eight faint overlapping images this time, including one of Kolya hauling himself up off the ground, stun gun in hand. There are endless whispers now – words said not here but in other timelines – but when it all comes together again, Kolya is lying there, perfectly still, his steaming blood pooling beneath him.

I hold the pendants up to Saratov, seeking an explanation. 'I don't understand . . .'

'No time,' he answers. 'Just get to the cart and put the damn things on the corpses!'

I don't hesitate. I just do what I'm told. Yet as I make to lift Katerina's head, I gasp. She's warm, despite the ugly grey pallor of her flesh, the small, dark circle of the chest-wound. So too is my other self. I put the pendants on and turn, but as I do so the scene appears to split, parts of it beginning to fragment.

The dark patches have spread, forming long ribbons of black emptiness. Three separate Nevskys can be seen, crawling away in different directions, their eyes staring madly, as if they've fallen into hell.

The air crackles with static and there are jumps, like reality has been cut into individual frames and edited back together badly. I know we have only seconds to go now, and as I look about me frantically, I see first Zasyekin and then Pavlusha vanish. Katerina, a look of utter surprise on her face, is next to go, and then Rakitin and the other Russian agent, Tyutchev. He looks to Saratov, who tells him to jump.

'Jump now!'

Only he can't jump and leave the two on the cart.

'Jump!' Saratov pleads. '*Please*, Otto. You've done all you can for them. You've put the pendants on. There's nothing else you can do. But if we lose *you* . . .'

Saratov's words are overlaid with slight variations in how he said it. Moment by moment the scene is getting darker and stranger, with echoes and doubled images and strange ghostly variants, and everywhere those streaks of absolute blackness, like three-dimensional tears in the canvas of reality. And all the while it flickers and crackles like some very poor-quality copy, growing grainier instant by instant.

'Now-now-now-now-now-now . . .' echoes from Saratov's throat, and then suddenly he splits and breaks and . . . shatters like a glass decoration dropped onto a hard stone floor.

I stand there, staring, the shock of it finally getting to me. And, putting my hand to my chest, I jump.

450

Into silence.

There is a moment's total disorientation and then I realise I am lying on my back in a cool, white room. Katerina's voice sounds gently nearby.

'Are you awake, my love?'

I turn my head slowly, and see her, sat there in the chair beside the bed.

'Were they . . . okay?'

Her smile reassures me. 'Yes,' she says. 'Now rest. You need to rest.'

'But I . . .'

She puts her hand gently but firmly on my shoulder, making sure I don't rise.

'It was close,' she says, 'but we all got back. All except Saratov . . .'

I swallow, my mouth dry, then ask. 'What happened to him?'

'Rest, Otto. Please. There'll be time for explanations. But not now. Not yet.'

I lie back, trying to relax, only how can I? I keep seeing Saratov splinter into a thousand tiny, jagged pieces. And then I remember. 'Kolya, he—'

An alarm begins to sound. Katerina is standing over me now, holding me down.

'He would have killed you,' she says. 'In some, variant worlds, he *did*. It was you or him, you see. It always was. Only Saratov swung the balance. Not that he should ever have been there. He shouldn't even have existed.'

'What do you mean?'

But even as she shapes her lips to answer, so others arrive, medical staff from Moscow Central and I hear and feel the hiss of a hypo-dart as they inject it into my arm.

Katerina meets my eyes, a sudden sadness in her own. 'Later, Otto. When they've made you whole again.'

451

They sent them in again, back to Himki, to be caught by him and shot and drugged once more. In a loop, in an awful bloody loop. Them? Katerina and I. Brought back from the ragged, tail-end of Time and 'cleaned up' and sent back in again, their memories of it erased. Round and round and round again. For ever. Otherwise it would never have worked, whatever Phil reckoned. Awful. Bloody awful. But here I am, alive. Thanks to Saratov.

He left us a file, explaining it.

'You had to believe you were dead, Otto, or you would never have gone in that far, never found out what was happening.'

'Which was?'

Katerina fills in the gaps.

'Kolya wanted the two of us who were outside the loop. That's what the exchange with Nevsky was about. Because he knew you'd worked it out. That you'd somehow found a way to survive his original trap. Only he got it wrong. He didn't understand the *sequence* of it. He saw it only from his viewpoint. That's why it surprised him when you were pulled out, because he didn't believe you would ever leave me there. He wasn't expecting that. Only you *were* still there.'

'Hold on,' I say, confused. 'I still don't understand the need for the exchange.'

'He meant to kill us and leave us there, time-dead, irrecoverable, while the others – our drugged selves – would become Nevsky's playthings. He had told Nevsky how to remove the focus from your chest without killing you. Not that Nevsky would have cared if you died or not. It was me he wanted.'

'Then Nevsky knew?'

'Who knows? He believed you were a sorcerer, certainly. A rival to Kolya.'

'I see.'

And I do. Because we'd have been doubly dead, even if we'd both lived in Nevsky's service for a hundred years. Dead at Krasnogorsk and dead in Moscow, or wherever else Nevsky chose to keep us: Katerina in his bed and I in his cells. In torment. Utter torment. Only Saratov intervened. *Swung the balance.*

I frown. 'You said something earlier . . . about him not even existing.'

Katerina is very quiet, then, softly, she says: 'He was our son, Otto. The child we lost. The one Kolya took from us. Only . . .'

'Only what?'

'Because it's impossible,' she says. 'That isn't how Time works. Unless . . .' Katerina meets my eyes. 'It's changed, Otto. You and

I changed it, when we met. That's part of the main trunk now, Otto. Folded back upon itself. *Defying* the normal flow of time.'

So all of the branches come off of that, I think. *All of the secondary worlds, we're in them all, now.*

Hundreds of Ottos and Katerinas, our love multiplied over a thousand worlds in a thousand variations. No wonder one of him survived. Sergei Ilya Saratov. Our son.

And I shed a tear, for my only son, who sacrificed himself so that *I* – Otto – might live. Yes, and how different is that from Kolya and his 'son' Reichenau?

Only I'm not satisfied with those explanations. It might be what had happened, only it doesn't fit with what I know of Kolya. After all, remember what Schikaneder said about Kolya being 'the ultimate control freak'? Why then would he allow himself not to be in control at the end, at Krasnogorsk? His surprise – which I think was feigned – is not like him at all.

Alone, I tour all of those places where I know Kolya has been, finding them all abandoned, not a trace of any 'brothers' anywhere.

Kolya, it seems, has effectively been erased from Time, a 'fact' confirmed by Old Schnorr, who reports that there's now not a single instance of Kolya's face in Time.

My last port of call is the underground fortress just outside St Petersburg, back in Catherine's era.

I go inside and walk about the abandoned spacecraft, and for once it sets me thinking.

So was that it? Was Kolya so easy to destroy? Or did we miss something? After all, he was so skilful elsewhere So careful. So maybe we didn't get him after all. Maybe the Kolya my non-existent son destroyed at Krasnogorsk was equally non-existent. One of many Kolyas, perhaps, or a clone, or . . . and I keep thinking this . . . *that there was another spaceship somewhere else. Not any place where we would find it. Not in a million years. And this? A 'red herring', as they used to call it. Carefully crafted to throw us off the scent.*

Only that's not satisfactory either, because – as several of my experts have pointed out to me – it would be virtually impossible for Kolya to extricate just *his* genetic line, because it interacts – and is constantly mixed up with – the genetic material of endless other families through the wives and mothers of his ancestors. To remove himself he would have to take the whole damn human race with him, and he clearly hasn't done that.

And yet his genetic forebears *have* all vanished from Time. Have been erased, just as if they'd never been.

Leaves from a tree.

Is it possible, then, that, through chance, we have managed to achieve the eradication of his genetic line? In killing him at Krasnogorsk, have I somehow killed all his 'brothers' too?

Perhaps. Only I'm far from happy with that explanation. It doesn't *smell* right.

I sniff the air. *Where are you, you bastard? Where the fuck are you hiding away?*

452

I walk the empty corridors of the craft, stand on its untenanted bridge, and recognise that there are no clues here. Or none that I would recognise as such. And so I return, back to Moscow Central, where news awaits me.

They have located the jump-in point into the world in which I was trapped. The alternate 1984 New York. From jumping into it from Moscow Central, we have created a doorway to it from our platform. Which means I can jump back in there, any time I want, knowing that I can jump straight out of there again.

'Well?' I ask, looking about me at the others. 'Do I go in again?'

It seems I shall. But first I warn them to maintain a state of high alert. Just in case my instincts prove correct and Kolya's tricked us somehow. Because now, more than ever, we need to be vigilant. Now that we're so close.

453

And so I go back, to New York City in the first days of the presidency of Philip Kindred Dick, to try and unearth the truth of what happened there, and why Kolya chose to strand me there of all places.

Because he must have had a reason. Kolya never acts without a reason.

Only this time I'm prepared. I've hired an apartment directly across from the one I was dumped into, from which I can watch myself and witness all the comings and goings.

Only I need to be much closer than that. Which is why I find myself, on that first night of exile, there in the apartment, standing over myself in the half dark, conscious of how vulnerable I was, how broken. I have cried myself to sleep and now I lie there, facing the wall, like one of the dead.

Lost.

For a time I sit there, across from myself, watching him, aware of the great gulf that separates my selves, a distance so immeasurable it makes the stars seem packed within the vacuum they call Space.

To have lost it all. Yes, I remember how that felt. Remember the pain, the sheer desolation, the fear . . .

I turn, thinking I hear a noise, but it's only the wind.

I go to the window and look out, the view familiar from the time I spent here before. It makes me think of how much I have experienced since those days. How much has changed. And, thinking that, it makes me think of something else. Turning back, I quickly search the room.

And smile.

There's no gun here. No box full of money. All of those things that helped me, first time out, are missing. Which means that I'm going to have to bring them in.

Jumping back, I'm greeted at the platform by Ernst, who hands me a package.

'Is this . . .?'

He nods. 'And spare keys . . . just in case you need them.'

I jump back, and look about me, tense suddenly, alert. But it's only nerves. If someone else was watching me, I'd know.

Wouldn't I?

Unless, of course, Kolya is watching me watch myself. In which case, maybe this is some kind of mad experiment. Only I don't believe that.

I go back to my apartment and make myself some dinner. Then, on whim, I go out, walking past Joe's bar, looking in to see, there in the corner by the bar, Kavanagh, sitting where he always sits. Only even as I watch, another guy approaches. Kavanagh turns and offers his hand, and the two of them shake, and I know, in that instant, that *this* is DeSario. The two of them working together.

I walk on, wondering what they know of me, and how? Or is that wrong? What if I'm not part of their plan? What if I'm some completely new factor that they're about to have to weave into their scheme?

I drop my groceries off, then return to the bar, watching from a nearby doorway as Kavanagh leaves. I follow, using all my skills not to be detected. Across Manhattan and down Seventh Avenue, stepping back into another doorway as he stops and, looking about him briefly, goes into a building; a big, anonymous-looking building that might once have been a factory, but which has now, I'm sure, a very different purpose.

I jump out of there, back to Moscow Central, where once again Ernst has anticipated me.

'He's part of a team of four,' he says, handing me a rather slender file. 'It's not entirely clear what their mission is, but our best guess is that they're attempting to track down the assassins of President Reagan.'

'And Kolya? How's he involved?'

Ernst produces another file. 'It's not conclusive, but it seems Kolya was working with the local Mafiosi. What the deal was we don't really know, but he's met them on at least three occasions.'

'So why didn't we hit him?'

'We did. Or rather, *you* did, when you first were here, when you took out their offices that time and killed the Big Boss. He *was* there. But the bastard slipped away, as ever. Disappeared without a trace.'

I shake my head. 'I still don't understand. Why would Kolya want Reagan dead?'

'He probably doesn't. Or, at least, it's of little concern to him. But think about it a moment. Placing you in that apartment – a man without any history, in effect, without an identity – was guaranteed to place you firmly in the frame. You'd be the number-one suspect, Otto. It's only your past connection to the new president that saved you. Anyone else and you'd have ended up in the chair.'

'The chair?'

'The electric chair. It's how they used to execute criminals back then.'

I shiver at the thought. But I'm still not sure why Kolya would go to such lengths. If I were him I'd be far more direct. But then I'm *not* him. I don't really have a clue what's happening in his head. And that's the problem. Only this other matter – regarding Reagan's assassination – can be sorted.

Jumping back and forth through Time, I find out just how Reagan was assassinated and, typing it all out, I deliver an anonymous note to the new president and leave it on the desk of the Oval Office, there for him to read.

And not just the details of Reagan's assassination. There's also information about myself – that is, the Otto who was trapped in this timeline. And it's this lengthy postscript that convinces President Dick, that time when he goes to visit me in DeSario's apartment. I know that because I was there, listening through the door, realising that, without my intervention, I would probably have been arrested and incarcerated in this age. I would never have got out.

Instead, I'm there to hear Dick's final words to my earlier self. Words which reverberate in the depths of my soul.

'Then find her again. And save her.'

454

Which, of course, I've done, the past being the future and the future the past.

And Kolya?

Of him there is no sign. No sign whatsoever.

We've discussed this one a lot, and the most popular theory is that he's trapped himself somewhere. Jumped to a place he can't get out of. What else could explain his sudden disappearance throughout Time?

Well . . . there are a lot of explanations actually, only none of them quite satisfy. None of them get close to suggesting how such an intelligent and ruthless man should make such an elementary mistake.

And yet . . .

It must be so. Because ahead of me lie years of peaceful and productive activity, back in Cherdiechnost. Long years spent fathering my girls and creating a humane environment in which they might grow up. Time which is guaranteed me. And how do I know that? Because it's on the loop. On it and in it. A loop so strong that it has changed the very nature of Time.

On the last day of the year, 2999, we throw a party, at the big farmhouse in Tannenberg. The majority of the inhabitants of Moscow Central are there, eating and drinking and enjoying themselves. Katerina and our daughters are there, along with many other children, such that it feels like one big family, its members chattering away in German and Russian and in the slang American of the thirty-first century – which, in an hour or two, it will be.

I stand there, drink in hand, along with Ernst and Svetov and Old Schnorr, looking on, bearing witness to this historic day, for today is the day when we will shut down our operations in Time. There will be no more changes after this, no, and no more meddling either. Our agents will be allowed to settle where they will in space and time, and though they'll be called upon, from time to time, to serve a period at Moscow Central, it will be to make sure Time is constant.

For our role has changed. From being agents and soldiers, we are now to become watchers and guardians. Vigilance is to be our key word. Vigilance against Kolya and his like. Because I know, for a certainty, that he is still out there somewhere, hiding, scheming possibly, filled as he is with hatred for me.

Yes, as long as I live, he will hate.

And here, at the end of the old regime, another group of people arrive, these from Up River – future agents: proud, upright young men and women of indeterminate race, the products of the system we have only today initiated. I greet them, then, speaking to them all, tell them I must leave them now – that I have an appointment or two in Time – and I wink at Katerina and my daughters and then jump . . . to Cherdiechnost, to be there with Katerina at the start, and to make the first of my daughters.

Part Fifteen
The World Tree

'Odin sat in his throne of gold listening through the stillness, unafraid, waiting for Ragnarok and his own doom. Waited he also for the song's end and the promise of Time's new morning, when evil would cease to be and Balder would come back.'

– Donald A. Mackenzie,
Teutonic Myth And Legend

And so here I am, home again. Here at the epicentre of it all; the place from where the loop derives. Cherdiechnost. I sit beside her on the bed, as, knees raised and legs parted wide, her brow sheened with sweat, she pushes one last time, her face contorted, her hand gripping my hand fiercely as she does, a pained groan escaping her. And there, suddenly, she is, the glistening crown protruding, pushing up and out into the world, the nurse helping her now, gripping the baby's shoulders and drawing her out, the umbilical dangling in the wavering torchlight before it's snipped, everything slick with blood and afterbirth. And even as the nurse lifts and cradles her, so she takes a breath and cries.

I take her from the nurse, holding her close and warm against me, cooing softly to her, as if she's the most precious thing I've ever handled. Which maybe is the truth. Tears are rolling down my cheeks now, and as I look to Katerina, I see how she too is torn by this moment, how she turns her back on us, looking away from her darling child, unable to bear it.

For this is Martha, our little lost one, whom we have never found, despite searching Time itself.

Ernst is there, and Svetov, and they solemnly raise a glass to toast me as I step out into the kitchen where they are waiting. Sensing my mood, each in turn steps close to hold me briefly, as if to comfort me.

'I didn't think it would be this hard.'

'No,' Ernst says. He really has no words for any of this, yet there's genuine grief in his pale blue eyes and a thorough love for me and mine.

Svetov shows no such restraint, but pulls me to him in a great bear-hug, which takes my breath, but, meeting his eyes, I see he shares my grief, my awful sense of loss that places a dark shadow over my love.

That evening, at the feast to celebrate the birth, many of the villagers are there, among them Iranov, the priest who, I know, will one day betray us all. But I must live with such knowledge. Live with the fact that, joyous as it is, it is only for a brief time before I am taken back inside the loop. Yet while I am here, at Cherdiechnost, I am living for the moment. Savouring my time here.

Yes, and that is what we decide to do with baby Martha. To cherish every waking moment with her. That night, when we lie down in our huge bed, I lay our darling girl, there, between us, her small, warm body between our own, and I feel blessed. Even for the short time we will have her. Loving her with an unlimited love that even death cannot take from us. For she was made from the powerful love that this German boy has for his Russian girl.

Our lost girl. Our little beauty, Martha.

456

Six months pass, and with it comes the harvest. These are golden days, when the sun beats down from a perfect cloudless sky and winter seems a million years away.

I am working in the fields, alongside my good friend Kebba Puskarev, the big African from the Gambia, whose freedom I purchased in Novgorod's marketplace eight summers back. As we cut and bundle, so we talk, of places we have been and people we have met, good and bad. Kebba's dark skin glistens as he swings the scythe, while mine, my upper body tanned by the sun, is a different shade of dark.

It is something I have never fully understood, this matter of skin colour. Why it should determine what a man is in life and how he is to be treated by his fellow men. Kebba, after all, is Kebba, and as he laughs, throwing back his head, his perfect teeth revealed, I am amazed that there are those who cannot see what he is. Cannot recognise how warm and kind and fair the man is. How *good* a man. And yet most of his life he spent in chains, *owned*, like a mule or any other beast of burden. Twenty years and more he lived that way. But now he owns himself. Skin and bone. Soul and intelligence.

'So where have you been, Otto? You say you liked to travel . . .'

That's a hard one to answer without making it all up, so I decide to tell him half the truth.

'Home is Germany,' I say. 'Or was, before I came to Novgorod. Berlin, to be precise. A big, sprawling city, where one might hear a dozen languages and more spoken on the streets and in the markets.'

Kebba rests a moment, his chin on the handle of his scythe. 'Was that where you spent your childhood?'

I hesitate. The truth is I spent my childhood in a *nichtraum* – a no-space – called Four-Oh, and in a place we called 'the Garden'. But I can't tell him that. He'd think me mad. And so I lie, as I've so often lied in the past. 'I lived in a big house, with lots of other boys. Boys who, like me, had lost their parents.'

Or didn't know who exactly they were.

'An orphanage?'

'Of a kind. Only one that taught us how to survive in the world.'

Kebba nods exaggeratedly as if he understands that only too well. 'That's where you learned how to fight, yes?'

I smile and nod. 'Yes, and by the very best of teachers. And then they sent me out, with others, older than me – men who had experience of the world – and that's when I began to travel. That's when I began to see the world.'

'The world is a dangerous place, no, Otto?'

'A very dangerous place indeed. But tell me, Kebba . . . where did *your* travels take you?'

Others are gathering about us now, sitting on the bundles, or leaning on their implements, keen to hear what we have to say.

'Oh . . . many places,' Kebba says, his eyes looking back. 'From Bergen in the far north, to Antioch in Asia. I have seen the great Middle Sea . . . rather too much of it, if the truth be told.'

I meet his eyes, a query in mine, and he laughs.

'I was a rower for a while, shackled to the oars. Many a time we made the crossing to Africa. To Alexandria itself. That was a sight. And then – in another life, it seems – I crossed the desert.'

'The desert?'

'What they called Arabia. Many died on that trek. Only I and three other slaves survived that. The slave master . . . that was a cruel one. If I ever meet him again . . . Well, let us say I have no love for the man.'

'And how is it you came to Novgorod?'

Kebba is silent for a time, then he looks up at me again. 'Fate chose it, I suppose. There were two of us, you see. Prime slaves, there in the slave market of Salonika, being auctioned. The other . . . what his name was I never asked for fear of being beaten . . . he was bought by a master from Thebes, which was to the south, while I . . . I was to be taken to Polotsk. Only by the time I got there, the new master had already taken on two new slaves, and I . . .' He grins. 'I was superfluous. The agent who had bought me was given me in settlement. He, in his turn, was heading north, to Novgorod . . . which is where I was blessed to find you, Otto.'

I smile. How can I not smile. Only now I've got him talking of his past I want to hear more. And besides, it's a good excuse not to speak of my own; of battles in Time and meeting Christ and . . . oh, so many things he'd think me mad to mention.

'Was there ever anyone, Kebba? A woman, maybe?'

'Oh, there were many women. The slave agents encouraged it. Making new slaves, we called it. But there never was a woman I was close to. You simply didn't dare. Not if you wanted to keep sane. They play dirty games, those men. Yes, and they treat you like you are farmyard animals. So no . . . there was never anyone . . . not until I came here.'

And as he says it, he wipes a tear away. And I am both moved and amazed by his words. There I was, thinking my life was rich – the things I've seen, the things I've done – but Kebba's life is just as rich . . . as are all men's. It's all determined by how you approach life.

As evening falls, I feel that tell-tale tingle in my nerves, and Katerina, recognising my brooding mood, takes me aside and asks me if it's tonight. And I say I don't know, but that's not true. I'm almost certain. That, after all, is what the tingling is. A warning in my nervous system that I am about to be taken back once more, into the loop, to fulfil some other part of it.

It might only be days, subjective, but the next time I'll be here years will probably have passed, and Katerina, knowing this, takes my hand and leads me upstairs, where we make love, the whole house listening – unable not to, there is such passion in our parting. And when we come down again, there are knowing smiles and nudges and, when we come into the kitchen, gusts of open laughter.

'Is Daddy going away?' young Natalya asks, and Katerina nods, as her other hand wipes away the tears that come unbidden.

'Be strong,' I say. 'I will be back.'

'I know,' she says, but her eyes are welling once again, and there is little I can do than bid them to prepare my cart. But they are used to that now. To me 'vanishing'. One day there, and the next . . .?

Gone. Off on another of my trading journeys.

And so it proves. That night I am taken back – stolen from my bed, my hand seeming to vanish in her hand, my naked body taking on form as it emerges onto the platform at Moscow Central.

What I've come from seems like a dream – a dream I can return to once this small fulfilling of the loop is done. Yes, and I know that there's no other option, for Time cannot be changed – not this part of it anyway.

'What is it now?' I ask Svetov, who throws a cloak over my nakedness then hugs me, there among the dozen or so who have come to welcome me back.

'Baturin again,' Ernst says, handing me another of his meticulously prepared files.

'Baturin?' And I want to ask what in Urd's name are we doing going back to Baturin, only Ernst's eyes suggest I look at the file before I begin sounding off. And he's right, of course.

And so I find myself in what were once Yastryeb's rooms, sat beneath the Tree of Worlds, the contents of Ernst's file digested.

Baturin. It's Hecht's suggestion. Yes, Master Hecht who's long dead. But this was in his notebook, awaiting discovery, and so I go to find out what he did, what he saw in Baturin that made him seek to warn us.

But not yet. Not necessarily yet. I have to go, but the timing's up to me. And so, for once, I choose not to. To complete one other chain of this loop before I venture out to Baturin again.

Because this once things are different. This time Katerina has written to me. A long letter, telling me about how it feels when I am gone. It was Zarah who gave it to me, the message sent through the women. And why them? Because the men don't want to 'upset' me. And part of me understands that. It's not easy knowing how vulnerable she feels when I'm absent, because one of these days – within this very loop – I will return to find that Kolya's taken them.

And yes, I know that that has happened, but it also still lies ahead. For this is pretzel logic, remember?

But right now?

Right now I want to go back to the one place in all Time and all Space I wish to be – Cherdiechnost after it was rebuilt, in the time after the loop. And it is there, now, that I go, reunited with Katerina and my four remaining daughters, who have come directly from the new millennium party at Tannenberg.

The villagers welcome us joyously, throwing a big feast to celebrate our homecoming, assuming that we have returned from a long physical journey, not thinking for a moment that we could have arrived back in any other way. But so it has to be. It's a secret my girls have sworn to keep, now that they understand the alternatives.

Only then someone asks after baby Martha, having noticed that she's not there among us, and – as we've rehearsed among us – I tell the villagers that she is gone, died of the fever on our travels and buried at the roadside. Only it's very hard to do – to utter those half-truths – and I break down, unable to carry on, knowing that this kindly lie is the only thing I can give them.

So it is that, the next morning, after a strangely subdued feast, Katerina and I come out to find the front garden of our dacha wreathed in flowers. The villagers have constructed a little shrine for Martha, the sketch of her I did a few months back at the centre of great sprays of camomiles and crocuses, azaleas, orchids and lilies, great swatches of them in reds and white, interspersed with painted wooden crosses and handwritten notes expressing love and loss.

Katerina finds this hard. The not knowing. The pretending that she's dead, when all she is is missing. Oh, and do not fool yourself – every time I say that 'all' I feel a pain of grief and longing so vast it threatens to unhinge me. But for Katerina it's more personal. She, after all, carried Martha in her womb for nine months and more. Gave birth to her knowing she would lose her. What in Urd's name could be worse?

But this – this celebration by our friends of Martha's brief existence – gives Katerina some solace. As she says to me, 'It's nice to have one single place we know is hers, where her spirit can lie.' And so it is. For the first time, that evening, I go to the shrine and, kneeling, alone there, talk to my baby daughter, finally accepting her loss, knowing that I will never see her again. And when I turn, meaning to get up, it is to find Katerina and the girls, there, kneeling alongside me, silent yet potent presences, there beside the shrine.

And before we leave that place, Katerina takes me in her arms and holds me.

'Is it okay now?'

I lower my head and nod. Only it isn't. It could never be okay.

458

Back at Moscow Central it is quiet. In the half-light it can be seen that only a third of the desks are manned – by both men and women, Russians and Germans. It is so quiet, in fact, that no one seems to notice the faintest glimmer of the platform, like sunlight glinting at the bottom of a rock pool. There is no power surge, no physical indicator that someone has just jumped through, and yet they have.

There is the faintest glimpse of them as they step down and move slowly towards the exit. It is done so casually, with such a lack of fear, that we might begin to believe that everyone in Moscow Central has been gassed or has had a spell placed over them, like in the ancient tales, yet it is really no more than a moment's inattentiveness. They have spent so long being vigilant that they have stopped looking. No one even bothers to look up as the tall, heavily built man in the long dark cloak moves past them.

In Yastryeb's room it is dark, but at a word of command the lamp on the far side of the room lights up. Not that our intruder needs light to see by, yet in its faint illumination we see more clearly who it is, and, as he stands, facing the clear and steady glow, the Tree of Worlds no more than an arm's length away, so we see how much he has aged since Krasnogorsk – how grey his long hair now is, how lined his ancient face. For this is the Master of Time himself, and he has come to check how things are in his domain.

He leans forward, placing his hand into the flow of energy, closing his eyes as the tingle of power runs over his fingers like water from a fountain. His lips, which never smile, tighten with concentration, and then he nods and lowers his hand and turns away.

Yet, before he goes, he walks across and, taking a book down from the shelf, opens it to the title page and, taking a pen from his coat pocket, writes a few words, then, below his message, signs with his customary mark, the lazy eight, the arrows pointing toward the centre – the same symbol that his ungrateful bastard son stole from him, along with so much else.

He puts the book back, the faintest ghost of a smile suggested but never surfacing on his lips. For a moment longer he looks about him, his fierce eyes seeming to take in everything about him in that room, and then, like a wraith, he vanishes.

The Tree of Worlds shimmers briefly, a single strand of its capillary-like branches pulsing a momentary brilliant carmine and then, like a stick of incense, turns to smoke. And then there's laughter, doubled, trebled in the room. Demonic laughter.

Epilogue
Six Endings

One

Sideways Twice and Back a Step

459

Kolya is after me.

I woke last night, snatched from the drowning pool of nightmare, to find a warning, written in blood on the wall beside my bed, from an agent of ours who has subsequently vanished from the map. 'Run,' it read. 'For Urd's sake, Otto, there's no time! Run!'

Only, even as I flee, going through my mind is the thought that there is *always* time.

But there is certainly no time to consult them at the platform, and so I adopt the emergency strategy our Great Men devised to deal with such a situation, using the special pendant to override the platform, jumping twice sideways and then back; each time the same, each jump taking me deeper into the maze that is the multiverse.

Twice sideways and once back? you ask. Why that?

The answer's simple. It's the knight's move in chess, and I use it to escape him. But at some stage I must return, or else be lost for ever. Hence the constant, easy-to-remember pattern.

The knight's move. So it is. Only this particular knight moves not on a board that's eight by eight, but one that is immeasurably larger, a four-dimensional board that is infinity times itself, then times itself again. The uncountable times the uncountable, and then again. And no. It is impossible to imagine it. The human mind hasn't the space – or inclination – to do so.

Ironically so, I think, as I make the first of a dozen tiny jumps, side-shifting through time, working my way slowly away from the central core into unexplored territory. My two eights and his two lazy eights. Now where have I encountered those before?

It is incredibly strange, doing this. It has a certain dreamlike quality. Because, from the first jump on, I've been effectively 'off radar', untraceable from Moscow Central, like a worm burrowing into the depths of the cosmic apple.

Only what kind of apple – cosmic or otherwise – would contain so much that's un-marked, unaffected, by intelligent life?

No. Don't answer that. The proper question is, what kind of multiverse is it that has any trace at all of intelligent life in it?

No, and don't try to answer that one either. Let's be more practical and ask why Kolya should be after me again? What's triggered this pursuit?

Maybe it's something I've done, or am about to do, elsewhere and elsewhen.

Or maybe the messenger simply got it wrong. Only I have been dreaming of Kolya these last few nights, since I've been away from Katerina. Dreams in which I die horribly.

On the tenth jump back, I stop, to 'catch my breath'. On all my previous jumps I've not stayed long enough to really register what's surrounding me, only a vague and generalised sense of things growing more wild and less human as I move further and further away from the main trunk of the World Tree.

But this once I take the time to see just where I am. To pause and turn 360.

When this is or where I do not know, but I seem to be in the depths of some great medieval castle, in a stone-walled corridor, lit by cresset-lamps, at the end of which is a massive, wall-length mirror.

I walk towards it, seeing how the other I – the mirror I – walks toward me. Which seems quite normal, only there's something wrong about this reflection.

My mouth opens, as I realise what it is. I am the same. Least, my mirror self mirrors me perfectly. But behind me . . .

Behind me ought to be the lamp-lit darkness of the corridor. Only it isn't. What is behind me – *beyond* my mirror self – is a landscape of scorched earth, the terrain, right to the horizon, burned to ash.

For a moment this is all. My mirrored self and the un-mirrored landscape. Only then a second figure enters the frame of the mirror.

Startled, I turn, looking behind me, only the flame-lit corridor is empty. Yet the mirror shows him clearly.

Him. Yes, Kolya. He looks about him, then comes across, standing there, two, maybe three paces behind me. He's wearing a long, pale blue cloak in this incarnation of himself. And his hair is darker, more lustrous, his face less lined. A younger version.

'So you've come,' he says, and the words, muted and distorted as they are, are out of synch with the figure that now faces me.

Can he see me? I wonder. Or does he only see my mirror image? Who now is he addressing?

He studies me a moment longer, surprised, perhaps, that I do not turn and face him on his side of the mirror, then comes closer, noting the fixed direction of my gaze. Looking past my mirror self to where I'm looking on. And I know suddenly that he cannot see me. That I am not present in his side of the reflecting glass, just as he is not present on my side.

Which is just plain weird.

Or is this just some property of Time at t⌐

the centre? Have I jumped so far from reality

natural laws have come into play?

Kolya moves past my mirror self and stand⊖

so close now that my fine hairs bristle with A

knows that someone's there behind the surfa

he cannot see me. Light is travelling in only o⊓

'Ah . . .' he says quietly, looking from wha

myself – to my reflection, and then back again, tⅠ

as before. 'I see . . .' And then. 'Or rather . . . I

aren't you, Otto?'

And as he utters those final words, he to u

surface with his left palm.

And there it is, his palm, imprinted on the su⊐

all clarity and detail; distorted, just as the sour

Instinct tells me not to say a word, not to ⊓⊓

any kind. Yes, and to keep him uncertain, even

there. Only, seeing those eyes, only an arm's le⊓

the imperfect imprint of his palm on the mirro⊐

skin stands on end with fear.

Can he get to me from there? Can he som⊔r

and pursue me?

Logic would say no. Only what's logical ab

If he can get at my reflection – which, it s⊖

he not also get at me?

He clearly has the same thought, for sud⊂⊃

pale eyes changing, registering some insight. Ta I

my mirror self, he reaches out . . .

Like Alice, I think, not sure from where th⊜

even as his fingers penetrate – pass through

shape of me, a faint electrical charge hissing

does.

Yet, before he goes, he walks across and, taking a book down from the shelf, opens it to the title page and, taking a pen from his coat pocket, writes a few words, then, below his message, signs with his customary mark, the lazy eight, the arrows pointing toward the centre – the same symbol that his ungrateful bastard son stole from him, along with so much else.

He puts the book back, the faintest ghost of a smile suggested but never surfacing on his lips. For a moment longer he looks about him, his fierce eyes seeming to take in everything about him in that room, and then, like a wraith, he vanishes.

The Tree of Worlds shimmers briefly, a single strand of its capillary-like branches pulsing a momentary brilliant carmine and then, like a stick of incense, turns to smoke. And then there's laughter, doubled, trebled in the room. Demonic laughter.

458

Back at Moscow Central it is quiet. In the half-light it can be seen that only a third of the desks are manned – by both men and women, Russians and Germans. It is so quiet, in fact, that no one seems to notice the faintest glimmer of the platform, like sunlight glinting at the bottom of a rock pool. There is no power surge, no physical indicator that someone has just jumped through, and yet they have.

There is the faintest glimpse of them as they step down and move slowly towards the exit. It is done so casually, with such a lack of fear, that we might begin to believe that everyone in Moscow Central has been gassed or has had a spell placed over them, like in the ancient tales, yet it is really no more than a moment's inattentiveness. They have spent so long being vigilant that they have stopped looking. No one even bothers to look up as the tall, heavily built man in the long dark cloak moves past them.

In Yastryeb's room it is dark, but at a word of command the lamp on the far side of the room lights up. Not that our intruder needs light to see by, yet in its faint illumination we see more clearly who it is, and, as he stands, facing the clear and steady glow, the Tree of Worlds no more than an arm's length away, so we see how much he has aged since Krasnogorsk – how grey his long hair now is, how lined his ancient face. For this is the Master of Time himself, and he has come to check how things are in his domain.

He leans forward, placing his hand into the flow of energy, closing his eyes as the tingle of power runs over his fingers like water from a fountain. His lips, which never smile, tighten with concentration, and then he nods and lowers his hand and turns away.

Only someone else has other ideas.

'Okay, Golubintzev, leave the man be. He's sorry he bumped into you, but that's no reason to kick ten shades of shit out of him.'

Straining my neck muscles, I see, past Golubintzev, a woman, her furs tightly fastened at the neck, her dark hair falling in ringlets.

'It's none of your business, Mariya Beskryostnov,' he says slurringly, glaring at me.

'No?'

'No. Now go back inside your shop and keep your nose out of things. Who is he, after all, your long-lost brother?'

The others laugh.

Only now she says something else.

'I saw him,' she says. 'This morning, in the cards.'

Golubintzev's eyes register surprise. 'In the cards?'

'In the cards.'

'It was him. Are you sure?'

'A *nemets*, yes.'

Ten seconds pass, and then he sheathes the knife, standing back to look at me, his eyes contemptuous. A *nemets*, that's all I am. A German. Why, he'd not sully his blade.

'He's yours, woman. I give you him.'

As they make their way away, I dust myself down, then look to her, my saviour. And find myself looking into a face of quite stunning beauty. Until that moment I had seen her only as a spill of dark hair against a white fur, but now . . .

'Well?' she asks, gesturing with her right hand, which holds a woven basket full of provisions. 'Are you going to stand there gawping or will you come inside?'

'Inside?' I follow the line of her gaze and see, there just behind her, a blue-painted wooden door, and over the door a sign. *Divinations*, it reads.

379

I look to her again, and see she's smiling.

'Look, thank you. For a moment there . . .'

But I fall silent again, struck by her beauty. Those violet eyes . . . now where have I seen *those* before?

Only as I take the first step there's a voice in my head.

'Ten jumps and then no more,' it says. *'You are at the very limits here, Otto.'*

Limits?

All I know is that I feel the growing strain of it, each time my body's rendered into atoms? And is that why I can't remember? Have I stretched my memories to an intolerable thinness? Stretched taut and then snapped back. To here. To Baturin.

She's staring at me now as if I'm a strange one. And maybe I am.

I take a step then stop. 'Look, I . . . I don't even know your name.'

I say that and instantly feel a fool, because I do. She's Mariya Beskryostnov. At least, that's what that rogue, Golubintzev, called her.

'Of course,' I say. 'You're Mariya.'

'And you?'

'I'm Otto . . . Otto the *nemets.*'

Yes, and Otto the forgetful.

463

Inside, embalmed, or so it seems, in a haze of sweet-scented perfumes and incense sticks, is her living room, a place of richly coloured silks and satins, of embroidered cushions and Persian wall-hangings, of comfy sofas and rich piled carpets, not to speak of the burning candles and the gold-framed mirrors and . . .

Divinations. I understand that now.

In the centre of it all is a low table. She makes me take a chair facing her across it. A table upon which is carved and painted a hundred strange devices, its rich decoration matching that of the room.

She smiles, then unfastens the fur at her neck and pulls it off to reveal a long, flowing dress of brilliant red, trimmed with an edging of blue and green and yellow. The kind of thing Russian peasants wear to church or on special days. Her earrings are large and colourful, while about her wrists are a dozen bangles that make a musical sound whenever she moves her hands, which is often. About her neck are a collection of various gold and silver charms. Only I am a man, and as a man my eyes are drawn to the curve of her breasts beneath the cloth, the fullness of her figure. Yes, and her eyes.

It's that last that disturbs me most – that throws me – because it reminds me, vaguely yet strongly, of other days and other eyes. But whose I do not know.

Seeing where my eyes dwell, she smiles and touches herself there, then turns away, moving across to a small wall of shelves, on which are many things – books, cards and trinkets among them.

'Have you travelled very far to come here, Otto?'

Have I? Damned if I know. Yet it seems so, so I nod.

'From Germany?'

Again I nod.

She turns back. In her hand now is an illustrated box of cards. I recognise them at once. The Tarot. Are these the cards she saw me in? If so, what significance has that?

She places the box between us on the table, then, seating herself across from me, tips the cards out and hands them to me.

'Shuffle them, Otto. Ten good shuffles, then hand them back.'

I do as she asks, taking the cards from her, and as I do, so my fingers brush against hers; that brief contact is like an electric shock, or a jolt of static.

We jerk our hands apart . . . and laugh.

'The power's strong in you, Otto.'

Only how do I answer that? And what kind of power does she mean? The power to change universes? I have that. But the kind of power that speaks of magic? In that I don't believe. I am, after all, a logical man.

I shuffle the cards – ten times – then hand them back to her.

'Have you ever had your cards read, Otto?'

If I have then it's completely slipped my memory.

'No, I . . .'

'It's all right,' she says, her voice softening, as she lays out the cards in what I recognise as a Celtic Cross. 'There's nothing complex about a reading, Otto. It's all . . . *intuitive*, I guess you'd say.'

Yes, and look where intuition has got you, Otto. Sat here with a gypsy woman in a town that's due to be burned to the ground sometime in the next twenty-four hours. What sense does any of this make?

Only I say nothing, just sit there, waiting to see where this road will lead.

I watch her reach out to turn the first of the cards, and notice, as she does, that her fingernails are painted with tiny gold circles against the red, like coins in blood.

For a moment I watch her hands, fascinated, then meet her eyes again.

She's watching me.

I look away. 'So?'

'So we begin.'

And she turns the first card.

'You must remember, Otto. The cards are all connected. Each one has individual meaning, but you must grasp the bigger picture. Nothing within the tarot is on its own.'

Only I'm not really listening. I'm staring at the turned card, reversed as it is to my view.

'Strength' it reads. Or, in German, *Starke*. Which is what we time agents would wish each other before we jumped from the platform in Four-Oh.

The first jump of ten.

For a moment I feel disoriented, like I've got up too fast. Only I'm still seated.

'Strength,' she says, her whole face lighting in a warm smile. 'See how the woman seeks to control the lion, the beast within, which represents our emotions. Note how patient she is. How courageous.'

'And the symbol?'

'The symbol?'

'Above her head. The infinity sign. The lazy eight.'

'Oh, that. That is the Lemniscate. It's a geometrical representation of energy, of its endless and eternal nature.'

'I see. And do any other cards carry this sign?'

She considers, then smiles once more. 'Well, there's The World . . . the Two of Pentagrams and, of course, The Magician.'

'But here . . . what does it mean here?'

'It means . . .' And she laughs – a pretty laugh – then reaches out to touch my hand. 'Our passions, too, are a form of energy. Let them run wild and they will damage us. Some Diviners call this card "Power", and the Lemniscate channels that power.'

'In a loop,' I say, and she nods and smiles and takes her hand away.

And turns the second card. 'This next card "crosses" you.'

I stare at it a moment, mouth open, then reach out and pick it up.

'Otto, you can't—'

'Where did you get this pack? Who gave it to you?'

The card is Death, but that is only half of it, for Death in this picture is Kolya, and his men, who fill the landscape beyond his unmistakable figure, are all his 'brothers'.

She takes it back from me, a touch perturbed by my reaction. 'I bought this on my travels in the southlands, from an ancient Ottoman . . . a Turk, you might call him . . . But why do you ask?'

'This one . . .' And I reach across to place my finger on the figure of Death. 'I know him.'

She laughs, slightly awkwardly this time. 'Everyone knows him. He is "The One Who Cannot Be Avoided".'

'Is that his other name?'

'Oh, he has many names. But that card, Death, is not death as you and I might experience it, but transformation. A transition to a new level of existence.'

'I see.'

Only I don't. Kolya is Kolya, and that's him on the Death card, and there has to be a reason for that. But I let it pass. I need to know just what the other cards have on them that relate to me.

She turns the third card. 'This card relates to the unconscious and to what's going on in the depths of us.'

The card is The Lovers. I look at it and nod. That's Hecht in the top half of the card, that fiery figure, like an Archangel, his wings spread wide.

I look at her anew. Is she just an innocent, or is she, like me, an agent?

She shakes her head; the barest of motions. 'This card . . . on its own . . . well, I would say that, while you appear to be very much in control of your passions, even, dare I say it, something

of a cold fish, beneath it all, in the very depths of you, you're . . .'
She meets my eyes. 'Who is she, Otto?'

'I don't know. It's like I've forgotten.'

'And yet she's there . . . in your subconscious.'

Yes, and if I close my eyes I almost see her.

The fourth card is Judgement.

'Another Major Arcana card,' she says, surprised.

But I'm not listening. This time I'm shocked, because beneath the figure of the trumpet-blowing angel is a peasants' cart and on that cart two figures, their naked bodies as pale as death as they wake to new life on the Day of Judgement.

Me and she, partners in death. Whoever she is.

'Are you all right?' she asks, suddenly concerned. 'Only you've lost all colour.'

'I'm fine, I . . . No, I'm fine.'

Only it's like I'm suddenly separated from her by a sheet of glass. Her lips move but no words seem to emerge.

The fifth card is . . . The Hanged Man.

'Odin,' I say. 'That's Odin and he's hanging upside down from the Tree of Worlds.'

'That's right,' she says, surprised. 'He's on an inner journey . . . one that links to the Strength and Lovers cards. All three of these suggest that you will only find wisdom through controlling your emotions.'

'And yet I seem a cold fish . . .'

'What you seem and what you are. They are different things, no, Otto?'

'So it would seem.'

The sixth card – the last of the first part of the reading – is The Tower.

This card surprises me. It's different in kind from all those that preceded it. So full of anger. So full of violence.

The tower itself is struck by lightning. Rain falls from a cloudy sky. As the tower bursts into flame, men fall to their death.

'The world re-cast,' she says.

The death of the old, I think. *Change.*

'Change,' she says, as if in echo to my thought.

The kind of change that erases worlds and puts others in their place.

She is staring at the cards, a strange expression on her face. 'All six in the Major Arcana.'

'Is that strange?'

But she doesn't answer, merely reaches across and turns the seventh – the first card of the four that run in a straight line from the past into the future.

The Magician.

She laughs, but it's a nervous laughter. This is clearly not going the way she'd thought it would.

I study the card. Over the Magician's head is the symbol for infinity. The lazy eight. The snake eating its tail, or the Lemniscate, as they call it.

As for the magician himself, he seems a relatively young man. No greybeard, this. In his right hand is his wand, while on the table in front of him are the implements of his pseudo-scientific powers.

'The Magician,' she says, her voice almost a whisper. 'The gateway to the Divine. The very conduit of the higher powers.' She looks to me. 'Just see what cards Fate has dealt you, Otto.'

Yet she seems perturbed, *shaken* almost by the reading. Seven cards and not a single one from the Minor Arcana. Not a single cup or wand, not one pentacle or sword. What were the odds on that? How likely was it?

This once she does not dwell, but turns the eighth card hurriedly. 'The High Priestess . . .'

I put my hand out. 'Can I see that?'

She hesitates. This reading is slipping away from her. Even so, she hands the card to me, then sits back, studying me.

I'm silent a moment, taking in the details of the card, then look back at her. My heart is racing. Was this my lover in some other past or future?

'I know this woman. I don't know where from, or in what circumstances, but . . . I *know* her.'

Mariya shakes her head. 'You cannot possibly know her, Otto. These cards . . . they are several centuries old. And the woman here . . . she's just the abstract of a woman.'

'No,' I say and shake my head. 'I know her.'

'You mean she *looks* like someone you know.'

Someone I know very well indeed. But where she lives and what her name is escapes me. In the card she sits on a throne between two pillars, surrounded by all manner of symbols, magnificent and powerful.

Mariya takes the card back from me.

'The Priestess speaks directly to the inner voice,' she says. 'Her domain is the unconscious. Perhaps that's why you think you know her, just as you think you know your Inner Self.'

'I don't believe that. I *know* her.'

Only I can see she doesn't believe me. But then, why should she? Unless she's a time agent like myself. But then, why this charade?

'Show me the last two.'

That flirtatious element has gone from her face. This reading has soured her mood.

She turns the ninth card. It's The Wheel Of Fortune. I see her intake of breath and know that this all means something to her.

'Fate,' she murmurs, in the quietest of voices. 'Destiny itself. It's all connected, Otto. Our fortunes rise and fall, as the great Wheel turns, but for some . . .'

She turns the last, the 'outcome card' as she calls it, impatient to see the whole of it. I see how she looks from one part of the spread to another, piecing it all together, a look of genuine, unfeigned awe in her eyes.

'Oh, Otto . . . The Star. It lights your way into the future. It . . .' She reaches across and takes my hands in hers. 'Oh my word, what a reading! I have never seen the like! You . . . you're very special, Otto. The Child of Fate. But you must look to what is inside you. Must follow what your inner self decrees, trusting that before all else. You see, The Star is a card of Faith, and its presence here in the tenth place is Fate telling you that you must have faith in the powers within you. Allied with The Tower, it is a powerful omen. Great change is coming to your life, but also great understanding. Few are given such an insight into the workings of Fate. But you . . .'

Mariya looks beyond me suddenly, and I turn, sensing someone else in the room. Her hands fall away from mine.

'Ernst!'

Ernst scowls at the woman, dismissing her at a glance. 'You must come, Otto. Things are happening.'

Mariya puts out a hand, as if to stop me rising from my chair. 'You can't go. Not now. I have barely begun—'

Ernst huffs impatiently. 'There's no time to waste with all this clap-trap! Come, Otto! We're needed.'

I nod. Yet I'm tempted to delay and ask the woman what else she sees in the cards. How she explains those aspects that seem to be intimately related to me.

I stand, pushing back my chair.

'You must go,' I say, looking to her. 'Leave Baturin right now or lose your life. Menshikov is coming, and he intends to raze the town to the ground and leave no survivors.'

She laughs. 'It cannot be. There was nothing in the cards.'

'Maybe. But then I came. And things changed, no?'

She nods uncertainly, then looks at the spread before her on the table. For a moment her whole being seems focused on the cards, as if she sees something other than what normal sight might reveal, and then she looks to me again. Meets my eyes and, almost without thought, hands me The Star.

'Take it, Otto. Let it be your light in dark times.'

'Oh, for fuck's sake,' Ernst says, uncharacteristically tetchy. 'Bring on the goat's entrails!'

But in the moment before we jump I meet her eyes and smile and let my lips say thank you, registering the shock in her face as first Ernst and then I vanish into the air.

Three

A Few Short Words in *Ge'not*

464

'Okay,' I say. 'So what's so important?'

'They're trying to change it, Otto. In the one place where it can't be changed.'

'Who?' I ask, wondering if Kolya has made an appearance during my brief absence.

'Germans . . . Russians, too. Dead men.'

I wonder what he means by that, but he quickly explains.

'Someone's gone back, way back, and left instructions. Brief notes in *ge'not*. And always for agents who, within hours, would be dead. Time-dead.'

'And have any of them been successful? Have any of them survived and made a significant change?'

'Not a single one, but—'

'But what? You know as well as I that part of the loop is woven so deeply into the weft of Time that *nothing* can change it. Not in its essence, anyway, and not without damaging reality itself. As for details, well, they don't really matter, do they? They change temporarily, and then change back.'

June 2747 we're talking of now. In the final days before the bombs fell.

Only in my head I'm still in Baturin, in 1708.

'The Tower,' I say, as if placing a piece in a puzzle. 'The same pattern. Eternally repeated.'

Ernst frowns deeply. 'What in Urd's name, Otto? Get all of that nonsense out of your head. It's superstition, that's all it is.'

I look to him. 'I'd agree, old friend, only there were things on those cards specific to me. There was a woman – I don't know where I've met her, but . . .'

'Katerina,' he says gently.

And I see her face again, in a flash that's just as quickly gone. 'Who was she?'

'Not now.'

'But . . .'

'Not now,' he repeats. 'As for this other matter, I don't think we can avoid it. It's failed so far, but that's not to say that they won't find a way . . .'

'How often are these intrusions?'

'One every fifteen minutes or so. But back in the Past. Our Past, that is.'

And suddenly it hits me. 'They've got access!'

'Access?'

'To the Haven. How else would they be able to track down dead agents? When they died, the link to the timeline they were in would have "died" with them. And the only record of their presence in those timelines would have been with Hecht's brother, in his archives at the Haven.'

Ernst shakes his head. 'We've looked there already. There's no sign of infiltration.'

'Oh . . .'

Then how was this being done, and – more crucially – why? After all, what could be achieved? Unravel that twisted skein and what would follow? Not time travel, that's for certain.

'What did they say, these notes in *ge'not*? Can I see one?'

'Only two have survived.'

'So?'

'I'll have them prepared for you. With translations.'

I nod. 'Incidentally . . . what was all that about just now, in Baturin? The stuff with the Gypsy woman?'

'She was an agent.'

'I thought she was. Only you were supposed to be with me. To jump in with me, and . . .'

Ernst looks away. 'I got delayed.'

'Delayed? No one gets delayed in Time. You can pick the precise spot. So what was going on? Why did you leave me alone with her? And why did I feel like I'd been hit over the head?'

'Our best guess is that it was the result of being catapulted back in Time. Those last ten jumps took things just a little too far. Your connection was stretched thin. We had a hard time tracing where you were. But then we located you. In Baturin.'

'But why leave me there alone?'

'To see if she's the one.'

'The one?'

'The one who's still connected to Kolya. When we realised it was her, we did a bit of digging. She's worked for all sides. For Reichenau and the Russians . . . why, she even worked for us, in the past.'

'You mentioned Reichenau before. Have I met him?'

Ernst stares at me, surprised. 'Reichenau? You don't remember Reichenau?'

I shake my head.

'Urd help us, Otto! Two brains sewn into one head? *That* Reichenau?!'

'It's a total blank.'

'Urd's sake! Did you leave your memory out there in the Wilds?'

'The Wilds?'

'Distant Time. That's what we call it. The Wilds. Don't you even remember that?'

And now I'm worried. What else have I forgotten? Who else? The woman in the High Priestess card for a start.

'As for the Gypsy woman . . . in some timelines she's a complete innocent. In others . . . she's got a twin, who works at Cherdiechnost.'

'Cherdie-what?'

Ernst stares at me, horrified now. 'Otto. Stay precisely where you are. Don't move and don't under any circumstances jump. Don't even *think* of jumping. We need to look at you. You've come back out of Time with half your memories missing!'

465

And possibly more than half. But first an aside.

In *ge'not* there are twenty-seven different terms for developmental control genes, and not a single one of them deals with the phenomenon of Time. We'll, not directly, anyway.

Developmental control genes?

DCGs are genes that have, as their primary function, control over development decisions. They regulate the fate of cells during their development, producing thereby the wide variety of life we witness on this planet. You see, genetics is entirely about *sequence* – about trigger events at the cellular level. The shape of a simple leaf is an example. The way it splits and branches. It is as it is because of certain natural decisions, decisions which are controlled by the DCGs.

And time travel?

Time travel bucks the rules of genetics. It is a kind of 'mutant'. That is, it ought not to exist in this unidirectional universe. And yet it does, the irony being that it depends on the transmission of DNA to function.

Oh yes, and there are forces that bond us to Time, and should we place too great a strain upon those forces . . .

Ernst, more than anyone, should know that.

I lie there, in the medical centre in Moscow Central, waiting for the results of the tests. Waiting to hear whether or not I've suffered a crucial loss of memory, and why, and what can be done about it, when I remember something.

I remember how it began.

When Ernst returns I tell him all I can recall of it, and he sits there, staring into the air a while, taking it all in.

'Are you sure?' he asks.

And I tell him I am. That what we thought was the culmination was in fact the start. That it began with my rebirth, raised from the cart – just as in the tarot reading – and carried from there to safety. From which point – and here it gets complicated – everything connected back. Back to the ending which we have been wrongly perceiving as the start.

Wrongly because that is the only way our brains have been genetically programmed to view it and interpret it. Whereas, in fact . . .

'That can't be so, Otto,' Ernst says, interrupting my chain of thought. 'That would be like . . .' And he shrugs, unable to come up with a likeness. No. The more I think of it, the more I am convinced. Time has two faces. It runs two ways, like the two circles in the lazy-eight symbol Kolya uses. And we can only travel within it because that is so. If it wasn't . . .

Only right there I start to shed my certainty. Because back at Krasnogorsk – and I remember its name now – reality itself was fragmenting. Put under too much pressure – too many tugs in too many directions – it began to fall apart.

As in that other card – The Tower.

Was that why she was there? To give me, in some palatable form, a series of clues, to help me understand just what has *really* been going on.

And Kolya?

We have been wondering all this time just how he could anticipate each and every move of ours, how he knew each time just where we'd be and when. It explains why we could never touch him. Never come close. It seemed like some kind of mind-reading trick on his part, only it wasn't. He was simply looking back over what had already happened – yes, and forward to what must be. Like Odin in the first and last days of the World.

Yes, it explains it all. The Past as Future and the Future as Past. Grasp that – attune your self to Time's twinned directions – and the rest was easy.

Only why, then, did he not kill me? What stopped him?

For that I have no answer. Not yet, anyway.

But it must make sense. It has to. How would any of this have happened otherwise?

466

I dream of moths, their wings painted in the colours of the woman, a dark red trimmed with blue and green and yellow. They flutter about the candle's flame and the light dances with them, casting shadows on the walls.

Of her – the Gypsy woman, Mariya – there's no sign.

The room is empty, silent but for the flapping of the moths.

And then I wake, to find myself in my own rooms once more, alone, the Tree of Worlds pulsing, shining in the darkness, the silence perfect.

And beside me?

No one. My bed, like the room, is empty. Katerina, Ernst called her, as if that should trigger some recollection. Only it doesn't. Not even at the deepest depths of me. I do not know her. She, who meant all the world to me. Why, she's not even an absence in my head.

Heavy-hearted, I shower and dress, then go out, searching for Ernst. And find him, poring over a map.

I go across and stand beside him. 'What's this?'

He looks to me and smiles, as if he's been expecting me. 'It's an estate in Russia, just north of Novgorod. A place called Cherdiechnost.'

'The place I didn't recognise?'

'The same.'

'And this woman? She lives there, yes?'

'We don't know. We presume so, only . . .'

'Only what?'

'Only this timeline is somehow flawed. Your failure to recognise it . . . that's troubling. Which is why we want you to study this and prepare yourself, ready to go back in. We need you to report back. To describe the place and how it functions and, well, to give us a portrait of the place to compare with what we know.'

'Cherdiechnost?'

'Yes,' he says, and there's a sadness in his eyes. 'Cherdiechnost.'

Four

Cherdiechnost B

467

Things have changed. That's the only thing I'm sure of. Reality itself seems now as changeable as the clouds, constantly forming and reforming. The question is, did we cause this? Is this the net result of all our meddling?

It is a warm, late summer day in AD 1237 and as I follow the broad and dusty path that leads down through the trees, I ask myself why I don't remember this. What's happened to me that could possibly have erased it? Because I've read the files and seen how powerful the time-change was. How she and I were central to it all. But now?

Now I cannot even remember her face.

The estate is up ahead, across the plank bridge and on another mile or so. It's harvest time and the serfs will be out in the fields, stripped to the waist beneath the blazing sun, gathering in the crops. While I . . .

I am an outsider, a youngish-looking man in my early forties, walking that broad path, wearing furs and carrying a heavy backpack, strangely over-dressed for this time of the year, sweat trickling down my brow and inside my loose-fitting clothes.

Ahead of me, beneath a cloudless blue sky, there where the ground begins to dip, is Cherdiechnost, a huge, sprawling estate, worked by over four hundred serfs and their families. It's a dour, unhappy place by all accounts, but not the Cherdiechnost that exists in our records back in the Haven. So let's distinguish. Let's call this Cherdiechnost B. The greyest of grey shadows of the place I once knew.

Not that I can remember much.

I am stopped at the gate by two big, brutish men, who keep me there while a boy runs across to the village to fetch the steward.

The steward turns out to be an elderly man in his sixties, his hair trimmed like a priest's, his whole nature slow, methodical, enough to make me wonder how he got the job. While he stands there, examining my papers, I look about me. I've seen all this before, of course, in the simulator; yet seeing it for real I get a much better sense of things.

The main *dacha*, the master's house, is to the left, no distance from the gate, surrounded by a scattering of smaller buildings, while the main village – a sprawl of cheaply built dwellings that edge the fields – is directly ahead of me. And there's a pond and a mill and a forge and a carpentry shop; enough to make the estate self-sufficient.

Finally, the steward looks up. 'Just what do you want?'

'I hope to get work.'

'Work?' He shakes his head. 'We have all the hands we need. Try the town.'

'I've tried the town. Someone said I might find employment here.'

He's about to tell me to move on before I get a beating, but just then a young boy runs up to say there's been an accident. Old Gregor has sliced off two of his toes with the scythe. It's his own fault, the boy is saying. He shouldn't have drunk so much last night.

Which leaves a vacancy.

'I can swing a scythe,' I say.

His eyes rest on me a moment, and then he shrugs. 'What's in the sack?'

I slip it off my shoulder and hand it to him.

He opens the neck of it and looks inside, then looks up at me again, surprised. 'Did you *steal* these?'

'They were my father's. He was a smith.'

'But you can use these, yes?'

'At a pinch.'

I nod. Smiths, in this age, are fairly high up the pecking order. It's an in-demand skill, and it makes the steward reappraise things. 'You worked with your father . . . in the past?'

I nod again.

'Come then,' he says quietly. 'Field workers I don't need, Gregor's toes notwithstanding. But smith's assistant . . .'

He dismisses the two guards, then gestures for me to follow him down through the knee-length grass and into the village, where, amid the dilapidated and decaying buildings, there's a forge. Not an impressive one at first glance, but that too is very much of this age.

The smith himself looks up from the horseshoe he's been making, his eyes suspicious. 'Who's this?' he asks, as he hammers out the red-hot iron.

I smile inwardly, for I can see at once that he's not the most skilful of smiths. There's a kind of awkwardness to him.

'This is Petr. He used to help his father out, in the smithy. I thought you might appreciate having a boy to act as a runner to you. To gather wood and feed the fire and pump the bellows.'

I see how the smith likes the steward's use of that word, 'boy'. It makes me less of a threat to him.

'Where's he going to sleep?' the smith asks, glaring at me, as if to put me in my place from the start.

'He can sleep here, in the back room. No need to impose on you, eh, Simon?'

Simon, eh? Not a traditionally Russian name.

'That be good with you?' the steward asks, turning to me.

I bow my head. 'Thank you, master, I . . .'

'Steward,' he corrects me. 'The master alone is the master.'

And he's not here right now. I know that from my briefing. But when he comes back he'll want to see me; to make sure I'm no troublemaker. Because troublemakers aren't welcome here in Cherdiechnost B.

'What about my pack?'

'You can leave that in the house for now. Until you leave us.'

'I thought, maybe—'

'Leave it,' he says. 'Unless you'd rather walk on.'

I bow my head. 'As you wish, Steward . . .?'

'Shepnikov,' he says and puts out his hand, taking the heavy pack from me, weighing it a moment before turning away, leaving me alone with the smith.

He's scowling still, appraising me, weighing up whether I'm a good thing or bad.

'Where you from?' he asks.

'South,' I say. 'But now I'm here.'

I see a flash of anger in his eyes. I'm rather too mouthy for his liking.

'Sorry,' I say, playing the conciliatory card. 'It's just . . . home was trouble. That's why I left, when I was seventeen. I came north. Tried my hand at trapping and hunting. Farming, too. I arrived here by chance. But now I need . . . well, I need to put down roots.'

'And you think this is the place?'

But I can see his attitude has softened. He gestures towards the wood stack. 'Build the fire up, Petr. I've eight more of these to fashion.'

468

As it turns out, the smith is not so bad, and for five days we get along just fine. He even lets me fashion a few things by myself, watching me with what I guess is admiration. But then the master returns from one of his trading expeditions, and things change.

On the second day back, the master summons me, sending his two brutes to fetch me.

Entering the room wherein he's sat, I fall to my knees, my head lowered.

The master is a big man. Six foot six and built like an ox, with a shock of long blond hair that gives him the look of a Viking chief, which is maybe what his ancestors once were. And then there's his son, stood just behind him, slimmer than he, but with the same shock of blond hair. A young man born to get his way. *Indulged*, the smith called it, when I asked. You can see it in his eyes, it seems, in the very way he holds himself.

The Sons of Odin.

'Master . . .'

My humility clearly pleases him. Behind him, his son smiles.

'Get up, man,' the master says. 'I'm told your name is Petr and you're a smith's son. Is that so?'

'Yes, master,' I answer, but make no move to get up. Like almost all the masters in this age, he likes the sense of his seniority. *Enjoys* it. And I want no trouble with him.

'And you want to stay here, yes? In Cherdiechnost?'

'That is so, master.'

'Smith Simon speaks well of you. My steward, too. But tell me . . . what trouble was it that set you travelling at so young an age?'

I look down. 'Do I have to say?'

'Only if you wish to stay.'

And so I tell him the tale I've learned by heart and, as I end my account, I see him nodding to himself.

'Families . . . there are ravenous wolves that behave better.'

The master eases back a little in his chair, then nods. 'You can stay, Petr, just so long as you behave and do what you're told. You're a free man, I understand that. You've bought your freedom, but if you want to stay you will work hard and do as you're told, when you're told. Do you understand?'

'I understand, master.'

'Good. Then go now.'

I hesitate. 'And my pack, master?'

He looks away. 'Don't worry. I'll take good care of it, Petr. After all, what safer place than with me, no?' And he laughs, as if it's all a joke and he hasn't already gone through the contents with a fine-tooth comb.

Back at the forge, the smith is curious as to what went on – what was said and what decided – but I'm not feeling like telling him. My task here is to find out why Cherdiechnost changed. Why my small utopian dream – my north Russian paradise – turned into a nightmare. Because perhaps there's a clue in that as to what has been happening lately. Particularly my loss of memory.

Not to speak of Kolya and whether he had a hand in this.

That night, the master throws a party, partly to celebrate, but also because – and word of it does the rounds within the hour – his son has his eye on a new conquest. A young maid who, with her family, arrived here from the town not two weeks past.

Oh yes. The boy means to get her father drunk, her mother distracted, and the maiden . . .

Well, let's not be coy about it. He means to fuck the maiden, virgin as she is.

All of which barely touches me. Masters are masters – with exceptions, and I count myself as one – and most will use what power they have to grab whatever it is they want, whether that be gold or land or flesh.

No. I am not here to save the maiden's virtue. I'm here to find out why – at approximately this time – things went wrong. And, with that, why the Tree of Worlds should undergo the convulsions of Time Change. Major Time Change.

I cannot afford to be distracted. Cannot, this once, let small things shape my course.

The smith gives me the day off to go and help set things up – carrying the big trestle tables and benches, then helping fill the bonfire and—

And then I see her. The maiden. Only I don't know it's her straight away, only that she is the most stunning woman I have ever seen.

I know her name even before I ask it. Katerina. And, for the first time, I wonder how I could ever have forgotten her.

She's helping lay a massive white cloth on top of one of the big trestle tables when I see her first, she and a dozen other young maidens, who, as one, throw the great white cloth high into the air, then spread it across the wooden surface, laughing as they do, their movements like the steps of a dance.

*She looks across and her mouth falls open in surprise. She knows me.
Just as I knew her the first moment I set eyes on her. I see her mouth
my name.*

Otto . . .

And turn away, disturbed, hurrying from there, my thoughts a
storm of confusion – for, much as I know her, I have never met
her before this moment. We have no past, no shared experiences.
And yet I know we have.

Cherdiechnost, and Katerina . . . how much more have I forgotten? No. How much more has been *stolen* from me?

It's as if they've been in my head and altered things. Tampered
with my memories.

That night, after the celebrations, the master's son goes to her,
and, her parents sleeping a deep and drunken sleep, he has his
way with her. In the darkness I hear her, crying out for help,
sobbing helplessly as he forces himself on her, her cries for help
no doubt arousing him.

There's a part of me who wants to go to her, no matter the
danger, to kill the bastard – big as he is – and free her, only I
have been given orders not to intervene. Not in any circumstances.
And so I lie there, beneath the rough sheet, my eyes squeezed
tightly shut, my hands gripping the wooden bed frame, like it was
I who was being raped.

Only what I really feel is shame. Shame and an overwhelming
hurt. Like I have violated my very soul.

469

I wake, and all has changed. My head hurts and, on investigation,
I find a bloody lump on the back of my skull that's tender to the
touch. But that's not the only thing. Other things have changed,

and that alone suggests that someone has been tampering with this timestream. Making those changes. And when my mother . . . yes, I have a mother now, a white-haired ancient . . . asks me where I went last night, I know at once where I went. To try to save her. Katerina, that is. Only I didn't.

Why, I was lucky not to die, the savagery with which that bastard clubbed me. And I realise that I'm in trouble now, thanks to my attempted intercession. I'll get a flogging at best. And at worst?

At worst I'll get my throat slit or a long time in the cells, my arms and legs chained to the walls, like a common criminal.

Which serves me right for not staying on message.

And, suddenly, Svetov is sat there at my bedside, placing his finger to my lips, whispering to my ear, explaining what's going on. That all this is somehow necessary. To protect things and keep this time-strand alive, to keep it 'growing'.

'Yes, but why did you permit that?' I ask, referring to the maiden. 'Why did you let that bastard rape her?'

Svetov looks down, as if ashamed, but his voice is clear and steady. 'Because in all other versions she dies.'

I consider that, then ask the question that's been bugging me since I came awake again.

'Something's wrong,' I say. 'My memories of other lives . . . they ought to have been changed, erased, even as my memories of Katerina have been erased. But that isn't so. I've a head full of partial memories. Of vague recollections and . . . flashes, I guess you'd call them.'

'That'll settle,' he says. 'But keep on in there. It will get better. You will pull through.'

'For what purpose?'

'To change it all back. What other purpose could there be? If they maintain this . . . if *he* maintains this . . . then he'll have

405

won. Because this place – Cherdiechnost – is the hub of it all. It's the reason why it all happens as it does. Or did.'

'He being Kolya?'

'Who else?'

'But how did it get like this? It was so strong. So . . . *permanent*. To transform it in this fashion . . . how did he manage that?'

Svetov shrugs. 'We don't know. But he did. So it's up to us to find out what he did and how he did it and change it back.'

'And if we can't?'

'Then we'll have lost.'

470

Svetov's words are still reverberating in my head an hour later when I'm dragged before the master. He's angry with me – furious – and inclined, I believe, to have me executed there and then. Only I plead with him, telling him I was mistaken, that in the dark of the night I didn't realise that it was his son, and, begging for his mercy, tell him I'll work for him for nothing for a whole year if he'll only forgive me. And I hate myself for grovelling in this fashion, but there's no other way to keep in this loop, and when he says two years, I agree to that – even though my true inclination is to choke the fucker with my bare hands, to gouge out his eyes and cut him into pieces for what he allowed his son to do to her.

In the end he proves 'magnanimous'. His word, not mine. It seems I'm to get ten lashes for offending his dignity. Ten lashes and two years of working for nothing. And all because the boy's a cunt.

Not that I plan to be here for that long. Not with things as they are. No. Somehow – and I don't yet know quite how – I plan to change things back. To make this the safe haven that it was. A nest for my six sweet darlings.

And so, as the sun nestles in the sky's heights, I am bound to the whipping post and, with the whole estate assembled to bear witness, receive my punishment, vowing after every stroke to kill the bastard slowly when the time comes.

Which it will.

They cut me down and, letting no one come to my aid, watch me stagger back to my hut where that stranger, my mother, is awaiting me, the blood on my back glistening in the sunlight, the pain – in my back and on the back of my skull – threatening to black me out.

For a moment I stand there, my hands gripping the frame of the door, my eyes closed, willing myself to stay on my feet, then go inside and, waving the old woman away, ease myself down onto my pallet bed.

My head swims, then vision comes clear.

What am I doing here? What in Urd's name am I about? Is Svetov right? Do I really have to stay here – for as long as it takes?

It makes no sense. No sense at all. But if Svetov says it . . .

Unless Svetov's one of them now. Those Sons of the Lazy Eight.

But even as I think it, I dismiss the thought. I'd trust Svetov every bit as much as I'd trust Ernst. More so, in fact, considering all he's done for me since our forces merged.

But just staying here. Not interfering. Can I really, honestly do that?

I wait a day, two days, helping out at the forge and staying silent, then, on the third day, venture out at first light.

If there's one thing the master doesn't expect it's for me to escape this place. Not while he has my pack and all the valuables inside it. Not to speak of that other treasure his son has been visiting these past few evenings. But if I've been contemplating running away, then my mind is quickly changed.

Coming to the top of the escarpment, I am faced by a great sea of mist, extending to the distant horizon. A thick white sheet of mist that seems to mark the edge of this world.

I return to the hut in time to meet up with Smith Simon. He wants to know if I am fit to work yet, and though I'm far from recovered, I say yes. But my thoughts are elsewhere.

What if this is a construct of some kind? What if this is not Cherdiechnost at all, merely another copy? A copy convincing enough to distract me while he goes about his evil work elsewhere?

Unlikely, I know, only this really is enough to make you paranoid.

I go out to get the week's orders for the smithy, keeping a watchful eye all the while, noting what changes our friend has made to the estate. There was a pretty little copse down at the foot of the big field, but that has gone now, cut back to build a hideous-looking barn. As for the school buildings, they have been torched and turned back into the soil. For there's to be no educating these serfs.

As for the serfs themselves, they're a surly lot. Not surprising considering the punishments that are constantly being doled out. But it's more than that. On my estate they had a stake in things. They worked hard because working hard meant that they earned a greater share of what we all produced. I would even say they were happy.

Back at the forge I find the smith seated by the unlit fire, biting on a thumbnail, looking inward at his thoughts. Seeing me he hurries across and, making sure no one can overhear, begins to question me.

'Why in God's name did you do that, Petr?'

I almost tell him, but draw back from the truth. 'I don't know. Something about her, I guess. Her innocence.'

'Yes,' he says, the look on his face surprising me. 'The bloody noise she made. I couldn't get to sleep afterwards. It's not the first time, but . . .'

'But what?'

'Nothing,' he says, clamming up, something about it suggesting to me that to even talk of this could get one punished. Or worse.

Angered, he tears the list of orders from my hand and studies it, then grunts. 'This'll take an age . . .'

'Then we'd best get started, neh? After all, I'm working on special rates now!'

It's a feeble attempt at humour, but the smith appreciates it and returns my smile. 'Just keep your head down in future, yes?' he says. 'As for the girl . . .'

I raise an eyebrow in query.

'Close your eyes and ears. He'll soon grow tired of her.'

'And then?'

Only he doesn't want to talk about this any more and turns his back on me, beginning to prepare the forge for lighting.

471

The next time I go there the mist has gone. Like it never was. But it's still not right. There's still something about the landscape that is unconvincing, some quality of vagueness, as if only the very minimum of effort has gone into creating this. It has . . . how do I put it? . . . an overwhelming sense of incompleteness. This is distinctly amateur. A job half done.

Only that seems totally at odds with what we know of our friend Kolya. This cannot, surely, be his work. It doesn't have the feel.

Unless . . .

Unless his resources are finally depleted. Unless he's quite literally running out of time.

I laugh, amused by the absurdity of that, then turn abruptly, sensing movement at my back. Kolya? Only there's nothing there, just a lack of sharpness.

Running out of time. What a notion. As if that were at all possible.

I walk back, up over the lip of the land, the great sprawl of the estate suddenly below me again, the image sharp and crisp. This had been home. The place I made. My great social experiment. All gone, as if it never was.

And still no clue as to why.

Only standing there, I have a thought. What if this *is* no more than a superior kind of backdrop? A screen of sorts. What would he be seeking to achieve by creating this? Is his purpose simply to confuse?

That night the young master pays the maiden one more visit, and for a while all seems peaceful. Only this time it's his screams, not hers, that rend the silent night-time air.

I've left the forge in an instant, joining the crowd of serfs and their families who quickly fill the big field before the master's *dacha*, anxious for news. And then it comes, but not as an announcement. No. The first we see of it is the master himself, down at the south gate to the field, where one of his men opens the latch and stands back as the master comes through, carrying something large and heavy; his muscles straining, his face . . .

No, I cannot see his face, but I know how it must look, for from the spill of golden hair it's evident who he's carrying. His boy. The vehicle of all his dark ambitions.

Next, dragged along between two ropes, comes the girl, stumbling and fearful, her face, when it comes in view, pale and distraught, her eyes unseeing. And beyond her, her parents, roped just the same, their pleas for clemency ignored, the mother falling once and then again, mud smearing her plain white dress.

Up the long slope towards the *dacha*, where, at the edge of the fenced garden, five great trees reach up into the dark.

And even as we watch, lamps are lit and, as the master nears the very top of the slope, so his steward makes his way down the slatted wooden path from the house toward him, gesturing to his servants to lay down a great padded bed-cover. It is barely down before the master staggers to a stop and, his legs almost giving under him, gently lays his boy down onto the blanket.

For a moment he simply stands there, swaying, as if in a daze. Then, life returning to his face, he turns and watches as the others are dragged up the slope toward him, the crowd angry now, spitting and cursing the trader and his family.

And now time itself seems to slow, as I see, over to my right, ropes being cast up into the high branches of the trees, barechested men following them, shimmying up the trunks to secure them.

There is to be no trial. No reckoning of who was right, who wrong. And, knowing that, my stomach clenches, knowing what's to come.

Those last few yards are awful, as I watch Katerina and her parents dragged and tugged into the open space beneath the trees where the master now awaits them. There is a moment's silence, and then the big man, his breath pluming in the air, leans close and strikes out, his closed fist breaking Katerina's nose.

She sinks to her knees, and as she does, so he draws his knife and grabbing her hair, lifts her head and draws the sharp blade across her face, left to right, then right to left, extending the

411

shape of her mouth from ear to ear, the soft flesh falling aside, blood bubbling down her neck and chin.

I howl. Her helpless screams break my heart. But he's not done with her. Standing back a little, he surveys his handiwork, then steps forward again, and with an obscene little movement, pokes the knife tip into her eye, blood spurting from the wound in a great spray.

I sway, feeling close to fainting, but there is nothing I can do, and even as the big man turns and gestures to his men, even as I step forward, meaning to stop it, I see how they're noosed, how more men rush to join the servants at the end of the rope, adding their weight as the three of them are jerked up off their feet, the nooses tightening as the bodies dance and sway in that lamp-lit space, moving up into the air.

Dead.

472

And I wake, the girl beside me, naked in my arms. I turn and stare at her and she says 'What?'

'Where are we?' I ask, remembering where I'd been but a moment earlier.

'Cherdiechnost,' she answers me. 'Where else?'

Where else indeed.

And then I notice it. Around her neck. A small copper pendant in the shape of an ash leaf. Beneath which, I know, is the lazy eight.

So why didn't she jump? Or did she? Damaged as she was.

But no. This is a much younger Katerina.

And part of me wants answers. Part of me wants to jump straight back to Moscow Central and find out what's been going on. Only I'm here, beside her, her warmth, the smell of her, intoxicating. And in a moment I am kissing her again and her arms go round my back and . . .

But you know the rest. It's what happens every time we meet.

And when we're done we lie there for a while, until she breaks the silence.

'What happened?'

'They killed you.'

'I thought they might. So what . . .?'

'Don't ask,' I say, putting my finger to her lips. 'It was awful.'

She's quiet again, then, 'Are we any closer to an answer?'

'No. But there was one thing . . .' And I tell her about the mist and my sense of incompleteness. That it wasn't all quite real. And she nods thoughtfully. And smiles.

'What?' I ask, puzzled by her amusement.

'I was just thinking. Maybe it's a peripheral world. One he's shunted us off into. One where – *because* it's peripheral – it's also less real. Less focused.'

'Okay. But why do that?'

'Because . . .'

Only that isn't an answer. That's just an admission that we have no answers. No. We haven't got a fucking clue what he's doing.

'So where next?'

She looks down, then meets my eyes again. 'I'm off up ahead. I'll tell you about it when we next meet up.'

'And me?'

'You're staying here. Svetov thinks you're close. Very close. That last time . . . the time before when we died . . . you literally shook the tree. There were BIG disturbances.'

That surprises me. Chiefly because Svetov didn't tell me.

'I should go back,' I say. 'See Svetov. Find out what else he hasn't told me.'

'You think that'd help?'

It always has in the past. But I don't say that. In fact, I change the subject. 'I had my tarot read. Did you know that?'

'I read the report.'

I wait. Then, when she doesn't answer me. 'And?'

'The cards are over there. In my knapsack. It was . . . interesting.'

I sit up, balancing myself against the stout wooden partition. 'Interesting? Is that all?'

'Sure. They're only cards.'

Only I don't think she really believes that. I think, if anything she's jealous of the gypsy woman who read them for me. But I'm not going to say that. Not while I have her naked in my bed.

I reach out and gently touch her neck. 'Do you want to . . .?'

Katerina smiles. 'What do you think?'

I smile, only there's a chill wind blowing out there and it's worrying to know just how many timelines there are that I don't know her in.

'Come here, my love. Come closer . . .'

For who knows how long it'll be until we meet again.

473

I find it. Or, rather, I trip over it and find it.

Why they didn't choose a better spot, I cannot say; only that it's hard to predict – from over a thousand years' distance – just what might grow there in between times. Especially when the timeline is changing so often.

A tree root, *that* was what it was attached to! And once I'd found it, my job was nice and straightforward. To watch it as long and as often as I could and see who came through. In both directions.

A platform. One small, man-sized platform, there at the very centre of Cherdiechnost. Un-noted, undiscovered, until I tripped over it.

Going where? And for how long?

Well, let's not rush. Let's take things nice and slow. Because we've all the time in the world to get this right.

I look about me, checking to see if anyone has seen my little accident, but it's early morning and there's no one, as far as I can see.

I crouch, examining it. It's small. Incredibly small, considering. It's almost certainly not from my age. No. This is as advanced as it gets. The only thing that gives away its function is its shape. That lazy eight we're now finding everywhere we go. The same shape that was there back at the start.

Looking at it, I realise that I need to get someone in here to look at it. Someone who might make proper sense of it. Who has the expertise. Just in case it's another time-trap, like the one that claimed Ernst. And so I jump, back to Moscow Central and to Svetov who is waiting beside the platform, as if expecting me.

Which, of course, he is.

'What is it?' he asks, and I blink, surprised by even this partial knowledge of why I'm there.

'It's a platform,' I say. 'A platform the size of a pearl.'

'Are you sure that's what it is?'

'Not one hundred per cent.'

And so we send in Hans Luwer, our artefacts expert.

He's back in less than ten seconds, nodding to himself and pulling at his new-grown beard. 'It's a real beauty,' he says, smiling broadly. 'I've never seen its like. The sheer delicacy of its fabrication . . .'

415

'A platform?' Svetov asks.

'A platform,' he confirms. 'Though I'd not advise any of our agents to try and use it.'

Svetov frowns at that. 'Then what use is it?'

'None at all, if we *want* to be cautious.'

'Then?'

'We take a risk,' I say, deciding there and then that if that's so then I'll be the one to take it.

Svetov is staring at me now, and then he shakes his head. 'No, Otto. You can't.'

'Can't I? I mean, aren't I the one all this has been designed for?'

'Precisely.'

'Well, then. Let's get whatever information we can. Send a few drones through – using my DNA – and try and establish where this links to, and what level of threat this involves. And then – and only then – I jump through.'

Hans Luwers shrugs. 'I don't know, it . . . it feels to me like Kolya's placed this there, right in your path.'

'Yes?'

'Oh, absolutely. He'd know you couldn't resist.'

And maybe that's true. Only I need to see where this leads, even if it means placing myself in danger one more time.

'This is our break,' I say. 'This, well, this could explain why Cherdiechnost changed. Where it all went wrong. If we ignore this . . .'

'I'm not saying we ignore it,' Svetov interrupts. 'I just don't want *you* to put your neck out this once. I mean, there's no need. Why not let our foot soldiers go in? Let *them* find out what it's all about and then jump through. To take any other action . . . well, it's just crazy, Otto. You're Master now, remember?'

And that's true. Or most of the time. Because that's another of those things I keep forgetting.

'Okay,' I say. 'So send me back in while you decide. Give me a day or two to see what I can see, then we'll address this matter again, in council, if you must. But don't pass on this. This is important. We need to see where this leads.'

474

They've always been protective. Always wanted to safeguard me against my wilder instincts. Only this time I can't help myself.

Reaching the foot of the great sloping field, I see them, there where night left them, their lifeless bodies dangling from the trees.

Pale and bruised, Katerina's naked body turns slowly in the morning breeze, like a great haunch of meat, her face disfigured.

I come closer, each step reluctant. Then, feeling a heaviness, an overwhelming hopelessness wash through me, I sink to my knees.

Dead. My darling girl is dead. In this world as in many others. Dead beyond recall. For I know we will have tried.

Ah yes, you say, but what of the Katerina I woke to? What of her?

Fewer and fewer of her kind remain. As if the night sky itself were shutting down, all those tiny pinpoints of light winking out, one after another, until . . .

I slowly haul myself back onto my feet, unsteady, afraid to look up again, lest my heart break once more.

And turn my back, for there's nothing to be done. No endless process of jumping back and forth in time can repair this.

I walk away, knowing what I must do, yet sensing a futility so profound that it takes my breath. Seeing her on the cart at Krasnogorsk was bad enough. But this . . .

This makes me want to end it now. To take a blade and . . .

Clenching my fists, I stop. For this is what he wants. My despair is his delight. My love . . .

But what *does* he feel? Or does he actually feel anything? The man seems inhuman, after all. So maybe he *doesn't* feel. Maybe . . .

I stop dead, noting the figure at the bottom of the slope, beside the gate. Is that Kolya? Come to witness my grief?

Only it can't be so, for, seeing me, this one raises an arm and waves and, as he begins the slow climb to where I stand, I realise that I know him, even if I cannot put a name to him. That for some reason I owe this one a life.

Saratov . . . is that it?

Only even as I put my hand out, even as I take my first step towards him, the air itself seems to shimmer and he's gone. Turned to smoke and ashes.

My mouth is dry now, a sense of nausea sweeping over me. He is playing with me, surely? Mocking my efforts. Showing me how easily he moves the pieces round the board. As in the old days.

Only I can't give up. I have to see this through.

Walking down to where the figure vanished, I have the strong sense of being watched. Stranger yet, in the place where the figure stood, the ground is now discoloured, a fine layer of ash covering that part of the pathway. And when I jump . . .

. . . it is not to Moscow Central, but to an old and bustling city. A place I'm sure I've been to, long ago now. I look about me, gathering clues. They speak English here, for a start. A broad countrified accent, like something from medieval times.

London. This has to be London. And as I start making my way to the river, so I am grasped through time and vanish from that crowded sidewalk.

475

'I'm sorry,' Svetov says, brushing me down. 'You weren't meant to go there. Not yet, anyway. We need to brief you first. Put things into context.'

'Context?'

'Some of it you know. Other parts . . .'

And for some reason he grimaces.

'Does it involve me dying?'

He hesitates, then nods. 'Once or twice.'

'So where was that? The place you snatched me from just now. It seemed . . . *familiar*. That river . . . I feel like I've been there before.'

Svetov looks down. 'We can't tell you. Least . . . not all at once. We need to feed it to you, piece by tiny piece. We've tried it other ways, but . . .'

He falls silent. Looks at me and shrugs. 'I can't say more, Otto. Only that if there are any answers to what's happening, then they're there. In the next place.'

'And Kolya?'

'We'll come to that. But first let's brief you. Or, at least, give you what we can. What you need to know. The rest . . . well, the rest is yet to come. It's all folded in, Otto. Realities like Russian dolls.'

'And the cards. The gypsy woman's cards?'

'They're in your sack.'

'You brought that back, then?'

Svetov smiles. 'I wasn't going to leave it there. Not that you'll need half of that stuff. But you never know.'

'So where exactly are we going?'

'Moscow Central.'

'And then?'

'London. Back where it all begins.'

Five

Of Time and Tides

476

Imagine this. Imagine living the best part of your life in one single, uninterrupted flow, having your children, loving your wife, and, on top of all else, building something – Cherdiechnost: that was utterly worthwhile; that thoroughly deserved to be guarded and preserved for all time. So it was for me in those days – those weeks and months and wonderful long years – that followed on.

Like one beautiful, endless summer.

Living life as if it would never end. Children's voices echoing across that sun-lit valley, joyful and high.

And then – unexpectedly and abruptly – out. Detached from it all. Some strange new urgency calling me back once more to that which I'd oh-so-gladly surrendered. Thrown back into the game, as if the rest were nothing but a dream.

Briefed and armed for war. That cherished reality reduced to little more than a distant memory. The loss of it so acute, so . . . *painful*, that to dwell too long on it might break a lesser man. Or is that true? For surely this is how soldiers have historically felt. Snatched away from everything they valued, everyone they loved.

Gone, and no immediate returning. Not until the job was done. Not until . . .

The incoming tide breaks against the rocks. There's a sudden slush of pebbles, like the indrawn breath of a giant, and then I'm there once more. Back there where I've been so many times.

477

Shakespeare is a big, heavy-set man, and as he climbs into the boat ahead of me, I catch a glimpse of his face, the flesh deeply lined, the eyes melancholy. It's June, but you would scarce believe it. The drizzling rain makes it seem like late October, grey cloud filling the sky, that same greyness reflected in the surface of the river.

It is 1609 and this is London, this the Thames, and, as we take our seats and the boatman casts off, so I find myself seated just behind Will, wedged in among a dozen others, poorly dressed in their brown and grey rags, the rancid smell of them reminding me once more that I'm in another time, another place.

The boat lies low in the water, the weight and number of its passengers surely unsafe, but this is the only way to cross, or it is for he whom I'm following.

He's silent, self-contained, but I know that his eyes take in everything. Yes, he's a living sponge. *Nothing* evades his notice. Unless it's me. But I'm fairly sure that he has registered my proximity; that he's worked out from my clothes, from the very way I move, that I'm the stranger here.

Only just *how* strange he does not know. For I have travelled fourteen centuries to be here, sharing a boat with him; here on this unseasonably dismal day.

I know precisely where he's been. Know why there's such misery in his eyes. He's been away from London eight days, staying with his sister in the Midlands, and now he's returning to all the same problems he left behind him.

No. Things have not been easy for him lately. But the boy's death has put everything into perspective. His sister's boy. Hence the journey north. Hence the sadness that pervades his every look, his every movement.

Six years old he was, and as sweet a boy as any you could ask for. Three days he was sick – only three days – and then gone. No breath of his, no trace of his spirit in the air. Back to clay and worms, the dried earth rattling on the child-sized wooden box, the simple sight of which was – in its very smallness – a reason for fresh grief.

We are out in the centre of the river now, the tidal current drawing us towards the distant shore, the boatman and his son pulling at the oars, every muscle tensed, straining to keep us from drifting too far downstream.

If I did not know already that we'd survived, I'd be concerned for us all, the boat's so heavily laden, but eventually we find ourselves drifting in towards the jetty on the Southwark side of the river, the boatman offering his hand to help me out, even as our man makes his way unassisted onto the old wooden structure, his heavy overnight bag slung over his right shoulder.

As I thank the boatman with a coin, I see how our man looks about him, hesitating. There are houses here, close to the jetty, clustered about an ancient-looking church, and an inn. I know he hasn't eaten since yester-evening, and as the day is rapidly drawing to a close, I see the change in his face as he decides to have a meal here and stay the night.

What difference will a day make, after all?

Oh, and I know what you're thinking. Why has he come this way when it would have been easier to come down through the city itself?

Only there's good reason for that. The man owes money. He is heavily in debt, and what with the work going so badly he has no means of paying back a tenth of what he owes. Yes, and if he came in through the north of the city, someone would have been sure to spot him. And then what? Debtors' prison and maybe even a beating before they dragged him away, and at his age he could be doing without any of that. Hence the long way round. Hence the boat. But tonight he'll stay in Battersea, and in the morning set out early, with whatever other company he can find.

Because this south shore of the Thames is dangerous. Cut-throats and footpads patrol the marshy river front, looking for easy pickings. Especially of a night.

I follow him inside; see him look about and note the one free table on the far side of that shabby, dismal room. Just the smell of the air in here would put you off eating. Only I can't be picky. I have a job to do. And so I make my way across, and, even as he sets his bag to one side and pulls off his cloak and takes his seat, so I step out in front of him, gesturing towards the empty place that's facing him.

'D'you mind if . . .?'

He simply stares at me a moment, weariness and hostility etched in the deep lines of his face.

'If you must.'

He wants to be left alone. I can see that. Only I can't let him. I need to get in close with the man, and this really is the only way.

'Thank you,' I say, setting my own bag down and pulling out the chair. 'I'd not bother you, only I haven't eaten since this morn-ing, and this looks like the only inn for miles . . .'

He looks down, silent for a moment. If he wants to spurn me, he'll do it now. Only he's not that kind of man. Not normally. No. Normally he likes nothing better than to meet new people and gather up their stories. It's all grist to the mill, as he likes to say.

'Forgive me,' he says. 'Only I've spent the whole day travelling. I'm tired and, well, not the greatest company.'

I put a hand up. 'I understand. I wouldn't have bothered you only . . .' I stop, then frown, as if, in those brief few seconds I've pieced things together. 'You're Shakespeare, aren't you? The playwright.'

'So?' he asks.

'So I can see you're having difficulties. Maybe I can help.'

Shakespeare laughs. 'You're a bold one. And no, I don't think you can help me. Unless you're my twin, separated at birth, and I'd say there was no real chance of that, comparing the two of us.' He pauses, then. 'What do you do?'

'I was a farm manager,' I say.

Shakespeare studies me again, nodding as he does. 'So I can see. Those arms of yours.'

I am about to say more when a serving wench approaches, a plump dumpling of a girl with greasy black hair and dirt under her fingernails.

'What you want?' she asks.

'Stew,' Will says. 'And make sure it's hot.'

'An' you?' she asks, looking to me.

'Same for me. Piping hot!'

And she goes away.

I sit, smiling apologetically. 'That accent?'

He softens. 'I'm a Midlander, if that's what you're asking.'

'I thought so. You visiting?'

'London? No. I live here. Been here since I was a young man.'

'Then why . . .?'

I meet his eyes, then look down, as if I've suddenly surmised what he's up to.

'Look, I'm sorry, cousin. None of my business. Only to say . . . any help you need. I mean . . . the river path . . . it's not the safest of ways.'

He's watching me now, the faintest trace of suspicion in his eyes. 'And you?'

'Me? I've come up from Wiltshire. Set off two days back. Got a brother not far from here in Southwark. Thought I'd stay with him while I seek out a job.'

It's all a lie, as you know. And it's not one I am capable of maintaining for too long. I'm not that good an actor – he'd see right through me in no time – but right now it works. I can almost sense him relax.

'What do you do?'

'Do?' I grin. 'Anything and everything, providing the pay's all right.'

He sits back a little. 'You should take care. London's a dangerous place.'

'So my cousin says. He was a stonemason, till he broke his hand.'

'That's foul luck.'

'It was indeed. Though some might say that borrowing the money in the first place was the worst of his luck.'

'Ah, I see . . .'

And we meet eyes, understanding.

'And your journey home? Bad news, I take it.'

'Who says I went home?'

'No?' I shrug. 'Just that I thought . . .'

I fall silent, even as the wench returns with two over-brimming bowls of stew, each with a crude wooden spoon, and sets them down on the table between us.

'Sirs.' And she bobs and turns and is gone.

I look up, seeing how thoughtful he is suddenly.

'I did, as it happens. My sister's boy, it was. She had him late, in her forties. Lovely little thing. Was as well as he could be one day. The next . . .'

I hate to think of it. Hate to think how easily we might have saved the boy – jumping back in time and tinkering a little. Keeping him from harm. Only we can't. Because this is the only sure way of getting in with the man. And I have to get in with him, or we won't have any chance of getting in with Kolya.

I lift my spoon and take a mouthful. The stew's delightful, as tasty as anything I've eaten.

'God, but that's good!'

He tries his own, then grins. 'You're right. That's really good. Whatever it is.'

And we both laugh.

'Will,' he says, when our laughter has subsided, 'late of Stratford.'

'Otto,' I answer, and clasp his offered hand. 'late of Westbury.'

And so the evening begins, as we slurp our way through the first of two bowls of stew. All of it on me, of course, because Will's not kidding: he might seem to be a rich man, but in truth he's as in debt as any man could be and still keep going, though neither of us mentions that.

Old age . . . who'd be contemplating old age in Stuart England? And yet that's his fate. Unless I can do something to help him out.

But first and foremost, Kolya. That is, if the bastard doesn't already know precisely where I am and when. And providing Old Schnorr is right about him being here, in London, in 1609.

478

The weather changes overnight. The next day's bright, the sky a cloudless blue. We make good time, following the river path, the Thames below us to our left, the water at low tide. We seem to be alone in that landscape, and the view across the river seems freshly painted by yesterday's rain, the air so clean and clear it's almost intoxicating.

Speaking of which . . .

I ought to feel slow and sluggish after all the dark brown ales I sank with my new friend last night, only I don't. As for Will, his whole mood seems to have changed.

'You should come see us,' he says. 'If you're looking for a job.'

'I don't know,' I answer, picking up a stone to skim across the water. 'Thanks for your offer, but I can't say that acting attracts me all that much.'

'You've tried it? Being a player?'

'No, but I was never a good liar.'

He laughs. 'Is that how you see us?'

'Well, you are, aren't you? Pretending all the while. I'd find that hard.'

And that's another lie, but he is not to know.

'Mind you,' I say. 'I'd make a good stagehand, if there were any vacancies in that line. I used to help my father with any carpentry work he'd need doing. When he was older, that was. And I can paint and carry and hand out bills . . .'

Will looks to me and smiles. 'We'll see, eh?'

We're silent for a time, enjoying the day, the open vista of the river, making good progress. And then he looks at me again. 'You know . . . I've never been any good with money.'

'No?'

'No. All the rest of it . . . well, all of that's been easy. Writing entertainments – I've never had to struggle with it. Not until lately.'

'What do you mean?'

'Oh, nothing. Just . . .'

Only he can't say. He thinks he's lost it for good. And without his particular talents, who is he?

No one is the answer. Without *that* – without the magical mastery of words he has – he does not really exist.

But that's not why I'm here.

Up ahead the ground falls away, the slope of the embankment descending to meet the river. It's low tide, so there's no problem. Except that I've been warned that if we're going to be attacked, it's here they'll set their ambush.

'What is it?' Will asks, sensing my sudden tenseness.

'Up ahead,' I say, keeping my voice low. 'The innkeeper . . . he said this is where they like to set their ambush.'

'If they're up yet,' Will says, then grows more serious. 'Do you think . . .?'

I point towards the trees at the top of the bank. If they're anywhere, that's where they'll be. I draw my knife and beckon Will closer.

'Let's go straight for it,' I say, keeping my voice low. 'I don't want to be trapped out on the mud.'

Shakespeare nods, then, unexpectedly, draws a knife from within his sock, a long, narrow stiletto of a blade which looks Italian.

'All right,' I say, and step forward, letting anyone who might be hiding up there see the knife. 'Let's shake the tree and see what falls from the branches!'

I can see that Will likes that. If he could he'd write it down for future use.

Only . . .

Only suddenly there's a good dozen of them, coming at us from all sides, and I realise I have made a mistake, that Kolya knew about this and set his trap, because two of them at least are 'brothers'.

Twelve on to two, and Will no fighter.

I jump out and then back in, this time to the jetty, two hours earlier, where I buy a passage upriver, just Will and I and the two boatmen, sailing past the marshlands and the ambush, to set us down at Southwark, not ten minutes' walk from the theatre where I know Will is based.

He's grateful for the trip, and as we part he tells me to meet him that evening at the Rose, just round the corner from the Globe, that they'll all be there and maybe – just maybe – they can sort out the small matter of a job.

'I'm not his favourite right now,' Shakespeare says, 'but he still owes me a few favours.'

'Thanks,' I say, not certain who he means.

And then he's gone, merged into the crowd, never knowing just how close he came to death.

479

I push the door open and hesitate, looking about me, and see them at once, twenty or more of them, there at the big table in the corner, beneath the leaded glass windows.

The Company of the Rose . . . but as of yet no sign of Will.

I go across and introduce myself to the players, hoping that he's told one of them about our meeting, but no one seems to have seen him since he's come back. No one, that is, except me.

I'm bought a tankard of ale and, before I can down a half of it, find myself sat between two of the 'actresses', both of whom seem to be vying for my favours.

It's then that Will arrives to rescue me – 'if you want to be rescued', he says quietly to my ear. I nod, then, making my excuses, join him at the bar. But if I thought I was going to get Will to myself, I was mistaken, because he is the hub of all of this. It's he they look to for their entertainment, both on stage and off.

'How was it?' one of his fellows – the big one who plays Falstaff – asks, as the rest fall silent.

'It was awful,' he answers, speaking to them all. 'You can't imagine. My sister . . . she's absolutely distraught. He was such a darling boy. Kindness itself.'

And so it goes, for the next few hours. Only then there's a lull and Will takes me aside.

'I've spoken to the man and he says yes, you're welcome to the job, starting tomorrow, if that's all right with you.'

'I . . . well, yes.'

Only I want to ask who 'the man' is, if it isn't himself. Is it the owner of the Globe? Or some other shadowy figure, maybe even Kolya himself?

I realise that I need to go back to Moscow Central, to see what else, if anything, they know, because all *I* know is that London in the summer of 1609 is an epicentre for Kolya's activities. Having disappeared altogether from our screens, he is suddenly here, back again in force, with two, maybe even three dozen of his 'brothers' and – if Master Schnorr is right – his own real self.

'So just what are they doing?'

Old Schnorr shrugs. 'I don't know. Teasing us?'

Teasing? Okay. But why here? What's the significance of this place, except that Shakespeare is here, too? How could Kolya possibly benefit from being here? I'd have said that this place – this time – had very little to offer him.

I leave early, returning to my room at the quayside inn. The landlady, a buxom woman with chestnut hair and hazel eyes, hands me a letter I've been left, then smiles.

'If there's anything else you need . . .'

I saw her husband earlier: a pinched little man, a good twenty years her senior, so I can imagine what she means.

'Thank you, but no. I'm tired, is all. And thanks . . . for the letter.'

Back in my room I open it. I don't know who I was expecting it from, but it's from Shakespeare. '*Meet me tomorrow morn,*' it reads. '*Six o'clock, at the stage door, Will.*'

I don't understand quite why he didn't just ask me at the Rose. There were plenty of opportunities. And why so early?

I put the letter into my bag, then slip into bed. I try to sleep, but it's one of the most uncomfortable beds I've ever lain in. Only just when I think I'm never going to get any rest, I fall asleep . . .

And wake, to find someone there in that narrow bed, squeezed in beside me, their hot, small, distinctly feminine hands, groping among my night clothes.

I'm only half awake, a fact that my assailant takes good advantage of, as she closes her fingers over my manhood. Surprised, I jerk back, grabbing her hand and throwing it aside, then realise just who it is there, naked, beside me in the dark.

It's her. The buxom landlady. It has to be – giving off that cloying scent of stale sweat and cheap perfume.

'Mary, Mother of God!' I cry out, thrusting her away, before she makes another assault on my cock. 'What in God's name are you doing?'

Only I know only too well what she's doing.

I've frightened her, it seems. Even so, she's not giving up that easily. Grasping my left hand, she places it on her breast, forcing my palm against the rock-hard nipple.

I pull my hand away and thrust her from me.

'Woman! Let me be! What would your husband say?'

'Fuck the old bugger!'

I almost laugh. Only this is a difficult situation. She's as determined as any woman I've ever met, and she's acting like she won't

432

take no for an answer. Noting my arousal, she makes another grab for the source of the problem.

'Woman! For our Lord and Master's sake leave me be! I really don't want you!'

Only my body is betraying me. Whether it happened before or after she slipped into bed beside me, I don't know, but I have an erection now as fierce as any I've ever had for Katerina.

'Jesus!'

I shove her back again, away from me, but it's like she's some kind of sex-crazed assassin. No sooner have I cast her off than she's back, clinging to me again, her right hand seeking out my manhood. All of this played out in the fetid dark.

As she lunges at me again, I jump right out of there, then jump back in a moment later, only this time into the corridor outside, the innkeeper – the pinched fellow – between me and the door, his back to me, a burning candle held out before him, forming a bright-lit halo of his thin grey hair.

'What the fuck . . .?' The woman sounds confused.

I was there . . . and then, suddenly, I wasn't. And she can't for the life of her understand how I managed to slip past her.

'Wife?' the pinched man says querulously, nudging the door open with his foot. 'What in God's name is going on?'

The wavering candlelight falls on the naked woman and the empty bed. She's yet to see me, there behind her husband, but then she does and cries out.

The pinched man turns and gasps. 'What devil's work is this?'

What work indeed? I scowl at the man, sudden understanding coming to me. This is a set-up. The little rat was *meant* to stumble onto us, me and his wife, naked, *in flagrante delicto*, as the Italians like to term it. And film it, maybe?

Only how can that be so? It's completely anachronistic. I mean, what reason could there be for that?

I push past the innkeeper, meaning to confront the woman, only as I do, so I see, hanging about her neck, a pendant. A lazy eight. It shocks me. Makes me reassess the scenario.

'Where did you get that?' I demand, pointing to it. 'Who gave it you?'

She doesn't answer, merely pulls the ragged sheet up, as if to cover her nakedness. Only this pretence of modesty comes far too late to be convincing.

'*You!*' I say, turning to face her husband. 'Give me that candle!'

The man takes a step back, meaning to refuse me, but I'm not having it.

'Give me that fucking candle!'

Like a sullen child, he hands it to me. But even now he has not finished. The nasty little weasel still cannot understand.

'You *want* her, master? If you do . . .'

But I'm not in the least interested in having her. No. I want to know two things. One, where she got hold of the lazy-eight pendant and, two, whether there's a hidden camera in the room.

Not that they'll necessarily know what a camera is.

Holding the candle high, I look for myself. It's hard to distinguish things in its wavering light, but suddenly I see it, there in the far corner, like some large beetle, squatting on the wooden frame. Only this is no insect.

I go across and, reaching up, pluck it down.

'Master?' the innkeeper asks, clearly wanting to know what I've found. But I've no time for his questions.

'Go!' I yell, turning to face the innkeeper again. 'You, too,' I say, looking to the woman. 'Get the fuck out of here, before I throw you out!'

Yet even then they persist, as if I'm going to change my mind, but that – that sordid, carnal act – will simply never happen.

'*Go*! Both of you! For God's sake, *go!*'

And finally they leave, cursing and muttering, the woman making obscene gestures to me and lifting the sheet to reveal her ageing sex.

When they're gone, I look about me, gathering up my things, then jump again . . .

480

Back to Moscow Central, and to a new and worrying thought. That Kolya himself might have set up that sordid little interlude. To film it and show it to Katerina. If I'd succumbed, that is. And why should I not? I am a man, aren't I?

Only he really doesn't know me, not if that's what he thinks.

And maybe I'm totally wrong. Maybe he had nothing to do with what happened back there. Only there's the camera bug . . .

'Get me back!' I say to Urte.

'What happened?' she asks. 'We weren't expecting you . . .'

'Just send me back,' I say, interrupting her. 'But not there. I can't stay there.'

'Have you met him yet?'

'Kolya? No. But the other, Shakespeare, I've got a meeting with him, only . . .'

And I explain what happened.

'We'll drop you back in there, Otto. Outside the inn. That way you'll not affect the timeline before then. The one you've already been in, that is. All of that good work with Shakespeare, that'll survive. That's if you don't mind wandering the streets of London for an hour or two.'

By which she means three, or maybe even four.

'That's fine,' I say. 'Just drop me back in. I'll do the rest.'

And in an instant I am back there, wearing new clothes, freshly washed and ironed, a stun-gun in my pocket, courtesy of Urte.

Just in case . . .

London, 1609. Seven years before the great man's death. Not that I'll ever let that slip. For what's worse than knowing when you'll die?

Only that makes me recall Hecht's death. *He* knew. It happened thus for him; there one moment, the next . . . *gone*. Thirty days condensed to thirty minutes. Or so it seemed, from our vantage point in Time. For him it must have seemed a small eternity, waiting for death to come.

But let's not think of that right now. The night is dark, the moon hidden by cloud, and as I walk away from the riverside inn, I think of Kolya, wondering why in the gods' names he should be here of all places.

For once I've not a clue. But I have gone less than a hundred yards – less than half the length of that darkly shaded road – when I see two of them.

'Brothers'. I'm certain of it. One turns, his face showing briefly in the light and the fact's confirmed. That's near enough Kolya's face and these are Kolya's men. Seeing me he cries out and the two begin to run.

Drawing my knife, I follow, along and to the left, towards the dark mouth of a narrow alleyway, which they turn into.

And are gone . . . like wraiths blown away in the wind.

I stand there, one hand pressed to the wall, getting my breath back, staring into the blackness of that narrow rat-run of a passageway. For some reason I feel a strong, insistent sense of recognition. And even as I do, so a light comes on halfway down, a warm, roseate glow spilling out from a ground-floor window.

Baturin!

Yes, the last time I saw this was in Baturin, a century from now, the shadowed, curving lane identical to this.

'*Urd save me . . .*' I whisper and step into the darkness of that narrow lane. And as I do, as I take my first, faltering step, so the door swings open and a woman steps out into the light, her eyes straining, looking for me in that darkness.

Waiting for me, it seems; one arm outstretched to summon me again.

I feel a shiver pass through me.

How does she know . . . ?

And yet she does.

Impossible, I think. But then again, why so? Why should this *not* be here? Maybe so, I tell myself, but then whose game is it that we're playing now? For I know the room from where that light spills out. Know it for a certainty. Remember how I had my fortune read that time.

The gypsy woman . . .

Two steps back, I think, *and one to the side.* That's the pattern of things. Only why hasn't he killed me? Why hasn't he sent in a pair of his 'brothers' – one to hold me down while the other parts the flesh of my throat with his stiletto? Because that's what I would have done. And yet might do. If that's at all possible. If he doesn't, as usual, slip away an instant before I act.

But why here? And why repeat this strand? Unless the purpose is to change it subtly.

Only now, as I step out from the dark, I see how she smiles and holds her arms out to me, and know I have no choice but to follow this through. To see just where in this strangest of universes this leads.

And see once more how the cards fall.

'Otto,' she says softly, as she takes me in her arms, embracing me. 'I knew you'd come.'

As the night watchman calls the hour, so, like a figure from a dream, Shakespeare steps from the darkness and approaches me.

'Otto?'

I take his hand briefly, then turn to follow, as he takes a heavy key from his belt and fits it to the lock.

The door swings back, revealing the interior of the theatre, lit faintly now by moonlight. The stage, the pit, the balconies: all as I recall them from a future time. The one time that I came here. Back when I was learning my trade. Before I was *Reisende* proper.

Ten thousand jumps through Time ago. But now I'm back. Where I began. And maybe that's why.

He locks the door behind him, then, as I follow him across the dirt floor, Shakespeare glances back at me.

'Sleep well?'

'Well enough,' I say, thinking it best to say nothing of the night's events.

Then, because it's been troubling me, I ask him why we've met so early.

'Because.'

And stops at the edge of the pit, beneath the overhanging stage, in the shadow of which is a tiny door that might have been made for a dwarf. Stopping, he searches at his belt again, and finds another key – longer, thinner than the other – and opens it.

And in we go, ducking beneath the lintel to get in.

Inside, he lights a lamp and holds it high. And as he makes a cursory search, I wonder what exactly's going on. He finishes his search and, content that no one's there, seems to relax, though there's still something about him that makes me think that there's something he's keeping to himself.

'Are you all right?' I ask, pre-empting him. 'You seem . . . *troubled*.'

'As well I might,' he says, then sighs. 'Today's the day.'

'The day?'

'That's right. Today's the day I have to repay them. By midday latest.'

'And you have no means?'

'Not for the amount I owe them, no.'

'They being?'

'A violent, brutish fellow and his crew.'

'Why did—?'

'Why did I borrow it in the first place from such a man? Because others would not help. No, not one of my so-called friends would aid me. Not so much as a bean. Why, you would almost think there was a conspiracy against me. First that business with the land documents up in Stratford, and then—'

'Whoa, whoa there, friend. Slow down now. Begin at the beginning.'

'At the beginning . . .' And he laughs, as if what I've just said is absurd. And I'm not sure why. I know he had money troubles. Our agents had established that. But nothing like as bad as what he tells me.

'Christ, Will,' I say, when he has finished. 'If I were you I'd have stayed in Stratford.'

'And have his men find me there? No. Here I've at least a slender chance of borrowing something. Back there, in Stratford, no one would give me the time of day.'

'I see . . .' And I wonder, as I say it, whether this isn't Kolya's doing. Isn't a means of drawing me into this man's fate.

Because I could solve Will's problem in an instant.

'The worst thing,' he says, 'is that it keeps me from writing.'

'How do you mean?'

'My plays have been very successful, up until recently. But now . . . well . . . I've just lost it, Otto. It's all a blank . . . up here.'

And he touches his forehead.

'I guess the two must be connected somehow . . .'

'What makes it worse,' he says, speaking over me, 'is what that bastard Thorpe has been up to. Stealing my poems . . . my sonnets . . . and publishing them as if he had the right!'

'No . . .' I say, as if horrified by the thought. As if I'd never heard of it before that moment. 'Couldn't you get some money from *him*?'

'He'd just laugh in my face. The man's a total crook.'

'Then you are well and truly—'

'—fucked.' And he laughs. 'Jesus, Otto. How did I get in such a mess?'

It's light now. Church bells are sounding seven.

He looks at the keys in his hand, then throws them to me. I catch them.

'And?' I ask.

'Do what you can here to make things tidy. Open up the shutters, then sweep the floor. Help should come sometime soon.'

'And you, Will?'

'I'll be gone an hour or two . . .' He smiles wistfully. 'I've got to see a man about a dog.'

'A man . . .' And I laugh, wondering if that's the first time anyone's ever used that term. 'It's okay,' I say. 'I'll make sure everything's spick and span . . .'

To which he smiles and then is gone, leaving me to look about myself, wondering how this is going to pan out.

482

There are five of us, busy cleaning up that big, wonderful wooden theatre when Will returns. If he looked bad before, he looks dreadful now. A man in deep trouble.

I go over to him. 'Do you want . . .?'

'Not now,' he says, brushing past.

I turn away, looking towards the big outer wooden door of the Globe, then walk across. Out there, just across the road from the theatre, three pugnacious-looking men are huddled together, talking.

Seeing me, their faces take on a scowling expression.

In trouble . . . You can say that again.

So what exactly am I going to do? Am I going to help him out, or just ignore his fate and get on with the task of locating Kolya?

Instinct tells me that things here are connected somehow. That it's no accident that I'm here in Stuart England, in 1609. Kolya is here because it's important to him, and if it's important to *him* . . .

. . . then it's important to me.

All right. Then I'm going to have to play it by ear.

Shakespeare finishes talking to the others and, without a glance back, heads off. I watch him go; watch the three rogues turn to follow. And then follow myself, not knowing where this will end; some strange shadowy memory of past events coming to mind.

I have been this – *done* this – once before. But once again my recollection is of the vaguest sort. Even so, I use all of my experience to keep the three rogues from noticing me. On through the maze of ancient London Town, until we come to the centre of it all.

Saint Paul's . . .

Yes. I have been here before. Many times. And yet remember nothing.

I shake my head, trying to clear it, but each step now seems to lead me further into a place I've been a hundred times, back in some other timeline. He and I. Younger, much younger than we are.

Before Krasnogorsk . . .

I stagger and nearly fall, my hand going to the cold stone of the cathedral wall, steadying myself, noting, as vision returns, how the three have now surrounded him.

Fearful, I make to shout out, to warn him, only in that instant I see something that surprises me. See the three men turn as one and, facing outward, knives drawn, form a defensive circle about our Shakespeare, even as a dozen men – Kolya's – rush in to try and settle matters.

I look on, admiringly, seeing how skilled, how ferociously efficient, the three men are with their weapons, and know – without a doubt – that these are agents, Russians at a guess, placed there to protect Shakespeare.

Only why? Why is this poet and playwright so important to us? It's not as if he were a Frederick or a Peter, a Napoleon or a Hitler. No. He's just a writer.

I withdraw into the shadows, making sure that I'm not seen, even as the last of Kolya's men – if that is what they are – fall to our agents.

What's going on? For Urd's sake, what's happening here?

And even as I turn to make my hurried way away from there, so the great church's bells begin to toll . . . And there, right there, immediately in front of me, is a stall, and on that stall are books, and those books are all one and the same.

Sonnets, by William Shakespeare.

And I realise something. That this really is *his* time, *his* age. But what has any of this to do with us? With Kolya and myself?

I jump back. To Moscow. To find Albrecht awaiting me on the platform.

'Come,' he says, taking my hand. 'I've something to show you!'

483

It is as before. Only different.

Which is to say that the Haven seems unchanged. Unchanged not from where we saw it last, but from the time beyond that, when Katerina and I first visited it, back when Master Hecht was still alive and the Neanderthal camp . . .

Well, there it is. Right there, before my eyes. Their huts have not been burned down – not in this reality.

And Albrecht . . . ?

I turn and look at him . . .

Albrecht seems younger than he was. Unchanged yet younger.

And I realise that something has happened here. Some profound change. One step backward, to when things were different. To when they were *better*.

Or is that so?

Albrecht is clearly happy with this. It was the more recent change he hated. The change that scattered the Neanderthals and brought about his brother's death.

But Change is Change. And even when we agents – and Masters – of Time seem to return, it is never ever *the same*.

It might look so, even to the most skilful of observers, but there is always something.

And so here.

'Have you been there, Albrecht?' I ask. 'To the Archives? Has it all been preserved?'

But I know, even before I hear his reply, that *something* has been altered. For the rest of it to have reverted, something must have been given in exchange.

Or been taken away.

We go and look.

The door is barred. It opens only to Albrecht's code. And inside . . .

Albrecht stands there in the doorway, sniffing.

Damp. It reeks of dampness. Only how can that be so? The Archives are a sealed unit, designed to be damp-free.

'1609, London,' I say, seeing how subdued Albrecht suddenly is. 'List the files.'

He sits and does as I ask, then sits back, letting me see the screen.

I catch my breath. There are a hundred files at the very least – each one representing a single timeline – whereas before . . .

'There should be six,' Albrecht says.

'You know that for a fact?'

He nods. 'They were training exercises. You were in two of them.'

'And now?'

Albrecht leans in again. For a time there is nothing but the tap of his fingers on the keys. Then he straightens.

'Look,' he says, and sits back so I can see again.

I pull up a chair beside his and look.

Albrecht has opened three of the files and, from the summarised notes, each one is different. Yes. These are very different Londons. Only one thing is consistent in them all – Kolya and I.

'It isn't possible,' he says. 'It really isn't . . .'

Only it is. For the last two hundred years the Haven has concealed these files, hiding them away, even from those – Albrecht

444

and his brother, the Meister – who thought they had a firm grip on it all.

Only now, for some reason, they have reappeared.

'Can you . . .?' I begin, not sure quite what I want Albrecht to do.

'I can provide a summary document for each of them,' he says, answering what I haven't asked. 'In fact, I could probably get that printed up straight away.'

'All right . . . then let's do that . . . And, Albrecht . . .'

'Yes, Meister?'

'Put them in chronological order if you can. The clue to all of this is there, in what happened between Kolya and I to create all of these timelines.'

Only, as he turns away to begin his work, I wonder just what gargantuan event set off this hidden chain. *More than a hundred.* No, that doesn't seem possible. And yet it's true. For it to exist at all it must be true.

A hundred 1609s. A hundred Londons. Just how was that possible, and we not knowing it?

And just why is Kolya showing us this now?

Most frightening of all, perhaps, is the fact that all this has already happened to me. Is in my past. And I remember none of it. No. It has all been erased. And now he gives it back to me. For what possible purpose?

I turn, even as Albrecht gives a surprised laugh.

'It's Kolya, Otto. He's left you a message.'

484

I am returned to the playhouse, to the Globe, as midday falls and the bells of London ring out, drowning the nearby cry of gulls.

Spotting me, Shakespeare comes across. 'Otto . . . Where have you been?'

In the deep past. Only I'm not going to say that to him. Instead I duck the issue and turn it round. 'Something's happened, hasn't it?'

He hesitates, then nods. 'I was attacked . . . in St Paul's.'

'Attacked?'

'Yes . . . only there were three men . . . these Russians, and . . .'

And so he tells me what I've already witnessed. But there's more to it than that. It seems he was on his way to meet a potential patron. Someone who might, if not resolve, at least *ease* his problems.

'I gave him my play.'

'Your . . .?'

But before I can query it, he turns and calls one of his players over.

Play? He has no play. That was the problem. Unless things have changed dramatically in the hour I was gone.

The player leaves hurriedly. Shakespeare turns, looking to me again, and, seeing my expression, laughs.

'Oh, I know. There is no play. Nothing *finished*, anyway. But he's not to know.'

'Then this is . . .?'

'A delay,' he answers me. 'It buys me time.'

'And he's taken you on trust?'

His face clouds. 'Ah, well . . . That's the only problem. He wants to see it. This afternoon, at two . . .'

'And?'

'They're rehearsing it right now.'

I look at him, incredulous. 'So you actually have something? Something new?'

'Not new exactly. More like fragments. Scenes I left out. Early drafts. That kind of thing. I've told him it's a work in progress.'

'But when he sees it . . .'

Will looks away. 'Let's hope he's not discerning . . .'

Only I know he will be. Else why buy Will's work when you could buy some minor playwright's work for half the price?

No. He needs a completely new angle if this is to work, not the patchwork he's suggesting. Only dare I suggest it?

'I've an idea,' I say.

Will looks at me uncertainly.

'For your play.' And, as I say it, so I see his expression change.

'Forgive me, Otto, but . . . have you ever actually *written* anything?'

'No, but I—'

'But nothing. Writing plays . . . it's . . . well, it's a complex skill. Few can do it well. And those that can have spent long decades honing that skill.'

'Maybe so,' I say. 'Only what you're suggesting . . .'

'Oh, don't worry about that. We'll bluff our way. Tell the man that it's always like this. That the first draft's there to be built upon. He'll know no better, and . . .'

Only I know he's beginning to doubt whether he can pull this off.

I place my hand on his arm. 'Will, please. Just hear me out. Over a beer, yes?'

He stares at me a moment, his eyes doubting me. 'This idea . . .'

'In the tavern,' I say.

485

'So . . . fire away!' Will says, wiping the ale's foam from his top lip. 'Let me have it, both barrels.'

I look to him, frowning. Was that an anachronism I've just heard coming from his lips?

'Will . . . I've a confession to make.'

'A confession?'

'Yes. What I told you . . . none of it was true. I was a soldier, you understand. A mercenary.'

Shakespeare laughs. 'You . . . a mercenary?'

'In the European wars. As a young man I fought for Wallenstein, and, lately for Maurice of Orange.'

'A mercenary? *You?*'

I nod. Then, standing, unbutton my shirt and show him the scars I've accumulated over the years. Some of which killed me, that is, before they brought me back again.

Will takes in the sight, then nods, his whole manner changed. 'So why . . . ?'

'Why the deception? Because I'd heard of you. Heard you were in trouble.'

'And?'

'And I think I can help you out. The things I've heard. The things I've seen. I know for a fact that someone like you could use them. Mould them. Give them shape and living motion.'

He nods. Only I can see he's not totally convinced.

'These things . . .' he begins, hesitantly. 'You mean battles?'

'And assassinations. Yes, and secret deals and betrayals. And in the midst of all a poignant love story, between rival families, rival races.'

'But I've already . . .'

'*Romeo and Juliet.* I know. But I was thinking more in the line of *Troilus and Cressida.*'

'You know my plays then?'

I smile. 'Not all of them.'

He stares at me now, as if he's making some kind of decision, and then he looks past me, towards the bar and the tavern keeper.

'Tom . . . bring me paper and ink. I've work to do.'

486

Shakespeare looks up at me and slowly nods. But it's not me he's seeing. No. Right now there's some other landscape in his mind. He's come alive, like someone's wired him up and plugged him in.

That someone being me.

For the past hour we've been talking about the endless things I've seen, and if at first he wasn't entirely convinced, the more he's heard the more he's relaxed his resistance to the notion that I was actually there amid the carnage of the battlefield. It's the fine detail that has won him over, as much as the long-healed scar tissue. That and the fact that I *was* actually there in many cases.

Because there's no more convincing a lie than the one presented by a man who's telling the truth.

Only right now it's not the battles that he's interested in – after all, where's the drama in a battlefield? No. What Will is fascinated by is the persistence of the old religions among my fellow mercenaries. In particular, he loves my tales of Odin and the Norse Gods, all of which are absolutely new to him.

'This World Tree . . . what's the significance of that?'

Again I smile. It's not even as if I have to try hard. And so I tell him about Yggdrasil, the eternally green ash tree, and about Asgard, home of the gods, and know that I have hooked him, like a fish. Even so, he still has doubts.

'I love it. This is all wonderful. Only . . . how am I going to fit all of this together? How structure it? How give it shape and form and dramatic beauty?'

'That's easy,' I say, wondering even as I say it that I might end by regretting this. 'You set it in the future . . . and in the past.'

Will stares back at me, then bursts into laughter. 'You're joking!'

Only I'm not.

And so we begin to put together a crude structure of the play. The potions that they drink to go forward or backward in Time. The disease-free future society, which our scurvy hero from the Present Day, unknown to himself, infects, causing a deadly, debilitating plague. The villain with the two heads and the strange monk-like villain, whom I name Kolya.

This last confuses Will. 'Why have two villains, Otto? One is surely enough.'

Only I claim it isn't, and as I gradually put flesh on the bones of these two different characters, so Will slowly changes his mind.

In fact, so excited is Will at this notion of setting the work both in a time that has long gone and one which is yet to come, that he begins to consider other connected matters. Like time paradoxes. Things that, had I not opened the door to them in the walls of his skull, would have lain dormant in human consciousness for another four centuries at the very least.

'Yes,' Will says finally, when I ask him whether he thinks it will work. 'Most definitely yes. Only . . . what do I call it?'

I tell him and he smiles.

'*Of Time and Tides*,' he whispers. Then, gathering all of his papers together, he hurries away.

To write the thing, I realise. My work here, it seems, is done.

Only I find now that I'm trembling, my hands shaking at the thought of the changes in thinking this will cause; just how radically it might influence the timeline we are in.

How? I don't know how. But it will. I'm certain of it now. And as I think that, I wonder also if this is why Kolya is here. To prevent this.

Only surely that can't be. Because, knowing our 'friend', he'd already have acted to erase it.

Or is that so?

What if he too wants this, for reasons of his own?

And as I think it, a great wash of understanding lifts me and carries me ashore.

This is it! This play was what gave our old enemy Kolya both the notion and the practical scientific basis of time travel!

My pulse is racing now; my heart thudding in my chest, because this – as much as Gehlen's equations – brought our world about. This isn't just a play, an entertainment, it's a theory. Who knows what theory, exactly, but one that worked. One that allowed Kolya access to a thousand worlds. That opened up the Tree of Worlds to everyone . . . but particularly to him.

Yes, simply by bringing the idea of it into the forum of human thought, at some stage someone invented it. The lazy eight. There in the tarot cards and there all along – or so it seemed – in my long unhealthy dealings with the man.

All of it spawned by Shakespeare's words.

I let out a long breath, then slowly nod. No wonder he is here. Not meddling this time, but *preserving*. Keeping us from changing this particular strand of Time.

Which begs the question, should *we* be interfering here? Changing things to prevent change? Or is it all too late?

If so, then why am I here again?

Sitting there in the minutes following Will's departure, I realise that I need to see Albrecht again, and Old Schnorr, and perhaps myself. To find out just what's going on and why we seem to be *collaborating* with our enemy. For what else is it?

I stand, then, making my way across the crowded room, venture out – out into the cold, wet dark – and jump. Back to Moscow Central and, I hope, some explanation for it all.

487

Only I have to be naïve to think that they have the vaguest idea about what's been going on. Albrecht, particularly, is bemused by what's been happening. He's used to knowing precisely what's transpired, even if at such a vast temporal distance, but the idea of all this new stuff turning up out of the blue just throws him totally. And the further notion that *Kolya* is behind it all . . . Well, that's just not possible, is it?

And I don't mean that he came up with the idea, only that he stole it, sometime in the past. Or had Reichenau steal it for him, back when Reichenau was still alive. The same way he stole both Gehlen *and* his equations.

Which is where all of this gets complex. If it wasn't already.

Albrecht takes me inside the vaults and sits me down and has me look at what he's prepared for me: one hundred and seven trips, in sequential order.

I've only been studying the pile for a minute when I look up at him. 'What *is* this? *Seven* seconds?'

'There're a lot that are shorter than that. That's when we dragged you out of there. After he'd killed you.'

He doesn't have to say who. I flick through the next dozen or so 'reports', finding little difference between them.

I say that, but then I look again. The timeline every one of them is in is . . . well, *different* doesn't come near describing it.

'So how did he know? How did he . . . anticipate?'

Only I realise, even as I say it, that these are the questions I have always asked about Kolya. I have never understood how he's always there, one step in front of me, anticipating my every move.

Like a savant or a mind-reader. Or has it . . . might it just be . . . a reading of the cards?

No. Even I'm not crazy enough to believe that my life is being dictated by the fall of the cards in a tarot pack. That everything I've done has been foreshadowed.

It can't be so.

So what then? Because there has to be an explanation that fits. One that . . . *explains.*

And if there isn't? If it proves just to be a madhouse? A malfunction of time itself?

What then do we do with the remainder of our lives? How live within the walls of bedlam?

One hundred and seven journeys back. And in how many of those did I die? Five-sixths of them, Albrecht tells me, and Old Schnorr nods in his familiar fashion.

'It was why you were always special to him,' Old Schnorr says, after a moment.

'Sorry?'

'To Meister Hecht.'

I give an odd laugh. 'But Meister Hecht didn't know. This was . . . after his time.'

'It was and it wasn't.'

'What do you mean?'

Albrecht takes it up. 'I mean that he came here once, when I wasn't here. I was having an operation and, well, anyway, he came here on his own. It was the only time. So if he saw them, he saw them then, and then destroyed them . . . or hid them, more like . . . and then made one single change, right at the beginning of this sequence, and by doing so erased it from my mind. Until the records were retrieved, that was.'

'And?'

'And here we are,' Old Schnorr says. 'Back at the beginning. When it was all fresh to you. Before all that other nonsense.'

I hesitate, then. 'You said there were four that ran full length. Four in which I wasn't killed and therefore presumably wasn't attacked.'

'That's so,' Albrecht says. 'They're near the end. In fact, they form the bulk of the reports.'

'Then leave them to me. I'll be out when I'm done.'

488

As I stand there at the water's edge, I wonder where all this will end. The tide is slowly coming in, covering the mudflats that edge the ancient Thames. As for London itself, it's just a blur in the fine mist of rain that's falling.

London, 1609. How strange it is to be here once again, at this time and in this place, waiting for something new to be born into the world.

It's all a mess. I know that now. All our meticulously careful schemes have come to nothing. Or as good as.

And now I wait. For whom? I do not ask. For whoever comes now, whether it be Will or the man himself, I feel it's fated. Yes, it all went wrong not in these last few years but long ago. And who can change it now? Not he and not I.

In fact it's Will who comes, making his way through the early morning rain, his papers hidden away under his cloak, to keep from getting soaked.

'Come,' he says, and while he looks tired, his eyes are more alive than I've ever seen them. 'Upstairs in the Rose. Now!'

We make our way, climbing the old stairs at the back to the private room. There, having shaken off his coat, he unfolds the papers and turns them toward me so I can read his handwritten manuscript.

It's clearly a rather large play, and, by the look of it – the absence of scrawled changes on each page – he wrote it fairly cleanly.

'It needs a scene or two,' he says, waving his hand over it, 'but otherwise . . .'

Otherwise it reads wonderfully. I'm six pages in before I look up at him and smile. He grins back, then nods, encouraging me to read on.

I read on. Act One is fluent and sets up the ideas with a sparkling clarity I have never encountered before now. I'm tempted to say that he understands Time and its qualities, only . . .

Only there are things that he gets totally wrong. Not many but . . . enough to dissatisfy anyone – like I – who has spent any time in Time.

Act Two raises the stakes and introduces our villains. There are some comic interludes, too, which make me laugh quite openly before settling to the text once more.

'Wonderful,' I say, as I come to the last page of it – the scene that sets up Act Three. 'You took that from me, yes?'

'Verbatim,' he says and nods to me, as if thanking me for my gift. But I can only think how he's transformed it. Turned life into art, yes, and great art at that. If this doesn't spur someone on to invent time travel, then what the fuck will?

Act Four slows, for here the plot takes hold, twisting and turning, hiding and revealing until there, in the penultimate scene – after the plague our hero has unwittingly spread – the two dead lovers are brought on stage on the cart, there at Krasnogorsk. There at that evil place where life and art collide. And I wipe a tear away and look up and see him watching me and know that this is it, his greatest play. Written in a single night, after drinking with a man who ought never to have been there. A man yet to be born.

I finish it even as the bells begin to sound outside. Two o'clock it is. Back in the Globe they'll be playing out that pile of shit he gave them yesterday, while this . . .

'We should do it,' I say. 'Now.'

'But I thought . . .'

'No. Do a reading, at the least. Then get some copies made. As it is. We can rehearse it overnight, while you catch up on your sleep. Then we can perform it tomorrow. Invite your new patron along. I know he'll love it.'

'If he understands it, that is.'

'Oh, he'll understand it, all right. Those arguments . . . they're the best you've written.'

'You think?' I can see, for that brief moment, how insecure he's been these last few months. But now . . .

'It's a masterpiece,' I say. 'And no flattery intended.'

'Maybe,' he says and laughs, then leans across and takes my arm. 'But your name must be on it with mine, Otto. The scenes you gave me . . . for instance, that one where he meets Katerina for the first time . . . and you end up jumping through Time again and again, killing Kravchuk, time after time . . .'

I look down. 'You should change her name, perhaps. Make it more English.'

'You think?' Only he doesn't look convinced. 'I'm tempted to leave that be. But there is one rather big loose end I need to resolve, and that's the fate of Kolya. Should I kill him, Otto, or does he live to scheme another day?'

I meet his eyes, then shrug. 'Give him a poem, maybe. Right at the very end. I mean . . . end the play itself on a triumphant tone by all means . . . but then clear the stage as if things were done, then re-introduce Kolya. Like some stock stage villain, only . . . not so. Present him as something a lot more threatening. Like a madman with a razor in his hand. Someone the audience will still be thinking of when all else is done.'

'You think so?' And he goes all thoughtful, his eyes staring inward. 'Maybe . . .'

'Then go. Get some sleep. I'll get twelve copies of this done.'

'Twelve copies? But I thought . . .'

'It's all right. I've come into some money. I heard last night, after you'd gone up. I would have said something, only . . .'

'Who died?' he asks.

'An uncle. I didn't think he liked me, but . . .'

Shakespeare raises his eyebrows, then begins to laugh. 'How life changes in a day, neh, my friend? Then let's do as you say and get twelve copies done . . . fifteen if you can afford it. And I'll do as you've told me to. I'll get some sleep. I'm sure it can't be hard.' And he laughs again.

489

We stand there, Will and I, watching as the players speak their lines, their fellows crowded about the stage, hanging on to every uttered word, every last one of them knowing that this is it, Will's finest play. Necks strain, eyes focus. There's sudden laughter from a dozen throats and then a sharply indrawn breath.

They're hooked. They're fucking hooked.

And our would-be sponsor? I turn and look and see how he too is caught up in this glittering spider's web of words as, wide-eyed and open-mouthed, he slowly nods to himself as the play rolls on, unstoppable, like the incoming tide.

Will presses close, his mouth to my ear. '*Well? What do you think?*'

I half turn and, gripping his elbow, smile and nod. This – written in haste and at a single sitting – is strangely beyond words. It isn't simply what is said, it's what the words allow us to glimpse . . . in that lies its magic. And in that regard it is truly magical.

I shiver, the hairs on my arms and neck rising. 'Don't change a word,' I say. Only I know he will. For having got this far . . .

I stop dead. I'd not noticed him before, but now I do, on the far side of the great half circle of the stage.

Kolya . . .

Will senses my sudden change of mood. Follows the direction of my eyes.

Only in the instant between me spotting him and Will turning to look, the man has jumped. *Vacated the air*, as Will terms it in his play.

What?' he asks, concerned.

Only how to explain?

I improvise a line. 'I need to go,' I say. 'I've just remembered . . .'

'Remembered?'

'I've a meeting. Regarding my uncle's estate. I'll be half an hour, an hour at most. Wait here. I'll be back.'

And I turn away, conscious of his eyes on me as I depart.

Exiting the gate I look about me . . . then jump.

'Otto . . .' Old Schnorr says, looking up from the desk, clearly expecting me. 'You saw him then? At the rehearsal?'

'I . . . Yes. Yes, I did.'

'And did you notice how young he was?'

I take a moment to think. Did I? I hesitate. 'I . . . I'm not sure I did. Just seeing him there was a shock.'

'I understand. Only it's important. Close your eyes and focus, Otto. What did you see?'

I close my eyes. He's there for the smallest flash, then gone. 'Yeah, maybe. I . . .'

Only I'm not sure. The only thing I'm certain about is that it *was* him. Kolya. But beyond that . . .

'How old was he?'

'Seventeen.'

I shake my head. The Kolya I saw could not have been only seventeen. His eyes, for a start. They were so experienced. Like he'd seen everything and done everything. Whereas I . . .

That first time I encountered him – when I was 'cutting my teeth', back before I was *Reisende* – I could only have been eighteen, maybe nineteen at most. And naïve. As unpractised as a newborn.

'What happened?' I ask.

'You took a step outside,' he answers. 'We even lost you for a time. And I mean lost. No trace of you. And then – days later – you came back. You flickered back into existence and we snatched you back. Before he could get to you. In less than an instant. That was Ernst's doing. He stayed awake all that while. Sat there with his hand over the response pad, waiting for the smallest glimmer of you on the screen.'

'And he reacted quicker than Kolya, yes?'

Old Schnorr hesitates, then. 'He guessed. And – impossibly – he guessed right. And there you were, saved.'

'Ernst,' I say and smile. 'I should have guessed. But where's Kolya now? Where would I find him?'

And, just as if he knew what was about to be asked, he reaches out and takes a file from the side, then hands it to me.

'Our closest approximation,' he says, sitting back, getting his old bones comfy again.

'What do you mean?'

'Only that it changes. Constantly.'

'Now he's there . . . now he's not.'

'Precisely.'

And, no doubt, the file will be the same, the very print on the pages changing moment by moment as Kolya jumps between the timestreams.

I open it; read the opening paragraph and look to Master Schnorr again. 'The *fading*?'

The old man nods. 'It's our term for what's been happening, out there at the periphery of Time.' He pauses, as if trying to find the proper words. 'To put it simply, Otto, it's all a question of how close to the hub – or distant – a timestream is. The further away, the less energy is involved. Whereas at the hub . . . that's where it's intense. That's where you'll find the highest energy levels.'

'And?'

'And you should speak to our expert on the subject. She can explain it much better than I do.'

'She?'

And, even as I say it, so she shimmers into being beside me. 'Katerina . . .'

490

She has explained it all. And now – post-coital, our 'expert' naked in my arms – I think over what she's said.

Put simply, we seem to have worn Time thin. So much so that, in the peripheral worlds – those timelines furthest from the cen-tre – things have begun to fade, to lose substance, their energy drained by the hub. It's apparently what happens after two centuries and more of constant misuse. And, because Time is Time, it was always so. Potentially, anyway.

All of it pre-ordained, if we are to believe what Katerina has told me.

Only I don't. I still think that Time is in our hands to change.

Not that I tell her that. But there is something I want to rehearse with her. An idea that's struck me as to why we're here, in 1609.

'Katerina?'

'Yes, my love?'

'What if all these other timelines are wrong?'

'*Wrong*?' She gets up on one elbow and looks down at me. 'What do you mean? They exist, don't they?'

'Yes. But what if they shouldn't? What if all of this is simply Reality repairing itself. All of the branches of the World Tree moving towards a single singularity?'

'For two hundred years?'

'Why not? I mean, that's just a blip in cosmic terms.'

I see how she thinks about that. How she goes to speak . . .

Only I don't let her.

'He's here for a reason, Katerina. To settle things for good. This is the End Game.'

'You think so?'

'I'm certain of it. Just as I am that nothing has been decided yet.'

'So this here, this now . . .'

'Is a contest to the death. To establish which of our realities is to prevail. Ours—'

'Or his,' she finishes.

'One hundred and seven times I've been here. And this the last.'

She looks down, contemplating that, then looks at me and nods. 'Done,' she says. 'And not done.'

'Precisely.'

I smile. 'But first the play.'

Katerina looks at me again, a query in her eyes.

'Will's play,' I say. 'About time travel.'

She laughs, a disbelieving laugh, then, seeing that I'm serious, leans closer.

'You've been meddling again, Otto, haven't you?'

'I wouldn't call it meddling. *Improving*, more like.'

But I say nothing of my notion of implanting the idea of time travel.

'Otto?'

'Yes, my love?'

'If this *is* the "End Game", then be careful out there.'

'I shall.'

'And mind the spirals.'

'The . . .?'

Only she's gone. Vanished from my arms, only the perfumed smell of her remaining.

Gone. And my heart aches to follow.

491

We spend the afternoon and early evening rehearsing. And every now and then new pages arrive. Fifteen copies of each, in six separate hands, Shakespeare's own among them. And each time the play improves, becoming funnier, more poignant, far more dramatic.

And the players?

The players love this play. Involved is not the word for it. It *fills* them. And, as the day progresses more and more people gather, intrigued by the news that Shakespeare has a new play – and not just new but *different*. Yes, by the time the sun begins to set the Globe is packed to the rafters, the host of watchers engrossed as they've never been before.

Yes, and their laughter when it comes is like a great wave of warmth . . .

The only shame is that Shakespeare does not witness any of this, for he's busy writing and rewriting, honing what was already magnificent into a work of paramount excellence.

The single best play ever written.

And then, quite suddenly and without a word, he's gone.

It's young Todd who raises the alarm. Young Todd who plays the boy-girl in most plays. Not finding Shakespeare in his room, the young lad hurries back to give the news that there's no trace of him. It's like he's vanished into the air, which I know with an instinctive certainty's the truth.

Kolya. I know it almost for a fact. And, just as soon as I'm alone again, I jump. Back to when I last saw him.

And wait.

And sure enough, our old friend makes an appearance, smiling at me as he turns and, opening the door, walks in on Will.

Six seconds I have to cross that room, and in the end I have to throw myself across the desk, spilling ink and clearing papers to the floor, but reach him I do, grasping Will's left wrist as Kolya jumps—

492

Sprawling out into a sun-baked harbour, thrown forward on to the cobbles.

'Where the . . .?'

I sit up, looking about me. There's no sign of anyone on the vacant quayside. Only the abandoned trappings of a small fishing port, the soft grey of distant mountains.

Is this another trick? A trick to trap me in one of Time's cul-de-sacs, like that time in New York City?

I stand, then close my eyes, a wave of unsteadiness passing through me, making me totter on the stones.

And then the light begins to fade.

I turn slowly and see it – *there*, twenty paces distant. It's like a tiny gateway, the light there more intense. I walk toward it, and as I do, so the gateway starts to pulse, the colour slowly bleaching from the rest of it.

And as I come closer, so there's a disembodied voice in the air. *'Come, Otto. It's time for you to see where it began.'*

Only I know where it began. And besides, when did I begin to trust Kolya or choose to do what he told me to do?

No. Turn your back on it, Otto. Jump!

And I jump . . . Only, apart from some vague tingling on the surface of my skin, it seems there is no power left to jump. Either that or there's some kind of jump suppressor set up hereabouts.

I look to the glowing portal once again. Discern, in its depths, a slow turning shape – a spiral, and recall what Katerina said. Her warning about spirals. And turn away, deciding to go back. We can proceed with the play, after all, even with its author missing. And my hunch is that he won't be missing for long.

I try once more to jump. And this time it works!

Only my sudden reappearance amid the crowd at the Globe causes general consternation. People stare at me and point. I try to make my way away from there with as little fuss as possible, only there's a whole mob of them now, hemming me in, shouting at me, their hands grasping, pulling me back, seeking to restrain me.

I'm going nowhere, it seems. Only suddenly I'm no longer there. Suddenly it's night, and cool, and across from me the Rose is brightly lit and welcoming and I heave a massive sigh, even as I realise that I've made an impact on this timeline that I really oughtn't to have made.

Which is unfortunate. Only what real harm could it have done?

I pause in the doorway, looking across to our regular table in the far corner and see a number of familiar faces. Will's players. Then, with a shock, I see others among them, people who really should not be there, drawn, no doubt, by my earlier hasty and ill-planned jump.

Blagovesh, the marsh pirate, is there, as is the young Russian time agent, Saratov. And there – smiling across at me – the gypsy woman, Mari-something, also known as Jamil. And there's another – a tall man in his forties, who carries a purse at his belt and the marks of surgery on his half-shaven skull – who I only part recognise and cannot put a name to.

None of whom should be here. So what are they doing here? Is this Kolya's work, once again?

I make my way across, looking for Will among that host, and find myself stopped by the tall man. He grips my arm.

'Do I know you?' I ask, looking down at his hand, glowering at him.

The tall man smiles. 'Not in this form, no.'

I'm about to ask what he means, when, with a shock, I realise that the purse at his belt isn't a purse at all but a shrunken head.

'Reichenau?'

The villain's eyes light up. 'The same. But not as you'd remember me, neh?'

'We killed you,' I say. 'Time-dead.'

He shakes his head. 'No one's time-dead, Otto. Not these days. It's all unravelling. Didn't you know that? Unravelling, and then . . .'

And then what? Only I don't ask, for at that moment Will reappears, grinning, Katerina on his arm.

Seeing me, she smiles. 'I saved him,' she says simply. 'I went in there and snatched him back.'

But seeing her there with Will, their arms linked, I feel a strong surge of jealousy.

Jealousy? Yes. Because I know how charming he can be. And because Katerina is an impressionable young woman. Didn't her reaction to young Nevsky prove that?

Only right then things grow more complicated, as the gypsy woman – what was her name? Mariya? – comes and joins us at the bar.

'Otto . . .'

Katerina looks to me for an explanation, but before I can say a word, the woman takes a small package from her shoulder bag and hands it to me.

'You forgot these,' she says. 'Last time you came to visit me.'

It's a tarot. But not a complete one. No. These are the special cards. The ones Mariya read for me that time. I flick through them, then look to her once more.

'I thought them lost.'

Her smile returns. 'Nothing's ever wholly lost.'

'Otto?' Katerina unlinks her arm from Will's then reaches across to take the cards. She studies them a moment, then looks to me, lifting one of the cards – the High Priestess – to display its markings.

'This is me.'

'I know,' I say, taking them back from her, noting once more how warm the cards are. Unnaturally so.

I flick through them once more, naming the twelve as I do.

'Starke . . . Death . . . The Lovers . . . Judgement . . . The Hanged Man . . . The Tower . . . The Magician . . . The High Priestess . . . The Wheel of Fortune . . . The Star . . . The World, and the Two of Coins.'

The last of these is perhaps the strangest, portraying, as it does, a weird two-headed man who's clearly Reichenau, but that's only a question of degree. For Kolya's here, as Death, and Master Hecht, there on the top half of The Lovers card, like an Archangel, his wings spread wide. And on the Judgement card there's Katerina and I, our pale corpses stretched out on the cart at Krasnogorsk. Dead.

And everywhere – so it seems – the symbol of the lazy eight. Kolya's sign.

Only what does this mean? That it was all – as Katerina claims – preordained? The working-out of Fate?

As I've said already, I don't believe that. Despite all I've seen, all I've experienced, I think we yet might shape how things turn out.

Later, when things have quietened down and we're alone, Will hands me a small sheaf of papers. 'Kolya's speech,' he says. 'For the end of the play.'

I read it through, then tear the paper up. 'It doesn't work,' I say, but I can see just how shocked he is at my reaction. Shocked and hurt. But it's true. It doesn't work. It ought to have done, only . . .

'Look,' I say. 'I've got to get some rest.'

And leave him there. Only halfway up the stairs to my room, I realise I have left the tarot cards on the side behind the bar, and turn back, meaning to get them. And it's there, from the doorway, unnoticed by them, that I see Katerina kiss Will. It's not a proper kiss, just a peck really, but I note how her hand lingers on his shoulder, how the two of them exchange smiles. Katerina, who, a moment before, was somewhere else in Time, returning specially for that kiss.

My stomach knots. I close my eyes in sudden agony.

And when she joins me, later, in my room, she sits by me and asks me what is wrong. And I cannot tell her. Only when she makes to take my hand in hers, I shrug her off, and she stands, angry suddenly. More angry than I've ever seen her.

'What in God's name is going on in your head, Otto? Did all those years together mean nothing?'

'Will,' I say, hardly daring to articulate my fears. 'You and Will . . .'

'Will? Will *Shakespeare*?' And she laughs, as if I could have said nothing more ridiculous. Only I saw them. Saw the way she touched him, that exchange of smiles.

'I love *you*, stupid!' she says. 'Don't you understand that? *You*, Otto Behr. Not him. *You*.'

'Then why . . .?' Only I can't say it. For there are no words for how I feel right then, and when I flinch from her touch a second time it's all too much for her. She glares at me, then is gone from the air once more. Gone where? I wonder. To him? To punish me?

Whatever, she is gone. Yes, and all is chaos once again.

493

Shakespeare knocks us up early. He has us gather in the bar, more than half our number well the worse for drink.

Swallowing my pride, my fears, I go down and join them, standing there, silent and surly at the back of the room as he begins.

Calling for silence, he announces what we're going to do today, producing, with a flourish, a letter from King James in his own handwriting, requesting our attendance at the palace of Whitehall for a private performance.

It's not the first time that they've performed one of Will's plays for the Court, but the very nature of the summons – in the King's own hand – makes this somewhat special. For Will, particularly, this is a chance to get new sponsorship – from the King, no less – as well as clear his debts, and so he rushes here and there, organising things, keen not to squander this golden opportunity.

Will's only problem is that his current 'sponsor' – the one he borrowed the money from – wants his money back and he wants it back now, not a day, or a week or a month from now.

Why does he want it? Because some bigger crook wants *his* money back, and he can't, it seems, wait.

Will seems to think that the problem will go away, but I'm not so sure.

'Why don't you go and see him,' I say, keeping my tone neutral. 'Give him something up front and promise the rest next week.'

Will considers that and, despite the fact that he hasn't finished organising things, agrees to take an hour out of his schedule to go and see the man.

Which is where I get my first big shock. Because when I get to the inn we've agreed to meet at, the man who greets me – the Big Boss of London in these Stuart times – is none other than . . .

. . .'*Ernst?*'

'Ernst' frowns at me and looks to one of his henchmen for an explanation. He clearly doesn't know who I am.

'Ernst?' he asks, his voice similar but different. Ernst but not Ernst.

And my immediate thought is that this is Kolya's doing – that he's taken an Ernst from another timeline and is now using him against me, to fuck with my head.

'You know this man, Otto?' Will asks.

I still find it hard to speak to Will. Not to grab him and accuse him of stealing my wife from me. But I keep it all in check.

'I do and I don't.'

'Meaning?'

'Meaning he's the image of an old friend. Only it isn't him.'

Our fake 'Ernst' looks from Will to me then back to Will. 'Well?' he asks. 'You have the money?'

'Not enough to pay you off today. But my fortunes have changed and—'

'Fuck your fortunes! You know the deal.'

I look down, wondering what's the best course of action. Whether to fight our way out or simply vanish. Because one thing's clear. This 'Ernst' isn't going to compromise.

Only Will has already decided what he's going to do.

'One day,' he says. 'That's all I ask. Then I'll pay you the full amount.'

'Ernst' smiles unpleasantly. 'What's this? Have you found some other gullible idiot to back you?'

'You might call him that, that is, if you didn't value your head.'

'He's an important man, yes?'

'No less than the King.'

'The *King*?'

'Come with me. We're performing at the White Hall, three hours from now.'

'Ernst' looks to his men, then looks back at me. Up until twenty seconds ago, I'd have said we were heading for a stalemate, that or a pitched battle, but this version of Ernst – from wherever Kolya's brought him – seems to like the idea of seeing Shakespeare's play in the King's company almost as much as getting paid the full sum of what he's owed.

'All right,' he says after a moment. 'But you keep in sight, right? My men will be watching you closely. One false move and . . .'

He smiles and makes the gesture of a blade cutting a throat.

And so we return, to find the handcarts stacked high with all our makeshift sets, the players anxious – and eager – to get going.

As it is, it's another two hours before all is ready, and as we anticipate the arrival of King James, so I look about me at the packed benches.

There's scarcely a member of the nobility who's not attended – at least, those who were here in the capital. Word has clearly gone out that something special's afoot.

And then, with a fanfare, the King himself arrives.

James is a deeply unattractive man, both in his appearance and his manner. His particular mix of arrogance and physical timidity is deeply unappetising, to say the least.

Seeing him, Shakespeare hurries across, head lowered, then makes a sweeping bow.

'Your Majesty . . .'

But Will's smile is stretched thin. Like all there, his eyes are drawn to James's rolling eyes, and to his tongue, which is far too big for his mouth.

Yes, *deeply* unattractive.

I watch James, see how he reacts; noting how defensive his whole manner is. He is a man who never knew his mother, and it shows. Raised as a strict Calvinist, his nature is cold and austere, but rumour has it that, wife and children aside, James likes boys. Attractive young boys.

'Mister Shakespeare,' he says, putting out a hand so that Will can kiss the ring. 'I understand you have something special for us.'

Will bobs his head. 'My Lord, I hope it . . . entertains.'

And if it doesn't?

Only it will. I know it will. Haven't I witnessed it once already, from my vantage point on the balcony at the very back of the packed banqueting house? Yes, and seen the King's enthusiasm for the play.

It will, quite literally, be the talk of the town.

But right now Will is uncharacteristically nervous. He knows how important it is that the King likes it. King and courtiers, too. And though he knows this is his finest work, he also knows, deep down, that his fate might yet depend on how much – or how little – this frail and often disagreeable man enjoys this evening's fare.

It is, one must remind oneself, something new. Entirely new.

Ahead of its time? Well, surely that's the point, isn't it? That's what makes it the work of genius that it is.

Bowing one third and last time, Will steps back, away from the King, and turns to face the crowded hall, his right arm forming extravagant shapes in the air as he addresses them.

'Your Majesty, lords, ladies and gentlemen . . . I am delighted to present to you a tale of strange invention. A tale that, we hope, will both amaze and amuse you.'

And, as he says these words, so six of the cast – dressed in matching black cloaks – move slowly out into the vacant centre of the stage, each tilting the dark-painted box they carry so that the pebbles inside each box make the slushing sound of pebbles on a beach.

Will allows this sound to be repeated, once, twice, a third time, and then turns to the King once more and, smiling, bowing low, addresses him:

'Of Time . . . And Tides . . .'

494

As it ends, even as the tall, pale shape of 'Kolya' steps from the stage into the dark, there's the briefest moment of absolute stillness, of focused concentration, and then a great eruption – an ear-splitting tumult of cheering and clapping and of throwing of hats into the air. Why, even the King is on his feet, applauding, those surrounding him – looking to him for their lead – whooping and grinning, liberated by their master's clear delight.

A triumph . . . There's no argument. It's a gem of a play. Truly one of a kind. And, as Will takes the stage once more, the volume goes up a notch or two, a deafening noise that just goes on and on, as, one by one, the players take the stage for their encores.

Later, in the crowded back room of the Rose, Will takes the seat beside me and, leaning across, embraces me.

'Otto . . . what would we have done without you?'

I look down, as if embarrassed, then meet his eyes.

Which is when I see it. How strangely he looks at me, that is. As if, in the depths of him, he finally knows the truth about me. As if finally, drip by drip, it has penetrated his consciousness with a tiny 'ah!' of realisation.

And how could it not? Only nothing is said between us. He knows, and knowing is enough. Knowing is . . . well, let's say that it's something neither of us expected.

And then there's also the possibility that Katerina's told him. And if she has?

'You want a beer?' he asks, as if, at that moment, it was the most normal thing he could say.

'My shout,' I answer, my smile mirroring his. Prolonged. As if smiling were the most natural thing. Yes, and no trace of what I'm truly feeling, no casual spoiling of the moment.

I turn and order two beers, then turn back, meeting his eyes again.

'Is she waiting for you, Otto? Wherever it is you come from.'

'Cherdiechnost,' I say, and see him take that in.

'So it's a real place?'

I nod, then, the beers having arrived, I take them and hand one to him.

'And Kravchuk?'

'He's real. Six times I killed that fucker and he still kept coming back.'

'The dead who won't stay dead,' he says, quoting a line from his play. And I nod and take a long sup of my ale, wondering if he knows how close he is to dying. How deep the instinct is in me.

He's silent a moment, then: 'There was this woman once. I . . . I fell for her, Otto. Lock, stock and barrel. Left my wife and family to be with her. And then she died.'

'I'm surprised,' I say. 'I mean . . . there's nothing in your poems . . . nor in the plays, come to that.'

'I couldn't,' he says. 'I . . . I just couldn't. To constantly remind myself of that. To have it paraded out in public . . . No, it broke my heart, Otto. After that, nothing was the same. My work grew darker . . .'

I nod. Despite what I feel, I understand. And as I do, so the idea of taking him back there to see his dead love once more fills my thoughts. Only I know it's a bad idea. One I need to keep to myself.

I change the subject. 'So how was our friend, the money-lender? Did *he* like your entertainment?'

Will sups from his beer, then laughs. 'He loved it. Gave me a full extra week to come up with the money.'

'And the King?'

'The King wants me to write an alternate version. Something more flattering . . .'

'Oh . . .' I say, wondering why I should be so surprised. After all, they all want to rewrite history and show their bloodline in a better light. And what better opportunity than this? To have Time conquered by the glorious Stuarts!

He's quiet a moment, then: 'Otto?'

'Yes?'

He reaches out and holds my arm, giving me his most charming smile. 'Thank you, brother. Without you . . .'

'It was nothing,' I say, even though I know it was in fact a great deal. Had I not arrived through Time to save his bacon, where would he be? Dead, probably, floating face down in the Thames.

But that's not my role here. My task is to find out where our nemesis, Kolya, is, and why he's here, in 1609.

'It's strange, isn't it?' Will says, and for a moment I don't have the slightest notion what he's talking about.

'Strange?'

'The idea of changing the outcome of things. I've never really thought to play with time and event in that fashion. But now . . . Well, I just can't see how I can ever write things in the good old way again. It's as if . . . well, it's as if there are doors – real, physical doors – connecting all the different timelines, and the more you use those doors, the more tenuous they become. The more . . . fragile.'

He pauses then. 'Do you see what I'm trying to say, Otto?'

I shake my head. 'Not really. It's just a device, that's all. A toying with ideas. It isn't real.'

'*Isn't* it?'

Shakespeare's face changes. His eyes grow more thoughtful.

'It's just that, as I was writing it, it didn't feel like it usually feels. It felt real. As if I was some kind of conduit . . . some messenger sent by the gods. And d'you know what? I've never felt that way. Not ever. There has always been a distance between me and the words. I was always – *always* – in control. But this time . . . this time I felt *immersed*, swept along by the immense forward momentum of the play. Carried on the tides of time, you might almost say.'

'Maybe,' I say, trying to interrupt him. 'Even so—'

'No, no buts and no maybes, dear friend. I was totally immersed. Lost to this world and its ways. Adrift, and no way home except to step back through the door I'd taken.'

I nod, unable not to. Because that's how it feels every time I jump. And he *understands* that.

'You saw the crowd tonight, Otto. Saw how they reacted. I mean . . . I'm used to captivating them. But nothing like they were tonight. They were *there*.'

And that too is true. Crude as our time-travelling devices were, they were powerfully effective. More than that, they were new. The gasp of surprise the audience gave when our hero jumped between the worlds was one of genuinely shocked surprise. And yet there was belief there, too.

'All right,' I say. 'I can't argue with you, only . . .'

'Only?'

I shrug. After all, what was the point of arguing? It's what I wanted, wasn't it? And Will has delivered in trumps. For years to come, poets and playwrights will be mining this territory, inspired by the ideas Will has introduced here to the world. Until one day . . .

Or am I being naïve? What if nothing actually comes of this? What if this remains a purely imaginative venture? What if it spawns nothing in the way of deeper rational thought, but remains an entertainment, as now?

What a waste that would be. What a let-down for the species.

And yet the gambler in me would place everything I own on someone, somewhere coming up with something. That's vague, I know – vague to the point of being almost incoherent – and yet I sense its existence close by. Up River.

Which is why Kolya's here. I'm more certain of that by the moment.

I look to Will again and see that he's lost in his thoughts. And once again I see him kissing her.

I look down. My choices are simple. To confront him or to let things go. To trust in what I have and not destroy it through my jealousy.

'D'you fancy another ale?'

He looks to me and smiles. 'I think we deserve one, no? My shout.'

And so the evening begins. An evening to remember.

495

Only it's all for the wrong reasons. I'd seen them kiss before, but this time . . .

I have to stop. I tremble just to say it.

The problem's thus. As I said, I'd seen her kiss him once before, a chaste peck on the cheek, the briefest touch of her hand against his upper arm, but this, glimpsed from where I stand in the un-revealing darkness at the top of the stairs, is in a different category. This time it's her mouth to his, her tongue against his tongue, even as their hands grip one another in the spell of passion, body pressed to body.

And so my heart breaks once again.

I want to go down there and kill him, the way I'd killed Kravchuk that time. Only this time it's diffcrent. This time it's

Will and Katerina who are doing this to me. And I can see in their eyes that they can't help themselves. That this is not just lust but love.

And how am I to cope with that? I who know what love can do to a man?

I watch till I can watch no more, then turn away, into a darkness so profound, so overwhelming, I stumble and fall, all power gone from my limbs.

I want to die. Without her I cannot live. Only how can I unremember this?

And with the thought comes the answer. Urte will know how. She'll juggle with Time until there's no trace of this abomination in my head. And so I jump. Back to Moscow Central. As so often I have jumped, in dire need. Though never as dire as this.

Yes, but what else will I lose if I lose this? What lasting damage will this alteration bring?

The truth is, I don't know. Maybe it will mar all that we've achieved. Only what is that? The play? Might this destroy that too? Make it as though it had never been spoken of, never crafted?

We can't allow that, surely? Only how then can I live? How can I function, having seen what I have seen?

No. I am better dead than have *that* in my head.

Yes, and here's the irony. That he who I would newly kill should have written such a play as *Othello*. Or is that yet to come?

No. He has written it already. I know he has. How then could he do this to me, knowing that?

Unless he had no choice.

Even so, I can't forgive him.

I stand unsteadily, looking about me at the thick and choking blackness of that room, hearing the noise from the bar below.

I know that they're standing there, right now, there at the foot of the stairs, their eyes drowning in each other's eyes, their bodies locked in that passionate embrace. And I want to cry out like a child, the pain I feel. Want to tear and rip and stomp . . .

Or simpler, end myself.

Only that's no solution. For no sooner had I done it than they would have whisked me back and made me live again. In some other timeline.

I try to jump. Only there's no response. My body stays anchored where it is. I try again and then a third. But nothing.

It seems then that I must go down. To confront those whom I love and hate the most.

Only they're no longer there.

Gone to his bed, I tell myself, the wash of sheer agony at the thought almost unhinging me, making me grunt with pain. Only even as I frame the words in my head, I hear him – Will Shakespeare himself – shouting over the noise of the crowd down there, drawing their attention, so that it grows quiet, the crowd of friends and players listening to hear what he might say.

Only he's barely said two lines before there's a fresh outcry at the main door to the inn. Men are shouting now, exchanging blows, and suddenly there's a scream. Someone, it seems, has drawn a dagger.

I hurl myself down the stairs, in time to see a small group of men – a dozen or more of them – pushing their way into the already crowded inn. They're spoiling for trouble, and I can see that people are going to get badly hurt unless I do something. Our players might be great fighters on the stage, but in real life?

In real life, they don't stand a chance. Not unless I intervene. Only when I try again, I find that I still can't jump, which makes me think there be some kind of suppressor in the room.

There's the flash of steel in the candlelight, and shouts and yet more screaming, and then . . .

And then – and the transition is sudden and abrupt – nothing.

Leaving silence and blackness and a full moon shining in through the smashed windows of the inn. Only I realise I am not alone in that moonlit room. There's one other, seated there, across from me, his pale blue eyes registering a cold disdain.

Kolya.

496

For a moment neither of us speaks. The silence is profound.

And the room?

The room is the same as that we were in in what seems mere seconds past, only the windows now are all blown in, as if by an explosion, and the tables and chairs are covered in a moon-silvered layer of dust.

This is one of his oldest selves, perhaps the most ancient I have ever met. He's a hundred if he's a day, and probably twice that. As old as the timelines would be my guess. Mind, the night-dark cloak and the shock of pure white hair don't help, nor the long ash-staff he grips in his right hand.

A wizard, that's what he looks like. And those eyes. Paradoxically timeless. So pale and grey-blue they seem to hold the winter sky in their orbits.

I take a step toward him, yet even as I do, so two of his younger selves, more my age than his, step from the air, to either side of him.

I stop, seeing that both are armed, and take a slow step backward.

'Very wise,' he says, showing that cold disdain and sense of invulnerability I've come to recognise as his trademark.

'What do you want?'

The old man laughs – the sound like a gust of sudden icy wind. '*Want?*' he asks. 'Why should I *want* anything?'

'Because that's how you operate. You're not a *giving* fellow, are you?'

His eyes harden. 'You understand, I take it?'

'Understand?'

'The significance of this place. What it meant to you and me?'

'I know you killed me here, a hundred times and more.'

There's almost a smile on his lips at that. Only it clearly bugs him that I kept on coming back, good as new, even if it was a long time ago.

'Let me ask you again,' I say, determined to have his answer. 'What precisely do you want?'

He seems to lean back a little, as if getting his breath. 'I wanted to warn you.'

'To *warn* me?' I laugh, genuinely surprised. 'Why, Kolya, dear friend, you almost make it seem as if you're *helping* me. A warning . . .' And I laugh again.

Laughter. He doesn't like laughter. Unless it's from his own lips.

His eyes seem suddenly colder. 'I could have killed you . . . This time, I mean. I had the choice.'

'Only?'

He hesitates, then. 'You never were my match, were you, Otto Behr? From the word go you struggled to understand it all.'

I shrug. That's maybe even true. I really never was Meister material. No. I was far too impulsive. Much too driven. But I'll be fucked if I admit that to him here and now. Show any weakness and he's guaranteed to exploit it.

'I was lucky,' I say. 'And I chose my friends well. Very well indeed. That's why I survived it – your plan to eradicate all trace of me.' I pause, thoughtful suddenly. 'Yes, but why was that? What made you choose *me*? Or was it just that I was the first of us you encountered?'

I don't expect him to answer, and he doesn't disappoint. No. He just sits there, glaring at me, as if my mere existence were an insult.

Which maybe it is. But why is he just sitting there? Why *hasn't* he used whatever powers he has to have done with me?

Is this just to be a talking shop? If so, then what really is the point?

He clears his throat then, with the very faintest of smiles, leans towards me again.

'Talking of choices. Where's your wife, Otto?'

I was intending to turn away, to leave him sitting there, but now I turn back. There's a strong tone of insinuation in his voice that suggests he knows something that shouldn't be known. Something foul.

'What do you mean?'

'You want to go to her? To see what she's doing, right now? I can show you if you like.'

I take two steps toward him, my fist raised, and as I do, so the two figures appear once more. His bodyguards. His selves.

Brothers . . .

I take a step back, away from them. And as I do, so they vanish into the air, like projections, leaving a second set of footprints in the dust. Footprints that lead nowhere.

'Well?' he asks. 'I can show it to you if you want. But no, that wouldn't satisfy you, would it? You need to know. To see. Maybe even to touch.'

I look down, horrified by the suggestion. Wanting and not wanting what he's offering, if only to confirm my darkest suspicions.

Only . . .

Urd make me wrong! I beg, feeling a sudden weakness in my limbs.

Which is, of course, just what he wants. To weaken me. To undermine me.

Because that's it, you see. Part of me recognises what's being done to me here. Just as Ernst wasn't Ernst, this Katerina is not my darling girl, but a fake, plucked by Kolya from the timestreams to betray me; to seduce my dear friend Will and break my heart.

I know this. Know it almost for a certainty – for isn't this just how Kolya goes about things? – and yet part of me still believes she has cheated on me; that same part that will not be content until I see it for myself.

And yet . . . to *see* it . . . No, I surely haven't the strength.

Kolya stands, his slow movements showing his age, then looks to me.

'What's up, Otto? Afraid to face the truth?' He laughs. A cold, mocking sound. 'You think she's *our* creature, don't you? And yes, it would be easy to do that. Very easy. Only you'd know, wouldn't you? You of all people.'

My mouth is dry now.

Walk away, I tell myself. *Go now, before this bastard pours his poison in your eyes and ears.* Only something stops me, makes me turn again to face the old man, seeing now how he holds a parcel out to me.

'Here,' he says, throwing it to me, making me take a hurried step forward to snatch it from the air. 'Enjoy!'

And he's gone.

497

Meister Schnorr looks back at me from where he sits beside the screen. 'You really want to do this, Otto?'

I nod, knowing that it's actually the last thing I wish to see, because once seen...

I've discussed this now with Urte, and it seems it's true. Once seen there is no removing it from my head. Not without removing *her*. For Katerina's central to the loop. And not just to the loop, but to reality itself. Core reality.

Over the years we have refashioned the Tree of Worlds and cannot undo now what we have done. Not without losing all that I most treasure.

In this it is Kolya's master stroke.

I look to Ernst. 'Does she . . .?'

'Know about it?' He shakes his head. 'As soon as we found out what was going on we . . . well, we made a decision. To keep it from her. Bad enough that they got to you, Otto. But Katerina would have gone mad.'

I nod, but my whole self feels cast down.

'You want us to stay?'

'No, leave me, I'll call you when I'm done.'

And so they leave.

I lock the door behind me, then walk over to the screen. I have only to touch it and it will begin. Whatever it shows.

Yes, but do I want to see?

The sensible thing would be to destroy this . . . this *fake*. Only – as I've said – there's a small part of me that needs to know. That almost needs to gloat over it, even as the larger part of my soul dies.

Because nothing will be the same after this.

The screen lights up. Too close to it, I move back a little, and for a second or two fail to recognise just what I'm looking at. But then I understand. It begins where I ended it, the two of them together at the foot of the stairs, in Stuart London, in

1609, locked in a passionate embrace from which I watch them break.

Eyes wide with wanting, he grasps her hand. 'Come . . .'

And she obeys, taking his hand as he leads her down the dimly lit passageway to another set of stairs that lead up into another part of the inn. One I've never seen before this moment.

Fakes, I say to myself, trying to convince myself of that, even as they pass the camera's vantage point. Only they don't look like fakes. Far from it. Because every little gesture seems familiar.

Familiar and authentic.

Will flings the door open, then pulls her in beside him, drawing her into an embrace, Katerina laughing now, excited.

And that alone makes me groan, That she should want him. Above all others at that moment. *Him.*

And on the screen now she is undressing him, even as he unlaces her from her dress. And as their clothes fall away, so I drop onto my haunches, groaning with the pain I feel, knowing that for all Old Schnorr denies it, this is them – my wife and my latest friend – naked on that shabby little bed.

I look away, even as the soundtrack grows louder, even as the noises of their foul enjoyment fill the room I'm in.

Urd save me, no.

I am compelled to look back, and as I do, so, with a gasp and an increased excitement, they begin to fuck.

This is hell indeed. To witness this. To watch her lose faith with me and fuck another. And to enjoy it, too. This is worse than all the small deaths I've ever suffered. Oh, much, much worse. And no mistaking this, these two seem real. Not actors, but my lover and my friend. And I fall to my knees, as I did once before, and, head in my hands, howl out my bitter agonies.

Katerina . . . My darling girl. How in heaven's name could you ever do this to me?

498

'Watch,' Ernst says, and turns the screen on once again.

I look to him and shake my head. There's nothing he could show me now that would convince me otherwise. Nothing that could make this any better. Except, that is, to erase all trace of her, even if I could. Even if this new reality we now inhabit allowed such changes.

But he is adamant. 'No, Otto. Just watch. And remember who it was that gave you this. This is his last throw of the dice. Just think how desperate he must be, resorting to this.'

I turn, looking at the screen. For a moment I'm silent. Then I look to him again.

'What is this?'

'Watch,' he says again. But this time it's an order. And when it's done and the screen goes black again, I look away, thoughtful.

I make to say something then stop.

'Well?' Ernst says patiently. 'You've seen now, how it was done.'

'Have I?'

And indeed I have. Have seen them afterwards, on the screen, sat naked side by side on the edge of the bed, smoking a post-coital cigarette, as the film crew – two of them clearly Kolya's 'brothers' – tidy up about them.

Making a blue film, as they used to call it. Hard porn. And there's part of me that believes the artifice. That this was all a set-up. But still a small part clings on. Believes it's really them.

Punishing me. Making me suffer as only such betrayals can. My soul destroyed by what I've seen. Never to be the same.

Ernst huffs and walks away. And, even as he does, so I hear the door behind me creak open, and turn to see Katerina herself, standing there in the doorway, a query in her eyes.

'Well?' she says, the slightest impatience in the words. 'They said you wanted to see me . . .'

She's clearly still angry from our last meeting, but her voice trails off as she sees what's on the screen on the far side of the room.

She double-takes, then looks to me. 'What in Urd's name . . .'

I turn my head away, unable to look at her. I feel disgust, and hurt . . . and an anger to match her own.

'It's you. Can't you see? *You*.'

499

She steps up close to the screen and looks, studying the frozen image as if it were a painting and she some connoisseur.

For a long time then she's silent, like she's considering what story to tell, what lies to trot out and make things right again. Only nothing can make this right.

'It's strange,' she says, not looking round. 'Seeing yourself like this. It's all rather indecent. And yet, at the same time, completely innocent.'

'*Innocent?*' I climb to my feet, unable to contain the anger – the bitter, spitting anger – that I'm feeling at that moment. 'It's you! It's *you* fucking doing that, not some stranger!'

'And yet not.'

And now she turns, her eyes uncertain. 'You shouldn't have shown me this, Otto. Now it'll be awkward . . . with Will, I mean.

Knowing that there are versions of us, out there in the timelines, that have done this.'

'And you?' I say, the bitterness growing by the second. 'You sure as fucking well enjoyed it.'

Katerina shrugs. She looks down, abashed. 'The me in the film? Sure. But what if I didn't know you in that world . . . that timeline? What if that was one of the hundreds of worlds you died in? In which you'd never met me, never fell in love? What then? Was I to live like a nun?' She pauses, then: 'I have a passionate nature. That's all this says of our relationship. That this is what I'd have been without you. A sexual adventurer, if that's how you'd like to call it. But that's only because I didn't have you in my life, Otto.'

Only how can I believe that, now that I've seen her with another? How can I ever shake that off? Fated we were. Only now . . .

Now I suspect every man she's ever met, every so-called friend, and ask myself which among them have fucked her? Has Ernst? Or maybe Svetov? And I imagine a long queue of men, there at her door, each waiting to be fucked.

Ridiculous, I know. The imaginings of a madman. But I simply cannot stop it. I've seen it now, the worst thing a man could see. A cuckold's vision of the world.

She turns fully, straightening up, and looks to me. Her voice is gentle now, conciliatory. 'So what *are* we going to do?'

'Do?' And again, it's angry. I can't help it, but I also can't sustain this. I still love the look of her, the touch of her, the smell. She is all I ever wanted in this life. But Fate has tripped us at the last.

'Urd help us,' I say again. Only this time it's a whisper, a coil of smoke about the sharpest of needles.

Urd fucking help us.

500

And then Time slips. The sky moves sideways, and just as suddenly she's gone. To come again? Who knows? Only that a messenger – a young boy, no more than eight or nine, is there now at the back door to the inn, bidding us follow him, down to the river's edge as dawn breaks over the city.

And there, at the quayside, we come upon him, floating face down in the shallows, drowned, his throat cut, his pocket picked.

Dead, I think, recalling how I'd felt, only moments before, seeing him in my darling's arms. As if the wish were father to this deed.

And Katerina?

I ask the boy. But there was no sign, it seems, of a woman with him.

I want to go back, to ask her, yes and confront her again, only it's at that very moment that I notice the paper trail, the pages of his latest play marked on the reverse with arrows, pinned to the wooden walls of houses, pointing the way. I follow, gathering up the handwritten sheets, hurrying to do so before someone else plucks them from the walls.

London, I think. 1609. Where it all began.

And suddenly I'm there, back at St Paul's, and the bookshop, where there's a huge stack of leatherbound printed manuscripts of *Of Time and Tides*, dated a year hence. And as I take a copy from the pile and turn it, facing me, so I recognise whose work this claims to be. Whose symbol is branded into the thick leather cover of the work.

The lazy eight.

Okay. But why? For this seems petty by his standards.

I turn the cover, looking, wondering why this path should lead here of all places. And even as I do, so someone grabs me, grappling with my arms, while another kicks my legs away, forcing me down onto my knees in the mud. And, drawing a blade, he cuts me from ear to ear, the blood gouting from the gaping flaps of flesh.

'Dead,' he says quietly, letting my head fall back, his pale eyes at the last staring into mine. 'And no way back.'

501

I wake to find myself in limbo. Or at least something closely resembling it. A white room. A perfectly white room, without a window or door to be seen.

More cell than room.

I reach up to gently touch my throat and feel the thick scar there.

'Where am I?'

It's Kolya who answers me, making me turn, to see his presence there where a moment ago there was nothing.

'Somewhere that the youngster can't get at you,' he says, which makes me wonder about a lot of things.

'Your younger self, you mean?'

He nods. 'They live within much smaller loops than us.'

I blink, surprised, but he continues.

'Oh, I'd kill you, sure enough. If it meant something. Only there's little point to it now. It all reverts.'

'And this?' I ask, tenderly touching the scar at my throat.

'Was just a gesture. The last move in a very long game. No. This loop is done, Otto Behr. Nothing can alter it any longer. No more births, no more deaths. Just repetition.'

'And Katerina?'

But he ignores that. 'Are you still curious, Otto?'

'Curious?'

'As to why it happened as it did?'

I hesitate then nod. Only I don't expect the truth from him.

'Tell me,' I say. And he tells me. About the world he ruled. The great globe-spanning empire that he built. And about his use of Shakespeare to write the history of that world – the same book that was there on Master Hecht's shelves that time. And how I took that world from him. Yes, and robbed him of a son.

And this is the nub of it. For he was the only son Kolya ever had in all those worlds he made his own. The one and only he considered *his*, anyway. A boy, little more than eight years old when I took him from Kolya. Out into the void, where I dumped him. Left him to die in the eternal cold, beyond Kolya's reach for once.

His single failing. No wonder he hated me.

'What about Reichenau?' I ask, but he shakes his head. 'That abomination? That was my sister's child.'

'But I thought—'

'Then you thought wrong.'

He is silent for a moment, then stands, leaning on his staff.

'Your day is over, Otto. Mine too, I guess, only . . . I have this unfinished business with your daughter. You know, the one you lost.'

'Martha?' And I try to sit up, only I black out, and when I come to again he's leaning over me, his face a hand's width from my own, his foul breath in my nostrils.

'It's many years since she called herself that,' he says. 'She's the lost girl now.'

I close my eyes, a tear rolling down my cheek.

Alive. My darling girl's alive.

I drift into sleep and wake to find the old man gone, another in his place.

'Aren't you dead?' I ask him, and he smiles back at me.

'Aren't you?'

Kavanagh is different from how I remember him. The bullet holes that killed him have healed over, but his scarred and shaven head is still familiar.

'Where's the other one?'

'Kolya? He's gone. Word is that he's dying.'

'Dying?'

'Old age,' he says. 'Or should we call it Time?'

'And me?'

Kav hesitates, then answers me, somewhat reluctantly it seems.

'You're dying too, my dear friend. You've got a cancer, there, in your head, wrapped about your brain stem – a glioma. Malignant and incurable. You've been having proton therapy...'

I look puzzled, shake my head.

Kav sighs. 'Apparently they put you into this huge scanner that uses high-energy beams of radiation to destroy the cancerous cells. Only, well, only sometimes it doesn't work.'

'And it's not working for me?'

He hesitates again. 'I don't know. I think you'd need to ask.'

Dying, eh? Well, that makes sense of it all.

I close my eyes and ask the question I asked earlier again. 'Where are we?'

'On the shores of Lake Michigan.'

'Your home town.'

'Yes, only things have changed.'

'Changed? In what way.'

'You'll see. But I'll leave you be for now. You need your rest, Otto.'

Only I don't hear half of it. I drift off again.

And wake to find Ernst sat beside the bed, holding my hand.

'Otto . . .'

492

There are tears in his eyes. My oldest friend. I squeeze his hand and smile weakly. It's good to see Ernst. He's always had my back.

'Is it true? That I'm dying?'

He gives a single nod. 'Least, that's what the senior consultant says.'

'Fuck . . . And no jumping back?'

'Those days are done with, Otto. At least, in our circles.'

'Then who's running the show?'

'Svetov, mainly. But the idea now is to contain time travel, not proliferate it. We've become watchmen, guarding the timelines.'

'And does it work?'

Ernst smiles. 'So they say.'

'But you're not so sure?'

There's a moment's silence, then I gesture to Ernst to raise me up on my cushions. He does, making me comfy.

'There,' he says. 'That's better, eh?'

I study him a moment, realising how much I love the man. How many lives we owed each other. Then ask what Ernst knew I would ask.

'Is she coming?'

He looks down, dark shadows crossing his face. 'You . . . said you didn't want to see her.'

'Did I? When was that?'

'Oh, a while back now. And then you had the stroke.'

'I have been busy.'

And he nods. Like he's run out of words.

'So when did I last see her?'

'I . . .' He pauses. 'Two years . . . maybe three. Objective, that is.'

I open my mouth and close it again, stunned by his words. Three years since I'd last seen her?

'So we never made up?'

'She tried. Only you didn't want to know. You . . . you couldn't forgive her, Otto.'

'No?'

Only I have no recollection whatsoever of any of this. In fact there's nothing since she left me that time.

Brain cancer and a stroke. That explained some of it, only . . .

'Where's she now?'

Ernst hesitates again.

'Can I see her?'

He looks up sharply at that. 'Can you . . .? Well, sure. I can arrange that. If that's what you want.'

I try to smile, but only find myself grimacing. 'Okay. Then do it. Ask her, Ernst. Ask her to come. I'll see her now.'

502

And finally she comes.

She hesitates at the doorway looking across at me, taking in the whiteness that dominates the room, like it's some kind of tomb and I'm already dead.

'Otto . . .?'

'Come here,' I say, amazed by how beautiful she looks. Older, yes, but still the woman I fell in love with in what seems like centuries ago now.

She comes closer, the smile on her face pained. *Three years*, I remind myself. *She hasn't seen me in three whole years.*

'Katerina . . . bring me a mirror.'

She looks down, then shakes her head, a tear coursing down her cheek. 'No, Otto. You don't want to do that.'

Only I do. I have to know the worst. Know what the cancer's done to me.

As it is, I look down at my hands and see how aged they are. An old man's hands. Like Kolya's earlier.

'Bring a mirror.' But my voice is frail, and when I look at her, there's a strange horror in her face and she turns and runs from the room. Katerina. My eternal love. The other half of me. Gone once more. Run from me again.

503

An hour passes before Irina, the eldest of my girls, makes an appearance. She's alone and carries something wrapped in a white cloth. A mirror, as it turns out.

Too weak to do it for myself, I have her hold it up, then stare.

Is that really me? That sad-eyed old man gazing languidly – stoically – into the glass?

If it is, I do not recognise him.

I look to Irina, seeking explanation, but she just bursts into tears. Wiping them away with the back of her hand, she sets the mirror down on the floor, then comes and sits by me, taking my cold, frail hands into the warmth of her own.

'It's so nice to see you, Papa. We didn't think you'd ever wake up. We used to come here – us girls, that is – once a week, every week. Only nothing ever changed. And I guess . . . I guess she just got *tired*. And Will . . . Will's a lovely man.'

Will's a cunt, I think, surprised by the sheer violence of my thoughts. *A total fucking weasel, slipping into her bed while I'm not there!*

I close my eyes, tears welling once again.

'Papa?'

'Yes, my love?'

'You know it's ended. The War, that is . . . or whatever you want to call it. Within *this* loop, anyway . . .'

'And Kolya?'

'Kolya? We've come to an arrangement. He leaves us be and we leave him be. And generally it works. Though there are days . . .'

'The youngster?'

She looks surprised that I know. 'I spoke to the old man,' I say.

'Ah . . .'

Irina hesitates, as if running some tricky calculations in her head, then gently squeezes my hands again.

'I need to go. But I can come back later, with whoever else is free. If that's what you want? You probably need to rest after all your visitors . . . I . . .'

'Irina . . . darling . . . will you do one thing for me?'

She smiles – broadly this time, 'Of course. What do you want?'

'I want you to get your mother to come back here. On her own. I . . . I need to talk things through with her.'

'But, Papa . . .'

'Just do it, yes?'

Looking grave now, she nods, and in an instant is gone, the imprint of her lips upon my cheek bringing me close to breaking down altogether. As it is a single tear forms on my eyelid then slowly falls, glistening in the whiteness before it settles on my chin.

Will she come? Will she really dare to come a second time?

Yes, and what must she be feeling right now? That she's betrayed me? That she has proved the point I made about her and that bastard Shakespeare?

Kill me now, I beg, my head fallen back on the pillow like a sculpted shape of lead. *Let me not be this awful parody of life.*

Only I have no choice. Death holds me in its hand. And no escaping it.

For a time nothing. Only silence and the whiteness. And then the door eases open once again.

'Otto?'

Her voice is soft and loving, almost a whisper.

I make a small snuffling sound and slowly open my eyes. 'You came . . .'

She walks across and, smiling, leans close and kisses me. 'Of course I came. Why would I not?'

'I thought you'd left me. Abandoned me to Fate.'

I look past her at the door, then back at her. I want to ask her about everything. How – particularly – she gave up me for him. All the stages of it. How her love for me shrank even as it grew for him.

Only that way torment lies. So best not ask. Best say goodbye . . . and die. For what's to live for if she's not in my life?

She sits, pulling the chair closer to the bed, then takes my hands in hers.

'All those times, Otto, All those times when you were gone. Months, almost years when you were elsewhere in Time. I was always faithful. But this was different. No one expected you to come back from this. He cut your throat, Otto, and there was nothing we could do about it. There was no way we could jump you out of there. And the blood you lost . . . When we got what we thought was your corpse back, it seemed to us all that Kolya had won. If not the War then certainly his personal altercation with you. You were as good as dead, Otto. And still I waited.'

'So when did it happen? When did you . . . stop being patient?'

'That's unfair. You were as near dead as makes any medical difference, you know that? I sat here most nights, hoping and praying for some sign of improvement, but there was nothing. I cried endlessly, until I could feel nothing. And Will . . . he waited.

He was patient beyond belief, despite all that stuff with Kolya's films.'

The reminder is too painful. 'How could you, Katerina? After all we went through, after all we shared?'

But when she makes to respond, I raise my hand. This much has worn me out. I have no energy left to argue more.

That much she seems to understand, however.

'I'll go now,' she says, 'Get some rest, I'll see you in the morning.'

'Morning?'

'Yes, it's night right now.'

'I see.'

But sleep is dragging me down once more, like a drowned man, and I succumb. And wake to find the doctor at my side, taking my blood pressure.

'Good morning, Otto. How are you feeling?'

'Alive,' I say. And he nods and unstraps the monitor.

'That's good. Alive is good.'

And we both laugh; he strongly, I weakly.

'Will I . . . improve?'

He looks to me. 'Now, that's a difficult one. You see, Time we can change. You we can't.'

'And?' I ask, sensing he's keeping things back from me.

'Well, to put things at their simplest, Time has fucked with your system, Otto. Which is why I'm going to put you on a new drug we've developed. We call it Kairos Ignis. "Time's Fire". It's something that our team conjured up. It'll act to stabilise your state.'

'Forgive me, but that's rather vague. What does it actually do?'

'It *delays* things. Stops you ageing quite so fast as you have been.'

'So it's a short-term solution?'

'You want the truth, Otto?'

I'm not sure I do, but I make a small, nodding gesture with my head.

'Okay . . . it's like this. Every day we lose a bit more of you. Motor activity. Memory. All of the normal functions of the brain. But this slows that down. Reduces the losses.'

'So I'm still dying?'

'Second by second, I'm afraid.'

I close my eyes, *Death*, I think. *It's been waiting for me all this time, Up River. As patient as ever Will was.*

And, thinking that, I come to a decision.

'Doctor?'

'Yes, Otto?'

'Can you leave me now? Oh, and would you send Katerina again. I assume she's out there, waiting.'

'You assume rightly. But do you really want to see her again? Last time you met your vital signs went through the ceiling.'

'I'll be okay,' I say. 'Really, I . . . I need to see her. Straighten things out.'

'Then see her you shall.'

He leaves. But for all his certainty, I'm not so sure Katerina *will* return. I mean . . . after what I said.

Even so, she comes.

'Otto?'

She seems . . . quiet, contrite. Looking at her, and remembering the image from the mirror, I can't see how it's her fault that she fell for Will. He's an attractive, talented man.

'Does he love you?' I ask, surprising her.

'Will?' She hesitates, but I sense that there's no real hesitation. Not in her heart. 'He loves me,' she says quietly. 'Yes.'

'I've been thinking,' I say, 'And I know one thing for certain. I'll never make love to you again. Not in this physical form.'

I see the pain that statement brings to her and look down. Saying this is breaking my heart, but it must be said. 'You see, the way I look at it, I have two options. To rant and rage and leave you with unpleasant memories of me . . . Or make my peace with you and give my blessing.'

'Your . . .?' Her mouth drops open, realising the significance of what I've just said. 'Your *blessing*, Otto?'

'Yes. My blessing.'

'Oh, Otto . . . you beautiful, beautiful man!'

Only I am tired now. 'Bring him,' I say, my eyelids closing once again. 'An hour from now.'

And as I close my heavy eyes, so she kisses each lid in turn, with the softest, gentlest of kisses, and I smile, the smile of a finally contented man, feeling blessed to have known her. To have had her there at the centre of my life.

And sleep.

504

This then is the last of it.

Yes, but first I must thank them for their drug, which has brought me both the time and the clarity of mind to make sense of all I've lived through. And now, perhaps, to understand some very small part of it.

And to Kav, who has become a frequent visitor in these final days, joining me in that white room, his dead eyes smiling back at me.

As for me, I am a ruin. A fallen building, made up from the broken stones of a former life. My girls still come to visit me. I see the joy and sadness in their eyes. The love. Survivors all of them. All that is but one.

As for she whom I love most in this world and others, she watches always from the doorway, at a distance now, humbled, so she says, by my act of generosity, my letting go of her.

But little does she know. In those nights that are not nights, in that blanched and featureless cell, how much I long for her, crying myself to sleep recalling all we were to each other. But so it is. It is gone. All of it gone. And no returning.

So this I offer you. This commentary, set in Time. And as it ends, so I end too. Otto Behr, who was *Reisende*, time agent. Who crossed time itself to win a girl.

Who loved and feared and died. And was no more.

Six

And the Ruination of Worlds

505

Twenty years pass.

Out on the blighted beach of an ancient sea, beside an ash-charred battlefield piled high with corpses, a single figure moves through the drifting smoke, making their way slowly between the battle-weary figures in full combat dress, who, at the figure's passing, kneel, bowing their heads.

The figure is clothed in dark, padded leathers and, as it comes closer, we see 'it' is a she, her long jet hair falling, curling, to her waist, a massive, high-powered laser clutched against her chest.

Beneath a torn and ragged flag, its oak shaft embedded in the clinging sand, she stops, looking down at the fallen warrior who lies face down beneath the fluttering banner, and, placing her boot firmly on his shoulder, turns him over . . .

Bloodied bone. Mud and ashes cling to his ruined face. She shakes her head, seeing at a glance that this is just another corpse, not the ancient and evasive one she'd hoped to find.

As she looks up, surveying the devastation, so we see she has her mother's eyes, and recognise just who she is. For this is Martha, the Lost Girl. The Abandoned Child. Empress of all the Minor Worlds. *Reisende*. Mistress of the Time Lanes.

A wave rolls up the beach, the water thick with sludge, oil flowing about her booted feet, washing past her and then back. Like Time itself. And as it does, so she looks up at the stars.

And jumps . . .

There is silence. And then another wave rolls up the beach and back, washing ash and blood back into the great ocean. But she is gone. Back into the Lanes. Back to her pursuit.

506

Years pass. Long years, and yet time's passage is the briefest *augenblick*, the merest flutter of the lashes.

We see it all as the gods do.

For have you any doubt? The gods exist, and they like to play their games. To stave off boredom, the sheer *ennui* of millennia; the dull drag of day follows day.

And maybe that explains it all. Maybe that's all there is to it. All of it games, mere games, and our human lives just moves upon the board, the click of bone against wood.

Yet among the spreading trillions of humankind who fill every nook and cranny of the explored galaxy, there is a single one who is unique. The Lost Girl, they call her. But she has other names – the King-killer for one; or the One Who Was Foretold.

And so we see her, surveying the destruction she has wrought, the dark scar of a million ruined craft; mighty ships that once were powerful, but now drift slowly in the vacuum, shutting out great swathes of the star-spattered night, from hub to rim, like spilled ink on a blackened page.

So it is. About her Space unfolds like Russian dolls, layer upon hidden layer; here where her pursuit ends; here where all trace of the one she followed vanishes, sinking down into the endless layers of nothingness.

Here, at what has been known since time began as 'the bottleneck'. Here in deepest space; where a thousand battles have been fought; where great emperors have wagered their massive fortunes . . .

And lost.

She smiles. Maybe this time she will capture him. Only how can she be sure? He has evaded her a thousand times in a thousand different ways.

The Master of Time, he calls himself. Lord Chronos. Or, in a simpler vein, Kolya. Here before all others and here when they have gone.

She stands there on the bridge of her craft – the most powerful ever built; the product of mankind's zenith – and sniffs the air, as if, like a dog, she can sense him, close now; closer than he's ever been. Yet still no trace.

Instinct, that's all she has. Instinct and a mastery of this latest phase of the game, where a single move might take a thousand years.

'*Picture this*,' she whispers, remembering her dead father's words.

But this is beyond picturing. For one cannot imagine the complexity of each move in this latest phase of things.

She turns, looking to the one who's ever there, his head shaven, the dark scar of the intrusive surgery he suffered eons past mimicking the greater scar in the heavens. The one whose name was lost. Her father's saviour. There for him and there for her also.

Picture this.

Only He who is her Enemy has gone well beyond picturing. Beyond simple imagining. Out there – somewhere and in some fashion – he has reconstructed thought itself; taken the Time equations and made a song of them.

Also available from Del Rey

THE BEAR AND THE NIGHTINGALE

Katherine Arden

'Frost-demons have no interest in mortal girls wed to mortal men. In the stories, they only come for the wild maiden.'

In a village at the edge of the wilderness of northern Russia, where the winds blow cold and the snow falls many months of the year, an elderly servant tells stories of sorcery, folklore and the Winter King to the children of the family, tales of old magic frowned upon by the church.

But for the young, wild Vasya these are far more than just stories. She alone can see the house spirits that guard her home, and sense the growing forces of dark magic in the woods . . .

Atmospheric and enchanting, with an engrossing adventure at its core, *The Bear and the Nightingale* is perfect for readers of Naomi Novik's *Uprooted*, Erin Morgenstern's *The Night Circus*, and Neil Gaiman.

DEL REY

Also available from Del Rey

THE ONE

John Marrs

How far would you go to find THE ONE?

One simple mouth swab is all it takes. A quick DNA test to find
your perfect partner – the one you're genetically made for.

A decade after scientists discover everyone has a gene they share
with just one other person, millions have taken the test, desperate
to find true love. Now, five more people meet their Match. But
even soul mates have secrets. And some are more shocking – and
deadlier – than others . . .

A psychological thriller with a difference, this is a truly unique
novel which is guaranteed to keep you on the edge of your seat.

DEL REY

Also available from Del Rey

THE END OF THE WORLD RUNNING CLUB

Adrian J. Walker

The Number One Bestseller, featured on Simon Mayo's Radio 2 Book Club

THE ULTIMATE RACE-AGAINST-TIME THRILLER

When the world ends and you find yourself stranded on the wrong side of the country, every second counts.

No one knows this more than Edgar Hill. 550 miles away from his family, he must push himself to the very limit to get back to them, or risk losing them forever . . .

His best option is to run.

But what if his best isn't good enough?

An original and powerful post-apocalyptic thriller, perfect for fans of *The Martian*

DEL REY